Critical Acclaim for *Brought t...*

"This wonderfully constructed story delivers unexpected twists and turns that will keep readers engaged until they reach the shocking, last-gasp reveal of the murderer....A well-plotted, often engaging murder mystery." —*Kirkus Reviews*

Minotaur Books/Domestic Best First Domestic Competition in 2012— Final Round Selection.

"In his debut novel, Wark creates a likeable protagonist, and readers will root for Tony to solve the mystery and end up with his smart, sassy love interest, a bartending law student named Julie." —*Kirkus Reviews*

And What Readers Are Saying...

"*Brought to Justice* is a thoroughly researched and captivating story that you can't put down to the very last page. It's not just another mystery book; the author explores the characters' complex personalities, conflicts and dilemmas. It's a great read that you can't stop thinking about long after you have finished the book."

Eva W. – Toronto, Ontario

"The book is fabulous and ranks among my top ten detective novels, and that is pretty tough competition!"

George K. – Toronto, Ontario

"*Brought to Justice* is a well-researched, tightly written crime novel from a terrific new mystery writer. The intricate plot moves along at just the right pace and commands the reader to keep going. The book has been positioned as the first in a series featuring detective Tony Deluca and his partner, Julie Travers. Here's hoping there are many more installments to come."

Glenn S. – Toronto, Ontario

BROUGHT TO JUSTICE

BROUGHT TO JUSTICE

KEVIN WARK

MAD CAP PUBLISHING

MadCap Publishing

ISBN-13: 978-0-9936724-0-8
LCCN: 2014912078

Front Cover Image Copyright Kirill Kuroshov - Shutterstock, reprinted with permission
Back Cover Image Copyright Suzanne Tucker - Shutterstock, reprinted with permission
Cover Design by Steve Lindsay
Typeset by James Arneson

Printed in the United States of America

ACKNOWLEDGMENTS

I started writing *Brought to Justice* in 2009, full of anticipation and excitement. Finally, I had started my first fictional novel and it was going to be great! After several months and only a few chapters being written, reality began to sink in. Writing is hard work, particularly when you are otherwise gainfully employed. Fortunately I had to the support of many people who kept me motivated to finish the book.

First and foremost was the encouragement of my wife, Sandy. Even though my devotion to working on the novel was taking away from our time together, she remained 100% behind the project. When she read the first few chapters and said, "it's good, keep going", and I kept going. She's been like that ever since, a push here, a pat on the back there. Sandy, I couldn't have done it without your support. I love you!

Next came the assistance of good friends and family, who initially offered words of encouragement, and later their proof reading skills and critical reviews. The final story has been dramatically improved due to your input. You're the best!

Finally, there was the guidance and advice of a number of people in the publishing profession (some who barely knew me) as I moved through the various stages of completing and having this book published. In particular I would like to acknowledge the efforts of Maureen Garvie, whose professional editing skills greatly enhanced the readability of the novel. Many thanks!

Kevin Wark,
June 2014.

PROLOGUE

The car lights picked up the maintenance road marked by the sign "Private – No Entrance." It turned in to follow the laneway, and the car's suspension strained to cushion its passengers from the dips and bumps of the seldom-used road. The vehicle continued for a short time before coming to a stop in front of an aluminum storage shed. As the driver turned off the ignition, the woman in the passenger seat tentatively smiled at him.

Before she could reach for the door handle, he pulled her towards him. He kissed her lightly, then more urgently. She tasted the alcohol on his breath and sensed danger. She tried to push him away, but he tightened his grip, forcing his tongue into her mouth.

No…. I don't want to do this!" she said and tried to squirm away. He ignored her struggles, pulling her closer, his fingers fumbling at her bra.

Anger mixed with fear made her desperate, and she used her nails to scratch at his face and neck. Wincing in pain, he loosened his hold long enough for her to break free.

Scrambling through the passenger door, she gulped in a breath of cool night air and started running towards the tree-shrouded lights of the highway. She thought of shouting for help, but the wind was suddenly knocked out of her by a vicious tackle. He was quickly on top, his hand now underneath her skirt. Breathless and in pain, she struggled against him.

Frustration suddenly turned to rage and he grabbed a fistful of her dark hair, slamming her head to the ground. She no longer offered any resistance, which emboldened him to hike up her skirt and rip away her panties. It was only after violently climaxing that he noticed her totally motionless body and the blood-soaked ground around them. Lifting her head, he saw the sharp rock that had pierced her skull like a ball-peen hammer.

Panic now displaced all other sensations. He was having difficulty breathing and his vision was blurred. He lay there panting like a dog, trying to marshal his thoughts. Finally, with effort, he pulled his pants up and got to his feet. For a moment he surveyed the lifeless body before starting to strip it naked.

He found his keys in his pocket and staggered back to the car. Opening the trunk, he threw in her clothes and searched for something to cover the body. Hoisting her over his shoulder, he tottered for a moment under the weight. Regaining his balance, he started down a narrow pathway and followed it through a heavily thicketed area. Another hundred yards and he saw the perimeter of the lake, the city lights sparkling across the water.

After disposing of the body he slowly and deliberately retraced his steps. Dropping heavily into the driver's seat, he took another deep breath and slowly exhaled. He caught sight of his own image in the rearview mirror. He didn't recognize the man who looked back at him, sweat running down from his forehead, mud splatters on his face, the empty emotionless eyes. He quickly looked away and started the engine. Time to get out of there before someone stumbled across the car.

Jennifer Harding

MAY 14, 2014

Chapter 1
11:40 AM

Tony steered his '67 Mustang into a parking space at Governor Nelson State Park. Less than an hour had elapsed since he'd pulled himself out of Lake Mendota, chilled to the bone. In that period of time he'd returned to the cottage, placed a 911 call, taken a steaming hot shower, and changed into dry clothes. He was now back at the park to help the police locate and retrieve the body.

Before he could get out of the driver's seat, another car drew up beside him. He immediately recognized the driver, Detective Bobby Andrade. The black unmarked police vehicle had barely stopped when she began talking on a cell phone.

While they had not seen each other in at least six months, Tony and Bobby had at one time worked closely together. They'd been partners on the Karen Sumner homicide investigation. From working with her, Tony knew Bobby was a formidable detective, confident, and ambitious with a keen inquiring mind. She'd also proven to be a very loyal partner. While others within the department had been quick to distance themselves from him when the Sumner investigation went off the rails, she'd stayed at his side to the bitter end. Fortunately, her participation in the failed investigation didn't have any negative long-term effects on her career. In fact, he'd seen a recent WMTV news broadcast where the chief of police praised her efforts in tracking down the suspect in a gang-related murder.

Bobby ended the call and stepped out of the police car. She was tall, almost 5 foot 10, with a solid but shapely build. Her dark blue pant suit hugged her body, a crisp white cotton blouse under her jacket. She was typically implacable, but today one look at her told him something wasn't right. There was a frown at the corners of her mouth, her green eyes seemed distant, and her short brown hair was in a state of disarray.

However, when she saw him, her expression brightened and she greeted him with a crooked half-smile. "Tony, it's been a while. How're you doing?" She spoke with a distinct mid-western accent.

"Not too bad. But I wish we could've met under better circumstances. How about you? You look like you're having a tough day."

"I guess you could say that." Her tone indicated she was not about to go into details. "I was just on the phone with a state trooper. Croft's his name. He expects to be at the boat dock in about five minutes. He has the dive team with him."

Tony reflected on the politics of the situation. Although Lake Mendota fell within Madison city limits, the State Police had jurisdiction over the waterways. If a death occurred on the lake, the State Police had primary responsibility for the investigation. On the other hand, if it could be determined that the victim had been killed on dry land and within city limits, the Madison Police would take over the investigation. In the meantime, City and State Police would work together to recover the body and establish the cause of death.

"While we're waiting, Tony, tell me what happened out there."

He looked at his watch. "About an hour ago I was in my boat, maybe a mile from here, near the entrance to the Yahara River. My lure got caught on something in about ten feet of water. I tried a couple of times but couldn't dislodge it. That lure was special, a gift from my father on my sixteenth birthday, so I decided to dive in after it."

Bobby gave him an incredulous look. "Water's pretty cold this time of year."

"That's an understatement." He tried to hold back a shudder at the memory. "Anyway, I followed the line down with the help of my lantern and discovered the lure had become entangled in a thick braided rope, the kind used to tie up boats. And it was wound around what appeared to be a large white plastic tarpaulin. I thought I'd hooked some garbage dumped in the lake by a boater."

Tony paused, knowing the recounting of his next actions could be contentious. "I used my fishing knife to free the lure and in the process unsettled the tarpaulin. It completed a slow roll on the lake bottom, exposing a tear in the plastic. I found myself staring at the white, bloodless face of a young woman." It'd been like a scene from a zombie horror flick.

"By then I was turning blue from the freezing water and lack of oxygen. I had just enough energy left to cut free my lure before going topside."

"Why'd you do that?" Bobby sounded incredulous.

"To make sure I got back my property," Tony replied, a defensive edge in his voice.

"Tony, you know better than that. Once you found the body, you should've left everything alone and gotten the hell out of there. You may have compromised a key piece of evidence."

She was right, but Tony wasn't about to admit it. "Listen, I know how it works. I leave it there and some asshole in the evidence room pockets my lure once the case is closed. Says it got lost. I didn't want that to happen. And let's face it, without that lure, the body would never have been discovered."

Bobby shook her head, showing she didn't care for his logic. However, she let it slide. "Okay. Is that everything, then?"

"There is one other thing. Remember I told you the body was covered in some sort of white plastic material? I originally thought it was a large tarpaulin, but when it rolled over, I noticed there was a design on the inside. Pink flowers surrounded by long green fronds. And there were round holes at one end. I'm pretty sure it was a shower curtain."

"We'll be able to confirm that when we retrieve the body. Let's head down to the dock."

As they made their way along the gravel path, Tony tried to get Bobby's mind off his messing with the evidence. "So how's the Big Dick?" he asked, referring to Rick Adelsky, Bobby's boss and lead detective in the Homicide Division. Adelsky had taken over the Sumner murder investigation after Tony had been unceremoniously turfed out on his ass. The case was still unsolved, primarily due to the complete disappearance of the main suspect.

"He's still an arrogant prick and one of the biggest ass-kissers on the force. That guy's got his nose buried so deep in Senator Caldwell's butt, it's a wonder he hasn't suffocated."

Tony chuckled and was about to respond when his attention was drawn to the throb of an approaching motor. A white Boston Whaler, about twenty-five feet long with an open walk-around cabin, was pulling into the public dock. A moment later a power-fully built man in a State Trooper uniform – presumably Croft – leapt from the cabin onto the wooden dock and tied the boat to the rusted cleats.

When they arrived moments later, the trooper was consulting with two people in black wetsuits seated onboard. Croft looked to be in his mid-thirties, with the barrel chest of a weightlifter. His short black hair stood on end, courtesy of some sort of mousse product. He wore dark aviator sunglasses that partially hid a jagged white scar above one eyebrow.

Bobby started introductions. "Trooper Croft, Tony Deluca. Tony found the body."

"No need to be formal here. Call me Greg." The trooper shook their hands. "Mike and Dave are here to help us find and recover the body." Both divers raised a hand in acknowledgement.

"Let's get everyone on board." Croft led the way, taking the pilot's chair, while Tony and Bobby found seats behind him. Tony pointed northeast, and a few minutes later caught sight of the white floating fender he'd left as a marker.

"There's a fishing line attached to the fender that'll lead you down to the body," Tony told the divers as the boat was being anchored. Mike and Dave moved into action. Mike opened a large aluminum box near the front bulkhead, removing oxygen tanks and diving equipment. He also took out a neatly folded piece of black plastic, which Tony recognized as a body bag.

They finished suiting up and packing gear into waterproof storage bags. Greg checked their valves and meters to make sure everything was in working order and gave them the thumbs up. The divers dropped backwards into the water from the gunwale, simultaneously breaking the surface with a loud slapping noise. A kick of their flippers and they submerged, their black shapes melting into the darkness of the lake. The only reminder of their presence was the fender bobbing on the water.

Tony had been involved in many homicide investigations, but this was the first he'd experienced where the body was located in ten to fifteen feet of water. That factor was going to complicate the collection of evidence that might help in determining cause of death and the identity of the killer.

At the front of the boat, Bobby was watching for signs of activity in the water. Tony moved closer to her, and she acknowledged his presence with a thin smile.

"It sure feels odd, even after all this time, not being able to participate in the crime scene investigation," he ventured.

She nodded. "Yes. I expect it doesn't seem fair."

Tony ran a hand through his thick black hair, still slightly damp from his shower. "I miss the challenge of the hunt, sorting through the clues and ultimately getting in the face of the bad guys.... Watching them sweat as you reel them in. But those days are behind me. Now I'm wet nurse to a bunch of drunken university students."

"So I heard – security at the Varsity Bar. How's that going?"

"I can't really complain. It's got me back into the real world and earning a regular paycheck. Better than some of the alternatives," he replied with a bitter laugh.

Bobby gave him a sympathetic glance before turning back towards the water. Several minutes later their attention was drawn to large ripples forming near the boat. Two heads and a black body bag popped into view.

Croft scurried to the stern and removed a cover from the floor of the boat, revealing a gas-powered winch. He dropped down behind it and connected two steel cables. After starting the motor, he leveraged himself back onto the deck, cables in hand. He threaded them through steel rings fixed to the side of the boat and let them drop into the water.

He shouted to Bobby and Tony over the pulsating noise of the motor, motioning at the divers. "Okay, they're going to connect the cables to each end of the body bag. I'll operate the winch to bring the bag up beside the boat. We can hoist it in from there. I'd like the two of you to act as spotters as it comes out of the water."

Mike and Dave were attaching the cables to grommets in the body bag. Mike signaled to Croft to start the winch. Greg dropped back down beside the winch and hit the power switch. There was a loud whine from the cables winding around the cylinder. The black bag appeared to levitate magically from the lake, rivulets of water cascading off it.

Satisfied that everything was going smoothly, the divers started swimming towards the boat ladder. It was Tony who noticed the problem. The zipper on the bag should have been locked into place. However, in their haste to retrieve the body, it seemed neither Mike nor Dave had completed this step. The zipper was open several inches. As Tony debated telling Croft to stop the winch, a powerful gust of wind buffeted the police boat.

The boat's violent rocking caused the body bag to sway back and forth, throwing its contents with force against the zipper. It gave way and the body began spilling out of the opening. Tony yelled and leaned over the back of the boat to grab at the bag. Bobby was instantly at his side, pulling on one of the cables.

As they wrestled the body into the boat, the head and shoulders of the dead woman came into view. Bobby let out an anguished cry and staggered backwards.

Tony turned and saw her staring at the body. The blood had drained from her face, giving it the same ghostly pallor as the dead woman's. There were tears in her eyes. Although the sight of death was difficult for even the most hardened homicide detective, Tony was surprised by her reaction.

"Bobby?" She wouldn't pull her attention away from the partially exposed body. He gave her shoulders a slight shake. "Bobby, look at me."

She slowly turned, her eyes glassy and unfocused. "Oh my god.... oh my god."

"Bobby, what is it? Are you okay?"

She was taking in deep breaths, her chest heaving. Finally she seemed to gain control. "It's Jennifer.... Jennifer Harding," she gasped.

"Jennifer Harding?" Tony couldn't place the name.

"She's a lawyer with the State Attorney's Office in Chicago."

Chapter 2
12:20 PM

Croft had killed the power to the winch and was back on deck. "Holy Christ! Are you sure?"

The color was slowly coming back to Bobby's face and she'd regained some of her composure. She ran a hand across her forehead. "Yes, I'm sure." Her voice was devoid of emotion.

Tony looked over at Croft, and his stare was returned with a puzzled look. "How do you figure she got down there?" Tony asked.

Bobby rose, went over to the body and gently pulled the top of the bag over Harding's head, zipping it back up. She stood and hugged her arms to her chest.

By now Mike and Dave were back on board, unaware of what had just transpired. Croft quickly told them about the crisis with bringing the body onto the boat, as well as Bobby's revelation of the dead woman's identity.

"Sorry, Greg, I must have forgotten to fasten the zipper properly," Mike said.

"Damn right you did. If it wasn't for the quick work of these two, the body would be back at the bottom of the lake. And you'd be going back down again, this time without your tanks."

Mike looked miserable, his expression clearly acknowledging his screw-up.

"Fortunately, there was no major harm done," Croft said, softening his earlier comments. "Now what'd you find down there?"

Tony inched closer to make sure he didn't miss anything.

"Well, the body was located about twelve feet down on the lake bottom, wrapped up in plastic and bound with rope, like Tony said. There's lots of sediment in the water, probably from the storm last night, but Dave and I took pictures anyway. We transferred the deceased into the body bag and left a GPS marker in case someone needs to return to the exact location. We swept an area about forty feet in diameter but didn't see anything out of the ordinary."

Croft nodded. "Hopefully forensics and the autopsy report will give us some clues as to what happened. Talking about that, I think it's about time for the coroner and his pathologist to join us." He got out his cell phone and walked a little distance away. At first Tony couldn't make out what he was saying, except that he was clearly becoming agitated by the conversation. He finally said in a raised voice, "Listen Bradley, I don't give a rat's ass about your golf game. Our deceased appears to be with the State Attorney's office in Chicago. In a few hours a number of very powerful people are going to be asking questions about how she died. I want to have some answers. I'm sending over a police boat to pick you up at the Country Club in ten minutes. Make arrangements for the pathologist to be there with you."

He snapped his cell phone shut. "I can't believe that guy. He wants us to wait until he finishes his round of golf!"

He then got back on his cell and gave instructions for a boat to be sent to Bishops Bay Country Club.

Tony surmised that Greg's anger was directed towards Jim Bradley, the Dane County coroner. While the Coroner's Office had access to the top medical and forensic experts in the region, Tony had always found it curious that the coroner was not required to have any medical background or experience. In fact, other than coming from money and having powerful friends, Bradley seemed to lack any skills that qualified him for the position.

Until recently he'd spent most of his time at Bishops Bay Country Club, casting about for a career. When he learned that the incumbent Dane County coroner was stepping down, he threw his hat into the ring. By tapping into the power brokers at the golf course, and running against a mediocre group of candidates, he became the youngest coroner in Dane County history. Knowing this background, and having worked with the man, Tony wasn't that surprised that Bradley wanted to complete eighteen holes before attending to his elected duties.

A gust of wind hit the police boat and jostled Tony back to the present. Mike and Dave were removing their diving gear now. Croft had spread a navigation chart out on a table, marking their location. Bobby stood at the stern, like a sentry under orders to protect Harding's body from further harm.

Tony decided it was time to find out how she knew the dead woman. He joined her, asking, "You feeling any better?"

"Yes, thanks. I'm really embarrassed that I lost it like that. Very unprofessional of me. but it came as a real shock. It's hard to explain." She trailed off.

Tony nodded. "I can imagine what you must've felt. Tell me, how'd you come to meet Harding?"

Bobby's sad green eyes focused briefly on his. "She's with the Criminal Prosecutions Bureau in Chicago. We met at a law conference about four months ago. She was one of the speakers. She covered some recent court decisions that have put limits on police investigation and interview techniques. You know, the stuff that makes a detective's job even more difficult. I went up afterwards and introduced myself. Since then I've consulted with her on some related issues."

"I wonder how the hell she ended up in our lake."

Bobby shook her head, looking troubled. They lapsed back into silence, waiting for the coroner's arrival.

Tony was checking the time on his watch when he heard an approaching motorboat. Even from half a mile away, he could see it was a twenty foot cuddy boat with an open cabin. As the boat drew closer he made out three people on board, a state trooper at the helm with a man and woman seated behind him.

The man was in his late twenties, with sandy hair and a well-tanned squared face, dressed in golf gear. He didn't look happy about the turn of events that had interrupted his activities at the Country Club.

The other passenger was a slightly overweight middle-aged woman in blue medical scrubs. Her long brown hair was being whipped about by the wind. On her lap she clutched a black medical bag. Tony recognized Carolyn Thomas, the chief forensic pathologist at the University Hospital.

Dr. Thomas had a distinct look of fear on her round face. "Our good doctor is not very fond of water," Bobby murmured. "If she had to choose between getting in a boat and walking on hot coals, I think she'd volunteer to light the fire."

Tony smiled, glad Bobby's sense of humor was returning. He watched as the boat came alongside. Greg threw a line to the pilot and Bradley, along with Dr. Thomas and her black medical bag, stepped aboard. Mike and Dave, their duties completed, hoisted their scuba gear into the other vessel and clambered after it. They gave a quick salute to Croft as their boat headed off again.

Bradley planted his feet, getting his bearings. Seeing Tony, his face furrowed into a deeper frown. "Detective Andrade, what's *he* doing here?" His tone suggested he'd discovered some rotting garbage on board.

"Mr. Deluca found the body. We needed him to direct us to its location," Bobby responded firmly.

"Well, he has no right being here now. I want him off this boat. We have an investigation to conduct."

I appreciate your dedication to the job." Bobby made no attempt to hide her sarcasm. "But I haven't finished his debriefing. In any event, the shore transportation just left."

Bradley looked like he was about to argue, but the other boat was already a distant speck. Fine, but I want him as far away as possible. Now, where's the body?"

Croft stepped in, directing Bradley and Dr. Thomas to the back of the boat.

Bobby muttered, "That man is in a tight race with Adelsky as the biggest jerk-off I know."

"No argument here. Thanks for standing up for me."

"Yes, well, I wasn't going to let him push either of us around. Unfortunately he does have a point, though. You'll need to stay here while I go watch the examination."

Tony felt the familiar stirring of resentment and anger. Maybe he couldn't be on the front lines, but damn it, he was going to keep an eye on things and make sure they didn't miss anything. He dropped into the pilot seat but swiveled around to face the stern.

Dr. Thomas was finishing up explaining to the other three the procedures she would follow. "Any questions?" There were none. She opened her bag, removing some items including a pair of latex gloves, which she quickly pulled on. Kneeling by the body, she unzipped the black bag. Jennifer Harding's head, and then the rest of her body, still wrapped in plastic, were gradually revealed.

Tony watched as Dr. Thomas tried to establish the temperature of the body, hoping to get an approximate fix on the time of death. She asked Croft to check the water temperature on the boat's instrument panel. Having recently experienced the cold waters of Lake Mendota, Tony knew body temperature wouldn't be a useful indicator.

The chief pathologist used a small, powerful flashlight to examine the body's ears, nose and mouth. Next, she used her fingers to feel the head for bumps, lacerations, or other injuries. When this review was completed, she took some scissors and cut away the plastic wrapping. The waterlogged body contrasted against the colorful design of the shower curtain. Dr. Thomas retrieved a camera from her bag and took a number of pictures of the body's condition, front and back.

After what seemed an eternity, but was probably less than ten minutes, Dr. Thomas concluded her initial examination and re-zipped the bag. The next step was to transport Harding's body to the hospital, where a full autopsy would be completed.

In most cases this would provide more concrete evidence as to how this young woman died, as well as the identity of her killer. But in these extraordinary circumstances, Tony had an uncomfortable hunch that this wouldn't be the case.

Chapter 3
2:15 PM

On the table in front of him was a thick sandwich piled high with authentic Genoa salami, mozzarella cheese, lettuce, tomato slices and a generous amount of hot mustard, carefully arranged between two pieces of whole-grain bread. Tony was about to take a bite when Samantha, who'd been taking an afternoon nap, made an appearance in the kitchen.

Samantha (Sam to her friends) was a long-haired tabby, a present to his daughter on her twelfth birthday. Carla had named her after the character played by Nicole Kidman in the movie *Bewitched*. While Sam continued to be part of Tony's life, unfortunately Carla was not. She'd moved back to Chicago to be with her mother almost six months earlier.

"Sam, you won't believe the morning I've had." He reached down to stroke her head. Sam let out a sympathetic meow just as the phone started to ring in the living room. He let the call go through to the answering machine.

As he chewed on a particularly spicy chunk of salami, he heard his pre-recorded message and then the sound of a familiar voice. "Hi, Tony, this is Drake. It's about 2:40 in the afternoon. I know we're supposed to meet in less than an hour, but I wanted to update you on some extremely important news. If you get this message before you head to my office, please give me a call. You know the number." The answering machine shut off with a click.

In the rush of the day's events, Tony had totally forgotten about his appointment with his lawyer, Drake Fields. Fields had been recommended by Jason Barclay, a senior criminal lawyer in Madison, one of the few lawyers that Tony had ever liked and trusted. Jason, a serious Chicago White Sox fan, had told him in his nasal voice that Drake was "the kinda guy you want at bat when the count is full and the bases are loaded." That was exactly the type of lawyer that Tony needed for his legal battle with the city, and he'd made arrangements to meet with Drake shortly thereafter.

Washing the last of his sandwich down with a Coke, he reflected on his first meeting with Drake four months ago. Drake's office was in a one-story building on the corner of Washington and Hancock, just outside the downtown core. He shared space and support services with several other lawyers specializing in real estate, corporate, and criminal law – a legal supermarket of sorts.

Tony checked in with the elderly receptionist, who in a shuffling walk escorted him to a cramped interview room. It was nondescript, containing a small round table with two well-worn leather chairs. There were no pictures on the sickly green walls. The only other piece of furniture was a scratched and chipped wooden stand in a corner, with an old conference phone on it.

Drake came in carrying a pot of coffee, two cups, and a legal writing pad. He put this all down on the table and held out a meaty hand in greeting. He was tall and hefty, with broad shoulders that filled the space around him. He towered over Tony, making him feel shorter than his almost six foot frame. While the big lawyer appeared to be only in his mid-thirties, his sandy hair was already retreating up his forehead. Piercing blue eyes were contrasted by his ruddy complexion, which Tony learned could turn an even deeper hue when he became excited or angry.

They'd started with small talk, using the time to size each other up. Tony was pretty sure Drake had already checked him out after his initial call. His contacts within the legal community likely provided him with varying accounts of the intrigues surrounding Tony's departure from the Madison Police Department.

But Drake feigned ignorance of his situation as he got down to business. "Tell me, why do you need a lawyer?" he inquired, his deep voice rumbling like a freight train in the night.

Tony hesitated, not sure where to begin. With Drake waiting for him to speak, he decided to start with some background on his career with the Chicago Police Force. "I'm not sure how much you know about me. Before I moved to Madison, not quite a year ago, I was a senior detective in the homicide division with the Chicago police department. In my last few years there I was the top dog, dealt with the toughest cases," he added with some pride.

Drake gave an appreciative nod. "I have some friends on the force and I know there's a real pecking order. You must've been quite the movie star there."

Although Tony laughed, there was some truth in the lawyer's comment. While he didn't have the million-dollar lifestyle or legions of tweeting fans, he could point to his bouts with alcohol and drugs, the recent separation from his wife, and forced retirement. These were all traits he shared in common with the rich and famous.

"I guess you could say that. But things started to collapse around me. I was being asked to handle an increasing number of cases without additional backup. The reality was that I was burning out, but didn't really know it."

"That's a real bitch." Drake nodded for him to continue.

"I reached my breaking point after taking a bullet while chasing down a suspect. I allowed myself to be pressed back to duty before fully recovering. There was this serial murderer whose MO was to rape and kill young women who lived in the low-rise apartments scattered through Chicago's outskirts. That bastard eluded us for several horrible weeks. The pressure kept on ratcheting up to find him before he killed again, and it felt like someone was jabbing a hot poker into my bullet wound. I didn't want to lose the case so I, uh, self-medicated with some stuff available through some friends on the force. At the same time, my marriage was falling apart. I was totally focused on apprehending this guy and being a real asshole to my family. We finally got a break and caught the killer, but by then I was hanging by a very thin thread."

As Tony talked, Drake kept his large head down, scribbling away on his notepad.

"With the urging of my wife, I took a voluntary leave of absence and checked myself into a detox center. After several weeks of hell my body finally purged itself of all the crap. I was fortunate; Joanna stuck with me through this ordeal. However, once the doctors pronounced me fit to go back home, she sat me down and said in no uncertain terms that things had to change or she was leaving me. There it was – I had to find another police job where I wouldn't be under constant pressure."

"Must've been a tough decision."

"You've got that right. I'd let the job become the center of my universe. But I was bright enough to know I needed Joanna and my daughter, Carla. They grounded me, gave my life perspective. Without them, the detective job would have eaten me up and spit me back out."

Tony felt like he was in a confessional booth, with Drake acting as priest on the other side of the partition. And while the lawyer couldn't offer him absolution, some of the weight of the previous year seemed to lift from his shoulders as he spilled out his story.

He went on to explain that after returning to work, he sent out feelers to police departments in several smaller cities and towns within an hour's drive of Chicago. Unfortunately no one seemed to be in the market for a good but well-used homicide detective, particularly one who no longer appeared to be interested in pursuing killers. After months of looking, he'd almost given up hope of finding another position that would allow him to slow down and restore some balance in his life.

"Then I got a long-distance call; Chief Dupree from the Madison Police Department was on the line. He'd heard through the grapevine that I was looking for a change of pace. He explained that he needed someone with my background for a special assignment with their homicide department. I agreed to come to Madison to continue the conversation.

"I'd never been to Madison and decided to do a bit of a background check. I was surprised to learn that it had a population of almost 250,000 people. And that in addition to being the state capital, it was also the home of the University of Wisconsin, which itself had most 50,000 students. At first blush, Madison sounded like the ideal spot to put down new roots with Joanna and Carla.

"When I met with the chief, I was very impressed. I'm not sure if you're aware of this, but he cut his teeth in the New Orleans Police Department, slowly working his way up the ranks to deputy chief. When Hurricane Katrina rode through and devastated the city, he decided it was time to relocate his family. He ended up being the first black chief of police in Madison. He then explained there'd been a rash of retirements within the homicide department and that a relatively young detective by the name of Rick Adelsky had been appointed to lead the division. The chief was concerned that a recent spike in gang warfare and other violent crimes might overwhelm Adelsky.

At the mention of Adelsky's name, Drake's head popped up. He grunted but said nothing.

"He thought Adelsky could benefit from the support of a seasoned homicide cop, and he'd obtained approval to hire a retired top gun to work as a consultant on a two-year contract. This person would be responsible for mentoring Adelsky in his new role, as well as making sure the Madison homicide division was state of the art. Dupree had spent months interviewing candidates, but he hadn't found the right fit. He'd heard about my recent troubles, and I assured him I'd cleaned up my act and was very interested in the opportunity. It took a couple more months of follow-up interviews and background checks, but I eventually got the job."

By now Tony was feeling a bit parched and asked if he could get some water. Drake used the conference phone to call the receptionist, who promptly appeared with a bottle of cold spring water.

"Feel free to go on when you're ready," Drake encouraged him.

Tony took a welcome swallow. "Thanks. I'm ready. The first few months in Madison were perhaps the happiest times I'd experienced with Joanna since first becoming a police officer. She was ecstatic with the change in scenery and enjoyed decorating our new home. Carla found a summer job at the Starbucks on State Street and was busy making plans to attend the University of Wisconsin in the fall. I was rejuvenated and threw myself into the new job. I spent a great deal of time with Adelsky, trying to help him in his new role. But this was a bit of a challenge. He grudgingly accepted my advice. He made it pretty clear that he felt he could manage the department without my babysitting. At the same time he played it smart, and didn't outwardly do anything to challenge my position. In fact, he adopted many of my recommendations on organizational structure and technology enhancements.

"I gained some insights into the man as we worked together. He told me he was a local boy who'd never strayed too far from home. He attended the University of Wisconsin and, in his words, was the star wide receiver for the Badger football team."

Drake interjected. "Yes, I had the pleasure of playing with Rick. He was quite the competitor." Tony sensed antagonism in Drake's voice.

"The first sign of trouble came when the disappearance of a third-year university student by the name of Karen Sumner was reported by her roommate. The chief assigned several detectives to follow up on leads, but after six days the missing student still couldn't be located. Her body was discovered later that week in a marshy area by Lake Mendota. That's when my newly discovered inner peace started to disintegrate."

Chapter 4

Tony picked up the phone and dialed from memory. The reception-ist put him through to Drake.

"Tony! Glad you got my message," the lawyer's friendly voice boomed. "I have some very interesting news for you." Drake paused for effect. "The State Police have recovered a body."

"Yes, I know."

"You do?"

"I was the one who found the body."

"Did I hear you correctly? You *found* the body?"

"Drake, your sources aren't very good if you don't know that. I was fishing this morning and snagged my line. For reasons I won't get into, I dived in to retrieve it. That's how I found the body – a woman bound up in a shower curtain. I just got back from helping the police pull her out of the lake."

Tony heard Drake exhale. "Listen, I'm not sure who you fished out of the lake, but we're not talking about the same body."

It was Tony's turn to be confused. "You'd better fill me in."

"Well, four days ago the State Police received a call from a distraught hiker. He was camping at Fox River Park in Waukesha County and went into the woods to get some campfire kindling when he stumbled upon a badly decomposed body. It'd been there for quite a while, and the park critters had been busy."

Tony wasn't sure what this all had to do with him, but was very curious. "So, who is it?"

Drake chose to draw out the story. "The state police weren't able to find anything in the vicinity that would ID the body, so it was taken to the Medical Examiner's Office for autopsy. It took a while, but they were able to trace him through his dental records. Now are you ready for this? The dead guy is Curtis Mansfield."

Tony's heart skipped several beats. Mansfield was, and continued to be, the primary suspect in the murder of Karen Sumner. However, he'd disappeared in the middle of the night, before his guilt or innocence could be established. In fact, her parents were still offering a reward of $50,000 for information leading to his arrest.

So how did Mansfield end up dead, his body rotting in a State Park less than an hour's drive from Madison? The day was turning out to be full of surprises.

"Tony, you still there?"

"Yes, just trying to process all this information. Did you get any other details?"

"Yes, my sources are well informed. The autopsy indicates Mansfield had a badly broken leg and a separated left shoulder. However, those injuries weren't the cause of death. Once the body was identified, the ME remembered that Mansfield had vanished without a trace last September. On a hunch he had someone check the weather records back then. I'm not sure if you remember, but around that time we had some freaky weather. The temperature dropped below freezing, and some areas outside the city got up to a foot of snow. The ME believes Mansfield got caught in a snow storm. The state police went back to take another look around and found his car rolled over in ravine, quite close to where his body was discovered. They figure he went off the road and managed to crawl out of the wreck, but then died of exposure."

"I assume the Madison police are aware of this development?"

"Yes, they were notified earlier today. That's how I got wind of it. The news is spreading through the Madison legal community like wildfire. There's a lot of speculation. The ME may have concluded that his death was accidental, but there are some conspiracy theorists who figure the whole scenario was staged and this was actually a retribution killing for the murder of Sumner. Who knows? There may have been a vigilante or two out there prepared to pronounce judgment on Mansfield. The police will have their hands full trying to get to the bottom of this one."

"Somewhat ironic that for the past nine months the police were hunting for a dead man."

"And that brings me to another important development…."

"What's that?" Tony felt close to his limit for dramatic news.

"Lou Driller called me earlier this afternoon. He'd like to get everyone together to discuss the settlement of your lawsuit against the city."

Tony slowly expelled his breath, taken by surprise for the second time in the conversation. Lou Driller had been retained by the city to defend it against his claim for breach of contract and defamation of character resulting from him being fired. Driller and Drake were on friendly terms, and early on in the proceedings they'd engaged in an off-the-record discussion of the merits of their respective cases. Driller confided that a number of people, in particular Chief Dupree, disagreed with the way Tony's situation had been handled. But there appeared to be a more powerful faction within the city that didn't want to settle this case at any price. Driller was not told the reasons why, but he had strict orders to vigorously defend the city's actions all the way to trial.

Tony couldn't help but wonder if the discovery of Mansfield's body had somehow triggered this change in legal strategy. "What do you think of this development, Drake?"

"Well, Lou admitted to being more than a bit confused by his client's sudden reversal in position, but it's not unusual for one party in a legal action to blink as the court date gets closer. Settling this would certainly save everyone a lot of time and legal fees. So I think we should see what they have to offer."

"Okay, go ahead and set up the meeting. You know I work nights, so the best time to for me would be early to mid-afternoon."

"Will do, Tony. And given this development, I really don't see the value of us getting together this afternoon."

"Sounds great. To tell you the truth, I wasn't looking forward to the trip downtown. Not that I don't enjoy your company."

"Don't worry, my feelings aren't hurt. I'll get back to you once we've settled on a meeting date."

After hanging up, Tony realized that they'd been so caught up with Drake's news that he'd forgotten to tell the lawyer about his own drama this morning. Well, that would have to wait. Right now, all he wanted was to get some rest before his shift started at the Varsity Bar.

Wandering into the living room, he picked up a Grisham novel borrowed from the public library. It was a change of pace for the author, about a NFL football quarterback who ended up playing in an Italian semi-pro league. Tony sat in an old overstuffed chair and flipped to the bookmarked page. However, his mind was still distracted, and he was having trouble focusing on the words. He made a second attempt to read the same page, then put the book down, deciding instead to pursue another one of his favorite relaxation strategies.

In the bedroom he pulled his exercise gear off a closet shelf. He'd taken up running on the advice of his rehab counsellor. *"You need to find something to channel your energies – like running, "* she'd recommended. He'd given it a try and it was now a staple in his exercise routine as well as an important balance in his life.

Leaving the cottage, he started down the gravel driveway to the main road, then followed a route that traced the outline of the lake. He was cooled by the breeze off the water and enjoyed the fragrance from the evergreens that lined the roadside. After several miles, he fell into a rhythm, his mind simply focused on moving one leg and then the other forward along the uneven road.

Back at the cottage an hour later, his legs were leaden and his shirt was soaked with sweat. But he felt mentally refreshed, ready to think about things other than dead bodies. In the laundry room he peeled off his running gear. His clothes from the morning's chilly dip were still on the floor in a small pool of lake water. He threw everything into the washing machine and took a bracing cold shower.

Once he'd toweled himself dry, he moved to the sink to shave. As he lathered up and ran the razor over the dark stubble, he assessed what he saw in the mirror. Courtesy of his Italian ancestry, he still had a full head of thick black curly hair, and his regular morning fishing trips had turned his complexion deep brown. Were the lines that had accumulated around his eyes over the past six months less pronounced? It could be just wishful thinking, but perhaps the security job was acting as some sort of balm to his soul.

When he finished shaving he took a step back from the mirror and briefly surveyed his naked body. He still had some of the extra pounds that had been acquired over his last few years on the Chicago PD. But he was definitely making progress. More noticeable was the angry red welt on his right shoulder, courtesy of a .45 caliber bullet.

He went to the closet and pulled on a pair of black chino pants and a white shirt with a button-down collar. The last piece of his "uniform" was a grey nylon windbreaker, the word "Security" on its back.

Looking at the jacket, he couldn't help but feel even a bit humiliated by his current situation. After almost two decades as a homicide detective, working security at a university bar was quite the come-down. At the same time, he was grateful to Josh Stein for giving him the job.

Karen Sumner

SEPTEMBER 12, 2013

Chapter 1

Karen Sumner, born and raised in Chicago, had majored in business and commerce at the University of Wisconsin, hoping to land a job with a New-York based investment firm when she graduated, her bio said. Photos provided by her parents showed a self-possessed young woman of medium height and build, with an attractive face surrounded by dark brown hair. However, what really caught Tony's attention when he examined the pictures were her lively blue eyes and friendly smile.

Her disappearance shortly after start of the fall term was reported by her friend and roommate, Teresa Munro. That Saturday afternoon the two had attended a Badgers football game. It had been a total blow-out, 48-0, over the Tennessee Golden Eagles. Later, the two girls headed out for dinner and then dancing at the Capital Club. Munro admitted that at the club she'd become interested in a fellow student, and Sumner had left to go back to their apartment.

When Munro got home in the early hours of Sunday morning, there were no signs of her roommate. Sumer had still not surfaced by noon, nor responded to messages left on her cell phone. Late in the day a worried Munro decided to contact her roommate's parents and the University Police to report her missing.

A police report was duly filed, but the University Police suspected that the missing student had gone off on her own amorous adventure and would reappear for classes on Monday. However, when Monday passed without a word from her, the University Police began to take matters much more seriously. At that point both the Madison and Wisconsin State Police became involved.

Sumner's parents arrived in Madison, upset and concerned, promptly offering a large reward for their daughter's safe return. The university newspaper ran photos of Karen Sumner, asking anyone with information concerning her whereabouts to notify the police. Although they assigned two officers to follow up on the deluge of phone calls and emails, Sumner was not located.

The following Thursday morning her nude and partially decomposed body was discovered in a marshy area just west of the city. After receiving a 911 call just after sunrise, the responding officer quickly surmised that he was staring at the body of the missing university student. He reported this back to the duty officer, who in turn alerted Chief Dupree.

That bright fall morning, Tony arrived in his office at his usual time, just before eight a.m. He was whistling a Santana tune from a CD that he'd been playing in the car, unaware of the tempest about to brew around him. That changed with the arrival of the chief in his doorway.

"Good morning, Detective Deluca." Dupree came in and quietly closed the door.

The chief's insistence on referring to his staff by their last names still struck Tony as a bit old school. Someone had told him it was the result of Dupree's stint in the military, where his training officer had drilled it in his head to refer to everyone by their surname, officers and non-officers alike.

Dupree sat heavily in the wooden chair in front of Tony's desk. At that moment he looked older than his fifty-two years. His dark skin had taken on an ashen tone. "I've just received some bad news. A body was found in the marshes on Lake Mendota near the university. We don't have a confirmed ID, but there's a good chance it's that university student who disappeared earlier this week."

"Accident or foul play?" Tony asked automatically and then realized it was a stupid thing to say. The chief wouldn't be sitting in his office looking the way he did if her death appeared to be accidental.

"All the signs point to it being a homicide. The first officer on the scene, a young officer by the name of Kelly, says she's been stripped naked and appears to have been dragged through the marsh. The body's in rough shape. Officer Kelly has the area locked down and I've requested additional back-up pending your arrival."

"My arrival?"

"That's right. I want you to lead the investigation. This situation has already received a lot of media play, with Sumner's parents posting that big reward and giving out press interviews. All eyes will be on us, and I want my best people on it. And there's no question you're the best we've got."

"What about Adelsky? Tony's chest felt constricted. "Shouldn't he lead the investigation? I can back him up and make sure he doesn't run into any trouble."

"Normally you'd be right. But not for this case. I've already had a quick call with the mayor and he's in total agreement – the city needs to be reassured we are taking this seriously and that a detective of your stature and experience is heading this up. Detective Adelsky will be your partner on the investigation, but he won't be in charge. He'll understand my decision."

Tony wasn't so sure this would be the case, but more than the possibility of hurting Aldelsky's feelings was causing him to hesitate. There were his own nagging doubts about his ability to manage another high-profile murder investigation after his last experience in Chicago.

He shoved these doubts aside. It could have been Carla who disappeared after a night in a bar. The thought both energized and angered him. He needed to find the person who did this, to make sure he didn't kill again. "Thanks for your confidence, sir."

"I'll talk to Detective Adelsky when he arrives. The two of you can then head over to the site to monitor the initial exam and sweep of the area for evidence. Make sure the both of you play this by the book. We can't afford mistakes."

After he left, Tony sat at his desk, feeling both disquiet and excitement at being back in the game. It dawned on him that he should speak to Joanna before she saw a report of the murder on TV. He picked up the phone and dialed home. "Jo, it's me."

"Is everything okay?" She clearly heard the tension in his voice.

"Not really. You know that university student who disappeared last Saturday night? They've found her body. I was just speaking with the chief. He's ... well, he's asked me to head up the investigation."

There was silence on the other end, and then a sigh. "And of course you accepted," Joanna said in a tight controlled voice.

"He really didn't give me a choice, and I need to do it." He tried not to sound defensive. "But this is the last one, I promise."

"Are you sure about this?"

"You don't need to worry. I'm not going to let this one get to me."

"Tony, remember, you've got to keep some perspective. You don't want this one to go like the last one."

"Jo, don't worry."

"But I do."

Before he could respond there was the soft click of the receiver. He exhaled, realizing he'd been holding his breath. He was a bit surprised Jo hadn't demanded he go back to the chief and refuse to take the job. It was certainly what she must've wanted, and he could tell it took a huge effort for her to accept the situation. He silently vowed to not let this case destroy the relationship they'd so painstakingly rebuilt since moving to Madison.

Chapter 2
8:15 AM

Back in his office, Chief Dupree put through a call to Kelly. To his satisfaction he learned that the additional officers had arrived and established a perimeter around the murder site. The chief pathologist was on the scene as well, waiting for the investigating officers to appear. Kelly also reported that a van carrying a reporter and camera person had just arrived in the parking lot.

How had the media managed to get there before his investigation team? Dupree wondered, not for the first time, if the duty officer might be feeding information to someone at the local TV station.

There remained one important task needing his full attention before the investigation started in earnest. Detective Adelsky had to be instructed that he would be taking, not giving, orders in this case. Dupree ran a big black hand through his short stubble of hair, not looking forward to the task. Despite what he'd said to Detective Deluca, he knew that Adelsky would need to be handled carefully. The man had a supersized ego and would not take lightly the usurping of his role as leader of the homicide team. Dupree was also aware that Adelsky was under a great deal of personal stress, being in the early stages of divorcing his wife.

A few minutes later Adelsky appeared at his doorway. He was a handsome man, slightly over six feet tall and well proportioned. His brown hair was cut short, almost military style, and he had piercing blue eyes that captivated a number of young women in the administrative ranks. One of those girls, barely twenty and now gone from the department, had been the final straw in his marriage falling apart.

Adelsky almost swaggered into the room and took a seat without being asked. "Mornin', Chief. I got here as soon as I could. Sorry to hear about that university student. I was pretty sure this would be the end result when she didn't show up, but it's a damn shame. I assume you want me to head over to the scene right away? I was planning to take Andrade with me. I think she's ready for the big times after that gang bang murder case she handled." Adelsky started to rise, expecting a quick approval from the chief before he was out the door.

"Wait a minute." Dupree motioned Adelsky to retake his seat. "I do want you to head over there, but not with Andrade. Given the profile of this case, I've asked Detective Deluca to participate in the investigation. His experience will be very important to bringing this to a quick and successful ..."

Adelsky cut him off. "Listen, Chief, I like Tony and all that, but he's a bit of an old dog for this gig. I need someone with fresh legs, who's prepared to do the grunt work and put in the long hours. Besides, I'm not confident he can handle the pressure. I've heard the stories about him imploding on his last case in Chicago."

Dupree felt his blood pressure rising. "Detective Adelsky, if you'd allowed me to continue, you would've learned that Detective Deluca will be running this investigation. Despite any stories you may have heard, he has an impressive record, and since his arrival has demonstrated that he can get the job done. This will be an excellent chance for you to learn from one of the best, while still playing a key role in the investigation."

The chief paused, waiting for a response. It was quick to come, and not what he'd hoped for. Adelsky's face turned a bright crimson, his mouth open in disbelief, and the powerful football shoulders rose to merge into his short neck.

"I knew it!" Adelsky spluttered. "That guy's been after my job ever since he got here. Trying to make it look he was helping me out, all the time plotting to push me out of the way. But Chief, listen to me – he's a real loser. He shouldn't be anywhere near this case."

"Be careful what you say here, detective," Dupree said sharply. "Don't be burning bridges with anyone in the department, including me."

"Let's make things clear." Adelsky's voice was now low and menacing. "I don't work with backstabbers. In fact, I'm not sure I want to be part of this team. This whole thing stinks."

"Detective! I know you've been under a lot of pressure at home, so I'm prepared to make allowances. But you've got to understand my position. With or without you, Detective Deluca will be leading this investigation. Now, what I want you to do is take the rest of the day off to reconsider your position. Report back to me tomorrow morning at nine hundred sharp to continue this discussion. Do I make myself clear?"

Adelsky barely nodded, pushing back his chair with a loud scraping noise. He jerked open the door and slammed it behind him with such force that it rattled the windows of the adjoining office.

Tony was distractedly reviewing a report when he heard the loud slam. He looked up to see Rick passing, his face frozen in anger. He stopped suddenly and returned to the open door. "Fuck you!" he shouted, embellishing his message with the middle finger of his right hand. Then he disappeared from sight.

Before Tony had a chance to react, his telephone rang. He saw the chief's extension on the call display and picked up. Dupree summoned him to his office without explanation.

When he arrived the chief was pacing, looking contemplative and somber. "Detective, come in and close the door."

Tony complied, and both men remained standing.

"My discussion with Detective Adelsky didn't go well. Quite bluntly, he has some issues with you leading the investigation. Don't take this personally. He's under significant stress from the separation with his wife. I'm no psychiatrist, but in my view he is – what do they say? – acting out his frustrations."

Tony remained silent, now understanding the incident outside his office.

"In any event, his reaction was unprofessional. I've given him the rest of day off to think about his situation. But given his uncertain status, we need to consider other options for the investigative team. What do you think about taking on Detective Andrade as your partner on this case? I know she's somewhat inexperienced, but otherwise she's an excellent detective."

Tony briefly contemplated the suggestion. He'd already spent some time with Bobby Andrade, getting to know her background and experience. She'd studied forensics and criminology at a college in Nebraska, joining the Omaha Police Department after graduating.

She had confided to him that initially things went well; she quickly moved up the ranks and into the homicide unit. There she met another detective, the so-called "happily married man," and they had an affair. She eventually came to the conclusion the relationship was going nowhere and, rather than continue to awkwardly work with him, made the decision to look around for another job. She had joined the Madison homicide department just over a year ago and had already successfully closed several difficult murder investigations.

Tony didn't hesitate. "I think she'd be an excellent choice."

"Very good, then, it's settled. You'd better go brief Detective Andrade and get going. There's a troop of people waiting at the crime scene for your arrival."

Tony made his way to Bobby's office. She was on the phone, playing with a strand of blond hair while listening intently to the other person on the line. Seeing Tony at her door, she held up a finger to indicate the call would end soon, motioning for him to sit down. The conversation, however, took longer than expected.

From what Tony could tell, the person on the line was an anxious and fearful witness to a homicide. Bobby was doing her best to calm him down and make sure he didn't recant the story he'd told the police.

Tony quietly observed Bobby as she continued her phone conversation. While not runway beautiful, she had a fresh complexion and fine features some would find attractive. She'd grown up on a farm in Nebraska, which probably explained her broad shoulders and well-toned body. He already knew from his limited interactions with her that she didn't take any shit and was always ready to speak her mind.

Bobby finally ended the call. "Sorry about that. Another gang murder … too many of them these days. That was one of my witnesses – his family has been threatened. Looks like they'll need protection. And to what do I owe the pleasure of your visit?"

Tony updated her on the events of the morning. Learning that he, and not Adelsky, would be leading the Sumner investigation, she raised her eyebrows but didn't comment. However, she couldn't disguise her excitement at finding out she'd be working with him.

As they drove toward campus, they discussed the significance of where the body had been discovered. The marshlands were part of a larger property, Picnic Point, owned by the University of Wisconsin, a mile-long peninsula jutting into Lake Mendota. The Point was a popular swimming spot for university students, Bobby explained. It was also frequented at night by romantically inclined couples. It seemed like an odd spot to dispose of a body, unless it was a crime of passion.

A small group of people were waiting for them near the entrance to the park. A young, fresh-faced police officer identified himself as Kelly and indicated he'd been the first person on the scene in response to the 911 call. Tony noted that his shoes and the hems of his pants were splattered with mud.

Kelly introduced Todd Preston, the associate chief pathologist at the University Hospital and head of the forensics team. Dr. Preston was in his late fifties, with overgrown furry eyebrows, a large handlebar mustache, and a red bow-tie clipped to his white shirt. If not for the dour look on his face, he would have appeared comical.

"What took you so long?" Preston asked sourly. "Even the press managed to arrive before you."

"Well, Dr. Preston, we're here now," Tony replied brusquely, not appreciating his tone. "Officer Kelly, please take us to the body."

Kelly led the group past the yellow police tape through a swath of cattails. Tony felt the greasy black muck sucking at his shoes, staining the cuffs of his pants in a similar pattern to Kelly's. They moved into single file, taking evasive measures to avoid pools of water and half-fallen trees. Finally they stopped in a small clearing where the ground cover had recently been trampled down.

Surveying the crime scene, Tony was overcome by shock and sadness. The young woman's face, ravaged by a week of exposure to the elements bore little resemblance to the pictures he'd seen of her. Her naked body was spread-eagled and caked in mud, as if she'd been dragged to this location.

Tony again battled the thought this could be his own daughter. He took a deep breath before giving orders for the team to move into action, telling two officers to search the surrounding area for footprints or other evidence that would be helpful to the investigation. Another officer assisted Dr. Preston in moving the body onto a plastic tarp.

As Dr. Preston prepared for the preliminary examination, Tony took Officer Kelly aside. "Tell me everything you know since you were called out."

Kelly flipped open a small notebook. "Okay. I was on early morning patrol, by myself. My partner had to go to emergency last night – thought he was having a heart attack. I'm pretty sure it's just heartburn from the double anchovy pizza we had last night after our shift."

Tony responded with a short smile.

"Anyway, I was driving along Campus Drive when I get a call from the duty officer. That was at, let's see, 7:14 a.m. He told me to get a move on to the parking lot nearest Picnic Point and meet with an individual named Jack Moffat. I was advised at that time about the discovery of a body and a possible homicide. When I get to the parking lot, there's a guy madly waving his arms. I pull over and it takes me a couple minutes to calm him down, he was in quite a state. Turns out he's a naturalist hired by Dane County to study local lakes for some sort of bacteria. He'd been out traipsing through the marsh since sunrise and stumbled upon the body. He called 911 on his cell phone, and that's about it from his perspective. I've let him go home, but I have all his contact information."

"Did you confirm that he didn't disturb the body?" Bobby asked.

"Yes sir. He was pretty scared and just slogged it out of there as fast as he could."

"Anything else to report?" Tony questioned.

"Not much. I called the Duty Officer at 7:25 and confirmed discovery of the body. He told me to lock down the location and said I'd be getting backup. Officers Johnson, Betz, Winter, and Groves arrived just before 8 a.m., and we established a larger security perimeter. Dr. Prescott arrived fifteen minutes ago … in a bad mood. I had a call from the chief and updated him on the situation. He told me to expect you and Detective Adelsky." He glanced at Bobby before returning to his notes. "That's about it."

"Good work, Kelly. The chief will be pleased with the way you handled this situation."

Kelly flushed at the compliment. "Thank you, sir."

"I'd like you to stay nearby and make sure we're not disturbed."

"Yes sir." Kelly moved about ten feet away and stood at attention.

Tony winked at Bobby, enjoying the opportunity to make Kelly's day. He turned back to where the pathologist was impatiently waiting for his go-ahead to start the examination. "Okay Dr. Preston, let's see what you can find."

"Finally," Preston muttered and knelt on the plastic ground sheet. He began with a careful review of the upper body, grunting at the discovery of a large wound on the back of Sumner's head, clotted with a mixture of dried blood and mud. He then worked his way down the body, trying to distinguish cuts and abrasions from the work of decomposition. His examination concluded with the collection of samples from under her fingernails. He nodded to Tony, and with the help of two officers, got the body into a body bag for transport to the hospital in the waiting ambulance.

"What are you initial conclusions, doctor?" Tony asked.

Dr. Preston ignored the question, removing his latex gloves and adjusting his bow tie, which had gone slightly askew during the examination. He retrieved a small steel comb from a pocket and swept it through his thick mustache. These grooming chores completed, he focused his attention on Tony.

"That's one nasty blow to the head, and at the very least knocked her out cold. But I need to get her back to the hospital before I can be certain that's the cause of death. There's the possibility she was still alive after being left out here, and she either bled out or just died of exposure."

"When can I expect your final report?"

"Let's see … two others came in last night. I'd have to say day after tomorrow."

"Dr. Preston, as you may have noticed, the press has been closely following the disappearance of this young woman. Her parents are in town and will be devastated. And the mayor has taken a personal interest in this matter. So I'm hoping you can do better than that." The inference was clear: *Speed it up or face the consequences.*

The pathologist knew enough not to argue. "Then you'll have my report first thing tomorrow."

Chapter 3
10:15 AM

The next step, Tony and Bobby agreed, would be to visit the last place Karen Sumner had been seen alive. The Capital Lounge was close to campus and on most evenings was crowded with rowdy students. However, it was still mid-morning when they arrived, and there was just a skeleton staff beginning to set up for lunch. Tony showed one young woman his badge and she said she would buzz the bar manager.

Moments later a man in his mid-thirties appeared. Short and slim, he was dressed casually in jeans and a silk paisley shirt. He had longish brown hair, and designer glasses perched on a slightly oversized nose.

Tony moved to greet him. "Detective Deluca. And this is Detective Andrade."

"Josh Stein. I own and manage this place. How can I help?"

"Is there a spot where we can talk privately?"

Stein looked concerned. "Of course. Let's go to my office." He led them back in the direction he'd come from, to a cramped office barely large enough for a desk and office chair. The walls were covered with autographed photographs of people taken at the bar. Tony didn't recognize anyone but assumed they were famous. On the desk sat a stack of file folders as well as a relatively new Apple computer connected to what looked like a portable credit card scanner.

Stein closed the door and squeezed around them to sit behind his desk. Tony and Bobby remained standing.

"Sorry, not much room in here, but it's the only spot in the place where we won't have staff barging in on us. Does your visit have anything to do with Karen Sumner? Has she been located?" Stein asked hopefully.

Tony nodded. "Yes, she has. Unfortunately it's not good news. Her body was discovered this morning, not far from here. She appears to have been murdered."

Stein's narrow shoulders drooped. "I still held out hope, you know, that she'd turn up okay. Worst case, I thought maybe she'd been kidnapped and would be released for the reward money offered by the parents. But this ... this is just terrible. Do you have any idea of what happened?"

"Not yet. We're at the very early stages of our investigation, trying to get up to speed with what happened prior to her death. I was hoping you could fill us in on her activities while she was here."

"Sure, it's all still pretty fresh in my mind. She entered the bar just after eight pm and left shortly before nine-thirty."

"How certain are you of those times?" Bobby interjected.

"Very certain." He picked up the device Tony had noticed on his desk. "This is an ID scanner, state of the art. Every person entering my bar has to provide their driver's license to security at the front door. It's scanned by this device, which, depending on the state of issue, can confirm whether the license is legit and the person is of legal drinking age. If everything checks out, they get in. Otherwise they need to find another spot to party. Every morning I download the information captured by the scanner onto my computer. In fact, I was doing the download from last night when you arrived. It provides me with a permanent record of everyone coming into the bar and confirmation of their drinking status. Very useful for audits by the Wisconsin State liquor authorities, or if some anti-drinking crusader tries to make the case we've been serving underage students."

"And your records indicate that Sumner entered and left the bar at the times you've indicated?"

"Well, partly. We only check IDs when people come into the bar, not when they leave."

"So how can you be sure when she left the bar?" Bobby asked.

"That's where the older technology comes into play. In addition to the front door, which in theory is always covered by security during operating hours, there are two other ways to get into or out of this bar. There's a fire door by the washrooms that leads to the back alley, and the loading door connected to the kitchen. There's an intrusion alarm on the fire door and I have security cameras covering the other doors. And another camera by the serving bar – to keep my bartenders honest."

"So the security camera picked up Ms. Sumner as she left the bar that evening?" Bobby asked.

"That's right."

"Do you have any video of her while she was actually in the bar area?" she quickly followed up.

"Unfortunately not. I asked one of my staff to review all the security footage for that evening. We have a recording of her when she arrived, but she wasn't picked up again until she left the bar. She came with her roommate, and I'm pretty sure she told the other detectives that they spent all their time on the dance floor. We don't have security cameras there."

"Okay," Tony said, "so she came in with her roommate, but I understand they didn't leave together. Doesn't the security video indicate Sumner might've have been with someone else when she left?"

"The camera by the front door is positioned to pick up the faces of people entering the bar, not leaving. Also, it was a Saturday night after a Badger's game, so it was extremely busy, lots of people coming and going. We were lucky to pick her out of the crowd on her way in."

"Can we get a copy of the security video and a printout from that scanner of yours?" Tony asked.

"They've already been provided to..." Stein opened a desk drawer and extracted a business card. "Let's see, Detective Thorsen. He was one of the officers investigating the disappearance. I can have additional copies made if you want."

"No need, we'll follow up with Thorsen. Just a few other questions and we'll be on our way. Does any of your staff recall seeing Sumner or her roommate during the evening?"

"Nope. Like I said, it was a busy night. Everyone had their head down and was working hard. Unless she did something to draw attention to herself, she would've been pretty much invisible. And evidently she didn't do anything remarkable. You might want to double check with Detective Thorsen to confirm all this. He and his partner interviewed almost everyone who worked that night."

"*Almost* everyone?" Bobby inquired.

"One of the bartenders who worked that night has been out of town due to a family illness. Not sure when she'll be back."

Bobby asked for her name and made a note.

"One final question," said Tony. "Did you or your staff see *anything* out of the ordinary that evening?"

Stein gave a shrug of regret. "It was just a regular crazy night after a big Badgers football win."

Jennifer and Karen

MAY 14-25, 2014

Chapter 1
MAY 14 6:25 PM

Tony left his Mustang at the back of the Varsity Club's lot. He couldn't even remember driving between home and work. His brain had been in overdrive, thinking about his conversation with Drake. What did it mean, Curtis Mansfield turning up dead? Would the investigation be reopened? And what impact would this have on his lawsuit? More unanswered questions....

As he passed through the service entrance, he reflected on the fact that he'd now entered his second month working security at the Varsity Club. He was grateful to Josh Stein for the regular paycheck. Ironic, he thought, that he was working for the owner of the bar where Karen Sumner had last been seen alive, even if this wasn't the same bar.

After the murder of Karen Sumner, the fickle university crowd had gravitated away from the now-infamous Capital Lounge to other local bars. Josh Stein had done everything he could to attract business back, with little success. Eventually he'd decided to branch out and purchased the Madison Restaurant, close to the university but in need of major renovations. Once the sale was completed, he closed the place and gutted it to the brick walls, rebuilding it into a trendy new bar, restaurant, and dance club.

Tony had seen a story in the newspaper that the Madison was about to be reborn as the Varsity Club and was hiring for security positions. By then he'd been without a job for almost six months. After some initial hesitation, he swallowed his pride and applied. Josh had personally met with him for the interview. After less than five minutes, Tony got a job offer.

Typically, he worked six nights a week, his shift starting at 7 pm and ending when the last bar patron was escorted out the front door. Tonight as usual, he was here early to take advantage of one of the few perks of the job – a free dinner. He also enjoyed watching the head cook, Leon Sanders, prepare what he called gourmet pub grub. Leon had no formal training as a chef, but no other local restaurant could match his cooking.

Leon was already hard at work, his forehead beaded with sweat from the kitchen's heat. The six-burner gas cook top was crowded with steaming pots, and the pungent aroma of heavily spiced food filled the air. Leon was barking orders at one of the assistant cooks, His normally jovial face was screwed up in a frown.

"Hey, Leon, what's got you so riled"? Tony called to him.

Leon's dark expression cleared a bit. "Eh, Tony. One of the fuckin' kitchen staff has called in sick again, and this dude here doesn't have a clue what he's doing. Other than dat, life's normal. How 'bout you?"

It didn't sound that bad to Tony after the day he'd just had, but he chose not to point it out. "Getting better, now I'm in your kitchen with all these interesting smells. What's the special tonight?"

Leon grinned. "I made up some of my Grandma's favorite recipes, grilled possum and fricasseed pigeon. If dat don't catch your fancy, I'm also cookin' up some meatloaf."

"No disrespect to Grandma, but I'll go for the meatloaf. It's one of my favorites."

"Probably a good choice. Possum can be tough, and the pigeon are scrawny this time of year. I still gotta dozen things to do, so grab a plate and help yerself. It'll be done by now."

Leon returned to berating the assistant cook while Tony got himself a heaping plate of meatloaf from the oven and a bottle of water. He savored the first bite, trying to identify the various ingredients that complemented the ground beef. There were mushrooms, onions, tomato sauce and something very hot – likely jalapeño peppers, combined with a sampling of Leon's special spices. The meatloaf was certainly good, but he preferred Joanna's. He thought about her and Carla, and for a brief moment felt the loneliness of his life.

He was brought back to the present by a young woman bursting through the swinging doors into the kitchen. Her eyes fell on Tony, standing with a fork in one hand and an empty plate in the other. "Can you please help me?" she panted.

"Why, sure," he said easily. "What's the problem?"

"I'm new here. I work behind the bar. The CO_2 tank for the draft beer dispenser is empty and I'm trying to attach a new one. Whoever replaced the last one must've been a gorilla. I can't turn the release valve. You look like a strong guy. I was hoping you could twist it open."

"Show me where it is."

"Follow me." The young woman made a beeline out of the kitchen with her new-found friend. In the bar area, she bent down to point out the location of several tanks. She turned to make sure Tony could see which one she was pointing at, and caught him staring at her ass.

Tony flushed. The moment quickly passed and she pointed again. "That's the offending tank. If you can replace it without breaking the release mechanism that would be great."

He took her place, kneeling down in front of the tank. There was the smell of stale beer and he moved carefully within the enclosed space to avoid a large sudsy puddle. He grasped the valve and gave a manly grunt as he applied pressure. There was the hiss of escaping gas as the valve gave way. He kept turning until it fully released and then pulled away the hose attached to the tank. "Mission accomplished." He stood and swung the empty tank out of its place, replacing it with the new tank.

"Should be fine now." Tony found a towel on the bar and wiped his hands.

"Thanks very much, I would never have been able to do that by myself, and serving flat beer would not be good for business. By the way, my name's Julie."

"Glad to meet you, Julie. Welcome aboard."

"And you are....?"

"Sorry – Tony. Tony Deluca. If you haven't already guessed from the big letters on the back of this jacket, I work security around here."

"Nice to meet you, Tony. I feel much safer knowing that you're around."

"Tony?"

They both looked around and saw Josh Stein. He was looking quite dapper in a blue flowered shirt, grey chino pants and leather sandals.

"Hi, Tony, Julie. I see you've met. Sorry to interrupt, Tony, but I'd like to talk to you before the crowd starts to arrive."

"No problem." Tony turned to Julie and felt her deep blue eyes connect with his. He had to force himself to move. "Well, duty calls. But if you ever feel harassed or in danger, just shout."

"Oh, I will. And by the way, you have a very nice ass." Julie gave him a mischievous smile as she headed behind the bar. Tony spent another moment admiring the swing of Julie's hips before turning to Josh.

Josh was smiling. "Hope I didn't interrupt anything important."

"Just helping a damsel in distress. What's up?"

"I had a call from one of my police buddies. He said rumors are going around the department that Curtis Mansfield has turned up. I was wondering if you'd heard anything."

Of course, Tony knew that Josh would be very interested in anything that had to do with Mansfield, given that he was the main suspect in the Sumner murder. The death had taken its toll on Josh, both financially and personally, after the bad press resulting from Sumner's disappearance from his bar. Tony had a lot of sympathy for Josh, given his own circumstances.

"Yes, I heard someone camping at a park in Waukesha County stumbled on the body. From what I understand, he was caught in that crazy snowstorm we had last September. Crashed his car and ended up freezing to death."

Josh shook his head. "Tony, I know you have doubts about Mansfield being the killer, but I have to admit to feeling a great deal of relief with this news. I don't want to wish ill on anyone, but the evidence suggests that at the very least Mansfield was a dangerous sexual predator, if not in fact a killer."

Tony could understand how Josh felt. Mansfield wasn't someone you'd want anywhere near your children. But while Tony had been in charge of the investigation, he'd felt there were too many unanswered questions to justify an arrest. With Mansfield's death, he wondered if the truth would ever be known.

"I expect this will bring the murder investigation to a close, and hopefully some closure for the girl's parents," said Josh. "Perhaps this is better for them than having to go through a trial. Anyway, if you hear anything more, let me know."

"Sure." Tony watched as Josh headed back to his office and decided it was time to officially start his security shift. At the front entrance, Dan Stockton was already checking IDs. They would work as a team through the evening, rotating between the front door and bar patrol.

Tony had shared a shift with Dan on many occasions. When they'd first been introduced, Tony couldn't help staring at his enormous belly. It was matched by his round chubby face, framed by short blond hair and uneven beard stubble. That generous paunch was the result of Dan's love for beer and total abhorrence of physical activity.

One night after one of their shifts, sitting at the bar enjoying their own last call, Tony had watched his new buddy consume six beers in just over an hour, without making a pit stop. He was not only amazed that anyone could retain that much fluid, but that Dan showed no obvious signs of being intoxicated.

During this exhibition of drinking prowess, they'd exchanged somewhat superficial life stories. Dan had related his attempts to graduate from several colleges in the Midwest. His parents had finally told him that any further educational pursuits would be on his own tab. He'd recently moved to Madison and was trying to earn enough money to enroll at U of W.

Dan had no inkling of Tony's background, and Tony preferred to keep it that way. So he'd simply said he was a retired police detective from Chicago who had decided to seek out the slower-paced life of Madison. At that point in their conversation Dan seemed more interested in complaining to the bartender about a short pour of beer than Tony's life history, so it was left at that.

"Any excitement, Dan?" Tony scanned the snaking line of university students waiting to enter the bar. Many were passing the time by texting friends or reading emails on their phones.

Dan paused from checking a young woman's ID. "Not really. But as they say, the night is still very young."

"How about I take over? You can make sure those frat boys who just came in don't try to take a box of Jack Daniels out the back door."

"Hell, if they cut me in, I might even help 'em. Then again, that sounds like too much work." Handing Tony the ID scanner, Dan shuffled off in the direction of the dance floor.

The next person in line was a pimply-faced young man with short hair gelled into spikes. While he didn't look old enough to drink legally, Tony was aware he thought the same thing about many of the people already in the bar. He knew he was getting old when the scanner confirmed that Mr. Spiky Hair twenty-two years old. "You're a winner," Tony said, and let him move into the bar.

When he next looked at his watch, it was almost time for Dan to return and take over the front door. He took the driver's license being offered by a short, buxom blonde in a tight cotton sweater and black jeans. She gave him a big smile, and the image of a young

Marilyn Monroe popped into his mind. He ran her license through the scanner and it emitted a high-pitched beep. An 'X' appeared on the screen over her personal information.

Tony held the license for a closer look. It was issued in Ohio to a Catherine Adams. The birth date on the license confirmed she was of legal drinking age in the State of Wisconsin. The picture on the license certainly matched the young girl in front of him. He was about to chalk it up to an electronic glitch and let her in when she opened her mouth.

"I'm not sure what your little machine says, but I really am twenty-one years old," she said confidently.

Tony looked at the license again. "How old did you say you are?

"I recently turned twenty-one." She thrust out her breasts as if to confirm the fact.

"Are you sure about that?"

"Of course I'm sure," she said, her voice rising.

Other people in line behind her stopped talking to watch what was happening.

"Sorry, your license says you should be twenty-two."

Catherine looked momentarily confused. Then a big smile formed on her face and she said, somewhat triumphantly, "Well, that's certainly old enough for me to enter the bar."

Tony had to stifle a laugh and in his most serious voice started to say, "Unfortunately, the state laws won't...."

A loud voice cut him off before he could finish his sentence. "Come on, Inspector Clouseau, give us all a break and let her in. You're cutting into valuable drinking time."

There was a titter of laughter from several people in line, but Tony was oblivious to it. He'd suddenly been transported back in time to another bar, where someone else had compared him to the bumbling French detective. He took exception to it then, and he planned to do so again. He looked down the stretching line of students, quickly identifying the person who'd made the comment by the smirk on his face. He took note and then returned his focus on the busty woman in front of him. "Okay, Ms. Adams. Sorry for the inconvenience. In you go."

She showed him a set of bright white teeth and moved quickly past him into the bar area. At that moment Dan arrived at Tony's shoulder. He did a full 360 turn as the young woman passed them. "That girl's got a beautiful set of knockers."

Tony nodded absently. "Dan, can you give me five more minutes? I have some unfinished business."

"No problem, man, take your time. I'll just make sure that young woman doesn't get into any trouble. Did you catch her name?"

"Yeah, but you don't have time for that. Be back here in five."

Tony quickly moved through the next six people in line, clearing them to enter without even checking their IDs. However, he held up his hand to stop the next person and asked for the young man's driver's license. He ran it through the scanner and was provided with his vital statistics: Jonathan Caldwell, age 23, 190 lbs, blue eyes, Suite 1104, 119 West Washington Ave, Wisconsin.

Tony took his time, examining the person in front of him. Caldwell stood just over six feet, with an athletic build, squared handsome face and very short blond hair. He wore a silky short sleeved shirt, linen pants and cowboy boots.

Caldwell returned Tony's stare, a patronizing look on his face. "How the mighty have fallen."

"What did you say?" Tony asked sharply.

"You heard me. From macho homicide detective to lowly door man. Must really hurt."

Tony felt a pang of anger. "You seem to know who I am, but I don't believe I've had the pleasure," he said icily.

"Well, you do have my ID," Caldwell smirked.

Tony examined the driver's license again. "Jonathan Caldwell. Then he put it together. The fancy downtown condo, expensive clothes and condescending attitude. "Let me guess. You're Senator Caldwell's son."

"Very good, Inspector. You *do* have some deductive reasoning skills."

"Well, there's one thing I can't figure out."

"What's that?"

"How'd you come up with Inspector Clouseau?"

"Well, I've seen the movie. You two seem to have a lot in common."

Tony flinched inwardly and decided it was time to gain the upper hand. "You seem to have strong opinions for such a young man. Or perhaps you're just parroting the words of your father."

Caldwell's smile faded. The words had clearly hit a nerve. "Don't give me that crap. I don't need anyone to do my thinking, especially my father. Now let me into the bar before I speak to the owner and get you fired... again." Caldwell was visibly fighting to control his own anger.

For a moment Tony considered blocking his way to see what would happen. But his better judgment told him that it would not end well for Caldwell or himself, and he needed this job. He jerked his head for Caldwell to enter.

"I thought you'd see it my way." Caldwell gloated as he pushed his way past.

"There's a guy who needs to work on his manners." Tony glanced around to see Dan right behind him. "What did he mean about you getting fired 'again'?"

"Oh, I had another job where I didn't see eye-to-eye with management." Tony said, glossing over the truth.

Dan still looked a bit puzzled by the angry exchange between Tony and Caldwell, but decided to leave it alone. "Five minutes are up. Are you ready to be spelled off?"

"Yes, I need a break and perhaps a shower after that little encounter. I'll see you in an hour or so." Tony felt the dryness in his throat and decided he needed something to drink. In the main bar, he observed Julie filling a stein with nicely foaming beer and realized he could take some credit for this.

Julie pushed some stray brown hair away from her bright blue eyes as she spotted him approaching the bar. "Ah, Mr. Security Man. You look like you could do with a beer – or perhaps something stronger?" Her smile almost made him forget his recent encounter.

"Would love a beer, but still on duty. For the moment I'll settle for a Coke."

"Coming right up." As Julie moved over to retrieve his order from a large glass-front fridge, she was hailed by someone who'd just arrived at the bar.

"Hey babe, don't you think you should serve paying customers first?"

The senator's son was standing at the bar, waving a twenty dollar bill in Julie's direction.

Julie frowned at him. "Hold your horses. I'll be there in a minute." She returned with a cold can of Coke and muttered to Tony, "Looks like the prodigal son has returned. Unfortunately, he doesn't appear to have learned any manners from boot camp. Let me take care of him and I'll be right back."

She went over to where Caldwell was standing. He spoke and then placed his hand on her arm. She pulled away from his grasp, took a Bud from the fridge, and set it in front of him. He winked and handed her the bill, walking away without waiting for his change. Julie shook her head in disgust and returned to where Tony was waiting.

"I take it you know him?"

"Well, sort of, but he doesn't seem to remember. I ran across him a while ago. He came into another bar where I worked and told me he was celebrating his last days of freedom before joining the army. As I recall, he didn't seem very happy with the prospect of serving his country. He ended up getting drunk and I had to put out the word that he was cut off. Fortunately he left without putting up too much of a fuss. I have to admit I'm surprised to see him back here in civvies. Thought it was a good thing that Uncle

Sam would be keeping him occupied, that a trip to the Middle East might help build his character.

"Maybe, but it certainly wouldn't have improved our relations over there."

Julie laughed. She then noticed one of the waitresses trying to get her attention. "Well, I'd better go."

Tony stole another look at Julie's swaying hips as she headed to the other end of the bar, and then shook his head with regret. *Buddy, she's way too young for you.* The clock over the bar said 8:15. "Oh joy, another five hours of babysitting university students," he said under his breath. It was shaping up to be a long night.

Chapter 2

The next morning Tony awoke with Sam nestled in her usual place on the pillow beside him, purring loudly into his ear. After showering and shaving, he made himself a breakfast of scrambled eggs, thick bacon, and whole-wheat toast. Taking it with a coffee to the front deck, he was content to eat and enjoy his view of the lake.

It was a real shame, he mused, that the owner of the cottage, a commercial real estate developer by the name of Frank Thomas, was in the process of getting approval from the city to tear it down and build a 4,000-square-foot monstrosity. The old place deserved better than that. However, he was thankful to have the opportunity to rent it until Frank was ready to build.

When he returned to the kitchen to clean up, he ventured into the laundry room where the garbage pail resided. He remembered then that he'd started a wash before going to work the previous night. As he pulled his jogging gear, assorted clothes, and fishing vest out of the machine, he felt a sharp pain in his left hand and dropped everything on the floor. A puncture wound in his palm was rapidly welling with blood. Carefully sorting through the wet clothes, he found cause of his injury. A sharp hook was sticking through the fabric of the fishing vest pocket.

He mentally kicked himself. After risking life and limb to re-trieve his prized antique lure, he'd managed to put it through a laundry cycle. He pulled open the vest pocket and closely examined the lure. It didn't seem any worse for wear. As he carefully extracted the hook, he noticed there was another object in the vest pocket.

It took him a moment to recall that he'd retrieved a circular piece of metal from the lake bottom just before resurfacing. At the time he'd thought it was one of the decorative bangles from the lure, pulled away in his efforts to disentangle it from the rope around Harding's body. It too had gone for a whirl in the washing machine.

Taking a closer look, he noticed distinct markings on both sides of the quarter-sized object. It had not come from the lure, he realized. It appeared instead to be a small medallion, with a broken metal loop at one edge likely meant for a chain. On one side was a faint outline of an elderly figure, with words running around the perimeter. On the other side was a short inscription partially obscured by a greenish patina.

He took his find into the kitchen and took a clean dishcloth from a drawer. Dampening the cloth, he carefully cleaned the medallion. When he was finished, it almost sparkled, and he could clearly make out the engravings. The figure was a bearded old man in flowing robes. He appeared to be carrying a baby on his shoulders while walking over water. Framing the picture was the inscription "St. Christopher, Protect Us." Although Tony hadn't been to church in many years, he realized he was holding a Saint Christopher's medal.

Turning it over, he read aloud the letters etched on the other side: "To J, Love R."

Based on where he'd found the medallion, could he assume that the "J" was for Jennifer? If so, this must have been a gift to the murdered woman. But who was "R," and was this person somehow involved in her death?

This was an important piece of evidence that should be turned over to the police. It was unlikely that forensics could have lifted any fingerprints or DNA from the medallion after it being in the lake. But now that it had gone through a wash cycle as well as a thorough polishing, there was no hope of forensics finding anything useful. If Bobby was upset with him for cutting the rope around Harding's body, she was really going to be pissed now.

He put this little problem aside for the moment and turned his attention back to the medallion. From his Sunday school days, he knew that St. Christopher was the patron saint of safe travel. Unfortunately the protective powers of the martyred saint had not been sufficient to protect the young lawyer from an untimely death.

It suddenly occurred to him that he was at a crossroads in his own travels. The events of the past nine months had pushed him far off course in his life journey, and he'd wondered if he would ever find his way back. He desperately missed Joanna and Carla as well as his life as a respected homicide cop. But those days, it seemed, were behind him.

He tried to throw off these negative thoughts. He still had the training and experience of a top-notch detective. There was plenty of time to start over and regain his old form. Perhaps he could even use his investigative skills to assist the police in solving Harding's murder. However, he quickly realized this was not an option: Adelsky would stand in his way. On the other hand, there was nothing stopping him from conducting his own little side investigation.

He gave the idea further consideration. Working outside the system offered some advantages. He didn't have to go by the book, worry about stepping on other peoples' toes, or waste time on administrative paperwork. And he still had his contacts in the Chicago PD, including his former partner. With some help from the right people, he might be able to cobble together enough information to crack Harding's murder before Adelsky even knew he was involved. And getting the upper hand on Adelsky would feel almost as good as finding the killer.

With a sense of purpose he hadn't felt in a long time, Tony went to the old oak desk in the corner of the living room. Sitting down in a well-worn leather office chair, he pulled out a police notepad, making notes of things that needed to be checked out. He was back in the murder solving business, and it felt good.

Chapter 3
MAY 15 1:30 PM

The small table at Starbucks was within spitting distance of the State Capitol building and police headquarters. Tony had selected the busy location to preclude the possibility of Bobby going ballistic when he outlined the real reason he wanted to meet.

"I appreciate you making time to meet with me. You must be extremely busy with everything that's gone down in the past couple of days."

"Yeah, it's been hectic, but you made it difficult to say no." She got right to the point. "Tell me, what information do you have relating to Harding's murder?"

"Before we get into that, I wanted to let you know I've been retained to carry on an independent investigation into Jennifer Harding's death."

"Retained? By who?" she asked incredulously.

"Sorry, I'm not in a position to divulge that." The conversation would come to a quick end if she discovered he was the client.

"Tony, the body was only recovered yesterday. We've barely started our own investigation. Why would someone pay you to stick your nose into this before the police have had a kick at the can?"

"Two reasons. First, my client knows your resources are stretched thin. And second, at this stage in my career I'm relatively cheap. Oh yeah, then there's that thing about me being a good detective. So that makes three good reasons." Tony held up three fingers.

"Well, this is an interesting development, to say the least."

Tony took a sip of his espresso before responding. "That it is. And I was hoping we might be able to share information as we move along in our respective investigations."

"Sorry, Tony, but you know that won't work. I'm not at liberty to share information with you, or anyone else for that matter, who's not associated with the police investigation. Adelsky would blow a gasket if he knew we were having this conversation."

Tony had anticipated her objections and moved on to the next phase of his pitch. "I understand your concerns about Adelsky, but he doesn't have to know about our deal. On the other hand, I still have my connections within the Chicago PD, and I could just as easily be talking with them. I don't think either you or Adelsky would be very pleased to have another police department getting credit for solving a murder in your own backyard."

He let this sink in. He could tell from Bobby's expression that she was wrestling with how to proceed. He felt sorry for putting her in this position, but he didn't have many other options.

Finally, with a frown, she said, "If Adelsky gets wind that I'm giving you information on the side, he'll have my badge. On the other hand, we certainly want to stay in control of the investigation. So I'm willing to consider some off-the-record information exchange. But there are conditions."

"And they are?" Tony tried to hide his excitement that Bobby was seriously considering his proposal.

"First, no one can know about our arrangement. That includes your client."

"Done."

"Second, if I feel you're not pulling your weight, I stop sharing."

"Of course. And I reserve that right as well," he said with a slight smile.

"Finally, you need to give me your word that you won't provide your client with any information pertinent to this investigation, from any source, without first discussing it with me."

While this third condition did not create any practical difficulties, Tony still objected. "What's this about? My client will want regular reports. What's your problem with my at least sharing the information I dig up?"

"Tony, let's be clear about what the stakes are. My career will be over if anyone in the department gets wind that I'm providing confidential police information to you. I know you won't deliberately screw with me, but I don't know who your client is, and consequently I can't trust 'em. So to prevent 'whomever' getting information that could be traced back to me, I want your client to be in the dark as much as possible. Tell him, or her, that you need to sift through the information before providing a report. Or make up another story. Just don't give any factual details unless I say so. This is non-negotiable."

"Okay, I get it. You don't want this little arrangement to come to light and deep-six your career. I guess I can live with that, and my client will understand when it's said and done, provided we get the results."

"Good. Then we have a deal. Now, do you actually have some information relating to the murder? Or was this just a ruse to get me here to strike this deal?"

Tony gave her a hurt look. "I'm surprised after all we've been through that you'd doubt me. I've discovered something that might be very important to your investigation." He dug into his windbreaker pocket and pulled out a clear plastic bag.

"Where did you get this?" She snatched it from his hand.

"At the bottom of the lake, by Harding's body. I thought it had fallen off my lure. I forgot all about it until this morning when I found it in my fishing vest pocket. You've probably figured out it's a Saint Christopher's medal. From the inscription, it was a gift from someone very special to her. Finding out that person's identity could be critical."

Bobby nodded. "I expect recovering fingerprints or DNA is out."

"I'm afraid so. In addition to handling the medallion, it was pretty dirty so I cleaned it up with soap and water. I would've been more careful had I known its relevance."

"See, this is a perfect example of why you shouldn't be poking around in this case!" Bobby snapped. "A number of people are going to be very upset to learn you've played around with more evidence."

The comment stung. "On the other hand, the body could still be at the bottom of the lake, with her family and friends wondering where the hell she got to. So let's focus on the benefits of my role to date and forget about the guilt trips."

She backed down. "Okay, you've got a point. I'll send this to forensics and see if they can make anything from it. I'll also notify the investigators in Chicago. They can talk to Harding's family and see if they know who this 'R' person might be."

Tony decided it was time to move on. "What about the autopsy report? Has it been completed?"

"Yes, Dr. Thomas dropped it on my desk just before lunch."

"How about giving me the highlights?" He saw hesitation on her face. "If this is going to work, Bobby, you'll need to fill me in on what you have. That's the whole concept of information sharing."

"Sorry, it's not that. I'm just very uncomfortable giving you this kind of information in the middle of Starbucks."

Tony looked around the crowded coffee shop. "I see your point. Let's get out of here."

They picked up their coffees. Once out on the street, Bobby followed Tony in the direction of the green space surrounding the capitol building. When she was sure no one else was within hearing distance, she started to talk in a lowered voice. "The cause of death hasn't been determined with total certainty."

"She didn't drown?"

"No, that's been ruled out. There was very little water in her stomach or lungs. It appears she was dead before her body entered the lake."

"Then what's the best guess on cause of death?"

"Could be one of two things. There was a nasty wound on her head, complemented by multiple cuts and abrasions over the entire body. But it's not certain if these were incurred before or after she entered the water. Then there is significant bruising around her neck, and the hyoid bone was broken – consistent with her being strangled. Unfortunately, Dr. Thomas can't determine which event caused her death."

Tony considered the information. Harding might have been hit on the head to render her senseless and then strangled. But this was only conjecture at this point. "Any signs of recent sexual activity?"

"Again, the good doctor couldn't come to any firm conclusion due to the body's immersion in the lake.

"How about time of death?"

"Best estimate, based on the body's condition, is she'd been dead for a max of forty-eight hours when you found her. This is consistent with information we've received from her office in Chicago. She was last seen by a co-worker on Monday evening around 7 pm, still working in her office. She didn't show up for work on Tuesday and didn't respond when her assistant called to find out when she was coming in."

"That would indicate she arrived in Madison sometime Monday evening or Tuesday at the latest."

"Yeah, that appears to be the timing."

"Is there anything else of interest in the report?"

"Dr. Thomas also ordered a tox screen. The report showed trace levels of Ecstasy in her system."

Tony stopped in mid-stride, surprised. Ecstasy, or XTC, was used by both the upwardly mobile and teenaged ravers. Users claimed to experience increased energy, euphoria, and intense feelings of sexual intimacy. However, the U.S. Drug Enforcement Agency had determined that Ecstasy offered no medicinal benefits and put it in the same criminal classification as LSD, heroin, and marijuana. This meant possible jail sentences for those caught dealing or using the drug. "So there may be some skeletons in her closet."

"Perhaps. But maybe it wasn't taken voluntarily. Her killer may have slipped it into a drink or forced her to take it."

"Right. I shouldn't jump to conclusions. Now, yesterday you mentioned you met Harding at a conference in Chicago. Do you know if she kept in touch with anyone in Madison?"

Bobby considered his question. "We really only discussed business. She gave me some background on several recent Illinois decisions relating to the admissibility of DNA evidence. The only thing I can say for certain is she would've had the chance to meet a number of people from the Madison Police Department at the conference. For example, I saw Adelsky talking with her after her session. But she didn't mention knowing anyone else from Madison when we spoke."

"Hopefully the Chicago police can figure this out from her email and phone records. What are your next steps?"

"I have a meeting with Adelsky in about an hour to discuss the current status of the case. I want to find out what aspects of the case the Chicago PD will be following up on and what we'll be responsible for. You know how it is: it always gets complicated when the investigation requires the cooperation of police in different jurisdictions. What about you?"

"I have a couple days off from work and plan to drive over to visit my dad in Chicago. While I'm there, I'll touch base with my old police partner. I'm hoping he can give me the inside scoop on Harding, the stuff that never makes it into the written reports. When I get back, I'll start mapping out a strategy for moving forward with my investigation."

"Why don't you give me a call then? I'll update you, and you can do the same for me."

"Sounds like a plan." Looking directly into her eyes, he added. "I'm glad you've agreed to this arrangement. I think I can help, and it's important that we find out who killed her before the trail gets too cold."

Bobby hesitated, then responded with a tentative smile. "Yes, agreed. And it'll be good to work with you again."

Chapter 4
MAY 15 5:35 PM

Tony's parents had moved to the suburb of Edison Park in north Chicago about fifteen years earlier, in anticipation of Joseph's retirement from his trade as a master electrician. Tony always thought it both ironic and fitting that his parents had moved to a place named after Thomas Edison, inventor of the light bulb. In truth, they'd been drawn to the area by the European character of the community, and the relatively inexpensive prices of houses. His parents had a well-kept home with a south-facing backyard, which was ideal for a large garden.

They did end up spending much of their time in the backyard; planting, tending and harvesting everything from cucumbers, tomatoes, and carrots to blackberries. In the fall it would take Tony's mom, Maria, almost a full month to can, bottle or freeze the fruits of their labor. They'd spend another month distributing the spoils to neighbors and friends. This job done, they'd enjoy Christmas with family and friends before driving south to Panama City in Florida.

This comfortable seasonal cycle of life was maintained until about four years ago, when . Maria started to complain about feeling tired all the time and began to lose weight. She was diagnosed with breast cancer. Despite a mastectomy, followed by chemotherapy and radiation, she succumbed to the dreaded disease. Almost two years had passed since then.

After her death Tony had tried to spend as much time as possible with his dad. Unfortunately, with his own recent problems, he hadn't kept in touch as much as he should have. This just added another layer of guilt to his already weighted shoulders, so he was glad for an opportunity to visit.

He parked in front of his father's house and unloaded several bags of groceries from the car – ingredients for dinner. Despite his dad now being in his early eighties, the grass looked freshly cut and well-groomed, the garden beds had been edged, and the perennials were in full bloom. Joseph was still keeping things ship-shape.

A moment later the door opened. Joseph was almost a half foot shorter than Tony and had become slightly stooped, taking on the appearance of a gnome. Thinning grey hair sat atop his brown wizened face, deeply wrinkled from exposure to the sun in the back garden. It looked like he'd lost weight, his faded jeans and checked shirt hanging loosely on him. But what Tony noticed most of all was the big smile spreading across his father's face.

Joseph opened the screen door. "Well, look what the dog dragged in."

"That's 'cat,' Dad, and good to see you too." Despite living in the States for most of his life, Joseph still struggled with English idiom.

Tony put down his groceries in the hallway and father and son hugged. Joseph continued to hold onto Tony's shoulders, peering intently into his eyes. "You look better, like you have purpose again."

Tony felt pleased by his father's observation. "Yes, well, it does feel like my life is slowly coming back together. And I've had plenty of time to think about things. There have also been some interesting developments I can fill you in on. But let's get this food in the kitchen and we can talk while I make dinner."

"I look forward to someone else's cooking. Mine is not so good."

Unlike the carefully kept front yard, the kitchen looked like a tornado had swept through. There were unwashed dishes in the sink, open boxes of cereal on the counter, grocery coupons and financial statements scattered on the kitchen table. A month's worth of old newspapers was haphazardly piled up in a corner. "Glad to see you cleaned up for my visit," Tony said dryly.

"You should've seen it earlier

"Why don't you clear off the table, Dad, and set it for dinner? I'll wash up these dishes and then get started with the cooking."

They both got to their chores and the kitchen was soon to the point where Tony felt comfortable unloading the food. From one bag he pulled out romaine lettuce, noodles, fresh parmesan, ground veal, and a loaf of bread. The next bag had fresh garlic cloves, balsamic vinegar and other necessities for the meal.

Joseph looked on with approval. "Ah, a real Tuscan meal. Your mother used to make pasta every Saturday. Those were good days." His voice shaded into sadness.

"I used to get up early on Saturdays and go with her to the market." Tony remembered his mother picking out the vegetables and meat she planned to serve that night. He'd help carry the bulging shopping bags. By noon she'd be in the kitchen making preparations for the large meal, bustling about, humming a favorite tune. Around four, the guests would begin to arrive. This was the signal for Joseph to move into action, serving his homemade wine and making off-color jokes, switching between Italian and his somewhat tortured English. After dinner Tony would be sent to bed. However, he couldn't sleep through the talking, shouting, and laughing that got louder as the evening wore on. Those were indeed good times.

He decided to change the subject before the both of them settled into a dreary melancholy. "How's the garden coming along?"

Joseph brightened. "The rain has been very good. I think we are a week ahead of last year. I am trying something new, eggplant. I should get a good price from the local restaurants. And the sunflowers are already two feet tall. Your mother loved the sunflowers in the fall."

"I want a tour after dinner. Do you still have any canned tomatoes from last year's crop? I'd love to put them in the meat sauce."

Joseph got up from the table, clearly pleased that he could make a contribution to the meal. He made his way slowly to the basement stairs and headed down to the cold cellar. Tony occupied himself washing the romaine leaves, getting out a frying pan and pot and turning on the oven for the garlic bread.

His dad was back several minutes later with two glass jars filled with red tomatoes. "This will really make a good sauce," he said proudly.

"Great. Now, stand back and watch the maestro."

While Tony focused on food preparations, his father pulled an old newspaper from the pile on the floor. He sat at the table and spread out the sports section, pondering the baseball box scores from several days before. Occasionally he would comment on a local news story or a political scandal.

Half an hour later Tony was ready to serve pasta with veal and fresh tomato sauce, accompanied by Caesar salad and garlic bread. The fresh aromas of garlic and basil filled the kitchen, and Tony suddenly felt very hungry. He put everything on the table and started hunting through cupboards. "Dad, I picked up very nice Amarone for us. Where did you hide your wine glasses?"

Joseph was already eating, red tomato sauce splattering the front of his shirt as he vigorously twirled the pasta with his fork and spoon. "They are all gone, too brittle. Use the juice glasses."

Tony shrugged in resignation and found two small glasses. He opened the bottle of wine and filled both glasses to the brim. "A toast; to sunny days, rainy nights, and an award-winning crop of eggplant."

"Ha, that would be good." Joseph drained his wine and pushed the glass back for a refill. This time Tony only filled it halfway, concerned that his dad was not properly savoring the expensive wine.

Joseph didn't seem to notice. "This is very good." Joseph pointed with his fork at the plate. "Joanna teach you to cook like this?"

"Dad, I've told you about our trip to Italy where we took cooking classes. I learned a lot about real Italian cooking, and in my present circumstances I've had lots of time to practice."

"You hear from Joanna or Carla?"

"No. I don't expect they want to hear or see me."

Joseph picked up his napkin to wipe garlic butter off his hands. "They visited me several weeks ago."

Tony raised his eyebrows. Joanna hadn't been that close to his parents. "What did they want?" He tried to keep his voice casual.

"I think Carla was behind it. She asked lots of questions about you. They both still care. You should call Joanna while you are in town and let them know you are okay."

Tony mulled this over. He'd had little interaction with Joanna since she moved back to Chicago the previous fall. At the time they'd agreed Carla would stay with Tony to complete her year at the university. After that, Joanna clearly wanted her daughter with her in Chicago.

Unfortunately Carla didn't even last with him until the end of the first term. Joanna's departure and the loss of his job made him angry and depressed. He started drinking again and became something of a recluse. His daughter by default became the centre of his life, and he clung to her like a lifeline. She began to resent the pressure he exerted on her to stay home and keep him company when she wasn't in class. Tensions hit a high point when she arrived home late one night and he drunkenly confronted her. The ensuing argument ended with Carla breaking into tears and retreating to her room. The next day, with her mother's blessing, she announced plans to move into an apartment with some university friends. Tony was shocked, feeling betrayed and abandoned. He responded without thinking, telling her that if she walked out the door, she wouldn't be welcome back. They hadn't spoken since.

Reflecting on these events, he wondered if it was time to take some tentative first steps to mend relations with both his wife and daughter. While he doubted that any apology he mustered could make up for how he'd treated them, it might at least reopen lines of communication.

"You're right, Dad. It's time for me to see if they'll forgive me."

"Son, I am glad to hear you say this. You need to put the past behind and get on with a new life. Now tell me, what is the news you mentioned? Have you found a girlfriend?"

Tony laughed. "No, still a swinging single. However, I went fishing yesterday with that antique lure you gave me many years ago. You know, the painted wooden fish with silver bangles?"

Joseph smiled. "Yes, very lucky lure. You caught a big pike with it?"

Tony shook his head and gravely recounted the events of yesterday. When he finished, Joseph was silent for a moment. The only sound was the ticking of the grandfather clock in the hallway. Finally, he said, "There are some very bad people in this world."

"Unfortunately, you're right. But I expect the police will find the person who did this." Tony said nothing about his plans to conduct his own investigation. He wasn't sure his dad would understand or approve.

They moved on to dessert – Tony had picked up some cannoli from a nearby Italian bakery. As they savored the sweet ricotta cheese in fresh pastry shells, the conversation shifted to neighborhood events and what was happening in the lives of relatives and friends.

Their dessert finished, there was still sufficient light for Joseph to give a tour of the garden. Tony was led through carefully maintained rows of plants, his dad proudly pointing out the different vegetables and in lowered tones sharing his horticultural secrets.

Afterwards they returned to the kitchen to set to work on the dirty dishes. Tony washed while Joseph dried. They did the task in silence, enjoying each other's company as well as the remaining red wine. When the last dish was put in the cupboard, Joseph announced it was his bedtime.

"I'll be leaving early next morning, Dad – I've got a breakfast appointment. Maybe we should say our goodbyes now."

Joseph solemnly shook his hand. "Good luck, and remember to call Joanna."

Chapter 5
MAY 16 7:40 AM

Tony sat alone in a booth at the Eleven City Diner, located downtown a few miles north of the Chicago Police Headquarters. It was part Jewish deli and part American diner, with high ceilings and an energetic vibe he enjoyed. Tony had stumbled upon the spot several years before, when he needed a quick shot of caffeine to get him through an 8:00 a.m. department meeting. He was surprised to be served a very passable cup of espresso. From that point on, the diner was one of his favorite breakfast hangouts.

Sipping a double espresso, he took in the sights and sounds around him. Most of the tables were full, with some patrons starting their day with a large breakfast of bacon, eggs and hash browns. Others appeared to be winding down their night with a smoked meat sandwich on rye.

His breakfast guest was late. However, he wasn't worried, as his former partner was habitually tardy. He almost always came armed with some fantastic reason for being delayed. Despite this shortcoming, Lonnie Tubman was the best partner Tony had worked with on the Chicago Homicide Division. Perhaps as a result of his childhood experiences, he seemed to have special insights into the criminal mind that often came in handy during a murder investigation.

Tubby, as he was referred to by his friends, had been born in Harlem to a mother who turned tricks to survive. His first thirteen years of life were lived in poverty and squalor, and he was gradually drawn into the life of a street-wise gang thug. His mother's death from an overdose turned out to be a blessing in disguise, as the boy was placed with foster parents who spirited

72

him away to a small town where he had the chance to pursue a different life.

The loss of his mother and his surgical removal from his neighborhood and friends at first made him taciturn and withdrawn. Over time, though, he rediscovered the joy of life by competing in various sports. In his first year of high school, he added an extra foot to his sinewy frame and learned the delights of dunking a basketball. He joined the high school team and in his final year led them to the state championship.

Five years after leaving behind a dead-end life on the streets, Tubman qualified for a basketball scholarship at Fordham University. There he encountered another piece of good fortune as his coach was a respected former NBAer. He took the young basketball player under his wing, telling him that even if he made it to the big leagues, his career could be cut short at any time by injury. He counseled his protégé to devote as much energy to getting good grades as to perfecting his spin-around dunk. Tubman took this advice to heart and by the time he completed university, he'd obtained a law degree as a complement to being a top NBA draft pick.

To the complete surprise of everyone but a few people close to him, he didn't take up a career in either professional basketball or law. He'd been pursued and ultimately recruited by the FBI, joining their organized crime division. For six hectic years he rotated between Miami, Detroit, Atlantic City, and New York in various undercover roles.

After a particularly difficult assignment, he decided to take a holiday at a Mexican resort. There, he met a strikingly beautiful woman by the name of Margaret. A week-long fling turned into a long-distance love affair, both of them travelling between various cities to keep in touch. When Tubman finally decided it was time to spring the big question, his prospective bride agreed to marry him, subject to one important condition. She wanted him to give up his dangerous undercover work and settle with her in Chicago. By then Tubman had begun to weary of his nomadic lifestyle with the FBI, so the decision was not that difficult. And with the expertise he'd gained investigating gangland murders, it was a somewhat natural transition to homicide detective with the Chicago PD.

At the same time Tubman was entering marriage and a new career, Tony's long-time partner was in the process of retiring from the Chicago PD. A meeting was arranged and Tony took an immediate liking to the ex-FBI undercover agent and his offbeat sense of humor. A new partnership was formed, and they quickly became the most effective investigation team in the homicide division.

Tony was startled out of his reflections by a tap on the shoulder. Turning, he saw a tall, athletic black man standing behind the booth, mid-thirties with a buzz cut, full round face and dazzling white smile. He looked a bit heavier than when they were last together at Tony's retirement party.

"Shouldn't let your guard down like that, buddy. I could've popped you one in the head, no problem." Tubman extended his finger and thumb like a gun.

Tony sadly nodded. He was getting sloppy in his forced retirement. He tapped his watch. "Tell me, why are you late this time?"

Tubby took a seat at the booth. "There's a lion on the loose."

"Lion?" Tony said, incredulous.

"Yup, one escaped from Lincoln Park Zoo. I expect some lion-keeper will be catching hell for that. It was sighted three blocks west of here. There are plenty of police and firemen who've formed a posse. Or perhaps it's a safari. Anyway, you're lucky I even made it. I had to take extreme evasive actions."

Tony laughed. "I have to tell you, that's one of your best ones yet. Next time, it'll be a herd of wild elephants stampeding down the Magnificent Mile."

"Not a chance. The zoo doesn't have any elephants. But I'm telling you the goddamn truth. Grab the *Chicago Tribune* tonight – you'll see I'm not having you on."

A middle-aged waitress plunked down an insulated container. The air filled with the aroma of strong coffee.

"Good morning, Sally." Tubman winked at her and filled his mug.

"Why, if it isn't the two hot-shot detectives! Been a long time since I've seen the both of you here," the waitress said with a bit of a Southern drawl.

Tony was glad to see Sally was still working at the diner. She'd been their favorite waitress and they always tried to sit in her section.

"The usual for y'all?"

"You bet," they said in unison. The "usual" for Tony was two fried eggs over hard, bacon and brown toast with strawberry jam. For Tubman, it was a bowl of fresh fruit topped with plain yogurt and granola.

After Sally departed with their orders, they surveyed each other. Seeing Tubman triggered memories for Tony of the two of them working long hours on some nasty homicides. They often got together over breakfast to review their findings and plot strategy for the upcoming day. Over the years, and through many difficult cases, a strong personal bond had been forged.

It was because of that close relationship that Tony felt comfortable reaching out to his old partner. He'd called Tubman before yesterday's meeting with Bobby at Starbucks. After spending five minutes listening to Tubby's update on work, Margaret, and the kids, they got down to the real reason for Tony's call. He explained his role in finding Harding's body, and outlined his somewhat wild scheme to find her killer. When he finished, there was silence on the line while his friend digested what was being asked of him.

After what seemed an eternity to Tony, the voice at the other end of the line responded by simply saying, "That's plain crazy… but I look forward to working with you again, partner."

Feeling immensely relieved that Tubman didn't try to talk some sense into him, Tony had outlined his game plan and the support he needed. Tubman said he would make some inquiries. They agreed to meet that morning for breakfast, at which time Tubman would report back on his findings.

Now Tony broke the silence between them. "Listen, thanks again for agreeing to help me out. I know what I'm asking could get you into a lot of trouble."

"Hell, I may be getting older, but my memory's still pretty good. I haven't forgotten all those times when you stuck your neck out to cover my ass. The most recent one almost got you killed. I'm glad you're giving me this chance to help out."

Tony unconsciously touched his left shoulder. In cold damp weather, it still ached. It was just over a year ago that they'd entered an apartment building to interview a suspect in a robbery/murder case. Tubman was in front when they got off the elevator and encountered the suspect making a hasty exit. A gun was pointed in their direction and Tony shouldered his partner away, charging forward. He knocked the man to the ground and fought for the gun. There was a thundering explosion and searing pain before he passed out.

Later that night, Tony woke up in the hospital with Tubby watching over him. Through the haze of the painkillers, he could remember his partner shaking his head in relief. He'd said, "You may be one crazy fuck, but you probably saved my life. Someday I'm going to pay you back." It looked like that day had arrived.

"If it gets to the point where I'm asking too much, let me know. You've got your career to protect. Now tell me, have you made any progress?"

"Yep, actually quite a bit. First of all, it appears that Madison homicide won the lottery and has overall responsibility for the investigation. Your friend Adelsky insisted it was their case. Appears he got support from some powerful people, as he managed to trump the Chicago State Attorney, who's totally pissed that somebody killed one of his lawyers."

"Adelsky probably used his pull with Senator Caldwell. But you've got to wonder why the senator would stick his nose into this."

Tubman nodded. "Good question. In any event, Adelsky agreed that Chicago homicide was in the best position to look into Harding's background and activities during the last few days before her death. Peters and Huffman have been assigned to that. You, of course, know those two. Real plodders, but eventually they get the job done. I was able to track down Peters late yesterday afternoon. He is totally stressed out. The case is extremely hot, and he complained that they have to report daily to the chief on their progress."

Their conversation was interrupted by Sally with their breakfast orders. She put a large plate in front of Tony. "Be careful, hon', it's very hot." She then set a smaller plate in front of Tubman and moved on to serve another table.

Tony started to chow down while Tubman continued. "Where was I? Oh, yeah, Peters said they already had a full dance card before this one came along. He was trying to figure out how to juggle everything. I told him a bit of a white lie, that I'd worked with Harding and was anxious to help out. I said I could do some of the grunt work, look at Harding's old cases for possible suspects, review phone records, even interview family and friends. This would allow them to focus on her activities before her death. Man, you should have seen his face. It was like throwing a life preserver to a drowning person. I've become an unofficial member of the investigation team."

"That's terrific. What's your plan?" Tony asked.

"Well, if you have the time, I thought you might want to join me in a visit with Harding's parents. They live in the Old Town, not too far from here."

Tony was surprised. Tubby was really going out on a limb asking him to participate in the interview. For a moment, to protect his friend, he contemplated saying no, but it was too great an opportunity to pass up.

"Thanks," he said gratefully. "Old Town eh? Pretty nice neighborhood."

"Yeah. Turns out Mr. Harding owns a commercial plumbing business with several locations – appears to be very successful. Jennifer was their only kid. He was pretty torn up when I spoke to him last night. He kept on saying 'Who'd do this to my girl?' "

"With any luck, we'll be able to find the fucker."

Tubman nodded, and they turned their attention to the plates in front of them.

Chapter 6
MAY 16 8:55 AM

A lawnmower droned in the background as Tony pulled to the curb behind Tubman's silver Passat. The large homes set back from the street were shaded by tall oak trees lining the sidewalks.

As he got out, Tubman pointed out a two-story red brick house, an older Victorian-style home on a corner lot. It looked to have been recently renovated with new windows and cedar shingles.

They reached the wood paneled front door and Tubman pressed the doorbell. A moment later the door was opened by a man in his early sixties, with grey receding hair and sad eyes. He was dressed casually in a short-sleeve shirt and brown cotton pants.

"Mr. Harding?" Tubman asked. "I'm Detective Tubman with the Chicago PD. We spoke on the telephone last night. This is my associate, Tony Deluca. May we come in?"

"Of course." Harding opened the door further to allow them into the front hallway. Tony recognized the familiar smell of fresh paint. The recent renovations had extended to the interior of the house, and included new limestone tile flooring, thick plaster cornice moldings, and oak wainscot paneling.

They were ushered into the living room. "Please, have a seat." Harding pointed towards two upholstered chairs. "My wife, Mary, is making a fresh pot of coffee. Would you like some?"

Tubman declined. Tony said yes, adding, "White, no sugar please."

Harding left them in the living room to go help his wife. Out of habit, Tony scanned the room for details that might provide insights into the lives of their hosts. Noticing a number of framed photographs on the fireplace mantle, he rose to take a closer look.

One of the pictures profiled a smiling young woman in a legal gown, book-ended by her beaming parents.

"That's Jennifer when she graduated from law school," a soft voice said.

He turned to see who was speaking. He recognized Mrs. Harding from the picture he'd just examined. She was bearing a tray laden with coffee cups. It was obvious where Jennifer got her good looks. Mary Harding was a striking woman with fine features and stylishly cut hair. However, her eyes were red and her face bore the sharp lines of grief.

"You both look very proud of your daughter," Tony said.

"Yes, that was a special day. Graduating from law school was a tremendous accomplishment." Her voice trembled. She caught herself and managed a small smile. "Are you Detective Deluca or Detective Tubman?" she asked Tony.

"Deluca," he responded, feeling a bit guilty for not correcting her.

"So by elimination this must be Detective Tubman."

Tubman stepped forward to take charge. "That's right. I would first like to convey our condolences for your loss. I know how difficult this must be for the both of you and appreciate you seeing us on such short notice. I want to assure you that both the Chicago and Madison police departments are devoting significant resources to finding your daughter's killer."

"Mary and I appreciate your thoughts and want to help in any way we can," said Harding. "But we still don't understand how this could've happened. Are you sure it wasn't an accident of some sort?"

"I'm afraid the evidence is fairly conclusive…"

Before Tubman finished his sentence Mrs. Harding started to totter. Her husband took her arm, guiding her to the nearest chair. She sat down heavily. "I just don't understand. What kind of person could've done this to our Jennifer?"

"That's what we plan to find out. We're here to ask some background questions that might help with our investigation."

Harding interrupted Tubman again. "What was she doing in Madison in the first place?"

"At this time we're not sure. As far as you're aware, did she know anyone in Madison?" Tubman asked.

"I don't ... think so," Mrs. Harding said haltingly. "But quite frankly, we haven't seen much of Jennifer since she stopped dating Daniel. In the last month or so she seemed to have become something of a recluse, totally immersed in her work."

"This Daniel you mentioned – can you tell us about him?" Tubman asked.

Mrs. Harding dabbed her eyes. "Daniel Jayman. Jennifer met him about four months ago at a charity dinner event. They were seated at the same table. Shortly after that they started to date."

Harding stepped in. "Jennifer brought him by several times. You could tell he was totally smitten with her. We thought he was perfect for our daughter. She was very much into her career and so was he. He's an executive at the Harris Bank."

"They just recently broke up?" Tony asked.

Mrs. Harding nodded. "Yes. It happened within the past month. Jennifer came over for dinner several weeks ago, by herself. We were having cocktails when she received a call on her cell. She took it in the kitchen, but she ended up speaking quite loudly. Bill and I heard almost everything she said."

Harding took up the story. "It was Daniel. She told him it was very busy at work and she didn't have time to see him. They argued, at least our daughter did, and she ended the conversation by hanging up. When Jennifer returned, she could by the look on our faces that we'd overhead everything. That's when we learned that she and Daniel had broken up. When we asked why, she said something about their lifestyles not being compatible. We tried to get more details, but Jennifer said she didn't want to spoil the evening by talking about it. Daniel was taking it badly."

"You said he works for Harris Bank. Is he in their main office downtown?" Tubman asked.

"Yes, I think so," said Harding. "I know his office is close to Jennifer's. She mentioned walking over to meet him one day for lunch."

"We'll track him down." Tubman moved on to another line of questions. "We are hoping to trace your daughter's movements the night of her death. We did a motor vehicle search and have her driver's license information, but it appears there's no car registered in her name. Is this correct?"

"That's right," said Mrs. Harding. "She had a car but sold it last year when she moved into a condo on the waterfront. They wanted $30,000 extra for a parking spot and she said it would be a lot cheaper to get around by taxi or public transit. She could borrow my car whenever she needed it. I gave her my extra set of keys. This arrangement seemed to work well."

"When was the last time she borrowed your car?" Tony asked.

Mrs. Harding tried to recall. "A while, perhaps a month ago. She did phone last weekend and mentioned she might need the car one evening this week. I told her she could take it as long as she had it back by morning. I typically get together with friends every morning for coffee," she added.

"Did Jennifer tell you why she needed the car?" Tubman inquired.

"No, she was in a big rush, and we didn't speak for very long. But she must have made other arrangements.... That was the last time we talked." Mrs. Harding winced at this thought.

Tubman paused sympathetically before continuing. "We'll see if we can find out where she was planning to go. Now, is there anyone else who is close to your daughter? A friend who might know something that would be helpful to our investigation?"

Mrs. Harding looked over at her husband. He shrugged. "Jennifer had several friends at law school but they've all dispersed to various firms across the country. I don't think they really keep in touch – too busy, I guess. There are of course her colleagues in the State Attorney's office."

"Yes, we'll be speaking with them. Did Jennifer ever mention being threatened by anyone? For example, a person that she'd prosecuted?

"No, she never mentioned anything like that," said Harding.

"Is there anything else you can tell us that might be relevant to our investigation?"

Mrs. Harding looked down at her clasped hands. Her husband gave a helpless shrug. "I'm sorry, I wish we could give you more to go on."

"Quite all right. You've been very helpful and we don't want to take up any more of your time." Tubman handed Harding his business card, then looked over at Tony. "Do you have any other questions before we head out?"

Tony hesitated. There was an important but delicate subject he needed to explore. Given the tension in the room, he had to be careful how he phrased his question. "Well, there is one other thing. The autopsy indicated that your daughter had taken a drug shortly before her death. It's a legally restricted drug with potentially serious side effects. We're not sure if it was taken voluntarily or given to your daughter without her knowledge. Did you notice anything that might have suggested she was taking drugs?"

Despite his best efforts, the question acted as a trigger for Mrs. Harding's barely controlled emotions. She raised her hands to her face and started to sob. Mr. Harding quickly moved by her chair and put a comforting hand on her shoulder.

"Detective Deluca, our daughter is a lawyer and a respected member of the State Attorney's office. If there were any sort of illegal drugs in her system, they must have been administered by someone else. Now, you'll have to excuse us. This has all been very difficult."

"Of course we understand," Tubman said quickly. "Thank you for your assistance. Don't worry, we can find our way out."

When they reached the sidewalk, Tubman spoke sharply. "What the fuck, Tony, you could've warned me about that. I didn't know anything about drugs. I hope to hell Harding doesn't call someone at the department to complain about the two insensitive detective pricks that just visited them. That will get me a visit to the chief and when he learns you were with me, my ass will be grass."

Tony was taken aback. "Sorry, I assumed Peters would've told you. The autopsy disclosed that Jennifer Harding had Ecstasy in her system."

Tubman took a deep breath to calm him. "Okay. I guess I should be venting at Peters rather than you. That sure adds a new twist to the case. Maybe she went to a bar on Monday night and the killer slipped it to her."

"Possibly. But that doesn't help explain how she ended up in Madison. I'd like to find the former boyfriend and hear his story."

"Agreed. Let me phone Dispatch and see if they can confirm his coordinates. We can arrange for an intimate little visit."

Tubman hit speed dial on his phone. He connected with Dispatch and starting talking. Tony decided to stretch his legs. Following the sidewalk, he noticed that the Hardings' garage was detached from the house, with the driveway on the street around the corner from the main door. A concrete walkway led from the garage to the house's side door.

He returned and waited as Tubman finished his conversation and snapped his phone shut. "Dispatch is going to contact the Harris Bank and locate Jayman. It should only take a few minutes, so we might as well sit tight."

"That's good, because there's something we should do before leaving."

"What's that?" Tubman looked puzzled.

"It's normal protocol to have forensics check out the deceased's residence, personal effects, and automobile, right?"

"Yeah, forensics went through her condo yesterday. A bunch of stuff has been sent to the Crime Lab for analysis. Peters said he'd let me know if they turn up anything of interest."

"Good, but we may be overlooking something. Mrs. Harding told us Jennifer phoned on the weekend and asked to borrow her car."

"But she never did."

"How do we know that for sure?"

"Mrs. Harding said she never came by. She would've noticed if her car was missing."

"Maybe, but come with me." Tony motioned for Tubman to follow him and retraced his recent route along the sidewalk. "Jennifer could've taken the car without her parents knowing. Maybe it was late and she didn't want to disturb them. Mrs. Harding told us her daughter had a set of keys."

Tubman looked skeptical. "Okay … let's assume she took the car the night before she was murdered. How do you explain it getting back in the garage before Mrs. Harding noticed it was missing the next morning?"

"I can't, but we should follow protocol and take a quick look at that car."

"Sounds like a waste of time. And we should see this Jayman guy pronto."

"Remember what happened in the low-rise killer case?" Tony countered.

Tubman sighed and rolled his eyes. "Fine, you win. But let me go back alone and get permission from Mr. Harding. I'm afraid you might create another scene."

While Tubman reluctantly headed back to the house, Tony reflected on the last investigation they'd worked together, involving a serial killer. They'd hit a brick wall, and the pressure to solve the case before the killer struck again had Tony near his breaking point. That's when Tubman came to him with a crazy idea to flush out the killer. Tony still remembered, word for word, saying to Tubman: "Are you nuts? We've got everyone breathing down our necks to catch this guy, and you want to waste valuable time going down a possible blind alley?"

But Tubman had stuck to his guns and eventually badgered Tony into agreeing to set an unusual trap for the killer. To his astonishment, the plan worked, and they were able to nab the killer before he struck again. The incident had demonstrated once again to Tony that no idea could be discarded as crazy and no stone could be left unturned when it came to solving a murder.

Tubby returned with car keys in his hand. "They were a bit confused by the request but said to go ahead. The side garage door is open. It's the Audi."

The garage was meticulously maintained, with gardening implements hanging on the wall and a narrow steel workbench at the back. The recent model silver Audi wagon was parked alongside a black Ford Explorer with the Harding's company logo on its side.

"I wasn't expecting to be going through a car looking for evidence. I don't suppose you have gloves with you?" Tubman asked dryly.

Tony shook his head.

Looking around, Tubman found a pair of rubber gardening gloves and forced them over his large hands. "Might as well do this right. There's no pair for you, so don't touch anything."

Tony nodded, recalling that he'd already disturbed enough evidence in this case.

The Audi was unlocked. Opening the driver's door, Tubman carefully examined the interior before moving over to the passenger side. He opened the rear passenger doors and went through the same routine. "Nothing here. Spotless, in fact."

He popped open the trunk lid. Tony looked over his shoulder. Like the rest of the car, the trunk was as clean as a whistle. Tubman was just about to close the lid when Tony pointed to the black plastic pull that provided access to the spare.

"Tubby, lift that up and take a look."

Tubman patiently complied. As he pulled on the lever and raised the carpeted trunk floor, the action dislodged something. It fell into the steel well around the spare tire, making a rattling noise before coming to rest.

Tubman peered in. After a moment he grunted and straightened up.

"What do you see?"

"Take a look for yourself."

Tony's eyes needed a few seconds to adjust to the trunk's darkness. Then he spotted it, nestled against the spare tire. It appeared to be a round piece of silver metal, resembling – a woman's bracelet? Too small for that.

He straightened up. "Partner, that looks to me like a shower curtain ring."

Chapter 7

Closing the trunk and locking the Audi, they returned to the house. Harding must have been waiting near the door, as it quickly opened when they rang the bell.

He scanned their faces. "Did you find something?"

"Yes, in the trunk. There was a silver shower curtain ring. Do you know of any reason why it might be there?"

Harding raised his eyebrows. "No idea. Why don't you come in and I'll ask Mary. She's in the bedroom resting."

He returned with his wife at his side. She was in a bathrobe now and her well-coiffed hair was a bit disheveled. Her eyes were puffy. "Bill says you found something in the trunk of my car." Her voice was slightly tremulous.

"We think it's a shower curtain ring," said Tubman. "Any idea how it got there?"

"Not in the slightest. Does this mean something?" Her voice was a bit stronger now.

The Hardings didn't know that Jennifer's body had been wrapped in a shower curtain, Tony realized. The police must be holding back this information as a means of verifying the story of anyone claiming to be the killer.

"Maybe." Tubman kept his voice neutral. "Have either of you had the interior of the Audi cleaned and vacuumed recently?"

Mary Harding glanced at her husband. "Bill must have done it earlier this week. I noticed the front mats had been vacuumed."

Her husband looked surprised. "No. It's been, let's see, at least two weeks since I took in Mary's car to be cleaned and detailed."

"That's very odd." Mrs. Harding looked at Tubman as if he might have an explanation.

"Looks like we need to investigate this a bit more," he said.

"I'm going to get a forensics team over here to take a closer look at the Audi. Sorry, but your garage is going to be off limits until they're finished."

Harding made a motion to protest. His wife touched his arm. "Bill, you can get one of your office staff to come by and drive you to work. These men have more important business to take care of."

Harding gave a nod of acknowledgement. "How long do you think this will take?"

"We'll be done by the end of the day," Tubman promised.

Tubman called Peters on his cell and told him he was at the Harding house. Giving an update on his visit, he requested a forensics team as soon as possible. Peters said he'd be there with them within a half hour.

Pending the arrival of Peters, Tony stayed out of sight in his car, killing time listening to an old Travelling Wilburys CD. He saw Peters and the forensics team arrive and speak with Tubman before they headed for the garage. One of the techs stretched police tape around the perimeter while the others went inside. Ten minutes later, Tubman reappeared and got into his car, motioning Tony to follow.

Tony kept tightly behind the Passat as they negotiated the mid-morning traffic to Harris Bank headquarters on West Monroe. He wondered if they were about to meet with Harding's killer. Pondering the questions that might trap Jayman into an admission of guilt, he almost missed Tubman's signal and had to brake hard to avoid a rear-end collision. When Tubman pulled into a street-level parking lot, Tony followed.

Tubman came over as Tony got out. "I was afraid your front bumper was going to end up in my back seat. You daydreaming?"

"Sorry, I guess I was. But I just about had Jayman ready to confess. Before we go in, though, what happened back there with Peters?"

"So far he's not convinced there's a link between the car and Harding's death. But he's going to stick around and give me a call if the techs come up with anything else."

"What do you think?"

"Well, assuming for the moment that what we found in the car was at one point attached to the shower curtain wrapped around Harding's body, this would seem to confirm your theory that the Audi was used to transport her body before it was dumped in the lake. It would also mean that Harding, or possibly her killer, drove the car to Madison."

"It would also suggest that her killer returned the car to the Harding's garage the same evening," Tony pointed out. "He'd need to know where the parents lived, which could point to the ex-boyfriend."

"Why take such a big chance by driving the car back to Chicago? It would've been a lot easier to remove the plates and registration, then dump it deep in the woods anywhere between Madison and Chicago. The car might never have been found. Even if it was, identifying the owner would be next to impossible."

"That part doesn't make sense to me either. Let's put this on the growing list of unanswered questions."

Tubman glanced at his watch. "We'd better get moving."

They walked towards a stately grey stone building, passing under two American flags flapping over the front entrance. In the lobby an armed security guard was patrolling near the bank of elevators. Tubman approached a second guard, in the marble enclosed reception area and pulled out his police shield. "Detective Tubman. We're here to see Daniel Jayman. He's expecting us."

The guard snapped to attention, like an army private being addressed by a commanding officer. "Yes, sir. I'll phone to let him know you are on your way up. Could you please sign the visitors' register."

Tubman entered their names in the logbook while the guard picked up the phone. After a short conversation, he said, "Mr. Jayman will be waiting for you in the reception area on the sixth floor." He passed them two security passes for the elevator. "You'll need these."

"What's with all the security?" Tony asked as Tubman pressed the up arrow and they waited for a car. "Are they trying to keep out irate customers?"

"It's no joke. They get threats from people who've been thrown out of their homes for defaulting on their mortgages, poor suckers. Anyway, these days it's not wise to let just anyone wander into your main headquarters."

The elevator doors opened. Tubman waved the security card and they were silently whisked up to the sixth floor, emerging into a glass-enclosed reception area. A young man who looked to be in his late twenties was waiting for them. He was average height and fit looking, neatly cut hair framing a narrow face. He wore a grey suit and a shirt with a pale blue paisley design.

"Mr. Jayman? I'm Detective Tubman and this is my associate, Tony Deluca. Thanks for agreeing to see us on such short notice."

"To tell you the truth, I've been expecting your call," Jayman responded in a light Boston accent. "When I learned of Jennifer's death I thought I might become a 'person of interest.'"

Tony resisted the urge to smile. The guy had seen too many police shows.

"We're certainly hoping you can help us out," said Tubman. "Is there some place where we can talk privately?"

"Of course. There's a small meeting room this way." Jayman took out his security card and swiped a reader beside a door leading to the inner hallway. There was an electronic click and he pulled open the door. They followed him into a room with a round table and four upholstered chairs. On the table were bottles of water, a pot of coffee, and several mugs.

"Would you like some coffee or water?"

Tony selected a bottle of water while Tubman helped himself to coffee.

Tubman started the questioning. "Mr. Jayman, I understand that until recently you were dating the deceased. Can you give us some details on how you got together and why the relationship ended?"

Jayman nodded. "Sure. I met Jennifer at a charity event sponsored by the Harris Bank for the Chicago homeless. Let's see, that was mid-January. I was hosting a table and Jennifer happened to be seated beside me. We spent some time talking. She told me she worked in the State Attorney's office. By the end of the evening I'd determined that she was currently unattached and I got her business card. I made several attempts to arrange a date. Eventually we were able to get together."

"She wasn't initially open to your advances?" Tony asked.

"I wouldn't quite put it that way. She seemed interested, but her job consumed a lot of her time and energy. She had to cancel a couple of times. I quickly learned that a relationship with Jennifer required both patience and flexibility."

"So tell us how things progressed," Tubman probed.

"It was slow going. We saw each other five or six times over the course of several months. I felt we were making real progress when she invited me to meet her parents, but about a month ago the bottom seemed to drop out of our relationship. Without any warning, she refused to see me … claimed she was too busy at work." His voice betrayed bitterness.

"Was there some disagreement that led up to this?" Tony asked.

"Not exactly. However, our last time together was a bit strange. In retrospect, I think it must have been some sort of test … and apparently I failed."

"Tell us about that," Tubman prompted.

"Well, Jennifer phoned me one afternoon and said she planned to work late. She suggested we get together for drinks afterwards at the Four Seasons. She said she'd booked a room, and if I played my cards right, we'd have a good time. It was an offer I couldn't refuse."

He laughed nervously and continued. "We ended up meeting around nine. She'd already ordered martinis. Those went down rather quickly, and we ordered another round. I knew I was going to regret it next day, but it did take the edge off. At that point Jennifer announced we were going to play 'Truth or Dare.' She wanted to get to know me better. You must know the game."

Tony responded. "Sure, used to play it as a kid. You tell the truth or perform a dare."

"That's right. The game got underway by her asking if I'd ever smoked pot. Since I was speaking to a criminal lawyer, I knew the correct answer had to be no. She called me a liar. Eventually, I confessed to smoking a couple of joints in college ... but I didn't inhale."

"Of course not." Tony and Tubman returned Jayman's smile. *Keep him at ease, and perhaps he'd reveal something he didn't intend to.*

"Anyway, she said I'd have to complete a dare at the end of the game. I tried to ask her a question, but she said it wasn't allowed. She continued quizzing me. The questions became increasingly ... well, *bizarre* would be the word."

"What type of questions?" Tony asked

"I don't recall them ... exactly." Jayman flushed slightly. It was evident that he was holding something back.

"This could be important. Please try to remember," Tony said encouragingly.

"Well, if you must know, she asked a number of questions relating to my sexual preferences. For example, had I ever made love in a public place, picked up a hooker, or ..." Jayman stumbled.

"Or what?" Tubman prodded.

"Had I ever been involved in a homosexual relationship. Actually, the question was whether I had ever given or received a blowjob from another guy."

"And how did the game end?" Tubman asked.

"Jennifer eventually ran out of questions and said it was time for my 'dare.' She said she was going to pick a woman in the bar at random. My task was to convince her to come to Jennifer's hotel room for a threesome. She assured me it was a joke, she only wanted to see if I had the balls. I tried to laugh it off, but she said if I wanted to get laid that night, I'd better do as I was told. She looked around and pointed out a woman sitting by herself at a table near the bar."

"Then what happened?" Tubman inquired.

"Well, somewhat fortified by the martinis, I went over to this woman's table and introduced myself. I apologized for bothering

her and said I'd been dared by my girlfriend to ask if she was interested in getting together for some sex. I told her all she had to
do was say no loudly and I'd leave her alone. I remember her quite
vividly. She was tall, attractive in a way, with these terrific green
eyes. She looked over at Jennifer, and then back to me. Then, to
my utter surprise, she said she'd be interested in getting together
with us. Well, I'm no prude but I admit this kinda freaked me out.
I mumbled something to her about it all being a joke and hurried
back to Jennifer."

Tony wondered how he would've responded if put in a similar
situation. He set this thought aside. "What did Ms. Harding say
when you came back?'"

"She wanted to know why I'd returned empty-handed. I lied,
said our offer had been politely rejected, and suggested it was
time to head up to her hotel room. She handed me the key and
told me to go get comfortable, she'd pay the bar bill and come up
in a minute. I headed up, got undressed and into bed. She never
showed and between the long hours at work and the martinis, I
ended up passing out."

"Did you ever see her after that night?" Tubman asked.

"No. I phoned, emailed, even tried to catch her outside her office. She seemed to be deliberately avoiding me. We ended up only
speaking once after that. I called her cell and she told me she was
too busy to see me. I knew it was just an excuse, but she wouldn't
explain. She hung up on me."

"That's the last time you spoke to her?" Tony asked pointedly.

"That's right. Look, I realize I must be a suspect, but you have
to believe I'd never harm Jennifer. I was extremely fond of her. In
fact she could've been the one."

Tony had been watching Jayman closely as he spoke, distress
clearly written on his face. He was either a very good actor or he
was telling the truth.

"Mr. Jayman, we understand your grief, but we do need to ask.
Can you tell us your whereabouts on Monday evening?"

He was clearly prepared for the question. "I've been working
on a big financing deal for the last two months. The deal closed

Monday afternoon, and a bunch of us went over to Morton's to celebrate. The party went on until about eleven. I wasn't in any condition to drive, so I left my car in the parking lot and took a cab back to my condo. I can give you the names of people at the restaurant with me, as well as the name of the concierge at my condo. He opened the door for me when I got back." He pulled a piece of paper from his jacket pocket and slid it across the table.

Tubman took it. "Thanks, that's a big help. Now, let's talk more generally. Did Ms. Harding ever mention knowing anyone in Madison?"

Jayman briefly closed his eyes in thought. "No ... well, wait a minute. She once mentioned she was looking into something involving a murder in Madison. But she didn't go into details."

Tubman raised his eyebrows. "To your knowledge, did Ms. Harding ever receive any threats to her life?"

"Nope. I'm pretty sure she would have mentioned it."

"Is there anything else you can think of that might be relevant to our investigation?"

"I don't think so. And, trust me, if I did know something, I would've contacted the police by now. I can't understand why anyone would want to kill Jennifer. It must've been a random act. Now if that's it...."

"I do have one more question," Tony said. "Were you aware of Ms. Harding taking any illegal drugs?"

Jayman carefully considered his words. "I never saw Jennifer take any sort of drugs. But that night in the bar ... I did leave out something. As she was asking me those questions, she started rubbing my inner thigh. This was very unlike her and kind of embarrassing, being in public. Her eyes were darting around, and she was kind of shaking with nervous energy. I chalked it up to her being a bit drunk, but maybe it was something else."

Tubman took over. "You've been very helpful, Mr. Jayman. If you remember anything else please call me at this number." He passed over his business card.

"Yes, I will. I hope you find the person who did this."

Tony and Tubman waited until they were out in the bright sunlight before discussing the interview. Tony broke the silence. "If you ask me, I don't think Mr. Jayman is our killer."

"I'll check out his alibi, but my gut says the same thing."

"I've also been thinking back to our conversation with the parents. Do you recall what Jennifer said to them when she was questioned about her breakup with Jayman?"

"Yeah, something about them not being compatible."

"Close. She said 'Our lifestyles are not compatible.' At the time I thought it was an interesting way to phrase things. But after hearing about the 'truth or dare' story, I believe Ms. Harding was referring to their sexual lifestyles. I don't think Mr. Jayman was adventurous enough for her."

"So Jayman didn't measure up to her expectations?"

"That's one way of putting it. Now where does that leave us?"

"I plan to head back to the Hardings' house and talk to Peters to see if forensics found anything else in the garage. I also want to make sure he's requested Jennifer's phone records and has assigned a computer tech to go through all her electronic gadgets. What about you?"

"I'd like to figure out what connection, if any, there is between the deceased and Madison. She said something to Jayman about looking into a murder there. Can you ask Peters to follow up with the State Attorney's office and see if they know what that's about? I'll also discuss this with Bobby Andrade and see if Harding mentioned it to her."

"Good idea. You planning to head back now?" Tubman asked.

Tony hesitated. "No, I have another stop to make."

Chapter 8
MAY 16 12:35 PM

Tony took his time driving into the suburbs of Chicago, going over what he wanted to say to Joanna, assuming she was at home. He turned into a residential neighborhood of modest 1960s-era houses. Checking the street signs and house numbers, he ended up in front of a small, tidy looking two-story brick house. The lawn needed a good cut, and the brightly colored perennials were beginning to overflow their beds.

Pulling up to the curb, he noticed an older blue Honda Accord parked in the driveway and heard the unmistakable voice of Andrea Bocelli floating from an open window upstairs. He almost stepped on the gas and kept going. He wasn't sure what type of reception he'd get or even what he'd say when she opened the door. But instead of pulling away, he took a deep breath and removed the key from the ignition.

He rang the doorbell. Upstairs the music stopped and after a short wait he heard the clack of high heels on ceramic floor. When the door finally opened, Tony saw the smile on Joanna's face instantly disappear.

"What are you doing here?" Her look made him feel like an intruder.

"Hi, Jo. Sorry to drop by unannounced. I was in town and, well, wanted to talk to you."

"You should've called. Another five minutes and you would've missed me. I don't have a lot of time, but please, come in."

Relieved, he followed her into the small, neat living room. "Sit down," she said, settling on the love seat across from him. She was wearing a black dress with high heels, her dark hair cut in fashionably short. Her small-framed body was lean and tanned, and she looked years younger than when he last saw her in Madison.

"Dad said you and Carla dropped by a couple of weeks ago. He was really pleased you came for a visit."

"Carla was anxious to see her grandfather. And quite frankly, we wanted to get some news about you. Joseph said you found a new job – some kind of security thing?"

"I'm working at a bar. Nothing special, but it's a start. I feel like I'm finally getting my legs underneath me again."

"I'm glad to hear it. I've been worried about you. You do look … more at peace with yourself. What else is happening in your life?"

"Not much, really. I'm still at the cottage – spending a lot of time fishing." Best to leave out the part about finding a body in the lake, he decided. "How about you and Carla?"

Joanna smiled for the first time since greeting him at the door. "Carla is doing great. Despite changing schools mid-term, she managed to get good grades and has some nice friends. She's got herself a summer job all by herself at MaxMara on the Magnificent Mile. My only concern is that she'll end up spending all her money on clothes. She's also made a major decision. She wants to go into law."

"Carla and law school? That's a shock. I didn't think she cared much for lawyers."

"Well, she learned that from her father. But recently she's had a change in perspective."

"I'm glad she wants to pursue her education. A legal degree will open lots of doors." He tried to muster some enthusiasm in his voice. "How're you doing?"

Joanna's body seemed to stiffen with this question. "I have to be honest, it's been tough going. Moving back here, finding a place to live, getting a job, and being there for Carla. There were days when I wasn't sure I could keep it together.…" Her voice trailed off.

Tony nodded. He'd had plenty of those days himself. "You have a job?"

"Uh, huh. Part-time, at a downtown legal firm. I fill in for reception, and when one of the secretarial staff get sick or go on holidays. They pay relatively well, and I have some flexibility. It certainly helps with the bills."

Tony knew money must be tight. Joanna had received all the proceeds from the sale of their house in Madison, but likely all of it had gone towards the purchase of this house. And while he sent her some money every month, it was barely enough to cover the cost of groceries.

"Sounds pretty good. And your parents?"

"They're doing well. Enjoying their condo and still travelling quite a bit. They were in Orlando several weeks ago. Dad totally loved Universal Studios and actually went on some rides. Mom watched. I hope I can keep as active at their age."

Tony smiled, recalling vacations with Gus and Lydia. Despite the bad rap against in-laws, he was quite fond of Joanna's parents and missed their joie de vivre.

Joanna started to fidget, and Tony knew his time was running short. He took a deep breath and stepped off the brink. "Jo, I've been thinking a lot about you and Carla. I know I put you both through hell and probably don't deserve to ask this, but – I was wondering if there was a chance for us to have a fresh start." He felt his heart pounding in his ears.

She looked down at her hands, now tightly clasped in her lap. Without making eye contact, she started to talk. "Tony, there've been many times over the past few months when I wished you were here with me. And I still love you … but we've acquired too much baggage over the years. I was planning to write and tell you. I recently met someone and it's getting serious."

Tony felt like he'd taken another bullet in his shoulder. There was a searing pain and a dark shroud settled over him, making it difficult to see or think clearly. Through the haze he managed to stammer, "You're … seeing someone?"

Hearing the pain in his voice, she raised her eyes. "Yes, just in the past month. He's at the legal firm where I work. One of the partners."

His stomach lurched. He now understood Carla's sudden plans to go to law school. The finality of the situation started to sink in. He didn't stand a chance of getting back his family or his old way of life.

He wanted to beat a hasty retreat, but there was more that had to be said. "Listen, Jo, I understand. I wish the past year never happened. Unfortunately it did, and I see now that we both need to move on. I honestly want you and Carla to be happy. Let her know I'll write, and tell her I'm hoping over time we can reconnect as father and daughter. Just remember I'll always be there for the both of you."

Joanna got up and hugged him. When they separated, he saw tears in her eyes. Fortunately, he was able to control his own until he got into the car.

Chapter 9
MAY 16 2:45 PM

Tony spent most of the trip back to Madison beating himself up. He replayed the final breaking point in his marriage, a few weeks after he'd been fired. By then he'd started to drink again, and Joanna was becoming increasingly concerned. One night after dinner, during which he consumed almost half a bottle of whisky, she sat him down and told him he needed to get some counseling.

The booze gave his tongue free rein, and he ended up calling her an unfeeling bitch. Joanna tried to ignore the insult and reason with him, but this just fueled his anger. He told her she was to blame for his current situation and he never should have left the Chicago PD. With this outburst, she caved in to her own feelings, responding through tears that he was an overbearing and egotistical pig. She stomped out of the room and that night they slept in separate rooms. Tony got up late the next morning with a raging headache, feeling horrible from the whisky and what he'd said to Jo. He went downstairs to apologize, but it was too late. She had packed her bags and gone, leaving a note that she was off to stay with her parents in Chicago.

He should have gone after her but managed to rationalize that a break might be good for them. He was wrong, as she never returned. Too many harsh words, and too few kind ones, he realized with regret. He swallowed hard to keep down the bile churning in his stomach.

Back at the cottage, Sam was waiting for him inside the door. She meowed plaintively, showing her displeasure with his being away overnight. He picked her up and she immediately started to purr. Well, at least someone loves me, he thought, realizing that he was feeling very sorry for himself.

With Sam suitably mollified, he put her back on the floor. She led him into the kitchen and stopped in front of an empty food bowl. He filled it with cat chow and then focused on dealing with his own hunger. Opening the fridge, he pulled out cheese, lettuce, assorted vegetables, and some leftover chicken. The end result was a satisfying mixed salad. After lunch he decided it was time for a run around the lake to cleanse his mind and stretch his legs.

Changing into jogging gear, he started down the gravel driveway leading to the wider paved road. This eventually connected with the County Road, where he turned west to loop around the lake. About a half hour into his run, he passed the entrance to Governor Nelson State Park. Despite his best efforts, the events surrounding his most recent visit to the park intruded into his thoughts.

His mind cycled through the information collected so far. Harding was last seen Monday evening, working in her office. She likely drove her mother's car to Madison, expecting to return it by the next morning. In Madison, she met with someone who killed her and dumped her body in the lake. For reasons unknown, the killer drove her car back to Chicago and returned it to Hardings' garage before it could be found missing. This might indicate that the killer knew Harding or extracted the information about the car from her. But why drive it back to Chicago?

Then there was the meeting with the ex-boyfriend. Daniel Jayman's account of their evening at the Four Seasons bar indicated that Harding was sexually adventurous. The autopsy report showed she'd received a strong blow to the head and was likely strangled to death. And there was Ecstasy in her system. The information Jayman provided suggested there was a good chance she'd taken this drug before. The final piece of evidence was the St. Christopher medallion found by her body, with the simple inscription and the initials "J" and "R".

He felt like he was chasing ghosts in the night. There were too many gaps in that meager evidence to draw any reasonable conclusions. Unless the two police departments could come up with something more meaningful, Harding's murder would quickly become a cold case. Tomorrow he planned to meet with Bobby and see if she had any new information.

His route was now taking him past Bishops Bay Country Club, one of Madison's more exclusive private golf clubs. It was here that members of Madison's business and political elite got together to enjoy a round of golf and share confidences....

AT THAT MOMENT, a table of three golfers was being served drinks in the Bishops Bay men's lounge. Two of the men were in their late twenties or early thirties, while the third man was older, in his sixties.

"Congratulations on that birdie, senator," Jim Bradley said to the senior person in the group. The man he addressed had a jowly but distinguished face, with smoky blue eyes, large furry eyebrows, and spidery veins in his nose and cheeks. His graying hair was slicked over with water from a recent stop to the locker room, to hide a growing bald spot.

Senator Caldwell smiled at the compliment. "Almost made up for my triple on sixteen. Now, what did you end up shooting?"

"Seventy-three," Bradley responded, satisfaction on his tanned face. He picked up the score card, looking at it attentively while running a hand through his blond hair. "You had a very respectable eighty-two, and, Rick, you shot a ninety-seven."

Rick Adelsky grimaced and wiped beads of sweat from his forehead with a linen napkin. "Those golf lessons aren't doing any damn good. Too bad Jack couldn't join us. Imagine running out on us to get ready to take his wife out to dinner and the theatre. He needs to show her who's boss. The guy's definitely pussy-whipped."

The senator raised his expansive eyebrows in reproof. "Now, now, Rick, be kind. Some of us want to keep our marriages in good working order."

"I suppose." Rick didn't sound convinced.

"A divorce would be extremely expensive for him," Bradley chimed in. "He told me his company just picked up another big contract in India."

"He's a mover and shaker – someone we should all try to stay close to," the senator agreed. "Now, I didn't want to talk shop in front of Jack, but I would like an update from you boys on all the excitement this week. Rick, what's the latest on Mansfield's death?"

"Forensics has finished going through the car wreck with a fine tooth comb. Nothing remarkable – road maps, sleeping bag, toiletries. But we already have all the proof we need to prove he's the killer of that university student. On Monday I plan to announce we're confident Mansfield is the killer and the Sumner investigation is officially closed."

"Great. Glad to hear that you've finally got your man." The senator turned expectantly to Jim. "Anything in his autopsy report that needs a mention?"

"Not really. The condition of the body is consistent with injuries suffered by his car going off the road and hitting a tree. Some broken bones and a couple fractured ribs. Now, the pathologist didn't feel he could rule out the injuries being the result of a severe beating. I had to spend some time convincing him that the city needs closure on this case and that he shouldn't add any fuel to the fire by offering any other interpretation of the facts. He saw the light, and his final report will confirm accidental death. A summary of the autopsy report will be issued to the media just before Rick's press conference."

"Excellent. You're both are to be congratulated on how this horrible event has been handled," the senator said appreciatively. "Now, let's turn to the Harding case. This appears to be more troublesome. Not good for the city's image. We need to deal with this quickly or it could draw the unwanted scrutiny of the media. What's happening there, Rick?"

Adelsky applied the napkin to his face again. "Thanks to your efforts, we have control of the situation. Andrade is on a very short leash, and I'm closely monitoring her activities. I also have my contacts set up within the Chicago PD. There will be no slip-ups."

"I'm counting on that." The senator's pale blue eyes focused intently on Adelsky. "Well, enough business. Let's sample some of this fine scotch."

TONY HAD LEFT the golf course behind and was now on University Avenue, the main thoroughfare that passed the University of Wisconsin campus before leading to downtown Madison. It was over an hour since he'd started out. His legs were heavy and his lungs burned. He just had to keep pushing himself, and eventually the discomfort would fade into the background.

In the heart of the university district, he turned at University Bay Road. Gasping for air, he stopped in front of a large map of the campus and traced the route along the promontory that went out into Lake Mendota. There it was, Picnic Park Point, the scene of Karen Sumner's murder. He took a mental snapshot of the map and started running again, eventually turning onto Lake Mendota Road and following it to a small parking area. There he stopped and looked around.

A young couple walking hand-in-hand along the pathway leading to the tip of the point were enjoying a romantic sunset. Once again Tony wondered why the killer had taken Sumner to that particular spot. It wasn't exactly a remote location, and there was a high probability of being observed, both coming and going. Orchestrating a murder in this location seemed to demonstrate the killer either had nerves of steel or was oblivious to risk. The whole thing didn't make sense. With Mansfield now dead, Tony feared they'd never learn the real story.

The sun was now on a steady downward arc. He'd better get a move on if he was to get to the bar in time for his pre-shift dinner. He wiped the sweat from his eyes and picked up the pace again. In fifteen minutes he was on East Washington Avenue, bounded on the west by Lake Mendota and on the east by Lake Monona. Normally he'd slow down and enjoy the view of both lakes, but he had to get back to the cottage to get ready for work.

Running under some tall willows, Tony felt something brush against his shoulder. He ignored it, thinking it was one of the dangling branches. He felt another tap, this time with more force. He turned his head and saw another jogger directly behind him.

"Hey, Mr. Security Guard ... slow down," she gasped. "I've been trying to catch up with you for the last five minutes."

It was Julie, the new bartender at the Varsity Bar. A white head-band kept back her long brown hair from her face, perspiring from her efforts to catch up with him. Her stretchy white t-shirt tried unsuccessfully to flatten her breasts.

"Julie! Sorry, I'm on a bit of a mission, trying to get back home to get ready for my shift. Are you working tonight?"

"Nope. I'm off for the next week. I have two exams left to write, and I've been cramming like mad. But I had to get out for a run and clear away the cobwebs. Do you live around here?"

"Not really, north side of Mendota. Some people sail around the world, I like to run around the lake."

"That's pretty good for someone...." Julie stopped.

"Someone ... my age?"

"For someone wearing those shoes." She pointed down at his feet.

Tony glanced down at his old scuffed tennis shoes. He gave her a wink. "Oh yeah, my Nike LunarGlides are in the shop being tuned up for the Boston Marathon."

Julie laughed. "You're pretty funny for a security guy."

"Thanks, but that's not really saying much."

Julie broke the brief silence. "I know you're in a hurry. I was wondering if you'd be interested in getting together tomorrow night. It gets a bit lonely, studying all day long."

Before Tony could reply, she rushed on. "I'd invite you over for a home-cooked dinner, but you can't swing a cat in my kitchen. And truthfully, I'm not that great a cook. So how about you take me out for dinner? Give me something to look forward to while I'm hitting the books."

Tony was more than a bit surprised by her invitation. She must be at least ten years younger than him, and with her looks she could have the pick of the pack. Then there was the fact that he was dripping with sweat, recovering from the news that his wife was seeing another man, and already scheduled to work tomorrow night. Put it all together, and it looked like a losing proposition.

"Come on. You'll be filled with remorse if you refuse and later on learn that I expired from loneliness and starvation."

"Okay, you've convinced me." He was intrigued by her directness. "What do you like to eat?"

"I could do with some good Italian. Whoops – food that is."

It was his turn to laugh. "I know the perfect spot. When and where should I pick you up?"

Chapter 10
MAY 17 8:15 AM

The next morning Tony got up earlier than usual, planning to make another attempt at fishing. However, he was disappointed to see the sky was filled with ominous dark clouds and a southwest wind had created choppy whitecaps out on the lake. He heard the distant rumble of thunder and decided he'd better occupy himself cleaning up around the cottage. While he was attempting to remove cat hair with a lint brush from the velour sofa in the living room, the phone rang. It was Tubman.

"Hey, Tubby, good to hear from you," he said, pleased. "I was planning to give you a call today. What's new?"

"Funny you should ask. Forensics finished up with the Harding garage late yesterday afternoon. They dusted for prints and lifted a bunch of partials from the steering wheel, driver, and passenger side doors. The lab worked overtime and got the results back to us this morning. Most of them belong to Mrs. Harding, of course, but at least one set of prints belong to the deceased. Unfortunately, no other prints were found. Our killer either wore gloves or tried to clean all the surfaces he touched. That might explain all the smudged prints."

"At least it shows the victim recently drove the car."

"Yes, although the techs can't confirm with any certainty when she left those prints. They agreed that the inside of the car had recently been cleaned. One of them discovered a hand vac being charged on a workbench in the garage. It had been emptied and wiped clean. The last time Harding remembers using it was several weeks ago. He doesn't recall cleaning it out."

"You're saying that the murderer not only returned the car to the Harding's garage but took the time to vacuum it out before leaving?"

"That looks like how it went down."

"That takes balls of steel. So with the exception of the shower curtain ring, the car really doesn't give us anything new."

"Not quite. The killer didn't go to the trouble of having the exterior of the car washed. Forensics found dried mud in the wheel wells they've sent off for analysis. It hasn't rained here in a week. I'm thinking it was picked up when the body was transported to the lake. Let's hope we get a match with your Madison dirt."

"I suppose that would help. I'm confident the car was used by the killer, given everything else we know. Especially if we can match the shower curtain ring from the car."

Tubman interrupted. "Oh yeah, I forgot about that. It's been sent to the Madison Crime Lab for comparison with the one found on the shower curtain. Peters expects to hear back in the next couple of days. But with your Madison police contacts, you may know about that before we do."

"I'll keep on top of it. Is there anything else?"

"We've requested video feeds from Monday evening to Tuesday morning for the toll routes leading from Chicago to Wisconsin. I'm hoping we can locate the Audi and get a visual ID of the driver. Unfortunately, that could take time to process. We're talking forty to fifty cameras and probably a twelve-hour window of time. That means up to twenty-five days of video footage to look at."

"I hope you can get more than one person working on this. You can't let the trail get that cold."

"Agreed. I spoke to Peters. He's received the go-ahead for overtime and has already put out the word. He figures he can get up to ten guys to look at all the video. They'll initially focus on the most likely time slots for the car leaving and returning to Chicago. With any luck, we should know the route the car took in a couple of days, and hopefully have a good description of the killer."

"Kudos to Peters."

"Yeah, we've all been busy. I also had time to check into Jayman's whereabouts for that evening. As we figured, he has a solid alibi. His boss confirmed they were out for dinner at Morton's until approximately eleven. The concierge at his condo clearly recalls seeing Jayman later that evening. The concierge says each resident has an individually coded access card for the front door and elevator, so it's possible to monitor all the comings and goings. Not much privacy there. His system log shows Jayman entered the building and took the elevator up to his condo around eleven-thirty. The next time he got on the elevator, it was early the following day, likely to go to work."

"Looks like we can strike him off the suspect list. Unless of course he escaped down the staircase, avoided the concierge, and snuck back in after killing Harding in Madison."

"I think that's highly unlikely."

"I was joking."

"Ha ha," Tubman grunted. "That brings me to the final and most interesting piece of news. I just got Harding's cell and work phone records for the past couple of months. I haven't had time to go through them in detail, but I notice there were several calls in late April to the same number. To a 608 area code."

Madison's area code. Tony felt a buzz of excitement. "Have you figured out whose number it is?"

"I did better than that. I tried it just before I called you."

"Ah, the direct route. Did anyone pick up?"

"No, I was put through to an automated reception system, and get this, for the Madison police department!"

Tony contemplated the significance of this discovery. "Business related?"

"Peters is going to check with the State Attorney's office and see if she had any files that would involve the Madison police."

"Any way of checking where the calls were routed?"

"Don't think so. If their system works like ours, the transfer from the main line to a particular extension is fully automated and not stored in the system."

"And these were the only calls to or from Madison that you found?"

"So far, but we have a lot more work to do on this. I've asked for Harding's home phone records and confirmed with Peters that the techs are going over her computers. If there's anything else, we'll know in the next couple days."

"That's great. Now can you do another favor for me?" Tony asked.

"Name it."

"Can you hold off telling Peters about this for a couple of hours?"

Tubman hesitated. "Shouldn't be a problem, but why?"

"I plan to set up a meeting with Andrade for an information exchange. It would be helpful if I could tell her something that hadn't already been passed over by the Chicago PD."

"Oh, I see. You want to demonstrate your value to the little partnership."

"That's the idea."

"Okay, but you've got to handle this carefully. Peters can't find out that I'm keeping you in the loop or that I'm holding back from him. He'll be extremely pissed. Next thing you know, I'll be cut off from the investigation. He could even lodge a formal complaint. Andrade can't act on any of this information until it comes through official channels."

"I'll get her word on it. Besides, I think she'd appreciate any information that gives her a leg up on her boss."

"I'll leave that for you to manage. Now I've got to go."

"Tubs – thanks, really."

"No worries. Almost feels like old times. I miss those days."

"Me too, partner." You don't know how much, Tony added silently.

Chapter 11
MAY 17 11:55 AM

The intermittent rain had progressed to a nasty storm, and the Mustang was sideswiped by a strong gust of wind. Heading along John Nolan Drive, Tony could see Lake Monona was being lashed by a driving rain. He was very glad to be inside a car and not on the lake. There was nothing worse than being caught in bad weather in a boat with a temperamental motor.

He turned his attention to the upcoming meeting with Bobby. He'd called her after speaking with Tubman to let her know the Chicago police had turned up new information on the Harding murder. She'd suggested they meet for lunch at the Heartland Grill.

The Sheraton Hotel parking lot was almost full. Tony finally located a spot in the far corner and sprinted through the sheet rain. His nylon jacket was soaked by the time he stepped into the hotel lobby. In the men's room he used some paper towels to dry himself off, then made his way to the dining room.

Bobby was already in a booth, studying her iPhone while sipping a Coke. She appeared to be both dry and comfortable. There was a large umbrella propped up beside the booth, with a small pool of water underneath it.

She waved him over. "You're looking a bit like a drowned rat."

"To continue with the small animal metaphors, it's raining cats and dogs out there. You were smart packing an umbrella." He slid into the seat across from her.

"The weatherman got it right for a change. It's supposed to clear up later this afternoon."

"That would be good. This weather has already screwed up my fishing plans."

"I'm glad to hear that. We already have our hands full from your last trip out on the water. Before we start, Tony, I don't have much time. Adelsky just texted and he wants to see me at 1:30. He just received some information from the Chicago PD that he wants to discuss. He's also asked for an update from my end. To tell you the truth, he's being a real pain in the ass on this one. He's constantly hounding me to see if I've found out anything new."

They were interrupted by the arrival of their waitress. Tracy, according to her nametag, had short blondish hair with wild streaks of purple. Her pierced nose contained a small diamond.

"Can I get you shomething to drink?" The girl's words were slurred a bit and Tony noticed flash of silver as she spoke. He figured she'd also had her tongue recently pierced.

"I'll have a cranberry and soda. We're in a bit of a hurry so we need to order as well. Bobby, why don't you start?"

Bobby flipped open her menu. "I'll keep it simple. A Cobb salad, hold the avocado, dressing on the side."

Tony ordered a western sandwich on brown, salad instead of fries.

"No problem. Anything elthe?"

"That's it for now." Bobby said.

"I'll let the kitchen know this is a rusthh." Tracy hurried away to place their orders.

"Yeth, you do that," Tony said to her retreating back.

"They're only piercings, Tony," Bobby admonished him. "All the teenagers are doing it. Along with tattoos."

"I suppose. I just hope Carla hasn't done anything like this - those tongue things really gross me out. Anyway, where were we? Oh, yeah, Adelsky has been sticking his nose into your investigation. He does seem very interested in this case. Tubman told me Adelsky used some political clout to maintain jurisdiction over the investigation. My guess is he got help from his good friend in the Senate – which is somewhat curious. Tubby also just provided me with some very interesting news." Tony let this dangle.

"Come on, what've you got?"

"Before I spill the beans, you have to make the same promise I gave you the other day. You can't share this information with Adelsky or anyone else until you hear it through the Chicago PD. If Tubman's boss finds out he's been talking to me, I'll lose my inside man, and he could be sanctioned or even lose his job. And what I'm about to tell you is hot off the press."

Bobby pondered his request only briefly. She could appreciate the risk Tubman was taking in trying to help Tony – she was in a similar position. "Okay, deal."

"Good. Yesterday I tagged along with Tubman while he interviewed Harding's parents. It looks like Harding took her mom's Audi to Madison the night she was murdered. And someone, we assume her killer, returned it early the next morning."

Bobby almost jumped out of her seat. "How do you know this?"

"Mrs. Harding confirmed that Jennifer didn't own a car but borrowed her Audi when she needed to. Jennifer asked to use it one night this past week but apparently never came by to pick it up. On a bit of a flyer, we decided to check it out. We found a silver ring in the trunk, lodged in a gap between the back seat and trunk floor. Looks like the other one on the shower curtain wrapped around Harding's body. It would seem that the killer used the car to dump Harding's body and missed the fact that one of the rings fell off. It's on its way to the Madison Crime Lab, and I'm betting it's a match."

"That's quite the discovery. Any theories on why the killer would drive the car all the way back to Chicago?"

"The only explanation I can come up with is that the killer didn't want the police to trace Harding's movements that night. If they knew she took the car, it might give them something to go on in their investigation of her disappearance. However, that's only speculation. More important, returning the car to the parent's garage suggests the murderer knew Jennifer, and perhaps her family."

"Hmm ... maybe. Were there any fingerprints or other evidence in the car?" Bobby asked.

"A number of partials, some from the deceased but mostly from her mother. No other unknowns were located. The techs think the killer wore gloves or wiped down the areas he touched. However, they found mud in the wheel wells. They're checking that out to determine if it originated from the Madison area."

"That seems a stretch."

"Yeah, but when it's all you have at the moment, you gotta run with it. Chicago PD has also requested the video from all the tollbooth locations the Audi might have passed through. They hope to track the car's journey that night and get a visual of the driver on the return trip."

Bobby sat back in her seat, assimilating the new information. "You got more?"

"We also learned that Harding had a boyfriend until quite recently, a banking exec by the name of Jayman. Her parents said they broke up about a month ago, quite suddenly. We talked to him and got his version of events. He told us things were going well until one night when they got drunk at a hotel bar. Harding challenged him to pick up another woman for a threesome. He wasn't up for it and, according to him, their relationship went stone cold."

Bobby raised her eyebrows. "The spurned lover. Sounds like a good motive for murder."

"That's what we initially thought. However, if you met the guy, you'd see he doesn't fit the profile. Well educated and definitely metrosexual. Plus he appears to have an air-tight alibi. I also asked him about her using drugs. Based on Jayman's description of her behavior the night in the bar, it sounds like she was on Ecstasy. Also, judging by the events of that evening, I wouldn't be surprised if she has more than one lover out there."

He saw Bobby flinch.

"Listen, I know this is tough to hear, given you knew her. But it's important for us to understand her, warts and all."

"I do appreciate that. It just sounds so … cold and clinical."

"Unfortunately, that's the way it has to be if we're going to find her killer. Now, you'll likely hear what I just told you in your little update meeting with Adelsky, so act surprised. What he won't know is that Harding made several calls in the past month to Madison police headquarters. The problem is the calls went through the main switchboard, and Tubman doesn't think they can be traced. You said Harding was at a conference you attended earlier this year. Was there anyone else there from the Madison PD?"

"Yeah, a whole gang of us. Adelsky, Mike Dambro, Eve Jackson, Judd Nixon … oh, yes, and Jim Bradley."

"Bradley? What was he doing at a police conference?"

"There were some sessions that might've been relevant to the Coroner's Office. However, I think it was more of a vacation than anything else."

"I wonder if Harding's calls were to any of these people?"

"I don't think so."

"Why not?"

"Because I'm pretty sure those calls were made to me," she said in a whisper.

Tony exhaled in surprise. "Bobby, what the hell is going on? Why was Harding calling you?"

Her inner debate reflected on her face. She came to a decision. "I think it's time to fill you in on some things. Harding was calling me about the Sumner case."

Chapter 12

Bobby put up a hand to stop Tony from interrupting. "I know you always had your doubts about Mansfield being Sumner's killer. However, the mounting evidence against him seemed hard to ignore. An eye witness placed him near the bar the night of the murder, he vanished before he could be arrested, and Sumner's clothes were found in a garbage bin outside his apartment. When you add in the fact that we didn't have any other viable suspects, it appeared to be a slam dunk." Her tone changed. "But I've recently learned some things that make me wonder about the integrity of the investigation once you left the scene."

Tony could no longer contain himself and broke in. "What kind of things?"

"Remember the security video from the bar that mysteriously vanished from your office?"

"Yes, of course." The officers who initially investigated Sumner's disappearance had been given a DVD containing security footage from the Capital Lounge on the night she went missing. This disk had been turned over to Tony once the university student had been found dead.

He'd signed for custody of the disk and placed it in one of the work trays on his desk. His plan was to get together with Bobby to review it once he'd finished some outstanding paperwork. He'd been called into an emergency meeting with Chief Dupree at the Mayor's office and when he got back to the station, the DVD was gone. Bobby and his assistant couldn't shed any light on its sudden disappearance. Finally, and with some embarrassment, he had to contact the bar for another copy. He'd been fired before receiving the replacement disk.

Bobby's voice brought him back to the present. "About a week after you left, I had a call from Josh Stein over at the Capital Lounge. He was following up on your request. He'd called your office to let you know the DVD was ready, and learned you were no longer with the department. He was redirected to Adelsky and left a detailed message on his voice mail indicating that the dupe of the video was ready for pick-up. Adelsky never responded nor did he send anyone over to pick up the package. Stein still had my card from our initial interview with him, and he called me. He wasn't sure if the video was still important to the case, but wanted to speak with someone in the police department before chucking it out."

Tony shook his head in disgust. It was unimaginable that Adelsky wouldn't have retrieved a copy of the security video. "You're kidding me, right?"

Before Bobby could respond, their funky young waitress appeared with plates of food. After putting their orders down in front of them, she said, "Plesth let me know if there's anything elth you need."

As soon as she'd gone, Bobby's continued. "I wish I was. But it gets better. I knew the video was important and said I'd come by the bar and pick it up myself. I took it back to the station and hand-delivered it to Adelsky. I even volunteered to take a look at it. He gave me one of his patronizing looks and said something like, 'No need, we already know who killed Sumner and we just have to find him'. Then he waved me out of his office. I saw him toss the video into an evidence box on the floor beside his desk."

"Are you telling me that no one in the homicide department has looked at the security video from that evening?"

"Not exactly, but let me return to that after I tell you about another incident. Recently I was contacted by an old friend from college. Her name is Connie Duncan. She studied forensic sciences and ended up with the Nebraska Crime Lab. We lost touch until she called out of the blue to let me know she'd just accepted a senior position with our Crime Lab. She was hired as part of the state-funded initiative to deal with their backlog."

Tony nodded. "I remember all the delays. Even with a high profile case like the Sumner murder, we were told it might take weeks to get back certain test results."

"That's right. In fact, most of the DNA tests for the Sumner's case weren't completed until after Adelsky took over. I had a call from Connie several weeks ago. She wanted to discuss some business matters in confidence. When we got together, she told me she'd been assigned to take a look at some old case files. Her boss wanted to make sure the Crime Lab hadn't missed anything critical during what she referred to as their 'out of control' period. She'd just completed her review of the Sumner case file. She knew from the documentation that I was involved in the initial investigation. She wanted my advice, off the record."

Bobby had Tony's full and complete attention.

"As you probably remember, we'd asked the lab to put a rush on the semen and skin samples collected during the autopsy. The results came back about a week later. The lab report indicated that the body's exposure to the elements and marsh water had contaminated the DNA samples, making a positive ID of her killer virtually impossible."

"Yeah, I remember you calling to tell me. It was a real disappointment. We discussed whether they could run other tests. Apparently there was nothing more that could be done."

"That's what everyone thought. However, as Connie went through the file, she saw a notation from the technician. It indicated that while the DNA samples were compromised, there were other tests that could be run by the FBI. They apparently had more state-of-the-art equipment that could identify certain genetic markers like race, ethnicity and age range. Not 100 percent reliable or conclusive, but this information could be useful in developing a better profile of Sumner's killer."

"And what were the results of those tests?"

"That was her problem. According to their files, a memo was sent to the Coroner's Office along with the DNA results, asking for written authorization to send samples to the FBI lab. However, Connie couldn't find a record of authorization or any other indication that the tests had been completed. She followed up with our beloved coroner and briefed him on what she'd discovered. Bradley said he'd discuss the matter with Adelsky, and get back to her. Connie followed up a week later by email, and then put in another call to Bradley. No response. She wanted my advice on whether to drop the matter or keep following up."

He leaned forward. "What'd you tell her?"

"At first I was going to suggest that she speak directly with Adelsky. Then I recalled his response on the security video. I was afraid he wouldn't take any action on the information. So I volunteered to bring her concerns to Chief Dupree and let him deal with it."

"And how'd he take this news?"

"He didn't appear that concerned. Thought Bradley must've discussed the situation with Adelsky and they agreed the additional tests wouldn't be helpful. But, between you and me, the chief hasn't been the same man since you were fired. I heard he really got knocked around by the Police Commission when he came to your defense. These days he doesn't want to do anything to rock the boat, particularly when it comes to matters involving Adelsky, or Bradley, for that matter. Dupree is well aware they're golf buddies with Senator Caldwell."

"Hmph," Tony muttered at the mention of Caldwell's name.

"After my conversation with the chief, I called Connie back and told her to drop it. But by then I had this awful feeling in my gut that the Sumner investigation had been fucked up by Adelsky. Both you and I know that unless you catch the killer in the act, the state prosecutor needs to demonstrate that the police have made all reasonable efforts to investigate any other possible suspects. It was becoming apparent to me that if the evidence didn't lead to Mansfield, it was being totally ignored." Frustration resonated in Bobby's voice.

"Yup. A good defense lawyer would destroy the prosecution's case with this kind of sloppy police work. That's the problem with having an inexperienced homicide cop leading the investigation. Mistakes get made and critical pieces of evidence are overlooked. Combine that with a coroner who's more interested in his golf handicap than doing his job, and you've got a recipe for the killer getting off scot-free."

Bobby nodded. "And I didn't want that to happen. So I decided to take things into my own hands and have a look at the security video."

"How'd you get your hands on it?"

"I'm in pretty good with Dan Vastic, who runs the evidence room. We work out at the same club. I paid him a visit and we chatted for a while, and then I mentioned I wanted to follow up on a cold case. I told him to keep it under his hat – it was totally unofficial and Adelsky wouldn't want me wasting my time on it. Fortunately, he's no fan. Calls him the 'A-hole.'" He turned his back while I rummaged through the Sumner evidence boxes until I found the DVD. I tucked it under my jacket and told Dan I'd be back for another visit in a few days."

"Good for you. Anything of interest on the video?"

"A few things," she said in a neutral tone. "First time through, I tried to focus on the activities of Sumner and her roommate. Unfortunately she only showed up entering and leaving the bar. There was no camera in the dance floor area where it appears she spent all of her time. I then watched more closely as she stood in line to get in and as she left. I wanted to track anyone she came in contact with. Again, I didn't see anything out of the ordinary. In my third viewing I widened my perspective and tried to take in the whole bar scene. That's when it hit me."

"What's that?" Tony asked, sensing her excitement.

"Do you remember how we got pointed in Mansfield's direction in the first place?"

Tony thought for a moment. "Adelsky actually did something to help us out. He pulled some pictures of ex-cons living in the Madison area who'd been convicted of sexual crimes. He suggested we go back to interview the bar staff and see if any of these characters had been spotted the night Sumner disappeared. We got lucky with one of the security guards. He picked out Mansfield from the photo array. As I recall, he told us he went outside for a smoke break shortly before Sumner left the bar, and was pretty sure he spotted Mansfield loitering near the front entrance."

"That's right. The security guard's name is Matt Riley. In my final time going through the security video, I recognized Riley checking IDs at the front door. According to the time-stamp on the video, he was there from approximately eight to nine that evening. Then, like he said, he was relieved by another security guard. I watched him pack up, but instead of going out the front door for a smoke, he headed back into the bar area. He's picked up again on the camera in that area. He sat down at a table and started talking with several women. He remained there until approximately 9:50, when he said his goodbyes. I went back to the video from the front entrance and Riley reappeared maybe thirty seconds later. He started speaking with the security guy at the door and eventually relieved him."

It didn't take Tony much time to figure out what this meant. "You're telling me that Riley never went outside for a smoke?"

"At least not when he said he did."

"Holy shit! What does he have to say now that you figured this out?" Tony was halfway out of his chair in excitement.

"That's the problem – he's gone missing in action. I searched the DMV database and found out his driver's license expired several months ago, with no forwarding address. I called Stein and learned that he'd fired Riley around the same time. Stein didn't have a clue where he might be."

Tony was confused. "I don't get it. Why would Riley lie about seeing Mansfield outside the bar?"

"I've been wondering about that myself. Maybe he thought he could get his hands on the $50,000 reward being offered by Sumner's parents."

"I don't know," Tony said, not convinced. Riley would have to figure there was a good chance that Mansfield had an alibi for that evening, or the real killer would eventually be caught. The police would then figure out he was lying, and that would really put him in hot water. But he let it slide, wanting to get back to the main topic of discussion. "Are we now at the point where you can tell me why Harding was calling you?"

Bobby nodded. "I was in a bit of an awkward spot. I had my doubts about Riley's ID of Mansfield, and I also knew there were some additional DNA tests that might shed more light on the identity of Sumner's killer. However, I didn't think I'd be able to convince Adelsky to investigate this further, and the chief appeared to be running a bit scared. I needed to speak with someone outside the whole mess and get some advice. Sorry, Tony, you weren't really an option."

He nodded in understanding.

"After giving it some thought, I narrowed down my options down to one person: Jennifer Harding. I thought she could give me an unbiased opinion on what to do, not being caught up in the Madison politics. It took another week to convince myself this was the right thing to do. I finally called and told her I had a somewhat unusual situation that I would like to discuss with her. I could tell from her voice that she was busy and perhaps hesitant to get involved, but she agreed to listen. I gave her a summary of the Sumner murder investigation and my concerns. I then asked her what she would do if she was in my shoes."

Tony took a bite of his sandwich and waited for Bobby to continue.

"She started by telling me about a murder case she prosecuted several years ago. The accused vehemently protested his innocence, and the evidence was a bit flimsy, but she got her conviction. He was given a life sentence. About six months later, the Chicago police arrested a guy for armed robbery. He said he had some information on another crime that he was prepared to barter for a lighter sentence. A deal was brokered and he ratted out a 'friend' for the murder that Harding had successfully prosecuted. The police pulled in the guy for questioning and he eventually confessed. Harding realized that she'd allowed herself to become so wrapped up in getting a conviction that was prepared to ignore the evidence and sent the wrong guy to jail."

"And the purpose of that story?" Tony interrupted.

"I'm getting to it. Harding told me this story to demonstrate that you can't take anyone's guilt, or innocence, for granted. She went on to say that at the very least the additional DNA testing should be completed. Otherwise the whole investigation would have the appearance of being a witch hunt for Mansfield. When I told her about the difficulties I'd have in getting either the Coroner's Office or my boss to order these new tests, she offered to help."

"Help?. In what way?"

"She had a rape case coming up for trial in a couple of months. The investigating officers had a hunch this was not the accused's first time. They'd been canvassing cold cases in the Chicago area to see if they could find other rapes with similar MOs. With Sumner being from Chicago, Harding thought she might be able to convince the officers to look into the DNA evidence for her case."

Tony shook his head. "Talk about a complicated way to get DNA tests completed."

"True, but her approach seemed easier than me trying to convince someone here to do the tests. And she was ultimately successful. The officers looked into the Sumner case file and learned that the initial DNA tests were inconclusive. However, they also learned that the additional profiling tests had not been completed. They discussed this with Harding and she gave them the go-ahead to have the samples sent to the FBI lab. Her calls to the Madison Police Department were to provide me with the test results."

"And?"

"The new tests indicate that Sumner's killer is male, Caucasian, and between the ages of twenty and forty."

"Not very helpful. Mansfield fits all those criteria."

"True. But the results also indicate that the murderer has a particular recessive gene. This gene is commonly found in people with red hair."

"Well, that's going to break the case wide open," Tony said sarcastically.

"Ah, but wait. I made some additional inquiries. It turns out this gene originates with an ethnic group called the Picts, who came from Scandinavia and inhabited Ireland and Scotland in the first century AD. Having this gene would indicate the killer is of Irish or Scottish ancestry."

"That's more interesting. Do we know where Mansfield's ancestors come from?"

"Glad you asked. I called Mansfield's mother on the pretext I was investigating her son's death. I asked a number of questions including where he was born and his family heritage. It turns out Mansfield is second-generation American. The grandparents on his father's side emigrated from Sicily after World War I. At that time they changed their surname from Manzotti to Mansfield. They didn't want any associations with the Sicilian mob. Mrs. Mansfield's family comes from southern Tuscany."

"Southern Italy. Dark skin and hair. It doesn't sound like Mansfield, or Manzotti, would have this recessive gene."

"Exactly. And we can probably confirm it, now that he's reappeared, albeit dead."

Tony thought this over, and a light bulb went on. "Do the Madison authorities know about these test results?"

"Yes. I called Connie after hearing from Jennifer. During our conversation I innocently asked if there was anything new relating to her review of the Sumner case files. She confirmed that an inquiry from the Chicago police had resulted in the additional DNA testing being completed. I asked if the results would be helpful to the Sumner investigation, but she hadn't seen them, and therefore couldn't comment. However, she did know the test results would be forwarded to the Coroner's Office for review."

"Well, that explains it."

"Explains what?" Bobby asked.

"Sorry, off on a bit of a personal tangent. This would explain why the city is now prepared to settle my wrongful termination lawsuit. By now the Coroner's Office will have reviewed the results, and this should have raised doubts about Mansfield being the killer. Since I was essentially dismissed for not arresting Mansfield, it puts their reasons for terminating me in a different light. It would be pretty embarrassing for the city if my case went to trial and this was put into evidence. I suspect they want to bury this whole thing. What they don't know is the price for settling my lawsuit just went up."

"I say stick it to them, Tony. You deserve every penny you can get. Your lawyer should remind them that if Adelsky and Bradley had been doing their job, it wouldn't have taken nine months to figure this all out." Bobby looked at her watch and then down to the barely eaten salad in front of her. "Unfortunately I've got to go. My meeting with Adelsky starts in twenty minutes. Can you pick up the bill?"

Tony said yes, but wished the conversation didn't have to end. This new information raised a number of tantalizing questions. Like, who actually killed Sumner? Did Mansfield really die of natural causes? And was there any connection between Harding's murder and her recent involvement in the Sumner investigation?

Bobby seemed to read his mind. "Let's plan to get back together tomorrow. I'd really appreciate your views on this new evidence and where it might lead the investigation."

"Good idea. That'll give me time to think all this through. How about we meet at my place around 10 am?"

"Should be fine. I'll give you a call in the morning to confirm." Bobby got up and headed towards the restaurant entrance.

Tony absent-mindedly took another bite from his tasteless sandwich while his mind moved into overdrive.

Chapter 13
MAY 17 6:50 PM

Julie had an apartment on the second floor of a four story walk-up on State Street. The rent was relatively cheap due to its location directly over a Taco Bell. She was now used to the constant hum of noise and occasional smell of greasy food emanating from the kitchen.

She did another spot check in the bathroom mirror. Not bad, she thought. Just a year shy of thirty and no sign of wrinkles. Moving quickly into the smallish bedroom, she opened the drawer of an ancient dresser and removed a light sweater in case the evening became cooler. Not wanting Tony to see the mess that had accumulated in her apartment after four days of cramming, she decided to head downstairs and meet him at the building entrance.

State Street was bustling with university students, window-shopping at the cheap chic clothing stores or heading to one of the many restaurants and bars in the area. There was a shoe store beside the Taco Bell, and she did some of her own window shopping while she waited for Tony's arrival. As she peered at the shoes, she felt a curious mix of anticipation and anxiety that reminded her of feelings she used to have in high school going on a date with a new boy. It struck her that she was on a kind of blind date, as she barely knew the man she was about to meet. But their two brief encounters had been like emotional teasers. Looking into his deep brown eyes had revealed a depth of sadness and strength that she decided to explore outside of work.

She caught sight of someone approaching Taco Bell, looking slightly confused. She turned and saw it was her date for the evening. He stopped in front of the building, searching for the entrance to her apartment building. She approached him from behind and lightly touched his shoulder. He quickly turned, surprised to see her. His black curly hair was highlighted in the evening sunlight behind him, and his cologne had a pleasant musky odor.

"Hi, Tony. I thought I'd save you the effort of walking up the stairs to my apartment. And it's such a beautiful evening; I just wanted to be outside."

She saw him appraising her and was pleased at his look of approval. She'd spent a good half hour picking out what she planned to wear tonight before deciding to go with the black cotton skirt that highlighted her shapely tanned legs, and the open-collar shirt that provided a glimpse of her full breasts. Her black sweater was now casually draped over her shoulders.

"Hello, there. I'm glad to see you're ready to go."

"A girl gets hungry after studying all day. Now, where are you taking me?" she asked brightly.

He looked up at the Taco Bell sign above them. "Do you like Mexican?"

"No way!"

Tony chuckled. "Okay, we'll go back to the original plan. Have you heard of Antonio's?"

"Are you kidding? I've always wanted to go there." Antonio's was one of the top restaurants in town.

"Then it's a good thing we have reservations. It's one of my favorite spots. And there really is an Antonio. If we're lucky, he'll be in the kitchen tonight. He's a real character. So let's go. Your chariot awaits."

As they approached the Mustang she let out a whistle. "Nice set of wheels. I bet it really moves."

"Yeah, I love the raw power and the sound of the exhaust. You can actually feel it in your gut."

Travelling east along State Street, the rounded dome of the State Capitol Building began to fill the skyline. "I'm still a bit awestruck by that sight," Julie said.

He nodded. "Yes, you'd swear you're in Washington, D.C., looking at a slightly downsized Capitol Building." He pointed to the gilded bronze statue of a woman at the top of the dome. "I understand the young woman up there weighs just over three tons. Must've been quite a challenge getting her up there, considering they didn't have the benefit of modern-day cranes."

"It's amazing what can get done with a bit of determination," Julie said with a grin.

Tony parked outside Antonio's, its entrance kitty-corner to the State Square. The restaurant in its historic century building had been a mainstay of Madison for over thirty years. Tony jumped out of the car and opened the passenger door for Julie. She smiled at his attempt at gallantry. "Thank you, kind sir."

They passed under a green canopy through the front door of the restaurant. The front tables were occupied, and several patrons were in the bar area waiting to be seated.

A hostess appeared and gave them both a big smile. "Mr. Deluca, welcome back. Let me escort you to your table." As they made their way through the restaurant, Tony exchanged a wave with a short, energetic-looking man in a chef's hat. He was talking with a couple at a table, waving his hands around animatedly.

"That's our host and chef 'straordinario,'" Tony explained. "Already chatting up the guests. I hope he gets back to the kitchen in time to oversee our meals."

The hostess took them to a private booth at the back of the restaurant and placed menus in front of them. "Your waiter, Vida, will be here in a moment to see about drink orders and explain tonight's specials."

Julie looked around. "I'm impressed, Tony. You must be a regular."

"If you have a name like Deluca, you'd better like Italian food. And Antonio is a wonderful chef. I try to chat with him every time I'm in here. I've managed to pry out some of his best recipes. Very useful when you're entertaining."

The wonderful smell of Italian cooking filled the restaurant and Julie's stomach gave a warning grumble. She picked up the menu. "I'm totally famished. What would you recommend?"

Tony spent some time pointing out some of his personal favorites. "But before you make any decisions, you should wait to hear the chef's specials. Antonio usually has several interesting dishes. It's also important to leave room for dessert. Antonio makes a tiramisu that some say is better than sex."

Julie raised her eyebrows. "I'll definitely have to give that a try."

As they both laughed, their waiter arrived. "Mr. Deluca, I'm glad you could join us for dinner. And welcome to your lovely guest. I believe this is your first visit?"

Julie nodded.

"Can I start you off with a drink?"

"Do you still have that 2004 Chianti Reserva from the small winery near Castellina, Vida?" Tony inquired.

"I think so, but let me double check. While I'm here, I'll go through the specials." Vida described three additional entrees, pasta, veal and chicken. "Let me look for your wine, and that'll give you some time to make your decisions." He headed off to look for the Chianti.

"I really like the sound of the Veal Florentine," Julie said.

"Good selection, one of my favorites. I'm going to try Insalata Alla Cesare followed by the Salmoneai Ferri. The food always sounds much grander in Italian."

Vida returned to their table with a bottle of wine. "You're in luck, Mr. Deluca, this is one of our two remaining bottles."

He showed the label to Tony and deftly pulled out the cork, pouring a small amount into his glass. Julie watched Tony swirl the wine, inhale the aroma, and take a sip.

Tony smiled broadly. "Excellent, just as I remember it."

Vida filled both their glasses and took their orders. After he'd departed, Julie held up her glass of wine. "To new friends and great Italian food."

She looked contemplatively at Tony as they clinked their glasses. Enjoying her first taste of the wine, she realized Tony was turning out to be a bit of an enigma to her. Working security at a bar and driving a muscle car, yet a regular at a swanky restaurant and well versed in food and wine. He definitely deserved careful consideration.

Chapter 14
MAY 17 8:20 PM

They were just finishing their main courses, as well as an interesting and sometimes emotional exploration of their respective pasts. Julie had learned about Tony's formative years in Chicago, his climb up the ranks as a homicide detective and a short discussion of the troubles that had caused the move to Madison. She saw the anger and pain in his eyes as he briefly recounted the investigation into the death of Karen Sumner, his sudden firing, and the events leading up to the separation from his wife and daughter.

She in turn talked about her crazy hippie parents who'd met at the University of Wisconsin in the early 1970s. After graduating, they moved to Denver where her father settled down and became a successful businessman. Her mother became a teacher and kept her flower child perspective of the world. She encouraged Julie to be her own person and experience life to the fullest. This had led her to postpone university and travel to Africa and South-East Asia, giving her a much better appreciation of her own life back in the US.

She'd returned home and got a business degree. Her father invited her to join his business and for two years everything was almost perfect. That all ended on the day he collapsed in his office from a massive stroke. She told Tony, tears glistening in her eyes, that the prognosis for her dad's recovery was not good and the business had to be sold. She'd worked around the clock with various lawyers until the deal was completed.

"It gave me a greater appreciation of having a legal education and I decided to go back to school – again – my parents' alma mater in Madison. Just another year and I'll graduate. Then only the bar ads stand between me and hanging out my shingle. And Dad's promised to be at my graduation," she said with pride.

Vida arrived with Julie's dessert, tiramisu, and a cup of espresso for Tony. Julie picked up a fork to take a bite and sampled the rich mixture. "Tony, you're right, this is incredible."

"I thought you'd like it." He smiled. "Now tell me, how did law school lead to bartending?"

"A matter of necessity. My money was starting to get tight and while my parents wanted to help out, there just wasn't enough to go around. I needed a job that would allow me to go to classes during the day. A friend suggested working in a bar, so I took a bartending course, applied to several local bars...."

"And ended up at the Varsity."

"Yes, but not right away. My first bartending gig was at the Capital Lounge. I was only there for a couple of weeks before that poor girl was murdered. Business slowed right down after that. I asked Josh if I could transfer to one of his other bars. I had to wait until there was an opening at the Varsity."

Tony pondered this information. "I take it you weren't working the night that Karen Sumner was murdered?"

"As a matter of fact, I was behind the bar the entire evening."

Tony looked at her in surprise. "We interviewed all the staff that worked that night. I certainly would've remembered speaking to you. My memory can't be getting that bad."

"No, we didn't talk. The day after that girl disappeared, I had a call from Mom to say that Dad was having a really bad time. I headed back to Denver and stayed there for a couple of weeks until I was sure he going to be okay. I didn't even know about the murder until I came back and Josh filled me in. By then the police were trying to track Mansfield down. The murder was old news."

Tony now remembered Josh mentioning the missing bartender in their initial interview. "So you're the staff person we never talked to. Did anyone else from the homicide department ever interview you about that evening?"

"No, but why would they? They'd already identified the killer and, honestly, I don't recall seeing anything out of the ordinary. Otherwise I would've gone to the police myself."

Tony looked directly into Julie's blue eyes. "I shouldn't be telling you this, but I think the Sumner case is going to be reopened. There's some new evidence that suggests that Mansfield wasn't her killer."

"No way!"

"Listen, I think it's important that you talk to someone I know with the Madison police and perhaps review the bar security video from that evening. You might see something you didn't think was important at the time. Would you be willing to do that?"

"Of course. I'll help out any way I can."

"That's great. Now, I have another favor to ask. I'd really appreciate if you didn't mention this to Josh or anyone else. At this point only a few people are aware of this new development. We should give the police a chance to manage the fallout from it."

"I understand. Mum's the word."

"Great. Now let me get the bill."

STATE STREET WAS crowded with university students looking to party and dance at the area's various bars. Tony got lucky as a car pulled out in front of them and he swung the Mustang into the vacant spot. He met Julie on the sidewalk. "Let me make sure you don't get accosted by a drunken student on the way to your apartment."

As if to prove his point, a young man, shirtless and painted with the red and white colors of the Badgers, ran by them and let out a raucous yell.

Julie shook her head. "Yes, I may need some protection."

Tony started down the street, Julie at his side. They didn't speak, simply enjoying the still warm spring night and each other's company. At the entrance to Julie's apartment building, they stopped and she turned to him.

"Tony, I had a wonderful evening. The meal was delicious and I really enjoyed our conversation."

"All part of the 'Save a Student from Starving' program sponsored by the city," he said lightly.

"Really, I mean it. You may not believe it from my youthful appearance, but next year I'll be hitting the big three-oh. By day I'm surrounded by law students, who are for the most part deadly boring, and then at night I have to deal with university kids who don't have a clue of what the real world is about. It's nice to spend time with someone who's experienced life and has interests other than drinking and getting laid. Not that there's anything wrong with either of those activities," she added, smiling.

"I have to admit I've been wondering why you picked me as your dinner date. I was kinda hoping it was for my devastating good looks, but I'll settle for my worldly perspective on life."

"Well, you are cute…. but I have another admission to make. Please don't take this the wrong way, but when I first saw you in the kitchen the other night, you reminded me of my father. Not in a physical way, you're very different. You had this sadness in your eyes, as if you'd lost something very important to you. But when I asked for your help, your whole demeanor changed. All of a sudden you became this take-charge kind of guy. And after tonight I understand why. Like my father, you've been very successful in your career. And like my father, you've experienced a tremendous setback. For a while it knocked my dad for a loop and he didn't want to get out of bed. But he fought his way back and he's now focused on restoring as much as he can of his former life. I get the same vibe from you. You've been stuck in this deep hole but you've dug yourself out. You're a street fighter, just like my dad." She stopped and gave him a tentative smile.

Tony was speechless, amazed by the depths of her insights from that single encounter. He was also a bit humbled to be compared with her father, who clearly had much bigger issues to deal with and somehow had managed to come back into the light.

"Sorry," Julie said with uncharacteristic shyness. "I didn't mean this whole thing to turn maudlin. And I certainly don't want you to think this some weird daughter-father thing. The attraction is based on something totally different."

"I feel the same way, the attraction thing, that is," Tony said hesitantly.

Julie moved closer and tipped her head towards his. Their kiss was both tentative and exploratory. Tony experienced something like an electrical spark coursing through his body. He pulled back and looked into her inquiring eyes, noting the flicker of desire within their blueness.

"Julie…" he started.

She seemed to read his thoughts. "Let me guess – you think we should get to know each other better."

"I guess that's right. Quite frankly, I've been on quite an emotional roller-coaster for the last few days. I'd like to take things slowly."

"I'm fine with that, subject to one important condition."

"What's that?"

"You have to promise to call me tomorrow."

"You don't have to worry about that," he said, exhaling in relief.

"Good," she murmured, and kissed him lightly before opening the door to her building.

The brush of their lips gave him another jolt, and he wondered if it was a mistake not following her through that door.

Chapter 15
MAY 18 7:55 AM

They were in bed, naked, and in each other's arms. She flicked her tongue in his mouth and his entire body responded. Their kisses became harder and more urgent, their bodies hot and sweaty with desire. At her urging he got on top, and they moved in unison with increasing tempo until he climaxed and collapsed in her arms. Afterwards she nuzzled her head into his chest, and he inhaled the gentle scent of her body. He felt at peace.

When Tony woke, sunlight was showing between the slats of the window blinds. He felt for the warm body, but the other side of the bed was cold and empty. He realized it had been a dream – an extremely vivid one at that. A mixed bag of feelings washed over him. Despite knowing his marriage was finished, he still harbored hope of reconciliation with Joanna. At the same time, while barely knowing Julie, she'd managed to enter his dreams in a very powerful and erotic way. He lay there a while, dissecting how he felt, but eventually gave up trying to rationalize his conflicting emotions.

As he got up and stretched, Sam rubbed against his leg. She followed him around, meowing until he got the message to refill her food and water bowls. Then, with a wave of her long bushy tail, she dismissed him and started to crunch on her food.

Tony wandered into the living room and saw the flashing light of his answering machine. He hadn't bothered to check for messages when he returned home last night. Curious, he hit the play button.

"Hi, Tony, it's Bobby. Sorry for not getting back to you earlier, but I was trying to juggle my schedule around. I just wanted to confirm I'll be at your place as planned at 10 tomorrow morning."

He was glad Bobby was coming over. Yesterday's revelations raised many disturbing questions about the Sumner murder investigation. Hopefully, by putting their heads together, they could come up with some answers. As he started to erase the message he was startled by the ringing of the phone.

"Good mornin', bud," a familiar voice said.

"Hey, Tubby, good to hear from you. How're things going in Chicago?"

"You know when you're looking through an evidence box for an important document and you can't find it? You're pretty sure it's in there, so you start all over again. On the third run through you find it paper-clipped by mistake to another report. By then you're really pissed off because you've wasted so much time?"

"I guess so...."

"Well, this time we found the document right away, near the front of the box."

"What the hell are you talking about?" Tony was totally confused.

Tubman laughed. "I suppose my analogy isn't very good. Let's start all over. Peters ran into some problems lining up off-duty officers to view the toll-route video footage. You may have heard that the President and First Lady are coming through town in a couple days and their visit is eating up all available police resources. It ended up he could only find two guys. I figured it could take days before we got though all the video footage, and we might not even locate the Audi being returned to Chicago. But one of the officers hit pay dirt around 4 am this morning. He spotted the Audi at a toll booth on the I-294. From there it was pretty easy to figure out its route and timeline. We have it going through four different toll locations from 1:15 to 2:30 am the night Harding was murdered."

"That's great news! It confirms our theory that the killer returned the car!"

"No, it confirms *your* theory. As you may recall, I wasn't that interested in taking a look at Mrs. Harding's car."

"Have it your way. Now, tell me, did you get a description of the killer?"

"Not so lucky on that count. The Audi's windows are heavily tinted and the lighting at the toll stations isn't that great. Whoever was driving was also smart enough to know there are cameras at each toll location and kept his head down. All we have is the silhouette of someone wearing a baseball cap and a dark jacket. Peters has asked the techs to clean up the video, but I'm not confident we'll get anything helpful."

"Too bad. But at least we have confirmation that Harding's car was driven back from Madison, presumably by her killer, between midnight and 3 am. This narrows down time of death to somewhere between 9 pm and midnight.'

"That about sums it up."

"Okay, the killer drops off the car at the Harding's house. What would be his next step?" Tony asked.

"Peters and I talked about that. Assuming her killer is not from Madison, and didn't have someone trailing him in another car, he'd need transportation. The bus system shuts down out there around 2, so that wouldn't have been an option. We've assigned an officer to canvass the taxi companies who service that area, to see if there were any pickups early that morning. We're also checking with all car rental places within a ten-mile radius of their home, just in case he doesn't live in the Chicago area. Unfortunately, if the killer used any other form of transportation, we're going to have a much harder time tracing his movements."

"What about the neighbors?"

"Yup, been covered. An officer went door-to-door yesterday. Unlike my own next-door neighbor, they all seem to be sound sleepers and mind their own business. No one recalls hearing or seeing anything out of the usual that evening."

"Anything else?"

"Yeah, one more interesting nugget of information. Peters went over to the State Attorney's office and talked to Harding's boss, her secretary, and a couple of her co-workers. He wanted to see what cases she'd been working on recently and learned that for the past month or so Harding was preparing for a rape trial. Nothing to do with Madison – the suspect is local and so was the victim. To Peters' credit, he followed up with the detectives working the rape case, and asked them if anything would link it to Madison."

Tony knew what was coming next, but didn't interrupt.

"The detectives told Peters that Harding had suggested they look at another open rape/murder case. She thought there might be some connection with their case and wanted to compare the DNA evidence. Guess what case we're talking about?"

"Karen Sumner's," Tony immediately responded.

"That's right. Wait a minute, you don't sound very surprised. What do you know about this?"

Tony updated Tubman on yesterday's lunch meeting with Bobby. When Tony came to the end of his story, there was silence on the other end.

"What do you think, buddy?" Tubman finally asked.

"To tell you the truth, I've had some distractions and haven't given this the thought it deserves. Andrade and I are getting back together this morning to discuss. Clearly the Madison police need to find the security guard and confirm his story. At the same time, all the evidence against Mansfield needs to be re-evaluated. There's something very wrong with the whole set-up."

"Yup, agreed." Tubman said. "Now, what about Harding's death? She touches the Sumner case and shortly afterwards winds up at the bottom of a lake. Do you think there's a connection?"

"As you know, I'm not a big believer in coincidences."

"Me neither. But how would Sumner's killer even know about Harding's involvement? And once the tests were completed, what benefit would there be to killing her?"

"It certainly doesn't fit neatly together. There's something we're missing. But we can't ignore this link between the two cases," Tony concluded.

""No, we shouldn't lose that thread. Now, anything else from your end?"

"No, but if something comes from my meeting with Bobby, you'll be the first to know."

"Sounds like we're both up to date. Our part of the investigation will continue to focus on tracing the movements of the killer once the car was dropped at the Harding's house. Otherwise we have nothing real solid at this point to go on. The techs have pretty much completed going through Harding's cell, phone, and email records. So far there's nothing out of the ordinary. I admit I'm a bit concerned that if we don't make better progress, the FBI might be called in."

Tony considered this last statement. The Harding murder was a high-profile case with cross-state ramifications. Of course the FBI would want a piece of the action. Their involvement would cut off Tubman, and indirectly him, from the flow of information. This would not be a good development. "How much time do you think we have before they try to force their way into the investigation?"

"I'd say if we don't get a big break real soon, they won't even need to push their way in. The State Attorney will ask for their help."

"So we'd better work quickly. How about we talk again sometime tomorrow? Unless of course something comes up and we need to speak before then."

"Sounds like a plan. Good luck, partner."

Chapter 16
MAY 18 9:55 AM

Tony was in the kitchen munching on cold Danish when Bobby knocked on the front door. "I was just about to pour myself a coffee," Tony said, opening the door. "Can I get you one?"

"Sure, sounds good."

In the kitchen, he motioned to her to take a seat at the table and filled two mugs. While she was fixing her coffee, he got down to business. "How'd it go with Adelsky?"

Bobby rolled her eyes. "He's so full of himself. He'd just had a conversation with Peters and dispensed the information like Moses coming down from the mountain. But the bottom line is that there were no developments in Chicago that we didn't already know about. He then gave me a dressing down about the lack of results at our end. I told him we're following up on all leads, which are very slim at this point. I mentioned that I'm still waiting to get back the analysis for the mud found on Mrs. Harding's car, and a tech has been assigned to collect soil samples from around the lake. That might give us an idea of where Harding's body was put into the water and we can canvass the neighborhood – maybe find someone who remembers seeing the Audi that night. The local media has also been briefed and given a picture of Harding for publication, along with a police hotline number." Bobby sounded a bit defensive. "There's not much more I can do unless someone here comes forward with some new information, or there's a break in Chicago."

"On that topic, I spoke with Tubman about thirty minutes ago and there have been some new developments."

The news about locating the Audi on the tollbooth video clearly got Bobby's attention. "That's a break. Have they been able to ID the person driving the car?"

"Not yet and maybe never. Between the Audi's tinted windshield and poor lighting, all they were able to make out was that the driver was wearing a baseball cap and dark jacket. Tubman doesn't think they'll get anything useful."

"Too bad." She looked thoughtful. "Did he have anything else to report?"

"Tubman did have a piece of bad news, at least from my perspective. He raised the specter of the FBI becoming involved in the case."

"The FBI? Has someone asked for their assistance?" There was a note of concern in her voice.

"No, but he feels it's just a matter of time. He believes the State Attorney will make the request if there's no further progress in the next couple of days."

"That doesn't give us much time. Did you tell Tubman about my phone contacts with Harding?"

"I did. It led to a discussion on whether there might be some connection between the two murders. We agreed there's nothing to suggest there is... at least at this point."

"It is hard to believe they're related."

"While we're on the subject of coincidences, do you recall that we missed interviewing one of the bar staff that worked the night that Sumner disappeared? We were told she had to go back home to help with a sick family member."

"Yeah, that rings a bell. What about it?"

"She just happens to be working at the Varsity, as a bartender. We exchanged some basic histories, and that's when I learned she was working at the Capital Lounge the night Sumner was murdered. Turns out her father got very ill that weekend and she returned home. Bottom line, she never was interviewed."

Bobby's eyebrows arched. "That's interesting. Does she recall anything from that night that might be helpful?"

"No, but there's been lots of water under the bridge since then. It might be helpful for her to take a look at the bar security video – see if anything stands out."

"Great idea. I still have the DVD. When do you want to set this up?"

"Let me check with her. But how about we tentatively say tomorrow morning around this time? We could do it here if you want."

"Doing it here makes sense. I certainly can't bring you both into the police department. Adelsky would hear about it and start asking questions I don't want to answer."

"Okay, I'll get back to you. I think we're both pretty much up to date on Harding's murder investigation. I have to admit I'm more interested in discussing what you've discovered on the Sumner murder. Where do you think this new information leads?"

"I'm not really sure. All I know is that we can't rely on anything that Adelsky did after taking over the investigation."

"My thoughts exactly. Maybe we should go back to ground zero, starting with the case against Mansfield. Review how he became the prime suspect and the evidence against him."

"Makes sense," Bobby agreed. "I guess the best spot to start is with our interviews of the staff at the Capital Lounge. That's when we got our first big break on the case. Or so we thought."

Chapter 17

"As I recall, it didn't start off so well."

Bobby nodded. "You're right. Most of the staff were university students and couldn't even remember what they'd eaten for breakfast that morning. I'd almost given up any hope of getting any useful information when Riley sauntered in, full of attitude. We showed him our handpicked gallery of sexual deviants, and he picked out Mansfield, no hesitation. So the key is to locate him and find out why he lied to us. But I'm not sure how to broaden the search for him without involving Adelsky. It's still technically his case, and despite the new DNA evidence, he continues to act like Mansfield's the killer."

"Yes, we need to track down this guy without going through official channels. It would make it a lot easier if we could get more background information on him. Might give us some idea of where he landed. I wonder if Josh Stein kept his original job application, or if someone on the bar staff got friendly with him. Why don't you let me check it out? Maybe I can narrow down where he might have gone."

"It's worth a try. The only other option is to go to the FBI, and that would certainly require Adelsky's approval. And right now, the less they're involved in anything to do with Madison the better."

"Yeah, let's leave that as the last resort and continue with our review of the case against Mansfield. As I recall, we interviewed Mansfield at the bookstore where he worked. He was extremely evasive and complained several times about police harassment. We finally got him settled down and asked him to give us his co-ordinates for the day Sumner disappeared. He claimed he worked until 5 pm, at a bookstore, if I recall correctly, and went directly home where he spent a quiet night watching TV."

"Yeah, and he was a good boy and called his mom," Bobby said sarcastically. "I spoke to Mansfield's mother and she told me they talked every Saturday night around 8 pm. She confirmed they spoke for about fifteen minutes the night in question – nothing out of the ordinary. However, we figured he still could've completed this call and driven over to the bar before Sumner left."

"Right, it's all coming back to me. We also knew from the pathologist's preliminary exam there were skin scrapings under Sumner's fingernails. We figured she'd put up a fight and scratched her killer. Mansfield didn't show any visible marks, but he refused to undergo a medical examination. At that point we ended the interview. It was my plan to get the full autopsy report along with the DNA test results before making any further moves. I was also a bit perplexed. The whole thing didn't fit with Mansfield's profile. He was a pedophile with a hankering for young girls. There was absolutely no record of his being violent. It seemed to be quite a leap for him to kidnap, rape, and murder a university student." Tony felt vindicated. His instincts had been right.

Bobby took a sip of her coffee. "Except that the following day the *State Journal* ran a front page story with a mug shot of Mansfield, identifying him as our prime suspect. It was pretty clear the reporter received this information from someone close to our investigation. It really spooked Mansfield, and with good cause," she continued. "The paper even published the name of the book store where he worked and he got a bunch of threatening calls. Someone came into the store and tossed a book at him. He claimed it just missed his head."

Tony chuckled, imagining it, but his mood sobered as he recalled what happened next. "He called me near the end of the day and said he was now prepared to submit to a full body exam. He wanted to prove his innocence and get everyone to back off. He asked that it be set up for the next morning. I told him we'd send over a squad car to take him to the hospital, but he refused – claimed he was suffering from nervous exhaustion and afraid to be out after dark. So it was agreed we'd meet him at the hospital the following morning." Tony grimaced. "Big mistake. I should've insisted he come in right then. A lot of things would be different."

He continued to fill in the blanks. "When I got into the office the next morning, I was told Mansfield had tried to contact me in the middle of the night. But the station clerk decided not to disturb me. How fucking stupid can you get? The prime suspect in a murder investigation calls me, and someone thinks my beauty sleep is more important." He remembered reaming the young officer out for this blunder.

"I tried to get a hold of Mansfield at the number he left, but there was no answer. I was getting worried and sent an officer over to his apartment. Mansfield wasn't there. The officer knocked on a few doors, and a bleary-eyed kid claimed he saw Mansfield leave in the middle of the night with a duffle bag. The officer confirmed that Mansfield's car was not in the parking lot."

Bobby ended the story. "So everyone came to the conclusion that he really was the killer and fleeing from arrest. Then the shit really hit the fan."

Tony nodded. "I still didn't believe it, but couldn't ignore the fact that our main suspect had gone missing. I put out an APB and updated Dupree. He went up the line and alerted the mayor. A short time later the chief and I were summoned to an emergency meeting of the Police and Fire Commission. They raked me over the coals for losing Mansfield, along with sundry other beefs about how I was running the investigation. I was then told to leave while they discussed matters with the chief. He returned about an hour later to deliver the bad news. Over his objections, the commissioners had decided my services were no longer required. I told him this was bullshit – that criminals got more due process than I received from the commission. I could tell he agreed with me, but he still asked for my gun and badge before escorting me from the building." Tony's eyes flashed with frustration and anger.

Bobby waited for him to collect himself, and then picked up the narrative. "Right after that, the chief called me into his office to let me know what'd gone down. He said Adelsky was taking over the investigation and he wanted to work the case with another detective. Apparently I was tainted by my association with you."

Tony grunted in disgust.

"The next thing I hear is that Adelsky had obtained a search warrant for Mansfield's apartment. They found a stash of child pornography under his mattress. Otherwise the apartment was clean. However, they hit pay dirt in the dumpster outside the building – a plastic bag of women's clothing. Her roommate later identified them as the clothes Sumner was wearing the night she disappeared. Adelsky was convinced Mansfield had tried to get rid of the incriminating evidence before skipping town. A manhunt was mounted, but Mansfield was never seen again."

"Until that hiker stumbled upon his body in a park." Tony added.

"That's right. Now, as far as I recall, that's the full case against Mansfield. We've now determined that the initial ID of him outside the bar is bogus. We believe the killer was scratched by Sumner, and Mansfield claimed he was ready to submit to a body exam. However, Adelsky says that was just a ruse to buy him time to get out of town. Mansfield called you in the middle of the night before vanishing. Why the phone call if he simply planned to disappear? And he didn't get that far – a state park just a couple of hours away. . And finally, we have the new DNA evidence that strongly suggests Mansfield couldn't have been the killer."

Tony jumped in. "And if Mansfield is not the killer, someone else planted those items in the dumpster. The real killer."

"That would make sense."

"The trash bin would be emptied on a regular basis," Tony went on. "If that happened, the incriminating evidence against Mansfield would disappear. So … the killer would need to know when the police were planning to make their move on Mansfield. How could the killer have this information?"

He pondered this question. If his theory was correct, the killer had to know the police were ready to swoop in for an arrest. He quickly put aside as too distasteful the idea that he killer was someone within the police force. Instead, he focused on another theory that fit with all the facts. There'd been threats against Mansfield's life – he was frightened and refused to go out that night. Then he'd tried to contact Tony before he disappeared.

"What if Mansfield wasn't trying to flee from arrest?" he ventured. "What if he received what he thought was a serious threat and was concerned about his personal safety? That might explain why he called me in the middle of the night – he was looking for help. When I didn't return his call, he decided to go into hiding. The person making those threats could've been Sumner's killer."

"Sorry, Tony, you've lost me."

"Put yourself in the shoes of the killer. You've read in the newspaper that the police are investigating someone else for a murder you committed. Wouldn't it be great if you could give the police some evidence against this guy – the victim's clothes, for example? You know where he works and decide to follow him back to his apartment where you see the dumpster. Maybe you figure out the schedule for the garbage pick-up. Now you have a time frame for planting the evidence. You don't know if and when the police will come to arrest Mansfield, but figure if you can scare Mansfield, he might do something stupid, like leave town. If this happens, the killer knows the police will be mobilized. That's when you plant the evidence."

"Sounds more like a fairy tale than a theory." Bobby sounded unconvinced.

"Think about it." Tony was now animated. "What does the killer have to lose? If he times it right, the police have a much stronger case against Mansfield. And if he doesn't, all the incriminating evidence goes to the dump. You know what? We need to see if Mansfield received any calls the night he tried to contact me."

"I don't know…"

"Come on, humor me. Get Mansfield's phone records from the night he disappeared."

Bobby saw the determined look on his face. "Okay, I'll follow it up."

"Thanks. Well, I think we have our marching orders. I'll contact Julie about viewing the bar security video, and I'll also ask around about Riley. You'll pull Mansfield's phone records. For me, it looks like the Harding murder will have to go on the back burner for the time being. Hopefully my client will understand," he added.

"That makes good sense. I'm as anxious as you are to solve Sumner's murder – her parents need finality. We've got lots of other resources on the Harding case, and you'll be kept up to speed by your two "partners." I just hope we get a break and keep the FBI out of this. I'll plan to be back here tomorrow morning to go through the security video. Give me a call if you hear anything new from Chicago."

Chapter 18
MAY 18 6:30 PM

Tony arrived at the Varsity Bar feeling famished. He went through the near-empty restaurant into the kitchen to see what Leon was preparing for dinner. His favorite cook was nowhere to be found, but he noticed a pungent odor that made his mouth water. It appeared to be coming from a covered pot on the gas stove. He was about to investigate when Leon emerged from the large walk-in freezer, grunting under his load.

"Hey, Leon, need some help?"

Leon smiled. "Evenin', Tony. You could close that door behind me. Kinda got my hands full."

The freezer door, insulated to keep out the heat of the kitchen, was as heavy as a bank vault door. Tony put his shoulder against it while Leon deposited a large quantity of steaks on the stainless steel table top. "Expecting a run on T-bones tonight?" Tony asked.

"You bet. The boys from Alpha Phi have booked the private room for their annual blowout. Those guys like their steak and beer and I'm gettin' ready for 'em."

"Sounds like it could be a busy night."

"Yup, and if it's anything like last year, yer goin' to earn dat big salary tonight. Now, is that your stomach that I hear growling? Would you like to know what the chef's choice is for tonight?"

Tony laughed. "I have to admit I'm hungry. What do you recommend?"

"You could have one of these steaks. It'd be good. Certified Angus, aged for thirty days. But you'd kick yourself for not trying tonight's special. Gen-u-ine Creole jambalaya. It's a real crowd pleaser."

"Sounds interesting," Tony said cautiously. The last time he'd tried jambalaya was while vacationing in New Orleans with Joanna, a year before Katrina had devastated the place. That jambalaya had been an extremely spicy mixture of rice, seafood, and steamed vegetables. It was so hot that he quickly downed several Hurricanes, a Bourbon Street concoction of dark rum and fruit juices. The next morning he'd stayed in bed nursing a queasy stomach and a hangover, leaving Joanna to explore the French Quarter without him. He certainly didn't want a repeat of that incident.

Leon sensed his hesitation. "Guar-an-teed tasty. You won't have no regrets."

"Guess you're right. Nothing ventured, nothing gained." Tony grabbed a clean plate from a shelf.

Leon removed the lid of the pot Tony had noticed earlier. "This here is called Creole rather than Cajun 'cause it's made with fresh tomatoes. Ya start up by cooking some onions, ham, spicy sausage, shrimp and chicken. Then ya throw in a bunch of vegetables – celery, bell peppers and carrots, or whatever. Put in tomato sauce, fresh tomatoes 'n chicken stock. Then, and this is why I'm willing to share everythin' to this point, I add some special 'gredients to give it some real good heat. Then yer going to let it stew for a while and enjoy the smells. Here, hold out your plate."

Leon dished out a steaming portion of jambalaya, handed Tony a fork and waited expectantly. Tony took a tentative taste. It was hot but not overwhelmingly so, and the flavor was outstanding. "Yum."

"See, I told ya."

Tony moved to a quiet corner of the kitchen to eat, watching Leon prep the steaks. After a few more forkfuls the "special 'gredients" were beginning to create a slow burn from his throat to his stomach, and he gulped a large glass of water. In less than five minutes, the plate was clean.

He still had ten minutes before the start of his shift. He decided to look for Josh Stein and see if he could fill in some details about

Matt Riley, the missing security guard. Josh's office door was open, but the only sign of his presence was a suit jacket on the chair behind the desk. He checked the bar area where he saw Dan Stockton speaking with Sue, one of the waitresses. As he approached they looked his way.

"Sorry to interrupt, but have either of you seen Josh around?"

Dan nodded. "Yes, he's on rounds, reminding staff that the frat boys are making their appearance tonight. He wants us all to be on our toes and take no shit. There's to be no repeat of last year's event, where the cops had to be summoned to evict them after last call."

Tony shook his head. "Why would Josh let them back here again?"

"After last year's fiasco, word got around. No other bar would book their party," Sue told him. "They got the message and came back to Josh to make amends. He finally agreed to let them back here as long as the party was on a Sunday night. The place would be quieter and staff have more time to deal with any crap. I also understand they had to put up a hefty security deposit, which would be forfeited if there is any trouble."

Tony could understand Josh's decision now. "Thanks. I'll see if I can hunt Josh down. Dan, did you want to do door or floor first?"

"How about I take the door? Just in case it takes a while for you to track down Josh."

"Thanks. I'll be around by eight to relieve you."

Tony spotted Josh heading to the kitchen and moved to intercept him. "Josh, do you have a minute?"

"Tony, there you are. I wanted to talk to you before it got busy. We may have some rowdy visitors tonight."

"I've been warned to put on my riot gear. I understand they got a bit out of control at last year's party."

"That's right – partly our fault for not taking a stronger line early on. I'm glad you and Dan are working security. I need guys with level heads who know how to handle themselves if things get out of hand."

"Don't worry; we'll keep a close eye on them. Now, there was something else I wanted to talk to you about. Do you have a minute?"

Josh glanced at his watch and nodded.

"There was a security guard who worked for you – by the name of Matt Riley."

Josh's expression hardened at the mention of Riley's name. "Yes, what about him?"

Tony didn't want Josh to know the real reason for his interest, so he'd come up with a story. "The other night while I was working the front door a woman came by asking for this Riley character. I said I'd never heard of him. She looked upset, so I asked why she was looking for him. Turns out that after they'd dated a few times, he gave her a story about needing some money for a trip to visit a sick aunt. She lent him a couple hundred bucks and it looks like he skipped town. She knew this bar was under common ownership with the Capital Lounge and was hoping someone here knew his whereabouts. I said I would ask around."

"Her story doesn't surprise me one bit," Josh said glumly. "I had to fire him for lying on his job application. I haven't seen him since. I won't go into details, but I'm pretty sure that girl can kiss her money goodbye."

"Any forwarding address?" Tony asked.

"Nope. He pretty much stormed out of here after I let him go, so there wasn't any time for the niceties."

"What about his original job application? He probably listed some references or former employers that might know where he's gone."

"I probably have it somewhere, but I don't think it will be of any help. In fact, everything he put on it was a total fabrication. I guess I can tell you that Riley is a convicted felon. He knew it would make it virtually impossible for him to get a security job, so he used an organization that creates false job histories. They back the service up with a call center to field reference checks. Very slick. Had me totally fooled."

"How'd you find out he was an ex-con?"

"I have Dan to thank for that. We have an annual after-hours party for staff at both bars. Last one was held at the Capital Lounge, early January. Dan and Riley were the last men standing. Riley got pretty drunk and let it slip that he'd spent some time in prison. Dan was sober enough to realize that an ex-con working security at a university bar wouldn't be good for business if it became public. And he knew I didn't need any more bad press after the Sumner murder. Dan swung by my office the next night and filled me in. I confronted Riley, and he basically told me to fuck off. Made it pretty easy for me to fire him. You might want to talk to Dan. Maybe Riley shared some other personal information that night."

AFTER ALL THE advance warnings, the Alpha Phi party turned out to be a relatively tame affair. The group stayed put in their private room, and only occasionally did the sounds of loud laughter spill out into the bar area. At one point Tony did become concerned when he heard the crash of glass from behind the closed doors. However, it turned out one of the staff had stumbled and dropped a tray of empty glasses. That was quickly cleaned up and the party resumed without further incident. Even so, the staff gave a collective sigh of relief after the last of the brothers had departed.

When their shift ended, Tony suggested Dan stick around and join him for some beers. In the empty bar area, Tony ordered six Buds in a pail of ice. He pulled two from the bucket, placing one in front of Dan and opening the other for himself.

"Those frat boys didn't put up much of a fight tonight," Dan observed, taking a gulp of his beer.

"Yes, Josh said he made it clear they weren't going to get another chance. Besides, who in their right mind would want to create problems with you and me around?" .

"Right you are. One look at this baby and they're quivering in their boots." Dan used both hands to jiggle his large beer gut. "So tell me. What did I do to deserve your generous offer of free beer?"

"I'm trying to get a lead on someone who used to work at the Capital Lounge," Tony admitted. "A security guard by the name of Matt Riley. An old girlfriend of his came by the other night looking for him. Turns out he stiffed her for some money and she's trying to locate him. I told her I'd ask around. Josh gave me a bit of a rundown on Riley, but doesn't know where he might have gone. I understand you were probably the last person working here to have a conversation with him. I was hoping you'd have some information on his whereabouts."

"Tony, best advice you can give that woman is to let sleeping dogs lie. That guy is a good for nothing low-life, and getting money from him would be like getting water from a stone. You know what I mean?"

"I've met the type, but can you fill me in?"

"I had the pleasure of his company at a staff party earlier this year – kind of a celebration for getting through the Christmas season. The party was at the Capital, and started just after closing. It was really cooking until about 4 am and then the crowd started to peter out. The diehards, including myself and Riley, settled in. Another hour goes by and we're the only two left at the party. He wasn't what you'd call a pleasant drunk. He was pretty mad at the world and how it'd mistreated him. He got into a bit of a rant about someone by the name of Curtis Mansfield. You probably heard about him. He's the guy who killed that university student last fall."

Tony gave a quick nod and Dan went on.

"Riley said he did the police a favor. He was expecting to pick up the reward being offered by the parents of the murdered girl. He didn't say what he did to earn this reward, but he was totally pissed that Mansfield disappeared before he could be arrested. He hoped the pervert would turn up soon and be sent to a supermax prison. He said something to the effect that in the pen where he spent time, the cons took pleasure in cutting the balls off child molesters."

"Did he happen to mention the name of the prison?"

"Let me see, yeah, he did. I thought it was a funny name for a prison. Fruit or vegetable or something like that. He said it was in Virginia."

Tony thought for a moment. "Red Onion State Prison?"

"That's it. Didn't sound like that bad a place – not like Alcatraz or Sing Sing."

Dan's observation couldn't have been further from the truth, Tony thought. Red Onion was one of a number of super maximum correctional facilities scattered throughout the country. These supermax prisons were designed to house violent criminals as well as terrorists who posed a continuing threat to national security. The prison had received a lot of media attention in the late 1990s due to allegations of prisoner abuse. Eventually a state commission had been formed to investigate and clean things up. However, Dan had been right on one point: if Riley had been incarcerated at Red Onion, he wasn't a person you wanted to mess with.

"I asked why he was in prison, and it dawned on him that he'd said too much. He told me to mind my own business and clammed up. I decided it was time to hit the road. I said I needed to take a leak and never came back. The next day I told Josh about Riley admitting to being an ex-con. Josh was pretty upset. Later I heard through the staff grapevine that Riley'd been fired." Dan took another long swig of his beer.

"Did you and Riley talk about anything else – family or friends? Something that might provide a clue to where he headed after being fired?"

Dan bit his lip, trying to remember. "Hmm, that was a while ago now and I had a lot of beer that night. But I think he mentioned something about growing up in Atlantic City. Yeah, he said he had to leave there because there were no jobs around, but one day he planned to go back and work in one of the casinos. That's about it."

"Thanks, Dan. I'll pass the information along to the ex-girl-friend. I'll also strongly suggest she write off the loan as a bad investment. Now, let's enjoy these beers and find something more pleasant to talk about. Do you think those Blackhawks can take the Stanley Cup this year?"

Chapter 19
MAY 19 8:10 AM

An intermittent ringing brought Tony out of a sound sleep. He opened his eyes and looked at the clock, thinking the alarm had gone off. Seeing the time, he knew it couldn't be the source. It was the phone. Who in hell could be calling him this early? He picked up groggily.

"Tony, this is Drake. Sorry to call so early."

He was surprised to hear the lawyer's voice. "I hope this is important. You've interrupted my beauty sleep," he said with a short laugh.

"I think so and hopefully you'll agree. I just got off the phone with Lou Driller. He was following up to arrange a meeting to discuss your lawsuit. He's going to be out of town for several weeks on another case, and he's under pressure to get your matter resolved before he goes. He wanted to know if we'd be available for a meeting this afternoon at two. I can free up the time and just checking on your schedule. He's even lined up representatives from the mayor's office and the Police Department to attend and get this lawsuit settled. "Now before answering, I should let you know this meeting is a bit of a departure from the norm. Ordinarily counsel for both parties would discuss settlement terms and then they'd come back with a written offer for you to consider. We'd go over it and probably make a counter proposal. It would go back to his clients, and there would be another round of negotiating. The whole process usually takes weeks and even months. Lou wants to short circuit this by getting all the decision-makers in one room to see if we can conclude a deal. I told him I was fine with that and figured you would be too.

Tony half-listened to Drake, mentally reviewing his schedule for the day. He had to pick up Julie for the meeting with Bobby at 10, and his shift started at 7 pm. Other than some odd jobs around the house his day was otherwise clear. "That time should work for me. Where are we meeting and how long do you think it will go?"

"Lou's agreed to bring everyone over to my office. I don't think it should last more than an hour, tops."

"Did he say who else will be at the meeting?"

"He's planning to bring the deputy chief of police, Barry Salzman. I assume you know him?"

"Yeah, Barry's a fairly decent guy."

"Lou wasn't sure who would be there from the mayor's office, but apparently the mayor has taken a personal interest in trying to settle the case."

Tony chuckled. "I think I know the reason for this sudden urgency to settle my lawsuit."

"Wonderful. Tell me about it."

"The police have new DNA evidence that provides a more complete profile of the killer. It would seem to indicate they've been chasing the wrong guy. It's a bit of a story, and I have to get myself and the cottage presentable before I pick up someone at nine. How about I come by a bit early and fill you in?"

"You're going to keep me in suspense until this afternoon?"

"I'm afraid so."

"Okay, I'll try to contain my curiosity."

Tony headed for the shower and had a coffee while giving the cottage a quick clean. He wasn't too concerned about Bobby's views of his home-making skills, but the imminent arrival of Julie was a different matter.

The previous afternoon he'd fulfilled his promise to Julie by calling her. They talked for almost half an hour. When he asked if she was available to view the bar security video, she readily agreed to come to his place. He'd volunteered to pick her up and bring breakfast with him.

He arrived at Julie's apartment building bearing Starbucks coffees and a bag of assorted pastries. He'd already opened the plastic cover on his coffee to take a sip, and walked slowly up the staircase to avoid spilling it. Knocking on Julie's door, he waited. When he heard her voice, he responded, "Room service."

He heard a laugh and the door opened to reveal Julie in a grey University of Wisconsin t-shirt and faded jeans. She'd recently showered and her damp brown hair had been loosely pulled back in a ponytail. She wasn't wearing makeup, and had an attractive girl-next-door look to her. "Sorry, running a bit behind schedule" she apologized. "I just need another five minutes to dry my hair."

"No problem. Here's a coffee to take with you. I'll warm up the pastries."

"I won't be long."

A few minutes later they were sitting at the small round dining table beside the galley kitchen. "Any excitement at the Varsity last night?" Julie asked between bites of chocolate-filled croissant.

Tony gave her a quick rundown on the frat party and said he'd got together with Dan after their shift.

"You had beers with Dan? For some reason I don't picture the two of you as drinking buddies."

"Actually, he kinda grows on you, but I did have an ulterior motive. I'm trying to track down one of the security guards who used to work at the Capital Lounge. You probably know him – Matt Riley."

Julie made a face. "Why are you trying to find that guy?"

Tony knew he had to be careful what he said. "It was Riley who told us that Mansfield was outside the bar the night Karen Sumner disappeared. His information resulted in Mansfield becoming the main suspect in the murder investigation. Andrade has some additional questions for him based on her viewing of the video. The only problem is, he got fired and seems to have left the city and possibly the state."

"Good riddance. He really creeped me out."

"Yeah? Tell me about it."

"When I first started at the Capital Lounge, he'd come over to the bar and try to use his so-called charm on me. I have to tell you, I got the shivers whenever he looked at me. It was like I was being mentally undressed, or something worse. I never gave him the time of day, and eventually he latched onto several women who were regulars at the bar. I thought he was getting too chummy with the female customers, so I wasn't surprised when he got fired. I didn't hear until later on that it was because he was an ex-con."

Julie's comments confirmed his growing conviction that Riley was not the kind of witness you'd build a murder case on. Surely Adelsky would've realized this – or perhaps he didn't want to. He checked his watch. "We'd better finish up and head out. I'd like to get back to the cottage before Bobby arrives."

Julie looked contemplatively at Tony for a moment. "This Bobby, is she good looking?"

"I guess you could say that."

"Have you ever dated? I mean, after you broke up with your wife?"

Tony laughed. "No, it's always been strictly business between us. She's already had previous experience with a married cop, and it didn't work out well. And while we get along, quite frankly, she's not my type."

Julie took his hand. "Sorry, I shouldn't pry when we barely know each other, but I'm already beginning to grow quite fond of you. I want to know if I have any competition."

Tony briefly contemplated his recent meeting with Joanna. "No, I'm pretty sure of that."

She squeezed his hand. "That's good."

Yes, I believe it is, Tony said to himself, feeling a warm tingle from Julie's touch.

Chapter 20
MAY 19 10:05 AM

Julie leaned forward in her seat, trying to get a better view of the cottage highlighted by the blue lake behind it. She suddenly turned to look at Tony. "I have a question. Why are we going to your place to watch the security video – I mean, instead of at the police station?"

"I've got popcorn."

"Seriously."

He paused a moment, pulling together his thoughts. His natural police instinct would be to tell her politely that he couldn't go into details relating to an open investigation. However, he was no longer a homicide detective. Still, he had to protect Bobby's position and shelter Julie from any responsibility for their unauthorized activities. He decided to take the middle ground.

"I can't go into details, but the head of the homicide department, who is Bobby's boss, is convinced that Mansfield is Sumner's killer. Bobby and I aren't so sure about this. Until we have more proof, we don't want to ruffle his feathers, so I suggested we get together at my place. Sorry, but that's all I can really tell you at this time."

"Okay…" Julie was looking intently at him, trying to read his expression. "You clearly know the politics of this much better than I do."

They were within shouting distance of the cottage now, and Tony could see an unmarked police cruiser parked under a large oak tree. There was movement on the front porch – Bobby getting up from one of the old wicker chairs on the deck. She held up a hand to shield her eyes from the morning sun and waved as she recognized his car.

Tony parked and they walked up to the porch. "Sorry to keep you waiting, Bobby. This is Julie." He noticed the two women giving each other a thorough inspection. Julie took in Bobby's flattering dark pant suit, a blue silk shirt peeking from beneath her jacket

"It's good to finally meet you in person," Bobby said.

"In person? Have we talked before?" Julie asked.

"No, no." Bobby smiled. "It's just that you figure prominently in the video we're about to watch."

"Let's go inside and I'll get everyone coffee," Tony said. Despite his clean-up efforts, he could see the living room was still a bit of a mess. There were fresh clumps of fur on the sofa where Sam had taken up residence after he left. Scattered on the pine coffee table were magazines and half-read newspapers from the past week. The old hardwood floors were pock-marked from hard use, and there was a patina of sandy grit near the front door that had been tracked in from his recent fishing trips. Topping it off, there was a noticeable musty odor, probably a combination of dry rot and over-ripe kitty litter. "Sorry, the cleaning lady's coming tomorrow."

"I hope she's bringing lots of help," Julie said, half-joking. She moved to the sofa to give Sam a scratch under her chin.

"More like a swat team," Bobby added, and they all laughed.

"Okay, I get the message. For now, feel free to find a comfortable spot where there's no cat fur. Bobby, the DVD player is under the TV, if you want to get that set up. I'll get the coffee going"

Tony went into the kitchen to turn on the espresso maker. When he reappeared a few minutes later with a tray, Bobby and Julie were deep in conversation, like old friends. It was only when he put everything down on the coffee table, which had been neatly rearranged in his absence, that they acknowledged his presence.

"How long do you think we'll need to go through the video?" he asked.

Bobby did some mental arithmetic. "This DVD contains video from three different security cameras, front door, bar area and back door. I don't think we need to review the back door video – nothing to see but kitchen staff throwing out garbage and taking smoke breaks. That leaves us with two cameras and with almost two hours of footage during the relevant period. We can fast-forward through a lot of it. Let's say two hours."

"So let's get started with the show." He sat beside Julie on the well-worn couch, while Bobby took up a viewing spot on the loveseat. As he played with the remote, a slightly grainy picture appeared on the screen. He vaguely recognized the front entrance to the Capital Lounge from his several visits there. The video showed a steady stream of students, many wearing Badger football jerseys, entering through the double front door. Their progress was slowed by the security guard, who was checking driver's licenses using a scanning machine. The camera angle provided a clear view of the faces in line.

Bobby started providing some narration. "Okay, you can see the video is time-stamped. This was taken at 7:30 pm, about a half hour before Sumner and her roommate arrived. I've gone through this section of the video several times and didn't notice anything of interest. I think you can safely fast forward to just before eight."

Tony pointed the remote and the images on the screen sped up and blurred. After about thirty seconds he hit another button. The time stamp indicated 7:47 pm.

"Close enough," Bobby said.

They watched in near silence as the screen filled with people lined up at the bar entrance to have their IDs checked. A new person arrived to relieve the security guard at the front door. "Okay, now it's getting interesting," Bobby said. "In case you don't recognize the new guy with the security jacket, that's Matt Riley. He's about to start his first door shift for that evening."

The security guard had a thin face, wavy dark hair, deep-set eyes, and a sallow complexion. His memory refreshed, Tony recalled when he and Bobby met with Riley two days after Sumner's body was found in the marsh. Josh Stein had made his office available from them to interview the bar staff. Riley came into the room, furiously chewing on a stick of gum. He sat down, anxiously shifting in his chair.

Tony had asked Riley if he recalled seeing Sumner the evening she disappeared. Riley said he couldn't place her face. Bobby then pulled out a number of pictures, several of known sex offenders living in the Madison area interspersed with a control group of photos. She'd asked Riley if he could recall seeing any of these people. He spent a moment examining each picture and then rather dramatically placed a finger on Mansfield's face. That's when he told them he'd seen Mansfield outside the bar during one of his smoke breaks, shortly before Sumner had left the bar.

Tony turned his attention back to the TV screen. Riley continued the monotonous routine of checking IDs. This went on for another ten minutes, as Tony sipped on his coffee and worked his way through two Oreo cookies.

Suddenly, Bobby straightened in her chair. She pointed at two young women entering through the front door. "There's Karen Sumner and her roommate, right on time."

Sumner was approximately 5'4", slightly overweight but with an attractive face highlighted by curly long brown hair. She wore a white blouse with designer jeans and heels. She was talking animatedly with a woman who was slimmer and several inches taller. Tony recognized Teresa Munro, Sumner's roommate. The two students continued in conversation, occasionally checking their phones and responding to messages, until they reached the front of the line.

Sumner was ahead of Munro and offered her driver's license. Riley swiped it in the scanner, then gave her a good looking over and said something. Sumner's scowled and grabbed her license from his hand. After moving some distance from the security guard, she stopped and waited for her roommate.

Bobby asked Tony to pause the DVD. "I forgot to tell you – it looks like Riley made some sort of comment that Sumner didn't appreciate."

"I'm not surprised," Julie interjected. "He was always trying to chat up women in the bar. I wouldn't say he was exactly Prince Charming."

Perhaps Riley had another reason for lying to the police, Tony thought as he restarted the DVD. Sumner and Munro disappeared from the view of the security camera and moved into the main part of the bar. For the next ten minutes they watched an endless stream of young adults go through the security line-up. Tony was beginning to lose interest when he spotted four young men take their place in line. One of them looked vaguely familiar. He was slightly taller than the others with longish blond hair. His mannerisms suggested he'd already been drinking.

"Oh god, there's that arrogant jerk," Julie said. "I'd completely forgotten that was the night he was in the bar."

"What 'jerk' are you referring to?" Bobby inquired.

"The tall blond guy in line. That's Jonathan Caldwell. You know, son of Senator Caldwell. God's gift to women, at least in his own mind. Tony, I'm sure you remember him from the other night."

Tony was closely examining the handsome young man with the rectangular face and slight cleft in his chin. It was indeed the same person he'd encountered at the Varsity Bar several nights before. He hadn't initially recognized Caldwell – in the video he looked much younger, almost boyish in appearance. His stint in the army had evidently matured him, at least physically. "Yeah, that's him all right."

When the time stamp moved to nine, the first security guard appeared and gave Riley a tap on the shoulder. Bobby spoke as the video continued. "Riley is now being relieved from his shift on the door. According to what he told us, this is when he went outside for a smoke and saw Mansfield."

Tony turned his full attention to the action on the TV screen. Riley held up his hand to stop the next person in line. He then got out of his chair, spoke with the other security guard and handed over the ID scanner. Then, instead of making a move towards the front door, he turned and walked in the direction of the main bar area.

"Could he have gone out any other door to have his smoke?" Tony asked.

Bobby shook her head. The only other way out is through the rear kitchen door leading to the back alley. As I mentioned, the only people I observed going out that door were the kitchen staff. Besides, as you will see, he was otherwise occupied."

As Tony considered this information, Julie put up her hand. "A bit off topic, but can we take a bio break? All the coffee is having its effect."

Tony pointed out the bathroom down the hallway. When they were alone, Bobby spoke quietly. "Tony, I'm pretty good at reading body language, and it tells me that you two are more than just co-workers. I don't have a problem with that. She seems very nice. But I hope you're being careful."

"Yes – in fact, we're practicing celibacy right now," Tony said with a crooked smile.

"You know what I mean. I don't want you to treat her as your confidante and share all of our business. If any news of what we're doing together gets out, it'll not only put an end to our so-called partnership but I'll be out on the street looking for a security job too. Sorry, but that's not my idea of career advancement."

For a moment he felt resentment at her words and look of reproach. He then realized that if their positions were reversed, he'd likely be giving her the same speech. "Bobby, I wouldn't do anything to jeopardize your situation."

"Good. Enough said on the subject, then." Bobby gave him a brief smile.

They both heard a toilet flush and a moment later Julie reappeared. She clearly felt the tenseness that still hung in the room. "Everything okay?"

"Sure," Tony said. "Just discussing some official police business."

"Okay," Bobby said briskly, "let's fast forward to the video from the main bar area. Julie, you're one of the stars in this part of the show."

Chapter 21

Bobby took the remote from Tony to cue up the video. The screen filled with the view of a long oak bar. Lined up along it was an assortment of young people, some standing while others were seated, enjoying their drinks and engaged in lively conversation. Behind the bar was a large display of liquor bottles and cocktail glasses on glass shelves mounted to the wall. Behind the bar were two very busy bartenders, one of whom was now sitting beside Tony. The time stamp indicated it was 8:48 pm.

Julie gasped.

"What is it?" Tony asked.

"My god, I positively look fat!" She put her hands up to cover her eyes in mock horror.

"It's the camera angle," Tony reassured her. "Everyone looks a bit stretched out …now tell us what you see."

Julie turned serious. "Okay, I vaguely recognize a few of the people at the bar. Everything looks normal as far as I can tell."

They watched the ebb and flow of people around the bar. There didn't seem to be anything of significance going on, so Tony excused himself to go to the bathroom.

When he got back Julie said, "You just missed my conversation with one of Caldwell's friends. That's when I learned he was celebrating his last night of freedom before heading out to boot camp."

Tony was a bit disappointed, but didn't want to interrupt the flow of the action by 'rewinding' the DVD. He planned to review the entire disk again in the next day or so anyway.

"No sign of Sumner or her roommate?"

"No, still on the dance floor and out of camera range," Bobby said. "We're really looking to see if any of the other people in the bar catch our attention."

A few minutes later, the time stamp indicating it was now shortly after nine, Bobby pointed at the screen. "See, there's Riley entering the main bar area. Less than a minute has elapsed since he was relieved from duty at the front door. He had to have come directly back from the front entrance."

Tony nodded, understanding the importance of her comment. He continued to track Riley as he went up to the bar and ordered a soft drink from the young woman working with Julie. Sipping a Coke, he gazed around the bar. His expression changed to a slight smile, and he moved to a table where two women were seated. They were older than the student crowd by several decades, attempting to make up for their years by wearing revealing blouses and lots of makeup. Riley engaged them in conversation and they motioned for him to sit down. He looked around somewhat furtively before taking a seat at their table.

"Ah, my two favorite cougars," Julie said under her breath. Bobby smiled.

Tony had other things on his mind. Here was a guy trying to hide his criminal record, and by all accounts he should want to shun any attention from the legal system. And yet he knowingly set himself up as one of the key witnesses for the prosecution. Was his motivation the reward money, or was it something else?

Julie patted his knee, trying to get his attention. "Watch the far left of the screen, over by the table where those three girls are leaving."

He diverted his attention from Riley to watch Jonathan Caldwell make an appearance with his three buddies. They sat at the now empty table, put down their beers and started to engage in a heated discussion. Caldwell didn't take part in the conversation, but instead surveyed the room, clearly sizing up the female talent. Then he picked up his beer, gave it a shake and put it down again. Getting up from the table, he walked with a slight sway to the bar where he waved to catch Julie's attention. She came over to him and they started to talk.

On screen, Julie's expression froze for a moment before she responded with a grim smile. Caldwell waited impatiently while Julie got him another beer. "He just propositioned me, and I told him he was within a beer of being cut off," she said with some satisfaction.

Caldwell lurched back toward his friends with his beer. Back at their table, he made a motion with his arm, and his entourage followed him in the direction of the dance floor.

Bobby paused the video. "We're now in the home stretch. As you can see, it's around 9:20. In the bar area, Riley is still seated with those two women, probably hoping to get laid after work. Sumner is about to head to the front entrance with the intention of going home. We'll watch the video of the bar area for another ten minutes to make sure we don't miss anything, and then flip back to the front entrance to watch Sumner leave."

She took the video player off pause. Riley was still deep in conversation with the two women. Tony turned his attention back to the bar and, in particular, to Julie. She seemed to glide from spot to spot with confidence and efficiency, serving a variety of drinks and chatting with the people around her. Then he saw her expression suddenly change to a frown.

Caldwell was tottering back towards the bar. On the way he stumbled over a chair and fell to one knee. With great effort he regained his feet, pushing his way to the bar until he stood directly in front of Julie. His actions drew the glares of several people patiently waiting their turn to be served. He spoke and Julie responded. Caldwell then appeared to argue with her, while she glared and shook her head. After another brief flurry of words, he picked up an empty beer bottle and slammed it hard on the oak bar top. With that he turned and marched away.

"Cut off!" Julie said triumphantly. Tony also felt some of her pleasure.

"Okay, I think it's time to go back to the front entrance video," Bobby said. "We'll start it around 9:20 pm and watch for Sumner as she leaves. Maybe one of you will spot something I didn't notice in my run-through."

After some stops and starts, she found the right spot on the DVD. The front entrance of the Capital Lounge came into clear focus, the time marker indicating it was 9:17 pm. This area was now congested with people, a snaking line of university students trying to enter the bar battling for room with others on their way out. Adding to the general state of confusion was the fact that the main washrooms were located in a short hallway off the far end of the entrance area. There was already a lineup for the women's washroom as well as a steady stream of men heading into theirs.

All this activity required Tony's full attention. Bobby was again the first to break their viewing silence. "There, at the far bottom of the screen. That's Sumner moving toward the front door."

Tony strained to find Sumner in the throng of people. He finally spotted her, but the camera angle made it difficult to see anything other than her side profile. She appeared to be alone as she made her way to the front door.

Her progress was slowed by the mass of bodies circulating around her. They could only see the back of her head; the camera now behind her, focused on the faces of the people entering the bar. She was closing in on the front door when Julie said excitedly, "Bobby, can you hit pause?"

Bobby froze the frame. Julie sprang up from the couch and went to the TV. She pointed at someone who was now near Sumner, also preparing to leave. "Does that person look familiar to either of you?"

All Tony could discern was the figure of a man with broad shoulders, almost a foot taller than Sumner. He appeared to be wearing a leather jacket with some type of logo or insignia on the back. In the poor light it was difficult to determine any other physical details. "See that crest there?" Julie said. "I noticed the same one on the back of Caldwell's leather jacket."

Tony felt her excitement. "Bobby, can you take us back a couple of minutes?" She complied, reversing and then starting the video again.

"Ok, let's focus on the top of the screen instead of Sumner's location," Tony directed.

Almost in unison they stood and huddled close to the TV, examining the faces of the people moving in and out of the scene. Tony couldn't see anyone matching Caldwell's description or anyone else in a leather jacket for that matter. He then noticed the men's room door open and a person appeared.

Tony experienced a familiar jolt of adrenaline, like old times when there was a break in a tough investigation. "The guy coming out of the men's room – he's wearing a leather jacket."

Unfortunately there wasn't enough light in the hallway to make out his face. A moment later the figure moved, stepping under a ceiling light, briefly illuminating the top of his head.

Julie was the first to comment. "Blond wavy hair, cleft in the chin. That's definitely Caldwell."

"Yup. Now let's see where he goes," said Bobby.

Caldwell paused by the wall near the men's room, using it as support after he tottered. He looked around, probably waiting for his pals to join him. He stood there for what seemed like a minute, impatiently checking his watch, then gave a drunken shrug, zipped up his coat and started to push his way through the crowd to the front door.

"It appears Caldwell's friends have abandoned him," Tony remarked.

They watched as he fell into line to leave, with Sumner almost directly behind him. As they both grew closer to the front door

Caldwell turned his head and appeared to see Sumner for the first time. His mouth formed unknown words, and Sumner nodded. Then they were both out the door, out of range of the security camera's watchful eye.

Chapter 22

The video had been stopped and the TV screen was blank. Julie, sensing that Bobby and Tony needed some private time, excused herself and went into the kitchen with a magazine.

Bobby waited for let Julie to move out of earshot before speaking. "Given what we just saw, I need to get to know Jonathan Caldwell a lot better. However, we both know this will be politically sensitive, being that he's the son of a senator. And that the senator is golf buddies with my boss."

"This whole thing could be much more than 'politically sensitive,'" Tony spat out.

"What do you meant?"

Tony realized that she still hadn't connected all the dots. Then again, maybe there weren't any dots to connect. In any event, he decided to forge ahead.

"Let's assume for a moment that Caldwell was involved in Sumner's death. Line this up with some of the other things we now know." He held up his hand, raising a finger as he made each point. "First, we have 'well-placed' media leaks concerning the murder investigation. Then, the security video mysteriously disappears from my office. Next, we have Mansfield taking flight, and Sumner's clothing finding its way into the garbage bin outside his apartment building. Additional DNA analysis is finally completed that seems to exculpate Mansfield. And now we discover that Riley lied about seeing Mansfield outside the bar. I think someone has been working very hard behind the scenes to cover up the fact that Caldwell is the real killer."

Tony closed his left hand into a fist, angered by the realization that he might inadvertently have played the patsy in this whole affair.

Bobby's eyes widened. "Whoa, slow down, Tony! Other than the fact that Caldwell left the bar at the same time as Sumner, there is absolutely no evidence of his involvement in her murder. We'll need a lot more before we can even consider what you're suggesting."

Tony backed down a bit. "Granted, we can't arrest anybody on this. But let's consider the other facts in light of this theory."

"Okay," Bobby said, "let's go with Caldwell as the killer. But there're a lot of other explanations for those things you just mentioned. Bad luck, bad timing, incompetence or maybe a very smart killer. You can't let your feelings about Adelsky or the senator cloud your judgment."

Bobby's last statement hung in the air. Tony wondered, not for the first time, if his deep anger and frustration with the system was coloring how he viewed the situation. But he shook off those feelings of doubt, confident his instincts were right.

"Bobby, things transpired during our investigation, and afterwards, that can't be dismissed by so-called bad luck or incompetence. There was a guiding hand behind everything that happened, and I'm pretty sure that hand is attached to the long arm of the senator. But he couldn't have accomplished this all by himself. He must've had someone close to the investigation helping him. It's got to be Adelsky."

Bobby still didn't look convinced. "Okay, Tony, let's take several giant leaps forward and assume the senator is somehow involved in a monstrous cover-up. Adelsky isn't the only person within the police department he could've reached out to for help. For all we know, Dupree or Salzman were enlisted, with the promise of more power or money. What I'm saying is we can't assume anything at this point."

Once again, Bobby's observations threw Tony on his heels. Was it possible that Adelsky was also a dupe in the murder investigation?

Certainly lack of experience combined with an over-abundance of confidence, or arrogance, could be the explanation for all Adelsky's mistakes. Perhaps he was being too hasty in jumping to the conclusion that he and the senator were working together to protect the senator's son.

"You might have a point," he conceded grudgingly. "Let's take a breather and examine the facts as we know them. That can guide us in where we should go from here."

"Exactly," Bobby said. "So here's what we know. The new DNA test results indicate that the killer has this rare recessive gene. We also have fairly conclusive evidence that Riley lied about seeing Mansfield outside the bar. Andy finally, Caldwell Jr. was in close proximity to Sumner as she was leaving the bar. Everything else is pure conjecture at this point."

"All roads keep leading back to locating Riley and hearing his story. Perhaps this is a good time to tell you what I've learned about our favorite security guard." Tony started to detail his conversation with Dan Stockton from the previous night.

"Red Onion State Prison? I wonder what he was in for?" Bobby mused.

"Unfortunately he didn't volunteer those details to Stockton. He did mention that he'd grown up in Atlantic City. He also told Stockton he wanted to go back there someday to work at the casinos. I expect the State Gaming Authorities would discover Riley's criminal record, but you never know...."

"This gives me a lot more to go on than I had a day ago. I'll start by contacting the warden at Red Onion. Good job, Tony."

"All in a night's work."

"There is one other thing I've been thinking about," she continued. "Sumner's clothing in the trash bin outside Mansfield's apartment: someone other than Mansfield must've put them in there. Maybe that person left behind a clue to their identity."

"Good point. The forensics analysis of the clothing needs to be reviewed."

"Easier said than done. I may be able to get the report, but I don't have the authority to request any additional analysis."

"True. Let's shelve that one for the moment. What about Mansfield's phone records for the night he disappeared? Any progress?"

"As a matter of fact…." Bobby pulled a folded paper from her jacket pocket. "I got this earlier this morning from the phone company that services Mansfield's apartment building. It's his phone records for last September." She handed it to him.

Tony glanced at the printout, which showed a series of phone numbers along with dates, times, and durations. They were arranged in two columns: incoming calls and outgoing. Four entries had been highlighted in yellow, presumably by Bobby. All the calls had been made in the early morning of the day that Mansfield disappeared. Tony felt a chill as he recognized two of the phone numbers. The first one, placed at 2:08 am, had been made to his cell phone. The second call, placed less than a minute later, had gone to the Madison Police Department's general number.

Tony had kicked the ass of the station chief for not contacting him at home when Mansfield called the police department in the middle of the night. He now realized that Mansfield had first tried to contact him directly on his cell phone. He thought back, remembering the incident with Bradley in the bar, coming home totally exhausted and going to bed.

"I'm sure you recognize my old cell number. I must've slept through Mansfield's call that night," he said in a flat monotone.

"Tony, it's no wonder. You were working 18-hour days and under a lot of stress. You needed a good night's sleep. Don't blame yourself."

He pushed aside his feelings of guilt and turned his attention back to the phone records. The two other highlighted calls had been made to Mansfield's apartment that same morning. They both originated from the same number, one being placed at 2:04

am and the second at 2:14 am. Both calls lasted less than two minutes.

"Have you been able to trace these two incoming calls?" he asked.

"Yes, in one respect a bit of a dead end. They were made from a public pay phone. On the other hand," Bobby paused for effect, "the fact that the pay phone is located less than a block from Mansfield's apartment could be significant."

"That's a bit of an understatement! I think we can safely assume these calls were the reason Mansfield tried to contact me. When I didn't get back to him, he decided to pack a bag and get out of town. I bet he received a threat on his life, by someone who was hoping this would cause him to panic. When Mansfield took the bait and disappeared, the caller planted the incriminating evidence in the garbage bin. I expect Mansfield getting into an accident and dying in that park was just icing on the cake."

"I've got to admit, it's hard to ignore the timing of these calls, Tony, as well as the fact that they came from a phone booth near Mansfield's apartment. In the absence of a better explanation, I'm prepared to go along with you on this. Too bad it's taken this long to figure this out. Back then we might've been able to pull some useful prints from that phone booth."

"Even still, this gives us a better idea of how things went down that night. It also reinforces the importance of getting access to the forensic analysis of Sumner's clothing," he pointed out.

"Okay, give me some time to think through the logistics of doing that. In the meantime, my first priority continues to be locating Riley. I also plan to do some quiet checking on Jonathan Caldwell. Then we need to figure out who we can trust in the department. This is quickly moving to the stage where we need to share what we've discovered and get some additional firepower working this case."

Tony agreed. "There's also another angle that I'm going to check into. Caldwell Jr. enlisted less than a year ago, but now he's back in Madison. A regular tour of duty is two years. I want to find out why he got an early discharge."

"That is an interesting question. I'm just wondering how you'll get the answer without speaking directly with Caldwell. The army won't release that kind of information, even if it's relevant to a homicide investigation."

"Six degrees of separation...." Tony said, almost to himself.

"Sorry?"

"You've never heard the expression? They made a movie about it with Will Smith"

"I saw it, but don't see how it works in this case."

"Well, in theory all I have to do is tap into my network. Eventually I'll find someone who knows why Caldwell was discharged early."

"Good luck with that one."

Julie appeared in the doorway. "Sorry to interrupt, but are you almost done? I really should get back to my studying."

Tony stood and looked at his watch, feeling a bit guilty. They'd monopolized enough of Julie's time. "Yes, of course, I'll get you back to your apartment. Bobby, I think we've discussed everything we need to cover?"

Bobby stood as well. "I can give you a call if anything else comes up. And Julie, thanks for your time. You've been extremely helpful."

Julie smiled. "Thanks, I'll be interested to see where this all leads."

"We all will," Tony said. "Bobby, can I keep the DVD for a bit longer? I wouldn't mind running through it again – the whole nine yards."

"Sure, another set of eyes would be good. I just need it back in a couple of days."

"No problem. I'll have some time tomorrow morning to go through it again. Julie, you interested in lunch before getting back to your studying?"

"Thought you'd never ask," she answered.

Chapter 23
MAY 19 1:30 PM

On the drive back into town, Tony steered the conversation away from their morning activities and his subsequent discussion with Bobby. Julie seemed to understand the situation, and instead of probing for details, discussed the merits of different restaurants for lunch.

They settled on the Kabul Afghanistan Restaurant on State Street. Tony had never eaten there and after looking at the unfamiliar menu items, suggested Julie order for the both of them. Soon a variety of plates, heaped with heavily spiced food, was being laid in front of them.

As they ate, Julie described her experiences travelling in Africa. In Kenya she'd lived for several months in a tribal village, integrating into their lifestyle and helping with traditional female chores such as finding clean drinking water and tending to the community goats. Over time, she said, the villagers began to treat her like a member of the community and shared what little they had with her. Her exposure to this way of life gave her a healthy respect for these people and also made her understand how lucky she was to have been born and raised in the United States. She still kept in touch with one family in the village, sending them money through a local mission.

Tony found himself totally intrigued by her stories, and with the storyteller. Although much younger than him, she'd already seen more of the world than he hoped to see in a lifetime, and had life experiences that he found difficult to comprehend. And yet, there was something fresh and still innocent about her.

She took his arm after they left the restaurant and suggested they walk the rest of the way to her apartment building. When they arrived outside the Mexican restaurant, she gave him a kiss on his cheek. "Now, call me after your meeting. I want to know how everything went."

TEN MINUTES LATER Tony was opening a heavy glass door etched with the name Madison Law Offices. He approached the receptionist, a bespectacled older woman with wavy gray hair. She appeared to be losing the battle of the paperless office, as client files and assorted court documents lay piled on her desk.

She raised her head from one of the files and made eye contact. "May I help you?"

"I have a meeting with Drake Fields. My name is Tony Deluca. I'm probably a bit early."

The receptionist peered over her glasses and gave him the once over, as if to make sure he wasn't an aggrieved client planning to debate his last legal bill. Seemingly satisfied, she pushed aside some of the papers on her desk and located her phone. She dialed an extension and announced, "Mr. Deluca is here for your meeting."

She nodded and hung up. "Mr. Fields will be out in a moment. You can have a seat." She pointed to a well-worn couch across from her. He sat and leafed through a *Sports Illustrated* magazine, pausing to read an article on the Stanley Cup playoffs.

After a few minutes a door opened. He looked up and saw Drake's bulky frame filling most of the hallway. Drake smiled and held out a large hand.

"Good to see you, Tony. You look a lot more relaxed than the last time we were together. Must be a relief knowing that your lawsuit is heading towards settlement."

"You've got that right. This is one more thing I'd like to put behind me."

Drake looked at his watch. "They're supposed to be here in fifteen minutes. Let's go to the meeting room and talk strategy before they arrive." He then turned to the receptionist. "Delores, I'm expecting Lou Driller and two other guests. I'll be in the meeting room with Mr. Deluca. Call me when they arrive."

He led Tony to a meeting room with a rectangular oak table and eight leather chairs around its perimeter. In the corner was a smaller table set up with bottles of water, mugs, and a silver carafe of coffee. The walls of the office displayed some pieces of original art, mostly bright oil landscapes. Drake motioned for Tony to take a seat on the side of the table farthest from the door. "Coffee or water?"

"I'll take some water, thanks."

Drake picked up one of the plastic water bottles and placed it in front of Tony. He filled a mug with black coffee and sat at the end of the table where a file and notepad were already in place. He had clearly staked out the power position where he could more easily control the meeting. "I've got to admit, our telephone conversation from this morning has me very curious. Let's hear it – why would the city suddenly be so anxious to settle your case?"

Tony took up the invitation. "Okay, but what I'm about to tell you can't leave this room."

"Of course, solicitor-client privilege."

"Good. As I mentioned on the phone, there's new DNA evidence that casts doubt on Mansfield being the killer. But more importantly, it turns out the security guard who originally pointed the finger at him is an ex-con. There's strong evidence that he lied about seeing Mansfield outside the bar that night. Even Adelsky isn't aware of this last piece of information," Tony added.

Drake did a double take. "Whoa, this is big news. Tell me more."

Tony filled in some more details without discussing his informal arrangement with Bobby. Drake listened in amazed silence. Before wrapping up, Tony once again cautioned his lawyer to not disclose this information to Driller or anyone else, noting this could jeopardize his contacts within the police department.

Drake nodded. "This is terrific – great for you and our settlement talks. Their decision to dismiss you was largely predicated on your failure to arrest Mansfield before he disappeared. As we've discussed, a jury might be swayed by evidence against Mansfield that came to light after your termination, such as the discovery of Sumner's clothing in the garbage bin. But with this new information, things start to stack up in your favor."

"Yeah, I'm pretty sure this is one of the things behind the change in tactics. But I've been thinking this through, and I believe there's more to it. When it finally comes to light that Mansfield is likely not the killer, there's going to be a real shit storm. Sumner's parents will raise a hue and cry, demanding to know why their daughter's killer is still at large. The media will love it, and it will become a source of great embarrassment for both the Mayor's Office and the Police Department. Remember, there are city and state elections this fall – the political hacks will want this whole mess deeply buried before then. If we proceed to trial, it will highlight how they all fucked up. The back-office boys understand all this and are likely behind all the urgency for a quick settlement."

Drake pounded a fist on the desk, animated by the thought of a sudden and crushing victory in the lawsuit. "Of course, that's it. We've got them by the short and curlies! This makes our strategy real simple. We stick to our guns in terms of damages – you get the remaining salary you're entitled to under the contract, plus interest and costs. We'll agree to keep the terms of the settlement confidential and not go blabbing to the press. We should have a deal wrapped up in thirty minutes or less."

"That would be great. Quite frankly, I'd be willing to take less if we can get this settled quickly. I'm not exactly flush with cash and it would be a good payday for you as well."

Tony was referring to the fact that Drake had agreed to work on a contingency fee basis, meaning that for the moment he was only on the hook for any out-of-pocket costs incurred in pursuing the lawsuit, like court filing charges, photocopies, that kind of stuff. Drake wouldn't get paid unless they won at trial or the case was settled, in which case he would be entitled to 30 percent of whatever Tony received. It was a fairly normal arrangement in litigation matters, and the only way Tony could afford to pursue the lawsuit.

"I appreciate the sentiment, Tony, but don't worry about me. I can put food on the table. Let's stick to our guns and relish the pleasure of seeing these guys cave in."

He looked like a shark that senses blood in the water, Tony thought.

The phone in the meeting room rang and Drake rose to answer it. He listened for a moment and replied, an edge in his voice. "Who'd you say is out there?" There was a pause. "Okay, put Mr. Driller on the line."

Drake rolled his eyes at Tony and waited a moment before speaking. "Lou, what's this about?" There was annoyance in his voice. Tony listened intently to Drake's response.

"Lou, you should've called earlier. There's some bad blood there, if you don't already know that. You'd better tell him to keep his mouth firmly shut during our meeting, or it'll be a short one. Okay? Good, I'll be right out." Drake put the phone down with a thud.

"What's up?" Tony asked.

"Driller told me that Barry Salzman would be attending this meeting on behalf of the Police Department. Unfortunately, he didn't turn up for work this morning – food poisoning. Lou didn't want to postpone the meeting, so he went to the next person in the pecking order. That just happens to be our friend Rick Adelsky."

Tony rocked back in his chair. "What the hell, Drake – he's the last fucking person that should be at this meeting. Are you sure about going ahead?"

"You heard me read the riot act to Driller. I promise you that if Adelsky gets one step out of line, that will be the end of the meeting. But, if you're not okay with this, I'll let Driller know and we'll reschedule."

Tony considered the situation. His desire to get the whole thing put to bed won out over his distaste for being in the same room as Adelsky. "Okay, let's proceed and see how it goes."

"Good. I'll go and collect our guests." Just before Drake opened the door, he turned back towards Tony. "Let me do the talking. If there's anything you want me to say or know, just write it on my notepad. I'll call a short break if we need to discuss anything."

"Got it."

Chapter 24
MAY 19 2:05 PM

Tony didn't have to deal with his unsettling mixture of nerves and anticipation for long. Drake quickly returned with the other participants in the meeting. The first to enter the room was an older man with well-groomed salt and pepper hair and a deeply tanned face. He was impeccably dressed in a tailored navy blue suit, starched white shirt and expensive-looking red silk tie. Tony quickly identified him as the hired gun, Lou Driller. According to Drake, he was one of the best litigators in the state. They had clashed in court on several occasions, and those encounters had given Drake a grudging respect for his opponent's legal skills.

Driller spotted Tony. "Mr. Deluca, I'm Lou Driller. It's a pleasure to meet you." Tony was surprised by the friendliness of the lawyer's greeting as well as the high pitch of his voice. He'd been expecting a rich baritone, like that of a radio announcer or game show host.

The two men shook hands. "Glad we're finally getting together," Tony said.

Following behind Driller was a petite Asian woman in a short yellow skirt and cream white blazer. Her jet black hair was pulled back into a tight bun that accentuated the sharp lines of her face. She looked to be in her late thirties.

Driller motioned her over. "Mr. Deluca, this is Ms. Fung, from the mayor's office."

Tony, still standing, gave her a quick smile. She lowered her head in a slight bow. Driller motioned her to sit on the other side of the table.

After a slight delay, Adelsky shuffled into the room. His blond hair now had flecks of grey at the temples and he seemed to be losing his boyish good looks. He was dressed a bit too casually for this gathering, in a short-sleeve shirt and dark pants. The expression on his square face clearly indicated he would prefer to be anywhere but at the meeting.

Driller again took the lead. "Mr. Deluca, I believe you know Detective Adelsky from the Madison Police Department. Detective, why don't you take a seat beside Ms. Fung."

Adelsky plopped down in the chair without acknowledging Tony's presence and took a writing pad from his briefcase. Head down, he started to write on the pad. Tony wondered if his note taking related to the meeting. Perhaps he was just working on a grocery list.

Drake slipped quietly into the room and offered coffee or water. Driller and Fung declined while Adelsky made no sign of hearing the question.

"Okay, help yourself if you change your mind. Now, Lou, you asked for this meeting, so why don't you start off?"

"Thanks, Drake. To briefly recap for everyone's benefit; Mr. Deluca is pursuing a lawsuit against the city alleging that his employment contract was terminated without cause. This case was recently set down for trial, and we expect to start after the summer break. It continues to be my clients' view that they acted appropriately in their dealings with Mr. Deluca. However, they are aware of the uncertainty inherent in a jury trial and have instructed me to attempt to settle the matter. The purpose of this meeting is to get all the parties together and see if we can come up with terms that will be satisfactory to everyone."

Adelsky gave a low grunt. Driller frowned at him before proceeding. "Drake, perhaps you can lay out your client's position."

Drake took this cue. "Well, to start with, I feel we can easily demonstrate that my client's employment contract was terminated without cause. As a result, he's experienced significant financial loss as well as harm to his reputation. However, to set the stage for these discussions, Mr. Deluca is prepared to settle this matter for a payment representing the salary and benefits remaining under his contract, as well as interest and his legal costs. In other words, and for the purposes of this meeting only, he's prepared to give up his claim for special damages relating to the loss of reputation and standing in the ...."

Drake was stopped in mid-sentence by another grunt, this time louder. The big lawyer narrowed his eyes and looked directly at Adelsky. "Detective, do you have a problem?"

Adelsky looked up, focusing on Drake as if for the first time. "As a matter of fact, I do. Your client doesn't deserve a penny. He screwed up a murder investigation and allowed the killer to get away. I'd say there was just cause for his termination, and any so-called 'harm to his reputation' was well earned." His tone left no mistake of the animosity he felt for Tony.

"Thank you for those insights, Detective," Drake responded sarcastically. "Since you've raised the specific issues of this case, it might be worthwhile to restate my client's position for everyone's benefit. From discussions with people who are familiar with this matter, I understand the Police and Fire Commission considered four incidents that they felt justified the dismissal of my client."

Drake referred to his notes. "Number one, that there were serious leaks of confidential information relating to the homicide investigation to the media. We fully concur with this concern, and acknowledge that such information must have originated from within the Police Department. In fact, Mr. Deluca was attempting to find the source of this leak when he was terminated. But the real perpetrator should have been identified and held accountable rather than my client." He looked pointedly at Adelsky.

"Number two: key evidence, a DVD containing security video footage, went missing. Again, my client shares the concerns of the Police Commission that someone removed this evidence from his office. However, the disappearance of this video had no material impact on the investigation as he was in the process of obtaining another copy."

Tony wanted to interject that if Adelsky had been doing his job, he would have looked at the video and discovered that his key witness was lying. However, respecting his lawyer's advice, he remained silent.

"The third allegation was that my client got drunk while on duty and precipitated a fight with the Dane County Coroner. As noted in our Court submissions, my client was in the bar to help celebrate the birthday of one of the officers in the police department. However, I have four witnesses including an employee at the bar who can attest to the fact that he consumed nothing stronger than a soft drink. As for the skirmish with the coroner, these same witnesses will confirm it was the coroner and not my client who provoked the incident. As I understand it, Detective Adelsky was nearby when the incident took place. I'm sure he can also corroborate this."

Adelsky glared at Drake but said nothing.

"That leads us to the fourth and most important reason for my client being terminated." Drake paused, enjoying the fact that all eyes were on him. "It is alleged that Mr. Deluca's hesitation in arresting the key suspect in the Sumner murder investigation gave him the opportunity to flee from the police. Again, as noted in our pleadings, while Curtis Mansfield may have been a suspect in the investigation, the evidence at that point was circumstantial and certainly didn't justify his arrest."

Adelsky chose this moment to interrupt Drake's monologue. "Listen, Counselor, Deluca is lucky he wasn't run out of town for letting Mansfield slip away. There's no doubt in my mind that he's the killer, and your client fucked up. Good thing he died in that park before he could rape and kill another university student."

This latest outburst cut through Tony like a knife. He couldn't restrain himself any longer. "Listen, Adelsky, the tide has turned, and you're the one that should be watching your back. How do you think everyone is going to react when it comes to light that all this time you've been chasing the wrong guy and the real killer is still out there?"

Adelsky pushed his chair back from the table. "What do you mean by that?" he hissed.

"You damn well know what I mean. And when everyone else finds out, you're going to understand the hell I've been going through for the last nine months."

Adelsky's body was tense, both hands clenched into fists. "Deluca, you're totally delusional and I've had it with your bullshit. I've half a mind to come over there and shut you up."

Tony rose from his chair and it toppled over with a bang. But before he could take a step toward his antagonist, he was fixed to the spot by the heavy pressure of Drake's hand on his shoulder.

"Slow down Tony, let me handle this." Drake turned to face Adelsky. "Rick, remember what I told you after the Michigan State game? You'd better get out of this room before I demonstrate what I meant."

Adelsky contemplated the imposing bulk of Drake for a moment, and then shrugged. "Fine. I didn't want to be here in the first place. This whole thing is a fucking joke." He grabbed his briefcase and left, slamming the conference room door behind him.

Driller and Ms. Fung were fixed in their seats. Driller opened and closed his mouth several times before finally speaking in a high, strained voice. "Drake, Mr. Deluca, I must apologize. I had no idea he'd act like that."

"Lou, I know this wasn't your fault, but I don't think we can have any fruitful discussions today after what just happened," Drake said. "Let's reconvene at a later date when you have appropriate representation from the Police Department. After that little display, your clients should also understand that we'll be reviewing the terms of our settlement offer."

Driller looked concerned. "I understand. I'm as shocked as you are with Detective Adelsky's behavior. Let me assure you there's a genuine desire to have this matter settled. Drake, maybe it would work better if you and I tried to iron out the details of a settlement. I can make time for a call while I'm out of town. You can then discuss our offer with your client."

Drake looked at Tony, who signified his agreement. "Okay, that works for us. Have your assistant contact my office with some times that work for you. Hopefully we can hammer something out before you get too immersed in your upcoming court case."

"Of course. I'll ask her to follow up." Driller stood. Ms. Fung followed his lead.

"Nice to have met you, Ms. Fung," Drake said, a wry smile on his face.

Ms. Fung nodded but did not respond, visibly upset by the display of hostility.

After they left the room, Drake and Tony resumed their seats. "Sorry for losing my cool," Tony apologized, embarrassed now about provoking the scene with Adelsky. "I just couldn't handle Adelsky insisting I screwed up the investigation when the facts finally prove him wrong."

"Yeah, well, no real harm done. Actually, I think today's abbreviated meeting will work to your advantage. Driller now knows that Adelsky is a loose cannon and could hurt their case if this goes to court. Imagine how the jury would react if we cross-examined him and he went ballistic like he did today." Drake chuckled.

"You're right about that. So, what was all that about the Michigan State football game?"

Drake gave him a knowing look. "You may recall I had the pleasure of playing university football with Rick for a couple of seasons. That was before I blew out my knee. I played middle linebacker and Rick was our star wide receiver, at least in his opinion. We had an important game against Michigan. They were divisional rivals and it was all tied up late in the game. We had possession and our QB hit Rick with a perfect pass and he got within field goal range. Instead of heading out of bounds and stopping the clock, Rick tried to get some headlines by going for the TD. He ended up being stripped of the ball by their cornerback. Fortunately the ball went out of bounds and we kept possession. Rick got a good dressing down from the QB when he returned to the huddle and was told he wouldn't get the ball again that game. He was pretty steamed.

"On the next play, I finished my block and saw Rick move down the sidelines with that cornerback in hot pursuit. Rick suddenly put on the brakes and as the cornerback went by him, grabbed his face mask. The guy's body kept accelerating forward while his head stayed put. Rick then let go and the cornerback hit the ground like a sack of potatoes. It took ten minutes for the poor guy to regain his senses. He was hauled off the field in a stretcher. Meanwhile, Rick is telling everyone within earshot how he showed that guy who's the boss."

"After what I've seen of Adelsky, I'm not surprised. But I assume there's more to this story?"

"Damn right. After the game I waited around for Rick to get showered and changed. I then went over to his locker and told him that if he tried anything like that again, he was going to have to deal with me. He laughed and made the mistake of trying to push past me. I grabbed him by his collar and tossed him back into his locker. His head put a nice little dent into the metal, but I had his full attention. I repeated my warning and told him if there was another episode like that one, he'd be the one going to the hospital. Rick got the message and minded himself on the field. However, I never trusted the guy after that. He has too big an ego, combined with a very hot head. Not a good combination in football or police work for that matter."

"You've got that right. Well, thanks again for stepping in and defusing the situation. I doubt either of us was going to back down.

I just hope he doesn't figure out I have some insider information relating to that DNA test."

"I don't think you have to worry. He had so much testosterone pumping through his body he probably can't recall what was said."

"Let's hope so." Tony looked at his watch. "I guess it's time for me to head out. Let me know how it goes with Driller."

"I'll be in touch. After today's show and the information you've provided, I expect Lou will come back with an offer you'll find hard to refuse!"

Chapter 25

The previous evening at work was a bit of a blur to Tony. It'd been a typically slow Monday night, giving him the opportunity to sort through the new information relating to Karen Sumner's murder. However, even after examining the facts from every angle, he was unable to form a coherent theory of the murder.

Returning home well past midnight, he got into bed, ready for a good night's sleep. Instead, he tossed and turned, his dreams filled with scenes from old murder investigations. The faces of the dead, men and women alike, all bore an uncanny resemblance to the young university student. He thrashed about so much that Sam was forced to retreat to a couch in the living room.

As the morning light started to peek into the bedroom, sleep remained elusive and he decided to get up. Still in pajamas, he padded into the kitchen and made himself a double espresso, then picked up a notepad and pen from the old oak desk in the living room. He sat on the sofa and started to work.

Thirty minutes later, he'd filled six pages with thoughts and questions. His initial notes were his recollections of the Sumner murder investigation, dulled as they were by the passage of time. This information was then lined up against his hypothesis that Jonathan Caldwell was the killer. This helped him to pick away at the holes in the theory and identify what additional information would be required to confirm or deny Caldwell's role in her death.

He remembered at one point in the investigation having a disagreement with Bobby on how Mansfield had managed to transport Sumner to the park without being noticed. He thought it was highly unlikely that Sumner would willingly accompany Mansfield in his car. Bobby was of the view that he'd taken her by force as she made her way back home.

Tony had expressed doubts. The Capital Lounge was on a busy street, and the most likely route back to Sumner's apartment was along a well-travelled thoroughfare. It would've been nearly impossible for Mansfield to have abducted her, even if she'd been a bit tipsy, without someone observing it. Yet no one had come forward to report a struggle taking place between a man and younger woman on the night she disappeared.

However, when Tony considered Caldwell as Sumner's killer, it put things in a totally different light. Caldwell may have been drunk that evening, but he was a handsome young man with an attractive pedigree. His story of enlisting and heading to boot camp the next morning may have struck a sympathetic, even romantic chord with this young woman. He could easily envision Caldwell charming Sumner into accepting a ride home, with the intent of having a sexual liaison with her. In his notepad he underlined the question, "Does Caldwell have a car, and did he drive it that night?"

The location of the murder had also confused both Tony and Bobby. Picnic Point Park was a well-known haunt for amorous university students. Why would Mansfield, with no known affiliation to the university, take Sumner to this location? In his notes he'd jotted, "See if Caldwell attended University of Wisconsin."

The recent DNA analysis indicated Sumner's killer had a recessive gene consistent with that person being of Irish or Scottish descent. While this type of DNA information would never be sufficient to obtain a conviction, it could be used to include or exclude Caldwell as her potential killer. Another note: "Research Caldwell's family background to confirm his heritage."

A final point he pondered was the timing and location of the phone calls made to Mansfield's apartment the night he disappeared. Tony had originally concluded these calls were placed by Sumner's killer. However, he realized it was virtually impossible for Caldwell to have made those calls. By then he was at Fort Bragg being indoctrinated into army life. And for that matter, who planted Sumner's clothing in the trash bin?" Tony made another note for follow-up.

This task completed, he turned his attention back to the security video from the Capital Lounge. Remote in hand, he spent the next three hours in front of the TV, reviewing various scenes from the bar in more detail.

While observing Matt Riley, he jotted down a detailed physical description: "Male, white Caucasian, approximately 30 years of age, 5'11, 185 lbs, brown eyes and hair, prominent mole above his lip and a small scar on the eyebrow over left eye." It was unlikely he'd need to rely on notes to identify Riley, but he felt some comfort in resuming his old habits as a homicide detective.

With Karen Sumner, he was less concerned about her visual appearance and more interested in what she'd been wearing that evening. He completed a description of her clothing, jewelry, and other accessories, planning to ask Bobby to compare this with the inventory of clothing that had been recovered. This would help determine if any of her personal items were still missing.

He completed a similar itemized list for Jonathan Caldwell. He scrutinized the leather jacket that Julie had recognized as he was leaving the bar, the "W" insignia for the University of Wisconsin stitched on the right arm. The crest on the back, the one Julie recognized, bore the logo of the Badgers football team. This appeared to confirm his connection with the university.

His final set of notes related to the three young men who accompanied Caldwell that night. One of them was tall and gangly, well over six feet, with short cropped hair. He looked like a basketball player. The second friend was of medium height and build, with intelligent eyes behind titanium-rimmed designer glasses. Tony pegged him as the rich kid, class president type. The other young man was the shortest of the four, with a barrel chest, well-muscled arms and a thick neck – a weight lifter or football team wannabe. He made another note to make sure Bobby retrieved their names and addresses from the security scanner records. Watching the four of them clowning around together, Tony wondered why Caldwell's friends hadn't gone with him when he left the bar. What information could they provide about Caldwell's activities for that evening?

The date stamp at the bottom of the TV screen now indicated it was after 10 pm the night of the murder. A good half hour had passed since Sumner and Caldwell had left the Capital Lounge. She may have already been dead by then, her body discarded in the boggy area surrounding the lake.

Apprehension and doubt now crept into Tony's thoughts. So much time had passed since her death. How could they possibly gather the necessary evidence now to make a case against Caldwell or whoever was responsible for her death? Pushing aside these negative thoughts, he decided it was time to take more positive action. Turning off the TV and DVD player, he went into the kitchen and picked up the phone.

"Pizza Pizza," the voice on the other end said in a monotonous tone.

Tony paused, thinking he'd misdialed. Then he heard a familiar chuckle. "Hah, that's good. How're you doing, Tubby?"

"Other than throwing you for a bit of a spin, not so great. We seem to be grinding to a halt on Harding's murder investigation."

"No luck with the car rental agencies?"

"Not yet. We're still checking out a few places, but so far we haven't found any place that rented out a car the day after Harding's murder with a drop-off in the vicinity of Madison. Looks like a dead end." Tubman's voice then brightened a little bit. "There's one bit of good news. The techs have been able to clean up the toll booth video. We've learned our killer must be a Minnesota Twins fan – that's the logo on the baseball cap he was wearing. That's it, though. They couldn't pick up the face of the driver."

"Wow, that really narrows the list of suspects," Tony said jokingly.

"I know." Tubman sounded a bit dejected. "But it's the only piece of new evidence we've turned up in the last twenty-four hours. Peters is worried about the lack of progress too. He's getting lots of heat from the paper pushers. The State Attorney is getting ready to pull in the FBI and see if they can kick-start this. Peters asked for a couple more days. It looks like he's got it, grudgingly. How about from your end?"

"Same problem, based on the latest update from Bobby. The only lead the Madison police are pursuing is the mud samples your guys found on the Audi. The analysis is going to take a couple more days. However, I'm pretty sure it won't break open the case. We need someone to come forward who saw something, like her body being dumped in the lake."

"That would be helpful," Tubman said almost wistfully.

Tony thought now was a good time to change the subject. "Can I bend your ear on something else?" He spent the next five minutes updating Tubman on the revelations from the bar security video and Mansfield's phone records. He mentioned that Bobby was in hot pursuit of Matt Riley and planned to do further background work on Jonathan Caldwell.

When Tony finished there was a long silence on the line. Tubman finally spoke, carefully choosing his words. "As they say down south, I think you're going to stir up a nest of rattlers by taking on the senator's son. Are you sure you want to do this? It's not really your concern anymore, and you're certainly not getting paid to do this. Why don't you let the Madison police sort through this and focus your energies on helping us solve Harding's murder?"

"Tubby, to borrow your analogy, I plan to sharpen a machete and wipe out those snakes. A young woman was killed and another person was set up to take the rap. Then there's the small point that my marriage and career were destroyed in the process. I just can't sit by and hope the police will figure it out. I need to get to the bottom of this. Besides, you never know – catching Sumner's killer might shed some light on Harding's murder as well."

"Buddy, we've already been over that. I thought you agreed it was too big a leap."

"Probably…. Bottom line, I'm not prepared to step aside for the second time and hope the police bring in the killer. This needs a real good push in the right direction. And you might be able to help me with a piece of the puzzle."

Tubman sighed. "Okay, what do ya need?"

"I'm looking for a copy of Caldwell's medical records from his induction into boot camp. I'd also like to know why he didn't complete his tour of duty."

"Sure, no problem. Everything will be emailed to you later today," Tubman said sarcastically.

"Come on, I'm serious. Caldwell entered boot camp the day after Sumner was killed. He would've undergone a standard medical to make sure he was fit to report. Sumner had skin samples under her fingernails from fighting off her killer. His medical records should indicate if he had any visible cuts or scratches. It's also very odd that he's back in Madison after less than a year in the army. I'd like my curiosity satisfied on this point as well."

"Listen, Tony, you know the military. They won't release that kind of information. Privacy and secrecy are paramount with those guys."

"I'm not talking about going through official channels, and this information wouldn't be used in any court proceedings. I just want to make sure we're chasing the right guy this time. Not needlessly stirring up that nest of rattlers that you warned me against."

"Off the record? That might make it easier. But I don't know anyone senior enough in the military that'd be willing to hang out his ass to get me this information."

"I was thinking…. You spent a long time with the FBI. I was hoping you still had some friends in there and might be able to call in a favor."

There was silence on the line. Then Tubman said, "Ted Price."

"Who's he?"

"My section chief while I was stationed in LA. A hard-nosed son of a bitch, but he took a liking to me. One day he told me he'd read my entire file. He was impressed I'd managed to make my way out of the gutter and get a law degree. After that we spent a lot of time together. He took a real interest in my career with the FBI. We still keep in touch. Last year I attended his retirement party in L.A., stayed at their house."

"And he has some contacts within the military?"

"Sort of. His son, Daniel, followed in his dad's footsteps, worked in the FBI's counter-terrorism section. I've met him a few times – a real smart guy. I got an update on his career when I visited last year. Ted told me Daniel left the Bureau to take up a position in Washington. He now heads up the Office of Intelligence and Analysis with Homeland Security. His group is the hub for all national intelligence, collecting and disseminating reports to federal and state agencies involved in protecting us against terrorist attacks."

"Homeland Security? Those guys have tentacles everywhere. This Daniel should be able to get the information we need."

"If he's sufficiently motivated."

"Do you know if Daniel has his own family?" Tony asked.

"Yup. Married, with two young teenagers. A girl and a boy, if my memory serves me."

"That's the hook. Tell Ted you're helping with the investigation into the murder of a young university student and need some background information that might confirm the identity of her killer. The suspect joined the army shortly after the murder, and maybe his son could make some inquiries, etc. etc. You know how to spin it."

"What about the fact that the suspect's father is a powerful senator?" Tubman asked.

"Tell him the truth. The person under suspicion is from a prominent political family, and we're doing this preliminarily work to avoid any unnecessary ruffling of feathers. Everything will be totally off the record with no attribution to sources."

"You're positive you need this information?"

"Yes, it's very important to the murder investigation ... and to me."

"Okay, I'll contact Ted and explain the situation. I'll let you know how it goes. Now, is there anything else I can do for you?"

The tone of his voice suggested that Tony he'd already asked too much. "No, after this little job, you can consider the debt for me stepping in front of that bullet has been repaid in full."

"With interest," Tubman muttered.

Chapter 26
MAY 20 11:15 AM

Tony returned to the couch with a fresh cup of espresso and sat reviewing his various lists of notes and questions. Satisfied that he'd captured all his thoughts, he took a break and headed for the shower. He didn't get more than a few steps when the phone rang. It crossed his mind it might be Julie.

He was surprised to see Bobby's cell number on the call display. "Hi, Bobby, what's up?"

"I was wondering if you'd like to take a road trip."

"Uh … where to?"

"Crown Point. It's a small town in Indiana. Seventeen miles from Gary, to be exact. You might recognize the town's name. John Dillinger escaped from its jailhouse in the 1930s. Johnny Depp played him in *Public Enemies*, not to be confused with Jack Sparrow in *Pirates of the Caribbean*."

Tony was indeed familiar with Crown Point. His dad had always been fascinated by the gangsters of the Great Depression era – Al Capone, Lucky Luciano, and of course, John Dillinger. When Tony was still in university, he drove Joseph to Crown Point to visit the small jailhouse, which by then had been designated as a historical site. He still had a photo of his dad standing beside the commemorative plaque outside, his thumb and finger cocked like a smoking gun. "And the purpose for our little trip?"

"To visit with Matt Fitzgerald, aka Matt Riley. He's currently residing in Lake County Jail. But we need to hurry. Visiting hours end at 4 pm sharp, and it'll take us a good three hours to get there."

"Wait a minute. You found Matt Riley?"

"Yes, and it wasn't easy. After I left the cottage yesterday I went back to the police department and got through to the Assistant

Warden at Red Onion State Prison. Clinton Powell's his name. I told him about Riley and said I wasn't exactly sure when he'd been incarcerated there. I could only confirm it was least a couple of years ago, given what we know about his time working at the Capital Lounge. Powell said all inmate records for the past ten years were now computerized, and if Riley was there during that period of time, they should be able to get his details relatively easily. He promised to get back to me when he had some information.

"I got a call this morning. Powell couldn't locate anything on an inmate named Riley. He'd also asked some of the guards who'd been there for a while. No one remembers someone by that name. He wanted to know if they should start going through their paper files. I had an idea and asked if they could just search on his first name. Powell got back to me in quick order, saying they released someone by the name of Matt Fitzgerald about three years ago. He was in there for armed robbery."

"He fits Riley's description?"

"Based on the pictures that were emailed to me, it's safe to say that they're one and the same person. Back then he looked a bit leaner and a lot meaner, but Fitzgerald is definitely our man."

"He must've changed his name to Riley after being released, probably to cover up his criminal record," Tony surmised.

"Not quite ... I'll explain in a moment. I asked for the arrest file and any other information that might be of assistance in locating him. Powell had it scanned and emailed to me. There was quite a bit of information in the file but I focused on a couple of the documents. The court sentencing report contained a nice summary of Fitzgerald's family history and prior arrests. He was born in Atlantic City to a James and Kimberley Riley. His birth parents were killed in a car accident when Matt was still in diapers. He was taken in by an aunt and uncle on his mom's side by the name of Fitzgerald. They lived in Richmond, Virginia, and eventually adopted him, changing his name to Matt Fitzgerald. While he was still a young teenager the aunt and uncle passed away in relatively quick succession. No other family members appeared on the scene and Riley became a ward of the state. From there he fell in with the wrong crowd and committed a long list of juvie misdemeanors. At the age of twenty-two he was arrested as the driver in an unsuccessful armed robbery. He got five years, to be served at the Red Onion."

"Sounds like he came from the school of hard knocks." Tony actually felt a bit sorry for the guy.

"Yes, but let's not shed too many tears for him. We all have choices to make in our lives – he made the wrong ones. It turns out he was given early release for good behavior, which as I said, happened just over three years ago. The parole board report indicates his hearing was attended by Trevor Fitzgerald, an older cousin who lives in Charlottesville, Virginia. He told the board he was prepared to give Riley a job in his construction firm. They agreed to an early release on the condition that Riley work for his cousin and not leave the state until the rest of his sentence had expired."

"Did the parole report contain any contact information on this cousin?" Tony asked.

"Way ahead of you. I spoke with Trevor Fitzgerald just before I called you. He was very hesitant to talk to me, said he didn't want to get his cousin into any more trouble. I explained that Riley was a key witness in a murder investigation in Wisconsin and we needed to clarify some of his statements. I also mentioned there was an outstanding reward of $50,000 being offered by the parents of the deceased. Fitzgerald became chattier at this point, as he figured I wasn't looking to throw Riley in jail."

"And you didn't dissuade him from this notion."

"No, of course not. Anyway, after his release from prison, Riley moved to Charlottesville to work in construction. Seems he wasn't very keen on the early hours or the hard work, and the day after his required work stint was completed, he moved on. He changed his last name back to Riley and put some space between himself and Virginia. He eventually settled in Madison and landed the security job at the Capital Lounge."

"Did the cousin keep in touch?"

"Yeah, they're still on talking terms. In fact, Fitzgerald was the first person Riley contacted when he got into trouble at Crown Point."

"What happened there?"

"According to the cousin, after Riley got fired, he decided to drive to Atlantic City to rediscover his birthplace and get a security gig at one of the casinos. He got as far as Crown Point and stopped at a bar for a drink and a friendly game of pick-up pool. He apparently pissed off several of the locals and a brawl ensued. At one point in the melee Riley picked up a pool cue and ended up rapping one of the combatants on the head. The poor sod went to hospital with a concussion. Riley was charged with aggravated battery causing bodily injury. Bail was refused on the basis that he wasn't a resident of the state and posed a flight risk, so he's on remand until his trial. Fitzgerald is funding a local criminal lawyer to represent him, and his lawyer thinks he can get him off on self-defense. Apparently it was three well-known local thugs who ganged up on him."

"And he still managed to get the better of them. Do the Indiana police know about Riley's criminal record?"

"Fitzgerald got very agitated when I asked him about this. At first he wouldn't give me a straight answer, but when I pressed, he said the police hadn't figured this out due to the name change. He pleaded with me to give Riley a break, especially since he's helping with our homicide investigation. I told him we'd take it under consideration."

"This means we have some very good leverage with Riley," Tony noted. And some great detective work, Bobby. So getting back to your original question, I'd be very interested in joining you for a visit with Mr. Riley. I'm supposed to work tonight, but let me see if I can switch with one of the other security guys. I'll get back to you."

TONY HAD THE MUSTANG in cruise control, travelling just above the speed limit along the Indiana I-65. Almost three hours had elapsed since Bobby had called with information on Riley's whereabouts. He was enjoying the Eagles' latest CD, *Long Road out of Eden*, the bass guitar booming from the car speakers. As he listened to a remix of "Guilty of the Crime," he reflected on what had transpired since their conversation.

He'd first found someone who was interested in changing shifts for that evening. His next step was to place a call to his dad. Chicago was only an hour west of Crown Point, and he hoped to work in a visit on the way back. Joseph was happy to hear from him and suggested he stay over. Tony gratefully accepted the invitation. It might give him the opportunity to accomplish something else on his bucket list the following morning.

He then called Bobby to confirm that he could join her at Crown Point but would be taking his own car. They talked about strategy for the interview with Riley, with Bobby making it clear he was merely going as an observer. She gave him directions to the jail, as well as a general overview of the facility. Based on her description, Tony realized the prison was substantially different from the historic jailhouse he'd visited with his father. The "new" Lake County Jail, built in 1975, was a six-story structure that housed more than a thousand inmates. This was a 200-fold increase from the five cell jail that once held one of the most famous gangsters in American history.

His last call before departing was to Julie. He let her know he was going out of town for a meeting relating to the Sumner investigation and that he planned to stay that night at his father's house. He sensed her disappointment that she wouldn't be seeing him for at least another day. She cheered up a bit when he said he'd call her in the evening to arrange a time to get together the following day. She wished him a safe trip.

An approaching highway traffic sign indicated that Crown Point was the next exit. Tony looked at his watch: 2:45. He'd agreed to meet Bobby in the front entrance of the jail by 3 pm. Assuming he didn't get lost now, he'd be there with a few minutes to spare.

Chapter 27
MAY 20 2:55 PM

The visitors' parking lot was nearly full. As he drove around looking for a spot he noticed a number of signs with various dire warnings. One indicated it was a serious offence to smuggle drugs or other contraband to inmates, another warned that visitors could be subject to body and property searches, while a third suggested it was unlawful to provide rides to hitchhikers in the area. Tony chuckled at the thought that an escaped convict would stand by the side of the road, thumb extended, in the hopes of catching a ride to freedom.

He did take particular notice of one sign. It indicated that all visitors needed to report to the Security Desk in the main reception area. An arrow pointed down a crumbling concrete walkway. He finally found an open parking space and headed in the indicated direction through a stand of tall trees. Lake County Jail was no great architectural marvel, a squat low-rise building constructed of grey concrete block with accents of red brick. There were large windows on the main floor, probably the visitors' reception and staff offices. The windows throughout the remainder of the building were much smaller and protected with iron bars.

At the front entrance another large sign confirmed this was the Visitors' Centre. In smaller lettering was another list of instructions and warnings for visitors to the jail. Tony didn't pause to read the fine print. Once inside he was greeted by a monolithic security guard behind a heavy steel desk. "Can I help you?" The guard suspiciously eyed Tony up and down.

"I'm here with a Detective Andrade from the Madison Police Department to see one of the inmates."

The guard's features relaxed and he pointed towards a hallway running behind his desk. "That way, first office on the right. The lady detective is already there. You'll need to show ID, fill out some forms, and go through a security check. Officer Denton will take you through the process."

Tony nodded, familiar with the security protocols of a high security jail. He walked in the direction indicated by the guard and found the visitors' registration office. Bobby was there with a cell phone in her hand.

"I was about to call you and then I realized you don't have a cell phone. They're very strict here about visiting hours – no one allowed in after three and everyone out by four. Another five minutes, and we'd have had to make a return trip tomorrow."

"And good day to you as well."

"Okay, sorry, glad you made it. Now you need to hurry up and sign in."

Tony headed over to another amply proportioned security officer in a small room off the waiting area, protected by a heavy security grill. Officer Denton slowly looked up from a newspaper he was reading.

"Good afternoon. I'm here with Detective Andrade to see a prisoner by the name of Riley."

"Right, fill out this form and sign at the bottom. I also need ID. Driver's license will do." Denton pushed a clipboard with an information form through an opening in the mesh. Tony quickly filled out the form with a pen attached by tape and by a dirty piece of string. When it was completed, he handed it back.

Denton thoroughly examined the form to confirm it was completed in full and the correct boxes were ticked. Satisfied, he said "Let's see your ID." He scrutinized Tony's driver's license. "Okay, so far so good. Now, remove all items from your pockets and provide me with your weapon."

"I'm not carrying." Tony rummaged through his pockets, placing his wallet, keys and loose change on the countertop.

Denton listed the items as they landed in front of him, and gave Tony a receipt for his surrendered possessions. He picked up his phone and punched a button. "Officer Starke will escort you through security and to the interview room we've reserved for you and Detective Andrade."

A moment later, a tall black man appeared. Starke weighed well over two hundred pounds with broad shoulders, thick muscled arms, and a chest that strained against the buttons on his uniform. Not a man you'd want to pick a fight with, Tony quickly concluded.

Despite his somewhat menacing appearance, he turned out to be the friendliest guard Tony had met in his short time at the jail. "We'll try to make this quick and easy so you can get on with your business," He said. He led them down a hallway into an area cordoned off by several X-ray scanning machines. Tony felt like he was about to go through passenger security in the Chicago O'Hare airport.

Starke stopped in front of one of the machines and asked Bobby and then Tony to walk through. Successfully passing this test, they were escorted along another hallway constructed of concrete blocks painted stop-light green.

Starke saw Bobby examining the walls. "The wall color is meant to signify the level of security risk in the area. Green of course means low level risk, yellow means there are convicts hanging around, and red means you're amongst the most dangerous criminals we've got. Some pencil pusher must have spent a week thinking that one up."

As they continued further into the depths of the prison, Tony couldn't help but notice a number of competing odors – the most discernible being bleach, urine and mold. How could anyone stomach this on a day-to-day basis?

Starke stopped in front of a heavy door with a small window reinforced with steel bars. "Your guy is already inside. He's cuffed and shouldn't be any problem." He then looked at his watch. "It's just about 3:15. Visitors' hours normally end at 4, but we can accommodate you until around 4:30, if you need a bit more time. The room will be locked up after you go in, but there's a camera inside and we'll be watching. When you're ready to leave, just wave at the camera. Any questions?"

"Is the room wired?" Bobby asked.

"Yeah, but we can turn it off if you want."

"Please do. There are some things we need to discuss in confidence with Mr. Riley."

"Rest assured, no one will be listenin'. But I should let you know that the officer currently monitoring the camera can also read lips. It can come in handy around here. Unfortunately, he can't be turned off..."

"Good to know," Bobby said.

Starke nodded his good-bye and Bobby reached for the door handle. Before opening it, she looked at Tony. "Remember what we discussed – I do the talking. If you have a question or think I missed something, let me know."

He nodded. This was Bobby's show, and he was just along for the ride. "Just don't forget the lip reader," he warned.

Chapter 28
MAY 20 3:15 PM

As the door opened, Riley turned his head in their direction. He was seated on a wooden chair that was riveted to the floor, as was the steel table in front of him. His hands were clasped together and resting on the table, the silver handcuffs around his wrists were attached by chains to the cuffs around his ankles. He was dressed in jail attire, his face white and gaunt, framed by long, stringy hair. Bobby had to admit she wouldn't have recognized him if they'd accidentally bumped into each other in the hallway.

No one spoke as Tony and Bobby both looked around the room and located the black eye of the security camera. Riley had been strategically seated to face the camera. Taking the chair directly in front of the prisoner, she slowly opened up her portfolio to reveal a notepad and pen. She waited for Tony to get settled beside her, then spoke to Riley.

"Good afternoon, Mr. Riley. My name is Detective Andrade and this is Mr. Deluca. I'm not sure if you remember us, but we met with you last September when we were investigating the Sumner murder."

Riley nervously licked his lips and nodded.

"We're here to ask you some additional questions relating to the information you provided to us at that time. But first, I want to let you know that at my request this interview isn't being recorded. We know there is certain information that you wouldn't want disclosed to the Indiana State Police. If you cooperate with us, we'll try to keep this information in confidence. However, if you lie to us, there will be consequences. Do you understand?"

Riley spoke for the first time, his voice low and gravelly. "Yeah, my cousin phoned and told me about — "

Bobby cut him off before he could finish his sentence. "Before you say anything further, you should also be aware that the person monitoring the camera that's focused on you right now is adept at reading lips. So please cover your mouth if you need to say anything you don't want the prison authorities to know about."

Riley looked up briefly at the camera and then tilted his head down towards the table, obscuring the lower half of his face from its view. "What I was goin' to say is my cousin filled me in and that ya know about my history. Now what da you want?" His voice was hoarse and muffled by the angle of his face.

"In our meeting last September you indicated that you saw Curtis Mansfield outside the bar the night that Karen Sumner was murdered. I'm wondering why you fed us that bullshit."

Riley's head popped up and she saw a fleeting look of fear in his eyes. He quickly recovered and put on a poker face. "Don't know what you're talkin' about. I saw him like I said."

"Watch it, Riley, or should I call you Fitzgerald? You're on a very short leash," Bobby snapped.

Riley's eyes focused on her face, clearly trying to figure out how much she actually knew. She was about to tell him.

"You may recall that the Capital Lounge has security cameras installed throughout the bar. We were able to track your movements for the entire evening. At no time did you go outside as you claimed in our interview. You couldn't have seen Mansfield that night. So I repeat, why did you lie about this?"

Riley shrugged, knowing he was trapped. "I think I need to speak to my lawyer."

"Cut the crap!. If you don't level with us right now, we're going to march over and see the warden, tell him about your prison time in Tennessee. Then for good measure we'll bring criminal charges against you in Wisconsin. One way or another, you'll be making a return trip to prison."

A vacant expression now appeared on his face, only broken by the quick fluttering of his eyelids. Bobby knew she had him on the ropes and was about to continue when she heard the grating noise of the chair beside her and the sound of Tony clearing his throat.

"Listen, Riley, let's be clear: it's not our plan to put you back in prison." Tony interjected. "We're just trying to understand why you picked out Mansfield from all the photos we showed you. We know it wasn't because you actually saw him that night. You give us a straight answer on this and we'll walk out of here. No one needs to be the wiser about your track record in Tennessee."

Bobby's first reaction to Tony's intervention was surprise. However, this quickly turned to anger. She visibly bristled. Tony had deliberately disobeyed her explicit instructions to keep quiet and let her run the interview. She shot him a sharp look to back off before turning her attention back to Riley.

The ex-con appeared to have come out of his funk and was gazing balefully at Tony, still trying to size up the situation. Bobby held back and waited, wishing her partner would do the same. He finally put a hand up to shield his mouth. "Before I tell you anythin', I want a letter from your State Attorney's office givin' me immunity. My lawyer tells me I'll beat the rap here. If that happens, I don't want you guys breathin' down my neck."

Riley wasn't as stupid as he appeared, Bobby had to grudgingly admit.

She put a warning hand on Tony's arm and took back control. "That's fair. We can probably arrange that. However, I can't go to the State Attorney unless we have some more information on how this went down. You need to give us something to get him interested in making a deal."

Riley nodded. His hand still over his mouth, he said, "Okay, first off, I'm not admittin' anything. But let's say … jus' between us, that just after that girl's body turned up, I got a phone call. The guy on the line says he has, what do ya call it? Oh yeah, a business proposition. Never met this guy but I recognize the name, so I agree to a meet. When we get together, I'm shown a picture of Mansfield and told he's a convicted sex perv who murdered that student. The guy tells me if I can identify this guy to the cops, he'll be taken off the streets and I'll be in line for a big reward. But he warned me about you two. Said you'd be in the dark about the deal and I was to keep it that way." He added in a whining voice, "He assured me I'd be doing the police a favor."

"We can appreciate your position." Bobby said, actually wanting to throttle him until he choked out the name of the person who'd fed him all this shit. However, she continued in an impassive tone, "What you just told us is almost enough to get us an audience with the State Attorney. But he's going to want the name of the person you made this deal with."

A bit of fight returned to Riley. "Hell, I give you that, n' next thing ya know, I'm a permanent guest in this hell hole. No, I need that letter from the Man before I say anythin' more."

She tried once again. "Give us the name as a sign of good faith. We get a name, and the next time you see us we'll have that letter you asked for, and our undertaking to not say anything about your past to the Indiana authorities."

Riley's eyes were darting around the room and his hands were twitching, the handcuffs rattling against the chain. He was clearly worried they were trying to put something over on him.

Bobby decided it was time to force the issue. She put her pen away and closed the portfolio. "That's it. I've got to get back to Madison for another meeting." She stood and motioned toward the security camera, signaling the interview was over.

"Wait!" Riley said urgently, his eyes almost bulging out of his narrow face.

Bobby paused. "What for?"

When Riley spoke again there was resignation in his voice and he forgot to cover his mouth. "Alright, I'll give ya this. He's someone ya both know, very close to whole police scene. But that's all I am goin' to say until I see that piece of paper."

Chapter 29
MAY 20 3:40 PM

Starke's head popped into view through the window in the door. A key rattled in the lock and the big guard stepped into the room. Bobby was still staring at Riley, digesting his last statement.

Starke hesitated, sensing something was not quite right. "Do you need a bit more time?"

Bobby arrived at a decision. "Sorry, we're done. At least for the moment." She turned back to Riley. "We'll be in touch." She moved towards the open door, Tony closely behind her.

"Riley, I'll be back in five minutes. Don't go anywhere." Starke closed the door with a laugh. Tony looked back and saw Riley wasn't amused.

Starke led them back to the visitors' office where Denton was waiting for them, anxious to close up for the day. He already had their personal items arranged in two piles on the counter. After signing the register acknowledging their return, they were quickly marshaled out of the office. Denton locked up after them.

Still in silence, they made their way outside. Tony spotted the security camera over the front entrance. "Let's get a bit further away." He didn't want the lip-reading guard observing their conversation.

They walked down the pathway towards the parking lot and stopped on a bench shaded by a large oak. Bobby turned on him. "Tony, I distinctly told you not to say anything during the interview. Not only did you disregard this request, but your intervention could've undermined the entire interrogation."

Tony was surprised by the vehemence of her tone, but he understood the reason for it. "Bobby, you did great with Riley. But at that point you were pushing him too hard and too fast. His body language was telling me he was about to retreat into a shell. If I didn't dial back the intensity, we could have walked out of there with nothing."

Bobby glared at him a moment longer, still not fully satisfied. "But we agreed I'd do the talking. You could've signaled me rather than taking over like that. I need to know you're prepared to play by my rules. "

"I'm sorry. I really didn't mean to step on your toes. It won't happen again."

"Okay. I'm sorry for jumping down your throat." Bobby looked a bit friendlier. "Anyway, let's get to the main issue. Do you believe Riley's story?"

"Yeah, I do. It fits with there being a cover-up of Jonathan Caldwell's involvement in Sumner's murder, and that someone inside the police department has been pulling the strings. You made a good attempt to have him finger the person before we left. I guess we'll have to wait a bit longer for that."

Bobby looked dubious. "There's something about your conspiracy theory that doesn't make sense to me. Why wouldn't the senator get his son to turn himself in to the police, and hire the best lawyers to defend him? Why risk his reputation and political career?"

"I've been chewing on the question and I don't think this is about the senator wanting to protect his son. Didn't you follow the state elections that were held last November? The senator was running for a third term up against a younger and very popular candidate. The polls indicated it was going to be a dog fight to the bitter end. I was so disappointed when I learned that Caldwell had held onto his seat by the thinnest of margins. Even the slightest hint of scandal could've turned the tide against him. Having his son in jail accused of rape and murder would have guaranteed his retirement from politics. And knowing the senator as I now do, losing his seat would have been devastating to him. He relishes the power of his position too much."

"So you think he covered this all up to protect his political hide?"

"Absolutely. I know it sounds like a big risk, but he would've weighed everything before choosing this course. He probably had his son go over in detail what happened that night and decided it was unlikely anyone at the bar would've noticed him leaving at the same time as Sumner. There was also a good chance that Sumner's body would never be discovered, at least not until the trail was too cold for the police to pursue it. And to cover off this contingency, he devised a back-up plan. He found an ally, someone close to the situation, who could help influence the investigation."

Tony could see Bobby mulling this over. "Okay," she said, "let's run with this for the moment. The senator discovers that his son killed Sumner. He's familiar with the way things work around the police department and anticipates that Adelsky will lead the investigation. Then he finds out you've been appointed. This would've thrown him for a loop."

"That's right." Tony picked up the thread. "He doesn't know me and so can't easily use his political influence. I'd pose a significant threat to his plan."

"So you figure he reached out to Adelsky to be his inside man?"

"I do. As we both know, Adelsky was really pissed off when he found out he wasn't going to head the investigation. He even threatened to quit. But the next day he's back at work, trying to help out with the case. This doesn't fit with his way of dealing with things. I believe the senator convinced him to move to the other side and work against the investigation. Remember, he was the one that researched all the sex offenders living in the Madison area. Hell, he gave us Mansfield's mug shot and rap sheet on a platter. Now think about all the things that went wrong: the media leaks, the missing security tape, Mansfield being scared away. It had to be your boss trying to make me look bad, so he could get control of the case. Then, once he took over, he failed to follow up on any evidence that might implicate the senator's son."

"Okay. I have to admit you've built a good circumstantial case. So we now have a big decision – where do we go from here?"

"My vote is for you to go speak with Dupree. I know you've got reservations about his ability to stomach another political brawl, but we need his support and advice. You've got to lay out everything we know and convince him to approach the State Attorney's office about an immunity deal for Riley. Assuming he fingers Adelsky, the next step would be to move in on Adelsky and see if he'll flip over on the senator."

"You really think the chief is up to this?"

"Yeah. He just needs to know our case is pretty solid."

"Okay. I'll speak to him first thing tomorrow morning."

"Good. In the meantime, we need to dig deeper … see if we can turn up more evidence that would implicate Caldwell Jr. I've written down some ideas that might help you with that. You may have already thought of these things, but just in case." He handed Bobby a folded piece of paper.

She opened it and scanned the contents. "Some of them. I hadn't thought about the car angle, though. I'll check this out. Are you still planning to head into Chicago for the night? It would be good if you could be around when I speak with the chief."

Tony briefly considered her request. "My dad would be pretty disappointed if I didn't show up, and it's probably better for you to speak with the chief alone. Things will be tense enough without me suddenly showing up. I'll call you when I get back into town tomorrow afternoon and see how things went down."

"I'd better head back and get a good night's sleep, then. Something tells me I'm going to need all my wits about me tomorrow."

"You can handle the chief, no worries." He just hoped his instincts were correct and the chief was indeed up to the challenge.

Chapter 30
MAY 20 6:10 PM

A large pizza box with "Gino's East of Chicago" on the lid lay in the center of the kitchen table. Inside were the remains of a deep dish sausage pizza. Tony looked over at his dad and observed a thin string of mozzarella cheese dangling from his mouth.

"Dad, did you forget your manners?"

"What, I can't enjoy my pie?"

"It's good to see you still like Gino's. You didn't ask for it when I suggested pizza."

"Yes, still my favorite, but too expensive for people on a set income."

"It does seem a bit pricier than I remember. But it's the best I've had in a long time."

"Now, tell me about Crown Point. Did you see Dillinger?"

Tony told his father about his visit to the jail and described the demeanor of the various security guards he met while he was there. They both laughed when he told the story about the hallways, being color-coded for security levels.

"The walls for Dillinger's cell would be blood red," Joseph said with a wink.

Tony decided it was time to move onto a more delicate subject. "Dad, I took your advice and saw Joanna."

"Good, like I told you. She looks nice, eh?"

"Yes, she's does. And she seems to be happy. But I learned she's dating another man – a lawyer in the firm where she works."

Joseph failed to hide his surprise and disappointment. Tony filled the awkward silence.

"It's probably for the best. I've put her and Carla through hell. They deserve better."

"No, you are a good husband and father. And my best son."

"Your only son," he pointed out. But he was still pleased by his dad's words and felt a lump grow in his throat.

Joseph suddenly got up from the table and picked up his plate, shaking several half-eaten pizza crusts into the garbage. "Let's clean up and go for a walk. It will be good for both of us to get some fresh air and see the old neighborhood."

Tony cleared the table while his father wrapped the leftover pizza in plastic and put it in the fridge. He washed up the few dishes they'd used, while Joseph dried and put them away. When everything was in its place, they headed out for their walking tour. As they strolled down the street, stopping in on several of the neighbors, Joseph took visible pleasure in introducing his son. Tony enjoyed the uncomplicated conversations that followed. An hour later the pizza had settled in his stomach. Back home they talked for a while in the living room. Joseph then pulled himself up from his lazy-boy chair and announced he was going to bed.

"I'm going to make a long-distance call before I turn in, Dad."

"Leave some money on the table." Joseph grinned and gave him a quick hug before disappearing into his bedroom.

Tony dialed Julie's number. She picked up immediately. "It's me. How's the studying going?"

"Tony! I was hoping it was you. I'm ready to ace my exam tomorrow. How did your day go?"

"Not bad ... I think we might have a breakthrough in the Sumner case," he replied, trying to say as little as possible without seeming rude.

"That's wonderful news. I won't ask you to breach any code of silence, but please tell me this doesn't mean you need to spend another night in Chicago. I was kinda hoping you'd be back tomorrow to help me celebrate knocking off another exam. Only one more to go after this one!,"

"That won't be a problem. I just have one thing to do tomorrow morning, and plan to be home by early afternoon. Look, I can't talk long – this call's on Dad's ticket. But when's your exam over?"

"I should be done by two."

"Why don't I come by your place shortly after that with a nice bottle of wine?"

"That sounds like a *great* idea."

Chapter 31
MAY 21 9:50 AM

Tony slowed down as he got closer to his destination, the so-called 900 Shops on North Michigan Avenue. This was a busy part of the Magnificent Mile, and the sidewalk was already filling up with affluent-looking shoppers. He turned into the multi-level garage attached to the shopping centre and found a spot on the second level.

At the courtesy desk in the shopping concourse, a young girl helped him with directions. The MaxMara store was larger than he'd imagined, its windows displaying the latest in Italian designer fashions. It had just opened, and the clerks were still arranging racks of clothing. A raven-haired woman behind a counter gave him a generous smile and said, "Welcome to MaxMara." Tony returned the smile and kept walking.

In a section of the store selling sports clothing, he spotted her. She was speaking with another young woman in tight jeans and a brightly flowered shirt. Not wanting to interrupt their conversation, he wandered through the display areas. As he stopped at a table of brightly colored silk scarves, picking one up, a voice behind him said, "Can I help you?" He spun around and saw the woman with the flowery shirt looking at him with an inquiring expression.

Before he could respond, he heard Carla's voice. "My god, Dad, what are you doing here?"

The other sales clerk retreated, sensing that father and daughter needed some privacy.

Carla looked shocked – not unreasonably, given that they hadn't seen or spoken to each other since late the previous year. In their last encounter, she had told him she was going to live with a university friend, angrily saying he'd become a miserable person to live with. Tony could now appreciate her perspective on the matter.

"Hi Carla. Sorry for sneaking up on you like this. I'm sure your mom told you I dropped by the house last week. She said you had a summer job here. I had to be in the area on business, and I took the chance you might be working."

"I'm glad you did. I was so disappointed when Mom said I'd missed you, Dad. I was going to call you, honest. I've been thinking about you."

"Me too," Tony said earnestly. "Would you get into trouble if we popped out for a quick coffee? I have some things I'd like to discuss."

"Just a minute." Carla excused herself to speak with her co-worker. "We're cool," she said when she came back. "If the manager comes around, Barb will tell her I'm on a short errand. But let's go out the street entrance so we don't bump into her."

Tony followed Carla as she navigated through the store and out onto the now busy sidewalk. "We'll head back into the mall. There's a nice coffee spot near Bloomingdales. We can sit there and talk."

Tony couldn't help but notice that in the months they'd been apart, his daughter had matured from a gangly teenager into a beautiful young woman. She'd learned how to use make-up to highlight her delicate features and large hazel eyes. Her long brown hair was now styled in wavy curls and lightly streaked. She wore a light silk dress that showed off her figure, and she seemed to glide along the sidewalk in her high heels. Once again he was reminded how much he'd missed her being part of his life.

Back in the mall, she led him to a trendy coffee bar sandwiched between two escalators. Its glass display case was full of muffins, croissants, and gourmet sandwiches. Carla ordered a green tea.

"Okay, one green tea, an espresso, and one of those double chocolate cookies," Tony told the barista, winking at Carla.

"Dad!" She rolled her eyes, and for a moment it felt like old times.

They took their order to a row of stools along a glass counter. Carla waited expectantly for him to say something. He wasn't quite sure how to start. "Your mom said you had a good term at U of C," he ventured.

"Yeah, it was pretty cool, all things considered. I had some awesome profs. That made it easier. Did Mom mention I took a law course? It was really wow. My prof thought I was a natural. I've started to look into what sorta marks you need. To get into law school of course." Carla finished her staccato update and waited for his reaction.

"Your mom said something about that. Sounds interesting." Tony tried to muster some enthusiasm in his voice, but he'd never been a great fan of lawyers. He was even less so now that Joanna was dating one. Then again, he was becoming involved with a soon-to-be lawyer and realized he would need to be less prejudiced on this subject. "I hope this works out for you. I know you'd be great at whatever you decide to do." He decided to change the subject. "Sam sure has missed you."

Carla smiled. "How's the fat cat doing?"

"She's fine, still likes her food. She's taken to sleeping on the bed with me. Everything is good until she wants her breakfast. Then she tries to wake me up by sitting on my head."

Carla gave an unladylike snort. "Charming. Mom says you've got some sort of security gig?"

"Yes, I'm working at the Varsity Bar. Have you been there?"

"Dad, you know I'm not legal yet! But I did hear it's one of the best dance spots in Madtown."

"That's a fact. I know it doesn't sound like much of a job, but it's got me out of the house and back into the real world. It's given me time to get a better perspective on things. I realize what a horrible job I did being your father after your mom left. Here you were, dealing with our split up, trying to do well at university, and all I did was make things more difficult for you. I can appreciate why you had to move out. The reason I dropped by the house last week was to apologize to you, and to your mom."

Carla looked intently at Tony, her expression neutral. "I've also had a lot of time to think about what happened between us, Dad. I had a lot of frustration and anger I needed to work out too. Believe it or not, Mom has been a very sympathetic listener. We've had long discussions, talking about what happened, and she's really tried to help me understand. I realize you must've been under awful pressure trying to solve that poor girl's murder. And then to lose your job and have Mom walk out on you – it must've seemed like a fucking nightmare. Oops, pardon my French!"

As they both laughed, the tension between them seemed to lift. She gave his arm a playful punch. "I'd like to try to put that awful time behind us and give us another chance."

"Ouch! That would make me very happy." He hesitated, then plunged on. "I was kinda hoping your mom would feel the same way. When we were together last week, I asked if there was a chance of reconciliation. That's when she told me she was seeing someone from work. I have to admit it hurt like hell. But she's right to move on, and I need to do the same thing."

She picked up that her father wanted to learn more about her mother's new boyfriend. "His name is Jacob. I haven't spent a ton of time with him, but he seems nice. Mom has been happier than I've seen her in a long time. And that makes me happy. Now, if you're wondering how that affects you and me, you don't have to worry. I've missed you horribly and wanted to see you, but I wasn't sure how Mom would take it. However, after your visit she encouraged me to make contact. I'm so glad you made the first move."

"Me too," he said, grateful for her words of reassurance. "I would like to find a way for us to stay connected, and for me to be a bigger part of your life. Do you think that's possible?"

She considered his question. "Well, why don't we start by my coming up for a visit?" she proposed. "We need to spend some time getting to know each other again. It would also be good to see Sam. I'm not working this Sunday. How about I drive up in the morning? Unless you have other plans, that is."

Tony felt like a huge weight had been lifted from his shoulders. "Next Sunday would be great. Can you make it up for around eleven? I can go to the Saturday market and pull together one of those large brunches we used to have – scrambled eggs, bacon, fresh fruit, pancakes – the works. We can spend the morning together stuffing ourselves and burping like crazy. If you like, afterwards we can head over to the university and explore some of your old haunts."

"That's way cool," Carla said in approval. "Now I'd better get back to the store before my manager starts getting antsy."

Chapter 32
MAY 21 10:20 AM

They said their goodbyes at the mall entrance, Carla quickly hugging him before heading back through the revolving door. Tony stood there for a moment, still on a high from their encounter. He felt immensely relieved that Carla seemed to understand what he'd been going through a year ago.

He was jostled back into motion by an impatient shopper. Seeing the line of pay phones along the entranceway, he pulled a handful of loose change from his pocket.

"Tubman. Who's this?"

"Hey, Tubs, it's me. You sound a bit harried."

"Tony! I didn't recognize the number. I'm up to my ass in alligators. I've been trying to reach you – left you a phone message at your house over an hour ago. Why the hell don't you get a cell phone like everyone else on the planet?"

"It's quite simple, Tubs. Until recently no one was calling, so it seemed like a waste of money. Now I appreciate the freedom of not having one."

"Hmph. I suggest its time you reconnect with the world. Where are you calling from?"

"I'm in your neck of the woods, at a pay phone on North Michigan. What's up?"

"I've got some positive news for a change. I was able to get through to Bill Copeland after we spoke yesterday. I explained the situation and asked if he was comfortable speaking to his son about your unusual request. He said he couldn't guarantee anything, but agreed to send him an email outlining the situation. I got a call from Daniel's assistant early this morning. She said he was looking into the matter I discussed with his father. He wanted to arrange a time to speak with me. The call's been set up for 11:30 this morning."

"Terrific. Any chance I can be part of the conversation?"

"Uhhh ... I don't think that's going to work, Tony. I didn't mention your name to Bill or Daniel, and this is supposed to be an off-the-record conversation. I doubt he'd feel comfortable sharing whatever information he's gathered with someone he doesn't know. Particularly since you don't have an official role."

"I guess you're right. Well, how about I come by your office and hang around until you've finished your call? That way you don't have to track me down to let me know what he had to say."

"Makes sense. Why don't you head over right now, and you can let me know what else you've been up to."

"Be there in fifteen."

CHICAGO POLICE Headquarters on South Michigan Avenue was only a short distance from the exclusive stores of North Michigan Avenue, but it was about as far away as you could get from the Magnificent Mile, Tony thought to himself. Except that they both had a lot to do with human greed.

The building was a modern four-story structure of brick, glass, and steel. Tony could still remember the opening ceremonies almost a decade before. Mayor Daley had proudly proclaimed that the new building housed the most technologically advanced crime-fighting unit in the nation. Ironically, it took another year for all the electronic gremlins to be exorcised.

Tony had worked out of the homicide division on the top floor. He was a member of the Detectives Division – Area 5, which covered criminal investigations in the downtown core. The division was part of the city's elite Bureau of Investigative Services, known as the BIS, which also included the Counter Terrorism and Intelligence Division as well as the Organized Crime Division. The BIS unit did most of the heavy lifting when it came to dealing with violent crime within the city.

Tony had lots of memories of the place, good and bad. However, he didn't have the time or energy to go down memory lane. Inside, the customary level of security was evident. He knew the drill for visitors and went to the front reception desk. The duty officer was speaking with a very agitated elderly gentleman who appeared to be somewhat inebriated. The officer, a young man with a blonde peach-fuzz mustache, was struggling to calm the man down and find out his problem. The old man shouted that he'd been accosted by a hooded teenager and robbed of his wallet and antique watch. Another officer was summoned, who led the man away to take his statement.

Tony was beckoned forward and explained that he was there to meet with Detective Tubman. The duty officer examined his ID, gave him a numbered security badge, and told to take a seat. No sign of recognition registered on the young officer's face. Tony realized he was already becoming a distant memory within the Chicago PD.

He picked up a day-old newspaper from a table and flipped through it while he waited. It was another ten minutes before his old partner emerged from an elevator. Late again, Tony thought, wondering what the excuse would be this time. "I just about finished yesterday's paper waiting for you."

"Sorry, Tony. We've been experiencing some technical problems with our new mind-reading and confession machine. Fortunately it's all fixed and ready for new customers. You interested?"

Tony snorted.

"I really am sorry," Tubman insisted. "But in a moment you'll appreciate why I was late. Let's head up to my office. We've got about twenty minutes before my call with Copeland. You can update me on what brings you to Chicago, and I'll give you an unfortunately brief report on the Harding murder investigation."

In the elevator with several other people, they limited their conversation to the weather and hockey. Stepping out at the fourth floor, Tony recognized several officers he'd once worked with, huddled together in a corner office. He kept his head down and followed Tubman, not anxious to get into any discussions about what he'd been up to since he'd retired.

Tubman's office was a small room with a large window overlooking the street. File folders were haphazardly scattered on the desk, and there were several pictures of his wife and children on a filing credenza. Tubman asked Tony if he wanted a coffee, and he declined.

"Sit." Tubman got started. "Okay, let me have it. What brings you to Chicago?"

"My destination was actually Lake County Jail in Crown Point. Chicago was just a side trip to see my dad and Carla."

Tubby raised an eyebrow. Tony wondered if he was reacting to the mention of Lake County Jail, Carla, or maybe both.

"It turns out that Matt Riley, the security guard who identified Mansfield, is at Crown Point awaiting trial on an assault charge. Andrade tracked him down and made arrangements with the warden to meet with him. She invited me along to observe. This isn't the first time Riley has been in prison. He spent three years at Red Onion under a different last name. The Indiana police haven't made the connection, so Andrade used the information to put the squeeze on him. Riley essentially admitted to lying about seeing Mansfield outside the bar."

"Did he say why?"

"He said he was contacted by someone who indicated the police had a pretty strong case against Mansfield. He was told he was going to be interviewed by the police and it would be very helpful if he happened to tell the investigating officers that he saw Mansfield outside the bar the night Sumner was killed. It was intimated that if Mansfield was convicted, Riley would be up for a large reward. He decided it was in his best interests to cooperate."

"Who the hell told him to frame Mansfield?"

"We don't know yet. Riley wasn't prepared to give up a name without written assurances that he wouldn't be prosecuted in Wisconsin for lying to the police. However, he did say the person was close to the investigation."

"Let me guess. You think it's Adelsky."

"It has to be him. He was in an ideal spot to help the senator. And I also think he put the fear of God into Mansfield. That's why he bolted in the middle of the night."

"Wait a minute, you just lost me. What's this about Mansfield?"

"Oh, yeah, I haven't told you. Mansfield tried to reach me the night he disappeared. Andrade got his phone records. Turns out he received two calls just before he called me and then the police department."

"And you think this proves that Mansfield was being threatened?"

"I do, and here's why. The two calls were placed from a phone booth a block from Mansfield's apartment. The caller would've been able to see Mansfield drive away from his apartment building. My guess is that's when Sumner's clothing was planted in the trash bin outside."

Tubman ran his hand across his chin. "It does sound like you're onto something. And this puts some information I've just received into a different light."

"You have something new on the Harding case?"

"Both cases, and they're related. Our techs just finished going through the rest of Harding's phone and email records, both at her office and condo. They were told to focus on any contacts with people in Madison. I've already told you about the phone calls to the Madison Police Department, which we now know were made to Andrade. They also found an email exchange between Adelsky and Harding, a week before she was murdered. Apparently he'd made inquiries within the Chicago PD and found out that Harding was behind the request for the additional DNA testing on the skin samples. His email indicated he was pretty

235

steamed about this. He told Harding she should've consulted with him as lead investigator on the case before requesting the tests and that he was totally taken by surprise when the results landed on his desk. Harding's response was pretty terse. Basically she told him to fuck off."

"Hmm. So Adelsky found out Harding was behind the request for the additional DNA tests. Were there any other communications between the two of them?"

"Not that we could find. But I think it would be wise for Andrade to quietly find out what Adelsky was doing the night Harding was killed."

"Holy shit. This is getting more complicated by the minute. I assume Peters is going to report this email exchange to Andrade?"

"He's planning to call her today."

"Good. Now, tell me, Tub, what's the status of the FBI's involvement?"

"They're going be called in tomorrow if nothing of consequence breaks in the meantime. But this new information about Adelsky and Riley may get us a bit of a reprieve. I'm not sure the State Attorney will want the FBI stomping around if there's the possibility of a dirty cop being involved."

"You bet. And it means there's even greater urgency for us to convince Riley to identify this mystery person and provide more details of their dealings. Andrade was planning to meet with her chief this morning to give him a full account of what she's learned and get his support. You can imagine she wants to keep everything pretty quiet until she has Riley's sworn statement. Once they have the information, I expect there'll be a flurry of activity on the Sumner case."

"I hope my conversation with Copeland will help the cause. Speaking of which – " Tubby let the silence stretch for a moment – "I got to thinking about your request to participate in the call. I'm still not comfortable with you being on the line, but who's fooling who? Once I get off the phone, I'll give you a play-by-play of our conversation anyway. So I've come up with a compromise. That's why the delay in coming down to see you. I've had a special conference phone hooked up so you'll be able to listen in, but the speaker will be muted. In other words, you'll hear the conversation but you can't participate. How does that sound?"

"Far exceeds my expectations, Tubby. I really appreciate it." At that moment Tony felt like giving the big man a bear hug.

"Great." Tubman looked at his watch. "The call is supposed to start in five minutes. Let me take you to the meeting room and get you settled."

Tubman led the way down the hallway before turning into a room on the right. "I'm sure this room looks familiar. It's now known as Meeting Room A, but some of us old-timers prefer to call it the Deluca Think-Tank."

Tony smiled. His old office had been transformed into a meeting room with a small conference table and four well-worn office chairs around it. On the walls were the framed pictures of Chicago landmarks he'd donated to his office's next occupant.

Tubman pointed to a phone on the table. "Line one is connected to my office line. When you see the green light come on, pick up. As I said, we've turned off the transmitter, so you can sing, laugh, cry, whatever you like, and we won't hear you. When the call's finished, I'll come back and we can discuss what Copeland had to say." He closed the door behind him.

Tony stood admiring the framed prints on display in the room. When he'd first moved into his new office, he decided it was time to replace his diplomas and certificates with some real artwork. Walking around during a lunch break, he'd stumbled on a gallery exhibiting black-and-white photos of the Chicago Navy Pier, Buckingham Fountain, the Chicago Theatre, and the Gothic Revival Tribune Tower. On a whim he decided to buy the four pictures for his office. He was now thinking he should've kept at least one as a reminder of Chi-town.

His attention was suddenly caught by the green light flashing on the phone. Tubby was already on the line with Copeland. How much of their conversation had he missed?

Chapter 33

Tony cupped his hand over the receiver, not confident with Tubby's assurances that he couldn't be heard. He soon realized the conversation hadn't progressed past the niceties.

"I had a nice chat with your dad. He said he's in good health and that he and Barb enjoyed their recent trip out to see you and your family."

An unfamiliar but friendly voice responded. "It was a welcome and past due visit. I don't get much opportunity these days to come out and see them in California. They're keeping me pretty busy here. Speaking of which, I've been called into a briefing and don't have much time. But I know you're anxious to get this information. I understand it's for a murder investigation." Daniel Copeland's chatty tone had changed, and he was now all business.

"That's right. A young woman from Chicago was murdered while attending the University of Wisconsin last fall. We're assisting the Madison police, who are pursuing some new leads."

"And the new information points towards this Jonathan Caldwell?"

"He and the deceased were at the same bar the night she was killed. We've found security video showing them leaving at the same time."

"I see. Interesting they didn't pick this up earlier. Is there anything else that ties him to the murder?"

"Nothing that would stand up in court. We do know that the victim scratched her killer, but unfortunately the DNA evidence was tainted by the body's exposure to the elements."

"That would explain why you're looking for the report of his medical exam. And tell me, why are you interested in learning about the terms of his discharge?"

"Let's just say we're curious why he didn't finish his tour of duty."

There was silence on the line and Tony wondered if the connection had gone dead. He then heard Copeland clear his throat. "I have to say you've put me in a delicate situation. You didn't mention to my father that your suspect is the son of Senator Caldwell. It would've been helpful to have this information before I started my inquiries. In your shoes, I also might've been silent on this point, but you must understand how sensitive this is. While Senator Caldwell isn't the political force on the Hill that he used to be, he's still someone you don't lightly fuck with." There was a hard edge to Copeland's voice.

Tubman jumped in to defuse the situation. "Daniel, I apologize for not being more forthright. I hope I didn't compromise you. The reason we're doing this background digging is to make sure we don't unnecessarily disturb the senator."

"I guess that makes sense." Copeland sounded somewhat mollified by the explanation. "Now, I have found out some information that might be useful to you, but you must assure me there will be no attribution back to me. I would disavow that we had this conversation, and if I had to, I would take other actions that would be detrimental to your position on the police force. Do you get my drift?"

"Absolutely."

"I'm glad you understand the situation. Let's first talk about Caldwell's medical records. I've been advised there's a notation from the doctor who examined Caldwell the day he reported for duty. It indicates that Caldwell said he had been in a bar fight the night before he arrived at camp. This was his explanation for several abrasions and scratch marks on his face and neck. An interesting coincidence, don't you think?"

"It certainly is." Tubman unsuccessfully tried to downplay his excitement.

"You were also wondering why he didn't complete his tour of duty. The official line is that he was honorably discharged due to personal reasons. My source was very hesitant to go into further details, but I got curious and pressed him. He finally told me that after Private Caldwell completed training camp, he was shipped to the Middle East. Over there, he was involved in several incidents indicating he wasn't suited for combat in an environment where the activities of US soldiers are under constant scrutiny."

"Could you fill in the blanks a bit more?"

"I'm limited in what I can say. However, it appears that Caldwell suffers from anger management issues that resulted in his causing injury to several local non-combatants. After the timely intervention of his father, combined with a psychological evaluation, it was decided that he should be discharged and sent back to the States."

"Did any of his transgressions involve local women?" Tubman guessed.

"I'm not in a position to comment further, but you can draw the appropriate conclusions. Now, as I said, I'm expected to participate in another urgent matter." It was clear that the conversation was over.

"Daniel, you've been extremely helpful. Thanks for expending some of your political capital on this."

"Lonnie, you know I have a teen-aged daughter. Go get him."

"Yes, sir!"

Tony heard a click and the line went dead. A moment later Tubman pushed open the door to the conference room. He was looking very pleased with himself, his dark eyes shining and teeth displayed in a big smile. "Did you catch all of that?"

Tony returned the grin. "Loud and clear."

"You heard the man. Go get the bastard."

Chapter 34
MAY 21 1:40 PM

Tony considered calling Bobby before he left Chicago but realized he'd better get on the highway if he was going to be back in time to meet Julie. Fortunately the traffic was relatively light and he didn't hit any major construction delays.

Back at his cottage, his first priority was to check his phone messages. There were two earlier ones from Tubman. The third and final message was from Bobby, asking him to call her when he got back. He looked at the clock over the fireplace and calculated that within the next forty-five minutes he had to shower, buy a bottle of wine, and get over to Julie's. Maybe getting a cell phone wasn't such a bad idea, he thought, picking up the phone and dialing Bobby's cell number.

"Tony, where've you been?" He could sense excitement as well as tension in her voice.

"Just got back. What's up?"

"Things are moving quickly. I caught up with Dupree this morning and told him we needed to talk, preferably outside the office. He was a bit taken back but arranged for a meeting room over at the mayor's office. It didn't start out well. I told him what we'd been up to, and he was very unhappy to have been kept in the dark about my unofficial investigation. He was particularly concerned to learn of your involvement. I reminded him that he'd given me the brush-off the last time I tried to discuss the Sumner case with him and that I was trying to gather enough facts to avoid the same thing happening again. Seemed to put him in a more understanding frame of mind."

"What happened after that?"

"Once I got him settled down, he asked me to go over everything I knew about her murder investigation. I gave him a timeline of events from the night Sumner disappeared until yesterday's meeting with Riley. He quickly figured out Adelsky had been grossly incompetent, or worse yet, working to subvert the investigation."

Tony was pleased to hear the chief agreed with his views on the situation but didn't interrupt.

Bobby continued with her update. "Once we'd gone through all the evidence, the chief was very upset. He muttered something to the effect that this explained why the senator was so interested in having you removed from the case. Dupree definitely smells a rat and wants to flush him out."

"Does it mean he's prepared to speak with someone over at the State Attorney's office?"

"I believe he's over there now, speaking with the head honcho. He's also asked me to quietly retrieve the Sumner case files from storage and go through them with a fine-tooth comb. He wants to know if anything else was missed or not properly pursued." She was now sounding full of confidence and energy. "This is it, Tony. I think we're finally going to solve this case."

"Great news and congrats. Full steam ahead!" Tony was happy for her. But he also realized, with a sinking feeling, that his role in the investigation would now come to an abrupt end.

Bobby seemed to read his thoughts. "Tony, things would never have got to this stage without your help. I made this clear to the chief at the end of our meeting. I told him that we needed you to be part of the ongoing investigation team."

Tony was completely taken by surprise. "You told him what?" he managed to splutter.

"I want you to continue to work on this case with me. It makes total sense. You're the most experienced homicide cop in the city and you're fully up to speed with the case. Besides, you're the only one I can trust in the department, other than the chief."

"Wow, I appreciate your vote of confidence. But how'd the chief react?"

"At first he raised all sorts of objections. He mentioned your lawsuit against the city, and not having the authority or budget to bring you on. Plus, there was the matter of police confidentiality and protocols to be followed."

Tony felt deflated as he heard the growing list of concerns with his participation in the investigation.

Bobby wasn't finished. "I told him, in a somewhat more diplomatic manner, that these were all bullshit excuses. You've already told me the city wants to settle the lawsuit and sweep it under the rug. I argued that giving you an official role in the investigation might make you more agreeable to working out a reasonable settlement. I also noted that the Mayor is almost next door, if he wanted to get support for this decision. In terms of confidentiality, I made the point that right now there was an even greater risk to the department's image if you decided to go public with what you know. This would cause more havoc than any potential breach of police protocols."

Tony had to give Bobby credit: she'd neatly dealt with all the chief's arguments. Right now he'd settle for a simple apology from the city in return for a chance to catch Sumner's killer. Hell, he'd even borrow money to pay Drake's legal bills out of his own pocket.

"I really appreciate you going to bat for me. How was it left?"

"The chief agreed to talk it over with the mayor. He came back with a rather grim look on his face. He said the mayor was not very happy with this turn of events and didn't like the feeling that he was being backed into a corner. However, as the chief explained, the mayor is above all else a pragmatist and he quickly realized the political risks if you were left out in the cold. Once he got over that hurdle, the city solicitor was pulled in. I now have in my hands an envelope containing a settlement and consulting agreement for you to review and sign. I was also asked to give you the message that time is of the essence, there's no room to haggle. Did you want me to drop it off on my way home tonight?"

"No, just open it up and read it to me."

"Tony, are you sure? There may be stuff in there you don't want me to know about."

"The chief's right. We can't waste time over this."

"Okay." He heard the sound of ripping paper. "It starts out with the typical legal mumbo jumbo. Then, it says the Madison Police Department agrees to engage you as a consultant on a per diem rate of $1,000 plus expenses for a period of up to one month, which may be extended at the option of the Chief of Police, and subject to certain conditions. The first one is that you agree to drop your lawsuit against the city for the sum of $100,000 plus reasonable legal fees. The second one is that you agree to hold confidential all information you have obtained or may obtain relating to the investigation of Karen Sumner's murder. The final condition is that you report to and take direction from Officer Andrade, who will be assuming the lead in this investigation." She gasped. "What the...? The chief never mentioned that to me."

"Well, congratulations again," Tony said with a laugh. "You can let the chief know the conditions are acceptable. I'll report for duty tomorrow morning, if that's okay with you. And as a show of good faith, I have some additional information relating to our chief suspect."

He quickly went over his information concerning Jonathan Caldwell's army medical records and the reasons for his discharge. In doing so, he took great care to protect Copeland's identity as the source of this information.

"So, you're saying we won't be able to use this information in court?"

"That was the deal that had to be struck to get people to talk. However, it doesn't stop us from using this information in discussions with Caldwell. I also have another interesting tidbit that Tubman shared with me. It relates to Harding's murder."

"What's that?"

"They found email correspondence between Adelsky and Harding that took place about a week before she was murdered."

"What? Why were they in contact?"

"Somehow he found out that Harding was behind the request for the additional DNA testing. Adelsky sent her a blunt message saying he should've been notified by her office of this request. She told him to fuck off. But there's no evidence of other communications between the two of them. Interesting, to say the least.'"

There was silence on the other end of the phone. "So Adelsky knew that Harding was poking around the Sumner case. Is it possible he figured out there was another agenda when she asked the Chicago Police to request the additional tests?"

"I've been wondering about that myself. The thought that the State Attorney's Office might be looking into the Sumner murder would've been extremely disconcerting even if Adelsky had nothing to hide. Harding's response wouldn't have been very reassuring to him. However, at this point there's no other evidence suggesting he played a role in her death."

"Yeah, I should take my own advice and not jump to conclusions," Bobby said. "We also shouldn't forget that the person with the biggest stake in this whole thing appears to be Senator Caldwell."

"Right. We need to follow the evidence, and that starts with getting the sworn statement from Riley." Tony looked at his watch. "Oh shit, it's almost two. Listen, I have to go. Can we plan to get together tomorrow morning, around nine? I can sign the agreement then and discuss what role you want me to play as the investigation moves along."

"How about we meet at the downtown Starbucks?"

"Starbucks would be fitting. As you will recall, that's where we first discussed our informal partnership. Your arm needed a lot of twisting."

"I'm willing to put up with that irony for the sake of their lattes. See you tomorrow."

Chapter 35
MAY 21 2:47 PM

Tony was still in a bit of a daze when he arrived at Julie's apartment – more that fifteen minutes late. He hoped the bouquet of spring flowers, bottle of California Pinot Noir, and cheese tray he'd picked up at Whole Foods would make up for it. When she answered the door, he extended the flowers. "I know I'm late. I'm sorry."

She accepted both flowers and apology with a graceful curtsy. "My exam was three hours long and grueling, so it's a good thing you were late. It gave me some time to catch my breath."

She led the way into the galley kitchen where two wine glasses and a corkscrew were waiting on the countertop. While Tony opened the wine and filled the glasses, she searched through cupboards for something to use as a vase. Meanwhile she gave him an update on her criminal law exam. "It was a series of case studies involving different crimes, and we had to assume the role of the defense lawyer. There were multi-part questions requiring a review of the elements of the criminal act, the procedures to be followed to get to trial, and the appeal process."

"Sounds familiar."

"I really enjoyed the criminal law course. Much more fun than contract law. That's my final exam, and I think it's extreme corporal punishment, clearly reviewable by the Supreme Court Justices, to schedule an exam on the weekend. But by Saturday afternoon I'll be *so* done. And I'm officially putting you on notice that you need to take me out for dinner that night to celebrate."

Tony made a mental note to find someone to take over his shift. He realized then that he'd likely need to negotiate a month sabbatical from his security job – if not longer. He'd deal with that issue tomorrow, he decided, after he signed the papers and it was all official.

By then Julie had located a wine decanter, filled it with water, and trimmed the stalks of the flowers before arranging them. Tony watched as she placed the decanter on the small kitchen table and then stepped back to admire her work. As she was doing this, Tony took the opportunity to admire the view. Her tight black jeans left little to the imagination. This was complemented by a v-neck cotton sweater that revealed her rounded breasts. Brains and sexy good looks – a killer combination, he reflected.

He picked up the two glasses of wine and handed one to her. "Here's to Julie Travers, one step closer to becoming the top criminal lawyer in Madison."

"Now that would be something. Maybe we could be partners. 'Travers and Deluca – Criminal Representation and Investigation.'"

"Change that to 'Deluca and Travers,' and you have a deal," Tony responded with a laugh. They clinked glasses and Tony enjoyed his first sip of the slightly fruity wine.

Julie was eyeballing the cheese tray resting on the kitchen counter. "I'm totally famished. Mind if we dig in?"

"Not at all. It should go well with the wine."

Julie put a generous wedge of Brie on a cracker. "You haven't said much yet, but I'm sensing this powerful aura around you. I'd like to think it's the excitement of being in my presence, but I'm beginning to suspect something's happened since we talked last night."

Tony smiled at the reference to his so-called powerful aura. Admittedly, his bruised ego was quickly in retreat and he felt a new sense of purpose in his life.

"Okay, dispense with the Cheshire cat imitation and fill me in."

He was glad to share the results of his meeting with Carla and their first tentative steps towards reconciliation. It felt good to have someone to confide in after what seemed a very long time. He updated her on his meeting with Carla and their first tentative steps towards reconciliation. "She's coming for a visit this Sunday." For a moment he considered asking Julie to join them, but something told him this might not be well received by Carla. He also didn't want to put unnecessary pressure on his relationship with Julie.

As if sensing his internal debate, Julie said, "It'll be good for the two of you to spend some time together. Give you a chance to reconnect. I hope I'll get a chance to meet her in a future visit, once you've put everything back on an even keel."

"Let's plan for that. I know you'll hit it off."

"We do have at least one thing in common." She gave Tony a nudge. "Now, what happened after your talk with Carla?"

"From there I ended up having an unexpected visit with my old homicide partner, Lonnie Tubman. He's helping me gather some additional information on the Sumner case. We're making some good progress."

He briefly related his conversation with Bobby upon returning to the cottage. "The chief is now fully briefed on our activities and supportive of the direction she wants to take."

"That's great. But where does that leave you?"

"Funny you should ask.... I'd already accepted that once Bobby went to the chief, it would be the end of the line for me. I wasn't very happy about it, but I figured it's the way it had to be. However, Bobby's convinced Dupree that I should be kept on as a consultant until the investigation is complete."

Julie's eyes lit up. "Tony, that's fantastic news!"

"It sure is. I'm supposed to get together with Bobby tomorrow morning to discuss my role and next steps in the investigation."

"Now we both have something to celebrate!" She looked at him expectantly. "It seems a shame to wait until Saturday. Why don't you grab the bottle of wine and follow me. We're going to explore that aura of yours in more detail." She took his hand and smiled.

When she led him towards her bedroom, this time Tony didn't feel any hesitation. What followed was much better than anything he could've ever dreamed.

Chapter 36

Tony closed the car door and began the short walk to Starbucks. He felt a sense of lightness and freedom that he'd not experienced in a long time. The black cloud that had persistently dogged him was gone.

As much as he needed to focus on his upcoming meeting with Bobby, yesterday afternoon continued to dominate his thoughts. His time with Julie, slowly exploring her body with growing excitement and abandon, had both exhausted and invigorated him. Afterwards, still in bed and sharing the last of the Pinot, had seemed both natural and disorienting at the same time.

Pushing open the coffee shop door, he looked around for Bobby but there was no sign of her yet. As he got in line to place his order, he took in the smell of freshly ground coffee and the loud chatter of people at tables. Once he'd picked up his espresso, he wandered outside to the patio to sit in the sun and watch for Bobby. As a steady stream of people came and went, he replayed his early morning conversation with Drake Fields.

While he was standing in front of the mirror, shaving, he'd realized his lawyer was still in the dark about his plans to settle the lawsuit. He called Drake just after 8:30 and related the sequence of events leading to the decision. Drake expressed concern about Tony being prepared to settle "for such a meager amount." Tony had explained that monetary considerations were secondary to his desire to stay connected with the Sumner investigation. He also told Drake that he was prepared to share a higher percentage of the settlement amount to make sure his lawyer was not adversely affected by the decision.

Drake had given a resigned sigh, realizing his client had made up his mind. "The original contingency fee arrangement is satisfactory. Send over the settlement papers once they've been executed by both parties." He promised to work with Lou Driller to finalize all the arrangements and have the settlement check delivered to his office.

Drake had concluded by graciously congratulating him on the successful resolution of his legal battle. He'd have to consider adjusting his opinion of lawyers, Tony thought. There were still a few decent ones out there.

He sighted Bobby walking along the sidewalk in his direction and raised his hand to catch her attention. "Beautiful day," he called to her.

She responded without much enthusiasm, "I suppose it is. I'll just grab a latte and be right back."

What's bothering her, he wondered? He had to wait almost five minutes to find out.

She plopped down in her chair. "Sorry, someone took my order by mistake, they had to make me another one."

"No problem. Is everything okay?"

She hesitated before responding. "Life is not without its complications. The chief was able to get an audience with the State Attorney late yesterday afternoon. I'm not sure if you're familiar with Paul Rosen. He was elected last November shortly after you left the department. Started out his legal career as a public defender, apparently a very good one. Before the election, he'd worked his way up to become the U.S. State Attorney for the Eastern District. He's earned a reputation for being very conservative and methodical. He won't bring a big case forward unless he believes his office is going to win."

"Sounds pretty typical to me."

"No, by all accounts he's more conservative than Rush Limbaugh. Anyway, the chief gave him a full report, including the possibility that the senator and someone in the police department might have worked together to frame Mansfield. True to form, Rosen suggested that the chief move with great caution until there's more evidence of Caldwell's guilt."

"Not a real surprise. Even the most aggressive prosecutor wouldn't want to take on a senator without a fully loaded gun."

"I suppose not. The good thing is that Rosen did agree that it's extremely important to find out what Riley has to say. He's prepared to send one of his senior lawyers with the chief to interview Riley and provide immunity from prosecution, if the circumstances justify it. However, he recommended that the chief not actively investigate the senator or his son until they've been able to evaluate what Riley has to say. If Riley's account of events demonstrates there has been any interference with the Sumner investigation, he'll commit the full support of the State Attorney's office to prosecute the matter."

"That last bit's a bunch of crap," Tony said angrily. "Regardless of what Riley has to say, there's clearly enough evidence to put Jonathan Caldwell under the spotlight."

"Yeah, I expressed the same sentiments to the chief. He's in total agreement and isn't going to let Rosen dictate how we run the investigation. However, he does want to proceed slowly until they've had the chance to speak with Riley."

"But when's that going to happen?"

"They've made arrangements to visit Lake County Jail this afternoon. Rosen's also asked that Riley's lawyer be present to ensure he's fully informed of his rights. We don't want him to rely on some technicality to withdraw his statement at a later date. So, in reality we're really only talking about a small delay, assuming Riley hasn't had a sudden memory lapse. However, Rosen raised another issue during their meeting that the chief has had to take more seriously."

Something in her look told Tony this meant trouble for him. "What's that?" he asked with some trepidation.

"The chief thought he should let Rosen know about your engagement as a consultant on the investigation. Simply put, Rosen wasn't in favor. He said that if the senator is dirty and we go after him, he'll end up hiring the best legal team in the state. They'll review every aspect of the police investigation with a fine-tooth comb. If there's anything out of the ordinary, they'll try to make that the focal point of the trial. He thought your participation could put a cloud of doubt over the objectivity of the police investigation. They could make it look like you were pursuing some sort of personal vendetta against the senator for his alleged involvement in your dismissal. He strongly urged the chief to withdraw the deal he's worked out with you."

"I'm beginning to take a real dislike to this guy." Tony felt his blood pressure rise. "What's the chief's position on all of this?"

"He told Rosen that he'd consider his views on this matter. He then came back and updated me on the meeting. He felt there was some merit in the concerns expressed by Rosen, but he also agrees that your experience and history with the case can't be matched by anyone else in the department. Eventually we hammered out a compromise arrangement that he thinks will address Rosen's concerns while allowing us to benefit from your expertise. The chief asked me to review the proposal with you."

"Lay it out for me," Tony said tersely.

"The actual police work – talking to witnesses, interviewing suspects, processing and handling evidence – will be left to me and others in the department, including the chief. You'll work behind the scenes on the investigation strategy and tactical operations and provide me with guidance and advice. It still allows you to play a significant role...." Bobby' voice trailed off, seeing the look of disappointment on Tony's face.

He sat for a while without responding, feeling like a cornered animal. "A significant role?" he finally repeated. "You've got to be kidding. It sounds like I'm being asked to contribute to the investigation with both hands tied behind my back and a sock stuffed in my mouth."

"Come on, it's not that bad. You don't need to be front and center to make this work. Think of yourself as a football coach calling in the plays. You'll help define the game plan and see everything as it develops on the field."

Tony was somewhat mollified by her description of his role. "Okay, I understand where the chief and Rosen are coming from, and I certainly don't want to be the poster boy for the senator's defense team. But they're asking me to take a big hit on my lawsuit, and now they want to neuter my role on the investigation. That doesn't feel right to me. But then again, I don't want to be hearing about Caldwell's arrest on the six o'clock news. So, for the moment, I'm prepared to play it this way. However, I'm going to fight like hell to be at your side for the final arrest."

Bobby met his determined gaze. "And I'll also be fighting to make this happen. You deserve that action." The sincerity in her voice helped take the edge off his disappointment. "If that's settled, let's take care of the paperwork." She retrieved a manila envelope from her leather portfolio. "This is the agreement we discussed yesterday, in duplicate. Dupree already signed off on it."

Tony opened the envelope and pulled out two documents, quickly reviewing them. "Got a pen?"

She handed one to him and he signed and dated each copy. He kept one and handed the other back to Bobby. "Okay, we're all official," he said, still feeling a nagging doubt with the change in arrangements.

"Welcome back, partner." Bobby held out her hand and Tony shook it.

So he was back on the case. He was suddenly struck by the enormity of their task. They had to solve a cold case where the main suspect was under the protection of a powerful senator. No doubt there were others within the department protecting his flank. They had their work cut out for them.

"I've already started some wheels in motion," Bobby was saying. "Rosen has allowed us to set up the command center in one of their meeting rooms to avoid prying eyes over at the Police Department. All the Sumner evidence boxes should be safely over there by now. My friend in the Evidence Room has agreed to let me know if he receives any inquiries on the Sumner case. The last thing we want is for Adelsky to find out all the boxes have been removed."

"That does raise an interesting point. How are you and Dupree going to handle Adelsky if he gets wind of the investigation being reopened without his approval or involvement? Something could easily get back to him, particularly once you start talking to witnesses."

"I have to admit, we really haven't had a chance to think about that. Any suggestions?"

"What you need is a plausible explanation." He thought for a moment. "I have an idea, but it would need the support of Sumner's parents ... and possibly her former roommate."

"Tell me."

"You could, uh, use the story that Sumner had a boyfriend in high school who got a bit nasty after they broke up. Let's say that Sumner's parents learned he's gotten into more trouble with another ex-girlfriend and they thought this was worth reporting to Chief Dupree. The chief could take Adelsky aside and indicate the parents are likely grasping at straws and he doesn't want to tie up his top homicide detective looking into this. He could indicate that with the Harding investigation losing momentum, you have time to show the boyfriend's picture around to some people who were in the bar the night Sumner disappeared. This cover story would also explain why both you and the chief talked to Riley, if that somehow gets back to Adelsky."

Bobby mulled it over. "That could work. It would mean that I wouldn't have to tiptoe around him. Let me speak to the chief and see if he has any concerns. We'd need to finesse this with the parents."

"I'm sure they'll be supportive if they know there's a chance of catching their daughter's killer. Now, how else can I help?" Tony asked.

"There are all those evidence boxes to go through. Soon as we're finished here, why don't we head over and take a fresh look at the files – see if we can find anything that supports the case against Jonathan Caldwell. In the files there should also be a report containing the driver's license information for all the people who were in the bar that evening. I want to track down Caldwell's friends and set up some interviews. I could use your story that we want them to look at some photos and see if they can identify a person we have an interest in."

"Sounds like a plan. And while we're on the topic of driver's licenses, have you had a chance to pull the DMV and licensing records for Caldwell Jr. and the senator?"

"I had someone do that for me this morning." Bobby pulled a computer printout from her portfolio. "The search goes back two years. It appears that Caldwell Jr. is licensed but hasn't owned a car in over a year. This may relate to the fact that he totaled his Corvette last summer. Coupled with several prior speeding tickets, it probably put his insurance premiums out of sight. So if he was driving that night, he was probably using one of his parents' vehicles. His bar buddies should be able to tell us."

"What do the senator and his wife drive?"

"Mom has a nice little convertible, a Mercedes SLK. Dad owns a fairly new BMW 7 series."

"How long has the senator owned his car?"

Bobby reviewed the printout in more detail. "It looks like he picked it up in August of last year. Probably one of the first off this year's production line."

"That's good news. I was afraid he might not still own the car that he was driving last September."

"There is one other thing I did this morning while I was in the office." Bobby passed over another sheet of paper. On it were a number of pictures of Senator Caldwell taken at various government functions. Each picture had a short paragraph underneath or beside it. One picture showed a slightly younger senator seated between a stern looking woman and a teen-aged boy who Tony recognized as Jonathan Caldwell.

"It's all taken from the Senator's webpage, with his biographical information," Bobby explained. "Check the text I highlighted."

Tony found the appropriate passage and started reading out loud. "The Senator has been married for over thirty-five years to Connie, and they have one son. Senator Caldwell is a third-generation resident of Wisconsin, his great-grandfather immigrating to the United States from Glasgow in the early 1880s. His son, Jonathan, is currently attending the University of Wisconsin where he plays for the Wisconsin Badgers football team. Although Robbie Caldwell is a proud American and Wisconsin native, he remembers his Scottish heritage and the need to work hard and be fiscally conservative...."

Tony stopped reading and looked at Bobby. "This confirms Jonathan Caldwell's attendance at the U of W, as well as his being a possible DNA match. You've saved us a lot of time in researching their family tree. And it's another indication we're on the right track."

Chapter 37

They checked in with security at the State Capitol building. After confirming their identification, an older security guard with a slight stoop escorted them to a conference room in the State Attorney's offices. He unlocked the door and gave Bobby the key. The room was furnished with a long table, leather chairs neatly positioned around it. The room had a conference phone, as well as an overhead projector unit and a retractable video screen. Displayed on the walls were pictures of distinguished-looking men in dark suits, who Tony figured had at one time headed up the State Attorney's office.

Seeing the file boxes neatly stacked in one corner, he went over to take a look. The boxes were numbered consecutively and dated, with "Karen Sumner – Dec'd" written in bold letters underneath. On the walk over from Starbucks, they'd agreed on their approach for reviewing the files. Bobby would go through all those relating to Sumner's disappearance and their initial investigation. Tony would go through the investigation files after Adelsky took over, looking for signs of any cover-up plot. Bobby reminded Tony not to handle any physical evidence collected during the investigation.

He set three boxes beside Bobby's chair, and then moved the rest to the opposite side of the table where he planned to sit. While he was playing moving man, Bobby phoned the receptionist to make arrangements for lunch. They took their seats and started to pull files out of their respective boxes.

The first file folder Tony opened was a report prepared by an Officer Stephens. He recalled that Stephens was the officer he'd sent over to Mansfield's apartment after he'd tried to contact him in the middle of the night. Stephens had reported him missing, setting off a fruitless manhunt to locate and arrest Mansfield.

The next file had been prepared by Adelsky. His notes detailed the results of the search of Mansfield's apartment. A shoebox of pornographic pictures had been found in a hall closet. A search of his computer hard drive disclosed that he was a frequent surfer of websites containing photographs and videos of young girls engaged in various sexual acts. The police really hit pay dirt when an officer was directed to search the trash bins outside the apartment building. Close to the top of one bin was a white plastic bag of women's clothing, later identified as belonging to Karen Sumner. For Adelsky, this was all the proof he needed to focus his efforts and police resources solely on capturing Mansfield. He didn't question why Mansfield, who appeared to be relatively intelligent, would leave such incriminating evidence so close to home.

Tony moved quickly through the next two files, which sum-marized the steps Adelsky had taken to locate the missing suspect. There were notes of interviews with Mansfield's family and neigh-bors. Another file contained documentation relating to a state-wide APB issued for Mansfield's 2003 Pontiac Grand AM. Yet another file was stuffed with arrest notices that had been provided to police departments and law enforcement agencies in nearby states. The file notations became less frequent as the weeks and then months passed by without Adelsky locating his prey. What he didn't know was that Mansfield would never be found – alive, that is.

After an hour of reading files in silence, they were interrupted by a knock. Tony looked up, rubbing his eyes. Like a cat, Bobby stretched her long body and got up to see who was at the door. She was greeted by a young man carrying two cups of coffee and a large white paper bag. Bringing everything over to the table she unpacked two sandwiches, chocolate chip cookies, a banana and an apple. "Take whatever sandwich you want."

Tony took the chicken on brown. "Discover anything of interest?" He popped the lid off his coffee.

"A couple of things. I've located the list of driver's license information scanned at the bar entrance on the night Sumner disappeared. From that I've been able to get the names, license numbers and addresses of Caldwell's friends. I was just going through our interview notes with the staff at the Capital Lounge when lunch arrived. You'll get a kick out of this, Tony – here's your description of Riley's interview." She picked up the file and started to read it. "'Subject interviewee appears jumpy and nervous. Might not make a reliable witness if required to identify Mansfield in court.' Now we know why. How's your review going?"

"So far I haven't found anything that would suggest Adelsky was involved in anything sinister. In fact, I'd give him a passing grade in his attempts to find Mansfield. I can't fault that part of the investigation. However, there's no indication he considered the possibility that somebody else could've been Sumner's killer. In addition to his failing to review the bar security video or follow up with the additional DNA testing, there's no record of the forensic examination of Mansfield's apartment. It either wasn't completed or the report has gone missing."

"Which raises the same old question – was Adelsky merely inept, or was he an active participant in a bigger plan to hide the identity of the real killer?"

"Exactly. Hopefully we'll have a more complete perspective on this by the time I'm done." Tony lifted another box onto the table. When he saw its contents, he stepped back in surprise. "Bobby, you should take a look at this!"

Bobby came and peered into the box. She started to pull out a number of sealed plastic evidence bags, which she carefully laid on the table. Each bag contained a separate piece of woman's clothing: a pair of black high-heeled shoes, designer jeans, short-sleeved blue cotton top, bra, and panties. The final item she placed on the table was an envelope marked "State Crime Lab."

The box emptied, she looked at Tony. "I believe this is the only physical evidence that was handled by her killer. Maybe you'll find something in the forensics analysis report of the clothing that others missed." She handed him the report and returned the evidence to the box.

Tony began reading the lab report on Sumner's clothing. The first thing that drew his attention was the analysis on the jeans and cotton top. The report concluded that the blood splatter on Sumner's clothing was consistent with her falling on her back immediately after receiving a violent blow to the rear of her head.

This was puzzling. If the killer had struck a blow to the *back* of her head, she would most certainly have fallen forward. Even if she was quickly flipped onto her back before being raped, there should have been blood traces on the front of her blouse. However, the report clearly indicated otherwise. Tony tried to visualize different scenarios involving Sumner and her killer. "Huh," he said, and Bobby looked up from her reading.

"Sorry," he apologized, "I just figured something out. Tell you later."

He was now pretty sure that whatever object had killed Sumner had not been wielded by her attacker. She must have fallen or been knocked backwards, hitting her head on a sharp object when she landed. This was the only plausible explanation for the blood-splatter pattern noted in the report.

He continued with his review. The report indicated that, while Sumner's jeans and blouse were heavily soiled, they had no trace of the brackish mud from the marsh. The simple explanation was that her clothing had been removed *before* her body was dragged into the marshy area. However, soil samples found on her clothing were consistent with those taken in the park area, supporting the conclusion that this was where she'd been raped and killed.

On the final page of the report he discovered what he considered to be the most revealing information. The lab tech had detected what was referred to as 'black trilobal fibers" on both the jeans and blouse. The State Lab's database indicated these fibers were made of a synthetic polymer frequently used in the manufacture of high-grade automobile carpeting.

The report also noted that small strands of a reddish woolen fiber were found on the cotton blouse. Unfortunately, the Crime Lab wasn't able to narrow down any specific common usage for this fiber, which apparently had many commercial and non-commercial applications. The report did, however, indicate that the dye-lot color would be an identifier. In other words, the dye lot could be of assistance in determining if a specific item was the source of those fibers.

Considering this information and what else he knew about the case, Tony chuckled.

Bobby looked up again. "What now?"

He handed the report to her, opened to the final two pages. He studied her face as she read, noting her eyebrows arch as she reached the description of the foreign fibers.

"Her clothes must've been put in the trunk of a car," she said. "That would explain the black fibers. We'll need to get a search warrant for the Senator's BMW."

Tony nodded, pleased she'd picked up on this. "Right on. But we shouldn't move too fast. We likely don't have a strong enough link to convince a judge, although we should have that soon enough."

"What about the reddish wool fibers? The lab wasn't able to identify the source."

"Think back to the last scene we saw on the bar security video. Then you'll see the connection."

Bobby closed her eyes, trying to visualize the final sequence in the video. Her eyes still shut, she said, "Caldwell was wearing a Wisconsin football jacket that night. Dark leather with red arms."

"It's known as a melton and leather jacket. I'll bet my badge that wool is used in the production of melton."

"Very funny. Now the big question: you think Caldwell still has the jacket?"

"If he's like any other football jock, the jacket might be put away, but it'll never be thrown away."

"Then we also need to get a search warrant for that jacket."

"Absolutely. And while you're looking, you should also keep an eye out for some other items. The night Sumner disappeared; she was carrying a blue clutch purse and wearing a sports watch with a silver band. Those weren't among the items discovered in the garbage bin. There's a chance Caldwell might've been kept them."

"He'd have to be pretty dumb." Bobby made a note on a pad of paper.

"Looks like I've gotten through all my boxes. I take it we're on hold with everything else until we hear back from the chief?"

"Yes, I guess that's right," Bobby replied with some frustration.

"I'm going to head home. I should be there until about six. Can you give me a call if you hear from the chief before then?"

"Sure. I'm going to stay a while longer and also take a look at those files from Adelsky's investigation. I want to make sure I'm totally up to speed on everything."

Chapter 38

The chief and Bobby were seated at the conference table deep in conversation when Tony arrived. He was perspiring and his heart was pounding from the sprint up the Capitol Building stairs in response to the urgent request for a meeting.

Chief Dupree stood up to shake his hand. Tony hadn't seen the chief since last fall, and his impression was that the intervening months had not been kind to him. The chief's posture was slightly stooped, his short dark curly hair had gone salt and pepper grey, and deep wrinkles were etched in his forehead. However, his eyes still had that intelligent twinkle.

His grip was strong and firm. "Tony, good to see you. It's been too long."

It was the first time Tony could remember the chief addressing him by his first name. For some reason it touched him. "Yes, it's been difficult to stay in touch, given the circumstances."

Dupree gave his hand another firm squeeze. "Personally, I'd like to turn the page on that chapter and hopefully we have time to write the rest of the book. Or perhaps rewrite it."

"That would suit me fine."

"Meanwhile, we've some pressing things to worry about. While we were waiting for you to arrive, Detective Andrade started to tell me about your morning's activities. I understand you've found new information in your review of the evidence boxes."

"That's right. I'll let Detective Andrade continue to fill you in." Tony felt a bit odd referring to Bobby by her formal title, but he knew this was the way the chief liked to do things.

Bobby started with a brief overview of the forensic analysis of Sumner's clothing. "The Crime Lab found two different types of fibers on the blouse and jeans." She gave the chief their theory on where these fibers might have come from. As she talked, Tony watched the chief's face for a reaction. He saw Dupree's eyes narrow and his features tighten as Bobby finished.

"This investigation has been an absolute disgrace," he growled. "Adelsky has a lot to account for here. Is there anything else?"

"Yes, we uncovered several other items of interest. I checked the senator's website and learned that his son went to U of W, where he played some football. That would account for the jacket he was wearing the night Sumner was murdered. It might also explain why she was taken to Picnic Point Park, which is near the university. The senator's website says that his great grandfather came from Scotland, so Caldwell Jr. could fit the genetic profile created from the new DNA testing. And finally, I've been able to identify the three friends who accompanied Caldwell to the bar that evening and complete preliminary background checks. They all come from prominent Madison families. Two of them have just completed their third year at the U of W and currently live at home with their parents. It looks like the other friend is no longer living in Wisconsin. I haven't had a chance to track down his current location. That's about it. Tony, anything else to add?"

"Yes, one other item. I haven't had a chance to discuss this with Detective Andrade, and I'm still not sure of its significance. As you may recall, Sumner suffered massive trauma to the back of her head, subsequently bleeding to death. With nothing else to go on, we were operating under the assumption that the killer came up behind her and delivered the killing blow. We were never sure if the rape occurred before or after this."

"Yes, the wound site was compromised as a result of the body being dragged along the ground, as well as by extended exposure to the elements," Bobby explained. "It made it impossible for the ME to identify what caused the blow to the head."

Tony nodded in agreement. "Now, the forensics report for her clothing, which we only saw for the first time today, noted that the blood from the head wound formed a pooled pattern on the back of her blouse. There was little evidence of blood splatters on the front of her clothes. This would suggest she was prone and on her back when the blow to the head occurred. What I think happened is that she either fell or was pulled to the ground and her head struck a sharp object, perhaps a rock."

"Interesting. But given the circumstances, does it really matter?" Bobby asked.

"Maybe, maybe not. But having a complete understanding of the events surrounding the crime is important. You never know when it might come in handy. Chief, I think you now have everything from today's activities. I'm interested to hear how your meeting with Riley went."

Dupree nodded, knowing Tony and Bobby had been waiting patiently for his news. "First, let me get something." He bent to retrieve some notes from his briefcase, then fumbled in a jacket pocket and pulled out wire-rimmed reading glasses. Slowly he looped them over his ears and settled them on his nose. Scanning the papers in front of him, he started to read in a deep voice, as if testifying before a jury.

"At approximately two pm on May 22, 2010, I attended a meeting with Wes Scott from the State Attorney's office, Matt Riley, and his lawyer, Lucas Gibson. This meeting took place at the Lake County State Prison in Crown Point, Illinois. The purpose of this meeting was to obtain clarification of certain statements Mr. Riley made to police during the investigation into the death of one Karen Sumner. We were prepared, if necessary, in return for Mr. Riley's cooperation, to provide him with immunity from prosecution in the State of Wisconsin for any actions he may have taken to impede that investigation."

The chief removed his reading glasses and winked at Tony.

"Sorry, I just wanted to practice that for when I get called as a witness for the prosecution. But I'm getting ahead of myself. It was indeed an illuminating session with Riley. After some preliminary skirmishing with his lawyer, who insisted we call him "Gibby," we got down to business. Mr. Scott gave assurances that the State Attorney's Office was prepared to grant Riley's request for immunity if he would identify the person who, in effect, recruited him to provide false information to the police. Gibson then asked Riley to provide his version of events. He confirmed that he never saw Mansfield outside the bar the night Ms. Sumner was murdered. However, within a day of her body being discovered, he received a call at home. The caller told Riley he had an important matter to discuss with him relating to her death."

"And I bet that caller was Adelksy." Tony interjected.

The chief slowly shook his head. "No ... it was Jim Bradley."

"Bradley!" Bobby exclaimed.

Tony said nothing, stunned by the news. However, it didn't take him long to adjust his thinking to this new reality. It was certainly plausible that the coroner was the inside man. For starters, the senator had supported Bradley in getting elected as coroner. Tony also noticed that Bradley had become very friendly with Adelsky during the murder investigation. The connection with Adelsky and his role as coroner would have given him full access to the inner workings of the Sumner investigation. Yes, Bradley was in the perfect position to manipulate the investigation and support the senator in his plan to get him removed from the case. And now it was payback time, he thought.

"That's right," the chief continued, "our good friend the coroner. He suggested they get together, and Riley didn't think it would be wise to say no. They met at a coffee shop near Riley's apartment. During their meeting, Riley was told the police had a good lead on Sumner's killer, one Curtis Mansfield. Bradley described the killer as a sadistic sexual predator with a long criminal record. He also indicated the police already had circumstantial evidence implicating Mansfield, but an eye-witness identification by someone at the bar that night would be extremely helpful to their case. Riley claims he told the coroner that he didn't want to get involved. It was at that point that he learned about the $50,000 reward being offered by the parents. This got his attention, and he asked what he was expected to do. It turned out to be quite simple. In the next few days the investigating officers would be talking to the bar staff and showing them some pictures. All he had to do was pick out Curtis Mansfield and tell the investigators that he was outside the bar that night."

"Wasn't Riley suspicious about all this?" Tony asked.

"He claims to have expressed concerns about what would happen if he was caught lying. Bradley then brought out his ace in the hole. Apparently Riley had been pulled over for a DUI a month earlier, on a drinking binge after being dumped by a girlfriend. If convicted, he could have lost his driver's license, and without any means of transportation, he'd probably lose his job. Bradley told him he could make the charges go away – a present from the police for his assistance. That apparently sealed the deal. He was then shown a picture of Mansfield and told to keep his mouth shut about their conversation – the investigating officers wouldn't be aware of this arrangement."

"And was that the only time he spoke to Bradley?" Tony asked.

"That's what he said."

'Were there any witnesses to their conversation?" Bobby followed up.

"Riley doesn't think so. There was lots of transient traffic in the coffee bar."

"Then Bradley can deny the whole thing ever happened." She frowned.

"He'd need to have a pretty good explanation for two things. First of all, there's this." Dupree slid a plastic bag from underneath his notes and placed it on the table. Inside was a manila envelope.

"I'll bite. What's in the envelope?" Tony asked.

"It contains a police mug shot of Curtis Mansfield. It was given to Riley so he could refresh his memory before meeting with the two of you. He held onto the picture as a memento, and it was still in a suitcase in his car. After our meeting I went over to the police impound center at Crown Point and retrieved it. This gives credibility to Riley's story, but more importantly, I'm hoping we can lift some fingerprints off the picture or envelope."

"This is a lucky break. Now, you mentioned there was something else that Bradley would need to explain?" Tony asked.

"Yes. On the way back from Crown Point I got on my phone and looked into the status of Riley's drunk-driving charge. I learned it was withdrawn approximately eight months ago. I was able to track down the officer who had pulled Riley over and asked him point blank what happened to the case. He vaguely recalls getting a message from the prosecutors' office saying they'd dropped it due to a technical deficiency. He was told they planned to re-file the charge, but this apparently didn't happen and he'd forgotten all about it. That's as much as I've been able to find out so far. However, there's little doubt in my mind that Bradley made the DUI charge disappear. A little more digging and we should be able to prove it."

"And if you do, down goes Bradley. Hopefully the senator too," Tony said with satisfaction.

"Yes, with any luck. Now let's talk next steps. Detective Andrade, how do you plan to proceed?"

Bobby hesitated for a moment. "I don't think we're quite ready to make a move on Caldwell. So, the next step would be to bring his friends in for questioning." She glanced over at Tony.

"I agree," he said. "Caldwell's buddies can confirm if he was driving that night and where he was planning to go after he left the bar. It would also be interesting to know if they've gotten back together since his discharge from the army. He might've said something to them that would be helpful to our case. Once we have this additional background information, we'll be ready to have a talk with Caldwell."

"And what should be done about the coroner?" the chief asked.

Bobby didn't hesitate on this one. "Let's continue to build our case. I'll send Mansfield's photo and the envelope for fingerprinting. We should hold off any further checking into the dismissed DUI charge – it could get back to him. I don't want Bradley alerted to the fact that his house of cards is about to collapse. We want to hold on to the element of surprise."

Tony nodded in approval; Bobby's instincts were good. He added, "Without making this into a witch hunt, we shouldn't discount the possibility that Adelsky was also recruited for the senator's team. He could've been working in concert with Bradley to make Mansfield the fall guy."

"Agreed," said Bobby.

Dupree packed up his briefcase. Okay, I'll update the State Attorney and tell him we're cautiously moving forward in the investigation of Jonathan Caldwell. Detective Andrade, as discussed, proceed with contacting Caldwell's friends for questioning. You'll need to go solo on this – any involvement on my part will raise eyebrows. If anyone asks what you're up to, I'll explain that you're merely following up on the lead relating to Ms. Sumner's old boyfriend. After you're done with Caldwell's friends, let's arrange to get back together. We can discuss what you've learned, and determine our next steps."

Chapter 39
MAY 23 7:45 AM

Silence enveloped Tony once he turned off the motor, with the boat bobbing up and down in the swells. He was several hundred yards offshore in one of his favorite fishing spots. He picked up his rod and cast. The lure hit the water, and he pictured it slowly twirling down to the sandy bottom where the fish should be feeding.

It was still relatively early, and the sun had just started to peek over the trees bordering the eastern shoreline. A cool breeze from the north cut through his windbreaker. He took a sip of steaming coffee from his travel mug and reflected on his shortened visit with Julie after work last night. She'd insisted he come over even though she was in the thick of studying. When he arrived, she was a bit punch drunk from lack of sleep and worrying about her exam. They snuggled together on the couch and talked about their respective days. Within fifteen minutes she was out like a light. He gently picked her up and carried her bed, then left a note on the kitchen table saying he'd call her today. After that he slipped out of the apartment and went home to his own bed.

Despite the cool weather, it felt pretty good to be out on the water again. His thoughts drifted back to the last time he'd been in his boat, somewhat surprised to discover that it was just a little over a week since his frigid dive to the bottom of the lake. What he'd discovered in the depths had set off a chain reaction of events that were still in motion.

He felt a pang of guilt, recognizing he was spending less and less time in search for Harding's killer. Truth was, he'd become consumed by the Sumner investigation. But in his defense, it didn't help that every promising lead in Harding's case had petered out into a dead end.

He checked off the facts that had been gathered so far. By day it appeared that Harding was an ambitious, hard-driving attorney who put in long hours at work. However, in her private life she seemed to exhibit a split personality reflected in the use of drugs and sexual experimentation. On the night of her death she'd taken her mother's car and travelled to Madison, where she met with someone who ultimately strangled her to death. Her body was then wrapped in a shower curtain and dumped in the lake. The killer drove Harding's car back to her parents' home in Chicago. His image had been picked up by tollbooth video cameras, but the only solid piece of identification was a Minnesota Twins baseball cap.

Something nibbled on the lure and pulled at his line. There was no pressure in response. False alarm, he thought. He continued with his review of the facts. Harding had only three known connections to Madison. The first related to her speaking at a conference attended by several members of the Madison police department earlier in the year. More recently, she'd been contacted by Bobby with her concerns about the Sumner investigation, which ultimately led to Harding having the additional DNA testing completed. Finally, there was the hostile email exchange between Adelsky and Harding the week before she was murdered. Tony then mentally kicked himself: he'd almost forgotten the St. Christopher medal. But again, it was a piece of evidence that apparently led nowhere.

As he moved the pieces around like a Rubik's Cube, he saw only one possible recurring connection. Adelsky had been at the conference where Harding spoke, he knew about her involvement in ordering the additional DNA analysis, and he initiated the email exchange with her. Could the "R" on the medallion stand for "Rick"? It was more than a rumor that Adelsky was a serious womanizer – his marriage had failed as a result of it. Harding was single and attractive. Was it possible the two of them had hooked up during the conference?

Tony continued to weave his theory. Perhaps they had a nasty breakup with the arrival of Daniel Jayman in Harding's life. Or maybe Adelsky ditched her for some local talent. Months went by, and all of a sudden Harding was handed the golden opportunity to make Adelsky look bad by ordering the DNA tests behind his back. He learned she'd helped turn up new evidence that put his career at risk.

Based on Drake's football story, it was clear that Adelsky didn't take kindly to being made to look bad. In fact, his natural reaction would be to get even. Maybe he enticed Harding to Madison on some pretext, where he confronted her. They had a violent argument that ended in her death. He then attempted to cover it up by dumping her body in the lake and driving her car back to Chicago. When by chance her body was discovered, Adelsky used his connections with the senator to assume control of the investigation and ensure his tracks were covered.

Tony shook his head in frustration. There wasn't a shred of evidence to support any of this. He couldn't tell if he was on the right track or just wasting his time with anger-fueled fantasies. Even worse, he realized, the police were running out of options and time on the case. Soon the FBI would be called in and take charge. Perhaps that was for the best thing for the investigation … and for him. But he wouldn't give up quite yet.

At that moment he felt another small tug on his fishing rod. He let the line play out and felt a stronger pull. Waiting another moment, he gave his rod a sharp upward yank. The pole bent in response and he leaned back to avoid being pulled out of his seat. The force on the line was now so strong that the boat began to strain against its anchor. Tony smiled in triumph – he'd finally hooked a big one.

The battle lasted more than twenty minutes. He had to continuously let out the line and reel it back in, until both he and the battling fish were close to exhaustion. The tug of war finally ended and he used his net to scoop up an enormous Northern Pike. It thrashed away in the bottom of the boat, its mouth opening and closing, gasping. He managed to keep its head down long enough to remove his lure. With great care he maneuvered it over the side and back into the cool water.

The pike stayed near the surface, taking a moment to regain its bearings. Then, with a splash of its tail, it plunged back down into the depths. It'd been a close call, but it had lived to fight another day.

Tony vowed that those involved in the deaths of Karen Sumner and Jennifer Harding wouldn't be so lucky.

By the time he returned to the cottage, he was shivering in the sweaty clothes that clung to his body. A hot shower was in order. Fifteen minutes later, the chill washed away, he dressed and picked up the Grisham book on the bedside table. He took up a spot on the couch in the living room and Sam jumped up beside him. In short order his eyes grew heavy, and a moment later the book fell into his lap.

Chapter 40

Tony was roused out of a formless dream by the ringing of a telephone. For a moment he was disoriented, not sure where he was. Then he saw Sam standing on the couch beside him, giving him an annoyed look at this interruption. He pushed himself up and walked into the kitchen.

Thinking it might be Julie, he picked up the phone, and said hello, feeling a raspy pain in his throat.

"Tony, you sound like hell." It was Bobby.

"Sorry. I passed out on my couch and you woke me up. My throat's burning. I caught a chill on the lake earlier this morning, I guess. What time is it anyway?"

"Almost 11:30. While you were getting your beauty rest, I was having interviews with two of Caldwell's friends, Robert Holmes and Sterling Everett. They were able to help me with a few more pieces of the puzzle."

"What'd they have to say?"

"I'll give you the highlights, but the chief wants to get back together with us as soon as possible. Can you be here in half an hour?"

"Sure, just need to put on some makeup. Now tell me, what've you learned?"

DRIVING DOWNTOWN, Tony went over what Bobby had relayed to him about her morning interviews. Despite the passage of time, Holmes and Everett had provided very similar accounts of their evening with Caldwell.

Bobby had learned that Caldwell had organized the pub crawl to mark his last night as a civilian before heading off to boot camp.

Everett thought that enlisting was part of some deal Caldwell had been forced to make with his father. He was very unhappy at the prospect of heading overseas to take part in the fight against terrorism.

The evening had started at Caldwell's house around 7:30 where they had some beers before heading out. Both friends confirmed that Caldwell had borrowed his father's BMW and was acting as chauffeur for the evening.

At the Capital Lounge they had more beers before checking out the dance floor. Holmes indicated that they were all having a good time until Caldwell struck out with a girl and decided to bolster himself with more alcohol. Everett commented that this was not a good move, as Caldwell had a tendency to become increasingly obnoxious the more he drank. This of course made it even more difficult for him to find a dance partner for the evening.

Both young men noted that not long into the evening their friend's drunken behavior caught the attention of bar management. Caldwell was cut off, and at that point he suggested they head to the next bar down the street. However, by then his friends were deep in conversation with a table of girls. Everett had suggested that Caldwell lead the way, and they'd catch up with him once they'd convinced their new companions to join them.

At that point Bobby had asked if they recalled meeting Karen Sumner that evening. She provided them with the young woman's picture to refresh their memories, but neither remembered her. Bobby then showed them pictures of several young men from the police files, sticking to the prearranged story that one of them was a person of interest in Sumner's death. Again, this drew negative responses.

She followed up by asking if they had reconnected with Caldwell that evening. Everett told her they'd been unsuccessful in convincing the girls to accompany them to another bar, so they decided to catch up with Caldwell. Their next agreed-upon stop was the

Stiletto Bar, a short distance from the Capital Lounge. When they arrived, Caldwell was nowhere to be found. Holmes had tried his cell phone but it went to voice mail. At the Stiletto they bumped into some other friends, but no one recalled seeing Caldwell. Everett figured Caldwell must have hooked up with someone after leaving the bar. Holmes thought he'd gone home to sober up before reporting for duty the following day.

Bobby also asked if they'd kept in touch with Caldwell since he entered training camp. They both indicated Caldwell had been given an early discharge for "health reasons" and was back in Madison. Holmes had seen Caldwell several times since his return and said that he seemed distant and aloof. He thought the experience overseas had changed him. Tony suspected it was more likely the sequence of events following Caldwell's departure from the Capital Lounge that evening.

Tony was nearing the State Capitol building now and pulled into a parking spot on a side street. He still felt a bit groggy and his energy level was low. No doubt it was the effects of the two cold pills he'd gulped down before leaving the cottage. At least his throat felt a bit better.

He made his way up the wide granite steps to the doors of the East State Capitol wing. After checking in at the security desk, he was cleared to go up to the conference room. The door was closed and he decided to knock. Chief Dupree opened it, looking more like his old self, his back straight and his bearing purposeful. "Tony, good. Come on in."

Bobby and a distinguished-looking man were seated at the table. The man appeared to be in his mid-fifties and looked vaguely familiar – jet black hair, a sharp nose, and hawkish grey eyes. He was wearing a dark grey power suit with a red tie, and his whole demeanor exuded energy and confidence.

The chief made introductions. "Tony, this is the State Attorney, Paul Rosen. He wanted to join us for part of our meeting.

Unfortunately, he's on a tight schedule and needs to leave in about ten minutes."

Rosen stood and leaned in Tony's direction, hand extended. Rosen was slightly taller and heavier than Tony, but clearly in good shape. "Tony, nice to finally meet you in person. Thanks for joining us on short notice." His slightly baritone voice probably played well in a courtroom.

Tony shook Rosen's hand, a tight smile on his face. "It's good to meet you as well. I certainly appreciate your support for my ongoing involvement in the investigation." He wanted to convey that he was fully aware Rosen had attempted to block his role on the case. He looked directly into Rosen's eyes, enjoying the slight discomfort he saw there.

Rosen dropped his hand. "Yes, well, let's get going. We have some important strategic decisions to make. Chief, why don't you start it off?"

Tony took a seat while the chief remained standing. He leaned forward, his large dark hands on the conference table, surveying the three faces looking back at him. "Here's a quick update for Tony's benefit. Forensics did a rush on the two items that were in Mr. Riley's possession. The envelope yielded a number of smudged prints, and unfortunately it was impossible to get a match. The picture, however, was a different story – it revealed three different sets of identifiable prints. With the assistance of our friends at the Lake County Jail, we've been able to confirm that one set belongs to Riley. Another set isn't in the system, but I asked one of my officers to pay a visit to the Coroner's Office early this morning to discuss a case with Mr. Bradley. They had coffee together, and Mr. Bradley's cup ended up in our possession. It was sent directly to the State Crime Lab, and the report came back about an hour ago. A positive match." The chief allowed himself a smile.

"And the third set of prints?" Tony asked.

"They were also in the system. They belong to Detective Adelsky. However, let's not leap to any conclusions."

Tony considered this information. Adelsky had provided him with pictures of known sexual offenders in the Madison area when they first started investigating Sumner's death. It now appears he also supplied Bradley with a copy of Mansfield's photo. Things were not looking good for Adelsky, he noted with satisfaction.

The chief continued to talk. "The other development is that Detective Andrade was able to interview two of the three gentlemen who accompanied Mr. Caldwell to the bar the evening that Ms. Sumner was killed. She obtained additional information that continues to support our theory that Caldwell Jr. is the killer. Detective, could you briefly review the highlights of those conversations."

Bobby recounted what she'd learned from her meetings with Holmes and Everett, information Tony was already aware of from their conversation just a short while before. She also advised them that Jonathan Caldwell was no longer living at home with the Senator and his wife. Instead, he'd taken up residence in an expensive condo in a new downtown development.

After she'd finished, Rosen spoke. "First of all, good work, everyone. As you indicated, Chief, all signs continue to point toward young Caldwell. Based on this new information, I'm ready to move forward with obtaining search warrants for the senator's home, Bradley's office and home, and Caldwell's apartment. I understand we're looking for Caldwell's football jacket, as well as Sumner's missing purse and other personal items. Is there anything else?"

Bobby stepped in. "Yes, we also want carpet samples from the Senator's BMW. We're hoping they'll match up the fibers found on the Sumner clothing that was recovered."

Rosen nodded. "We'll include that in our request. So, we're in agreement?"

Tony cleared his sore throat. "Actually, I don't think this is the best course of action at the present time." He felt three sets of eyes on him. Bobby and the chief looked puzzled, while Rosen was clearly frowning.

"And why do you say that? Rosen asked impatiently.

"Let's take a step back. We now have a pretty good idea of what went down with Caldwell and Sumner after they left the bar. He somehow convinced her to join him for a ride in Dad's BMW. They went to the park where they had sex and she ended up dead."

Rosen interrupted. "I already understand all of this. Why don't you get to your point? I have another pressing meeting."

Tony felt the blood rush to his face. "Well, one point is that we shouldn't be trying to force a key decision in a nine-month-old murder investigation merely to accommodate your schedule."

The chief quickly stepped in. "Cool it, Tony. The State Attorney is on our side. We spent some time before you got here discussing strategy. There was a strong consensus to proceed with getting the search warrants. However, Mr. Rosen agreed to delay his next meeting to hear your opinion on this matter."

Tony ran his hand through his hair, regretting he'd let his personal feelings for Rosen get the better of him. "I'm sorry, you didn't deserve that," he said somewhat contritely to Rosen.

Rosen evaluated Tony for a moment and, seeing that his apology was sincere, gave him a nod. "No harm done. I can appreciate that you're emotionally invested in this case. Give me a second." He pulled out his BlackBerry and tapped in a message. "Okay, I've asked my secretary to push back my next appointment. Take your time and tell us how you think this should go down."

"Thanks," Tony said gratefully. "Assuming we can match the fibers on Sumner's clothing to either his football jacket or the senator's BMW, Jonathan Caldwell is going to be spending a lot of time in prison. Now let's turn to Bradley. Right now you have a pretty good case against him for interfering with a police investigation. I assume a conviction would also be sufficient cause to have him removed as coroner. This, however, is just the tip of the iceberg.

If we're correct, he's been actively involved in the cover-up of a murder and should be charged with accessory after the fact. The problem is, we don't have any solid evidence to prove that, and we have even less that ties the senator to any criminal acts."

"Tony, I don't disagree with you, but that's why we want to get the search warrants," the chief interjected.

"I know, but what happens if you don't find anything substantive?"

"Well, we can then proceed with the case we have against Jonathan Caldwell and Bradley. We'll offer a deal to one of them in return for testimony against the other and the senator," Rosen responded.

"Yes, but by then the senator will have seen your hand. He'll circle the wagons, call in political favors, manipulate the press, and bring in the best lawyers he can buy. In addition, he'll make promises to Bradley and his son for their silence. In these circumstances, I doubt that either of them would rat out the senator."

He waited for a response. Rosen looked over at the Dupree. "I have to admit Tony has identified a potential soft spot in our approach. If it played out this way, we'd be left with the son going to prison and Bradley getting a relatively mild slap on the wrist. Although the senator wouldn't emerge unscathed, he'd likely keep his seat and wouldn't need to worry about prison time."

Bobby was nodding, and the look on Dupree's face indicated he'd also been swayed to Tony's way of thinking.

Rosen directed his next comment to Tony. "Okay, how'd you suggest we play this?"

"We need to use the element of surprise to get either the son or Bradley to flip on the senator before he knows what's happening. We also need to be prepared, as you've already indicated, to offer a deal for testimony."

"And who's your choice for 'Let's Make a Deal'?" the chief asked.

"That's a tough one. On the one hand, you have a rapist who caused a young woman's death and then left her body to rot in a bog. On the other hand, you have a public official who deliberately set out to protect a killer by framing an innocent person. They both deserve long stays in prison. But if I had to pick one, I'd go with Caldwell."

"Why's that, Tony?" Bobby asked.

"I think he can be more easily manipulated than Bradley."

The chief turned to Rosen. "I'm not sure how familiar you are with Tony's record on the Chicago homicide division, but it's impressive. As I recall, he had the highest success rate of all their senior detectives in solving homicide cases. More importantly, by the time he arrested a suspected killer, the case was iron tight. So if he thinks this is the way to go, I fully support that decision."

Rosen eyes narrowed as he considered the chief's comments. Then he said, "Okay, let's go with Tony's recommendation. Is there anything else?"

Tony didn't hesitate. "Yes, there is. I want my shackles taken off. I deserve a chance to be front and center when we go after Caldwell, Bradley, and the senator." He looked defiantly at the State Attorney, challenging him to object.

Rosen returned his stare, an inscrutable look on his face. For a moment Tony thought he might have pushed too hard. When Rosen spoke, he did so in a hard deep voice. "All right Tony, you clearly know that I had some reservations about your involvement. I still have them. But now that we've had this chat, I have to say I like your style."

Rosen gave him a clipped smile before turning to Chief Dupree. "This is really your decision, but if you want Tony to play a more active role, you'll get no argument from me. And heaven help those that get in his way." The State Attorney stood, straightened his tie, and fastened the top button of his suit jacket. "Thanks for letting me sit in on this strategy session. Good luck with Caldwell. Let me know when you need those search warrants." He nodded at each of them before departing, his eyes meeting Tony's for a split second more.

When the door closed, Tony realized he'd been holding his breath and slowly let it out. The chief gave him a nod of congratulations before they settled down to business.

Afterwards, Tony and Bobby spent several hours discussing strategy for the upcoming interview with their chief suspect in the Sumner case. Even though Tony was now a full-fledged member of the investigation team, they agreed he shouldn't actively participate in the meeting. It would only serve to raise Caldwell's suspicions and make him a more difficult interview subject. Instead, Tony would continue to play a back-room role and support Bobby if she ran into problems.

However, after another hour of role-playing with Tony portraying a recalcitrant Jonathan Caldwell, he was fairly confident she was prepared for anything that might be thrown her way.

Chapter 41

Next morning found Tony in a windowless interview room at the police department. The smell of stale cigarettes hung in the air, evidence of someone stealing a forbidden smoke break. Elbows on the table, head cradled in his hands, he was feeling miserable. His attempts to fight off a cold had been unsuccessful; his symptoms now included a sore throat, runny nose, and dull headache. He raised his head to gulp his coffee, hoping the caffeine would counteract the drowsiness caused by the cold pills.

Bobby knocked and came in, quickly closing the door behind her. She gave him a quick once-over. "You don't look so good, Tony. Are you sure you're up to this? "

"I feel like crap, but the show must go on. What's happening?"

"Caldwell should be here soon. Let's get you into the observation room and make sure everything is set up."

Tony grabbed his coffee and followed her down the corridor. Turning left and then right, they entered a long hallway punctuated by a number of solid steel doors. Bobby opened the door into a room slightly larger than the one they'd just left. Across from the door was a rectangular one-way mirror that looked into a brightly lit interview room. Underneath the mirror was a long table with several hard wooden chairs. To the right was a metal shelving unit that contained audio and video recording equipment. On the table was a wireless headset like a receptionist might wear in a high tech corporate office.

"Let's make sure we can communicate with each other." Bobby picked up an ear bud beside the headset and put it in one ear. It was well hidden despite her short brown hair. "Now try this on and say something. But not too loud – this thing is pretty sensitive."

Tony slipped on the headset. He adjusted the cushioned receiver and repositioned the transmitter. "Domino's Pizza, can I take your order?"

Bobby smiled and gave him a quick two thumbs up. "Good, everything seems to be in working order. A tech by the name of Denzel will be in here in a few minutes. He'll stay with you to monitor the equipment. If there's a problem, let him know, and he'll take care of it. You might as well get comfortable while I go back to my office and wait for Caldwell."

Tony put the headset back on the table. "Sounds like a plan. And good luck."

"Thanks. I have to admit, I'm a bit nervous."

"Just remember, all top performers have a case of the nerves before they go on stage. And Caldwell has a lot more to be worried about than you do."

Bobby gave him a short smile in appreciation of his words of encouragement before leaving. Tony turned back towards the one-way mirror and took a seat, staring into the room where Bobby would soon be trying to outwit Caldwell. There wasn't much to see, a steel table and four uncomfortable looking chairs illuminated by harsh fluorescent lighting in the ceiling. Reviewing their game plan once again, he realized he'd feel much better if he could be in there too. But he had to put his faith in Bobby and their carefully laid plan.

There was a knock on the door and a young man in his twenties entered. He was dressed casually in a t-shirt with the name of a rock band on the front. His khaki pants had about ten pockets and hung so low that the top of his underwear showed.

Tony stood to greet his new roommate, noting his dark face, long black hair twisted in dreadlocks and probing brown eyes. "You must be Denzel." He extended his hand.

"You've got it. And you must be Deluca." Denzel pronounced Tony's name with a Caribbean accent. Then, instead of shaking his hand, he gave it a bump with his fist. "The lady detective asked me to let you know your guest has arrived, they'll be here in a few minutes. Did she explain I'll be takin' care of the equipment?"

"Yes, she did. We've already tried out the headset with the ear bud. They appear to be working fine."

"Good man. I'm goin' to check out the rest of the audio equipment and try to stay out of your way. But if you can't hear what's goin' on, let me know and I'll get things sorted out."

"Will do." Tony sat down again, his various aches and pains forgotten, while Denzel fiddled with the audio equipment. Finally he was satisfied everything was in good working order and sat back in his chair. They waited for Bobby's arrival.

Chapter 42
MAY 24 10:30 AM

Bobby's phone buzzed and the Duty Officer advised her that Jonathan Caldwell was in the waiting area for their appointment. She picked up her portfolio and took a deep breath. She'd confidently handled many interrogations with suspected felons, and wondered why this one in particular was giving her a case of the nerves. Admittedly, the events of the past two weeks had left her anxious and upset, but that wasn't the cause. And it wasn't because Tony would be watching her through the one-way glass, critiquing her every move. No, she realized, it was because Caldwell represented the first domino in a series that could ultimately topple the coroner, a powerful senator, and perhaps her own boss.

She went out to greet her visitor. While introducing herself, she gave Caldwell the quick once-over. He looked like he was going into a GQ photo shoot rather than a police interview, dressed in a brown suede jacket, blue paisley shirt, designer jeans, and coordinating suede loafers. She wondered if he had plans for an important lunch date after this meeting. He just might lose his appetite if things went according to plan, she thought, her confidence returning.

"Mr. Caldwell, I want to apologize in advance for our meeting accommodations. My office is overflowing with boxes from cases I'm working on, and our regular meeting rooms are all booked. So we have to use one of our more formal interview rooms. I hope you don't mind."

"No problem. I don't mind spending time with you." Caldwell gave her a wink.

Bobby suppressed a frosty retort and merely said. "Please follow me."

When they entered the interview room Caldwell looked around and sniffed at the stale air. "This reminds me of an old detective movie. Now, are you the good cop or the bad cop?" he asked with an easy smile.

"The good one, of course." Bobby laughed. Caldwell looked pleased with her response to his joke. Perfect. She wanted him comfortable and at ease.

"As I explained on the phone, we have new evidence that has eliminated the main suspect in Karen Sumner's murder. Her parents have now suggested we take a look at one of her old boyfriends. The Chicago police have talked with him, and they can't substantiate his alibi for the evening of the murder. We're now following up with a number of people who were in the Capital Lounge around the time Ms. Sumner was there. We're hoping someone might have seen this person in the bar or nearby."

"I'm glad to cooperate. What happened to that girl is a real shame. Why don't you show me the picture of the boyfriend, and I'll let you know if I saw him that night."

"Yes, we'll get to that. Unfortunately, protocol requires me to go through some preliminary matters. First of all, would you mind if we make an audio recording of our interview? That way I won't have to take notes and can focus on our conversation. Also, if you did happen to see the boyfriend that night, it will be important to demonstrate for any criminal proceeding that we followed the appropriate procedures. Are you okay with this?"

Caldwell sat back in his chair, his arms folded, clearly enjoying the feeling of being in control. "Sure, absolutely no problem. As I said, I want to help out any way I can."

"Great. I'll just get you to sign this recording disclosure form so there are no misunderstandings." Bobby pulled the consent form from her portfolio and passed it to Caldwell along with a pen. He quickly read through its contents and signed with a flourish.

"Thanks. Now, for the record, can you state your full name and date of birth?"

It looked as if Caldwell would object, but he merely shrugged and said "Jonathan Darcy Caldwell, June 23, 1987. Would you like my Social Security number as well?" he asked in a slightly sarcastic tone.

"No, that won't be necessary." She gave him a courteous smile. "Now, I'd like to establish who you were with at the Capital Lounge the night that Karen Sumner was murdered, and what happened while you were at the bar. If you were there with some friends, I may want to speak with them and see if they saw anything that might be helpful to the investigation. So please excuse these rather mundane questions."

This was one of several critical moments of the interview, and Bobby watched for Caldwell's reaction. The big question was whether the two friends she'd interviewed yesterday, Robert Holmes and Sterling Everett, had been in touch with Caldwell. This would have given them the chance to compare notes and for Caldwell to prepare for this meeting. She noted with satisfaction there was no tell-tale change in Caldwell's facial expression or body language. She was positive that he wasn't aware of her earlier conversations with Holmes and Everett.

"First of all, were you with anyone else that evening?"

Caldwell sat upright and placed his elbows on the table. He then gave an account of his organizing an evening out with three friends. He noted that was off to army training camp the next day, and this was intended as his going-away party. Caldwell also indicated that he was the so-called designated driver, and had made arrangements to borrow his father's "Bimmer."

Bobby had to stifle a smile at the irony of Caldwell being the DD for the evening.

Caldwell's review of the evening's events went quickly, and she let him talk without interruption until he got to the point in his story about arriving at the Capital Lounge.

She broke in. "As you may recall, your driver's license was scanned before you entered the bar that night. The records show you arrived just after eight pm. Does that sound right to you?"

Caldwell looked thoughtful, trying to recall the timeline for that evening. "You know, I can't really remember the exact time, but that's in the ball park."

"No problem. The bar also has a camera that takes pictures of everyone as they enter. For the record, can you confirm this is a picture of you with your three friends?"

Bobby pulled out a picture from her portfolio and pushed it across to Caldwell. He picked it up. "Yup, that's me and the three amigos." He slid the picture back toward Bobby.

She picked it up and nonchalantly examined the picture, as if for the first time. "Hey, that looks like a Badgers' football jacket you're wearing. Did you play some football?"

Caldwell's chest visibly puffed out. "Yes, I made third string QB in my rookie season. I got to play in a few games and threw a long bomb for the big TD."

"Wow, that's great. My nephew goes to U of W and would kill for one of these jackets. He says they're impossible to come by. He's been trying to buy one on eBay."

"Well, good luck to him. I don't think anyone who played for the Badgers would part with his jacket for any amount of money – not unless they were down to their last dollar. It's a real honor to make the team and be awarded a jacket. Besides, it's a real chick magnet," he added with a sly grin.

"So you must really cherish yours."

"I plan to be buried in it." Caldwell looked half-serious.

There was a slight crackle in her ear and she heard, "Good work, Bobby". She'd almost forgotten about Tony listening in, so intent had she been in her questioning. Bobby gave an almost imperceptible nod to acknowledge his encouragement. They'd both worried that the football jacket might've been discarded or destroyed in the aftermath of his encounter with Sumner. Apparently the jacket meant too much to Caldwell for him to part with it.

"Sorry for taking us a bit off course. Can you describe what happened while you were at the bar?"

Caldwell told Bobby that he and his friends spent their time drinking and partying on the dance floor. But after a while he'd became bored and wanted to move on to the next bar. He spoke with his friends and they made plans to leave. He conveniently failed to mention that he'd been cut off by Julie for being drunk and disorderly, and Bobby chose not to raise this point.

Instead, she asked, "Now, about what time was it when you decided to leave?"

"I don't know exactly. I would guess around nine-thirty or so."

"Okay. As I noted, we know Karen Sumner was in the bar around the same time as you and your friends. I have a picture of her that I'd like you to take a look at. Think back and tell me if you recall seeing her that evening."

She passed Caldwell another picture, this one a color head shot of Sumner. His expression didn't change as he looked at it. After a moment he said, "Sorry, doesn't ring any bells. I would've noticed her, she's cute. But there were lots of people in the bar that evening."

"Yes, the night following a Badger's football game, the place must've been packed," Bobby acknowledged. "Now, I'd like to show you some other photos. Let me know if you bumped into any of these people while you were in the bar." From an envelope she pulled out pictures of four young men that had been taken from the police data bank. The plan was to make Caldwell think that one of them was Sumner's former boyfriend, now under suspicion as her killer.

Caldwell carefully lined up the pictures in front of him and scrutinized each one closely. Finally he put his finger on the third picture in the line-up. "That guy – I'm pretty sure he was in the bar."

She had to give it to him. He must've figured he had a 25 percent chance of picking the phantom boyfriend. Even after all this time, he was still hoping to place the blame on someone else.

"Very good." Bobby handed Caldwell a pen. "Could you turn it over and sign and date it? This will confirm the picture you selected."

"Is that him, the ex-boyfriend?" Caldwell asked hopefully.

"Let's just say you've been very helpful," Bobby said with a smile. "Now, let's finish things off. You indicated you left the bar around nine-thirty. Where did you go from there?"

Caldwell hesitated and she held her breath waiting for his response. "I've got to admit that despite being the designated driver, I was a bit drunk by then. But let's see, I'm pretty sure I went to the Stiletto Bar. It's just down the street from the Lounge."

"You went there with your three friends?"

For the first time in the interview Caldwell looked uncomfortable. He made a show of looking at his large sports watch. "Listen, I think we've covered what happened while I was at the Lounge. And I've got another appointment I need to get to."

"You've been very patient, Mr. Caldwell, and I appreciate that you're busy. I'm just trying to establish the timeline while you were at the Capital Lounge. You weren't quite sure when you left and the bar camera can't confirm this. Perhaps if I speak with your friends, they'll remember." Bobby was now firmly in control and setting the trap.

"Oh. Okay. Well, as it turns out, they stayed behind. They were trying to pick up some girls and told me to go ahead. They said they'd catch up with me, but it didn't happen."

"So you were there by yourself at the Stiletto. How long did you stay?"

"Probably a half hour or so. Enough time to finish a drink."

"And did you see anyone else there that you recognized?"

Caldwell frowned. "No, I sat by myself and minded my own business," he said sharply.

Bobby decided it was time for a change in direction. "There's another thing, relating to your time at the Capital Lounge, that I forgot to mention. Another person we interviewed said they remember seeing a fight in the bar that night. Your name was mentioned. Were you involved in some sort of altercation?"

"No, of course not." Caldwell's voice grew louder as he lost a bit more of his composure.

"Not there or in any other bar that night?"

"I was out to have a good time, not get into a brawl," Caldwell responded indignantly.

"A hard body blow," Tony said into Bobby's ear bud.

Bobby gave another subtle nod. "Clearly this person didn't have his facts straight. Don't worry about it. Now just a few more things before we wrap up. I have a few more photos to show you."

Bobby pulled another marked envelope from her portfolio and made sure it was the correct one before handing it to Caldwell. He looked puzzled as he took it from her. She could see him stiffen as he removed the pictures and lined them up in a similar fashion to the pictures of the four young men. He was now looking at a timed sequence of photos lifted from the Capital Lounge security video. They showed Caldwell first exiting the washroom, moving to the front entrance of the bar and exiting through the revolving door. That last photo showed him just before he headed out the door, his head turned toward someone who was almost beside him.

Bobby waited a moment for the significance of the pictures to sink in. "Mr. Caldwell, these pictures were taken by the security camera at the front entrance of the Capital Lounge around nine-twenty pm. So your recollection of the time you left the bar was fairly accurate. However, for some reason you don't seem to recall bumping into Ms. Sumner. In fact, it appears that you may have been engaged in a conversation with her. Can you could explain this?"

Caldwell swallowed hard. "Listen, I'm as surprised as you are. I must've been drinking more than I thought that night. I honestly don't recall meeting her." Sincerity dripped from his voice.

Pretty good, Bobby thought. The guy definitely has potential as an actor, albeit a bad one. It was time to move into high gear. "I'd very much like to believe you, Mr. Caldwell, but there are other things that need to be explained. Like why you lied about going to the Stiletto Bar after leaving the Lounge."

"What do you mean?" Caldwell's eyes narrowed in concern.

"I mean you'd do better to keep in touch with your friends. I spoke with Mr. Holmes and Mr. Everett yesterday concerning your night together. They both indicated they left the Lounge shortly after you did and went directly to the Stiletto Bar. They didn't find you there and when they called your cell phone, you didn't pick up. We're in the process of getting the Stiletto's security records for that evening. Like the Capital Lounge, they scan all drivers' licenses and retain those records. I think we'll be able to establish you never went there that evening."

A bit of a white lie, Bobby knew. The manager of the Stiletto advised her yesterday afternoon that their records were purged every six months. But Caldwell didn't know this.

"Okay, like I said, I was drunk. I must've gone to some other bar along that strip."

"No, that's not what happened. As you left the Lounge, you engaged Ms. Sumner in a conversation. You convinced her to go for a ride with you. You took her to Picnic Point Park where you raped and murdered her."

There was total silence in the interview room. Caldwell glared angrily at Bobby, it finally dawning on him that he'd been set up. She gazed back at him without a flicker of emotion. He finally dropped his eyes and sullenly said, "I want to talk to a lawyer."

"Yes, I thought you might. However, before you make that call, I'd like to have ten more minutes of your time. This could be the most important 600 seconds in your short life. You don't have to say a word, just let me speak. Will you allow me this time?"

Caldwell's expression was heavy with suspicion. "Ten minutes? I'll give you five, so you'd better speak fast. But don't expect your little talk to change anything."

Chapter 43

Despite Caldwell's bravado, Bobby was pretty happy with the way the interview was progressing. She'd been patiently following the script they'd developed and moved Caldwell closer to the breaking point. But in truth, the interplay between her and Caldwell had to this point only represented some preliminary skirmishing. The war would be won or lost in the next five minutes.

"Good work, Bobby. Now show him what you've got," Tony whispered into the transmitter. She gave a very brief smile before starting to speak again.

"By now you've probably figured out you were brought here under false pretenses. Let me set things straight. We know you raped and killed Karen Sumner and then dragged her body into the marsh, hoping it would never be discovered. We have an air-tight case, I am very confident you will be convicted and go to prison. But right now you have the ability to influence the length of your sentence and the type of institution you'll stay in. That of course depends on whether you cooperate with us or not."

Caldwell shook his head, and his face seemed to say, "In your dreams."

"Yes, I can certainly understand your cynicism. You need to be in the right frame of mind to appreciate my perspective. First, I need to convince you that we've sufficient evidence against you to obtain a conviction. A case so strong that even your father can't bail you out, as he seems to do on a regular basis. More importantly, I have to demonstrate the potential rewards of you providing your full and complete cooperation."

"The so-called 'carrot and the stick,'" Tony whispered into her ear.

"Are you with me so far?" Bobby asked.

Caldwell held up his wrist to display a chunky expensive watch. "Tick tock."

"Right, time is moving along. So let's first talk about the case we expect to build against you. The night of Sumner's murder, it was your plan to hit the bars with your buddies, get drunk, and get laid. You were wearing your prized Badgers football jacket, which you so aptly referred to as a chick magnet. However, you really weren't in the mood for a party. In fact, you were pissed off with your father for forcing you to join the army. You started to drink, a lot. One of your friends labeled you an "ugly drunk" that night, and you weren't even close to getting to first base with any girl at the bar. It got so bad that you were cut off by the bar. To make matters worse, when you decided to leave, your best friends appeared to abandon you for some pretty students they'd just met." Bobby paused for a moment. "How am I doing so far?"

Caldwell said nothing, but the smug expression had been replaced by a sullen glare.

"That's what I like, the strong silent type. Now, before you left the bar you decided to take a piss. I mean, relieve yourself of all that beer you'd consumed. Upon exiting the men's room you noticed an attractive girl in line getting ready to leave the bar. You followed her to the door and struck up a conversation, probably telling her you were heading off to war or something like that. This grabbed her attention and you turn on the drunken charm, asking if she'd like to join you for a drink and dance at the Stiletto. She declined the invitation, telling you that she was heading back home. You countered, asking if she'd like a ride home in your Dad's fancy car. She probably hesitated, and you of course assured her there was no need to worry, as the great Senator Caldwell is your father. You seemed like a nice guy, so she accepted your offer."

"You've got it all wrong." Caldwell was trying hard to muster some conviction in his voice.

297

"I certainly wasn't there eavesdropping on your conversation. But I'm pretty sure that's how it went down with Ms. Sumner. She's now in the car and you're feeling pretty hot and horny. This girl may represent your last chance for a score before the evening ends and the nightmare called boot camp begins. You suggest a bit of a detour, a trip to the park. She may have protested, but you're driving and in charge. When you get to the park, it's still pretty early – the moonlight walk crowd hasn't arrived yet. You find a secluded spot where you attempt to take advantage of her. She fights you off, scratching your neck and face in the process. After escaping from the car, she falls and hits her head, suffering a fatal wound. But this doesn't matter to you; you rape her even while the life is draining from her body. It's only when you've done the dirty deed that you realized she's seriously hurt, perhaps already dead. You of course do the Christian thing by stripping her naked and pulling her body into the marsh. You leave the body there, hoping no one will discover what you did to this poor girl."

Bobby paused again, looking directly at Caldwell. "I'm trying to figure out how you can live with that guilt. It's gotta be a tremendous burden."

She felt a tear forming in her right eye and quickly wiped it away. Caldwell was looking unsettled, squirming on the hard wooden chair, blinking under the harsh lights.

"You're now thinking this cop knows how it all went down, but there can't be a shred of hard evidence. Otherwise you'd already be under arrest. I'm here to tell you that's just wishful thinking. First, we have you lying about meeting Karen Sumner that evening and going to the Stiletto bar. Then we have you lying to the army doctor about the scratch marks on your neck and face. You told him your injuries were the result of a fight that took place the previous night. But you've just confirmed to me that you weren't involved in any fight."

Caldwell visibly jumped at the reference to his army medical records. Although they wouldn't be available for use in any criminal trial, he wouldn't be aware of that.

"Oh, yes, we have your medical records. They add up to a very guilty mind, and the jury will eat that up. Perhaps your lawyer can argue you were too drunk to remember any of this. However, he'll have a much more difficult time with the DNA evidence. That's what's really going to put you away for a long time. But let's not go there quite yet. There's something else you need to know. You're probably thinking that your father, the great senator, will pull his usual political tricks and make this all go away. Like he did after you got into trouble with the locals when you were overseas. 'Honorable discharge' – that's a joke."

Caldwell's eyes widened, registering his shock. "How'd you find out about that? Those records are supposed to be sealed."

Bobby gave him a generous smile. "Mr. Caldwell, you should know that we live in the era of the Internet, where news spreads like wildfire. It's interesting, television networks now rely on private citizens rather than journalists to report breaking news. They get their video feeds from the memory cards of cell phones. Did you honestly believe that the reason you were given the boot from the army wouldn't come back to haunt you?"

Now it was her turn to look at her watch. "Five minutes do go by rather quickly. Would you like to make that call to your lawyer, or perhaps your dad? Or are you willing to listen for another five minutes? I think you'll find it a good investment of your time."

Caldwell seemed to have shrunk into his chair. He nodded for her to continue.

"Good decision. Now, I was saying that you shouldn't rely on your father to help you out. There are a couple of good reasons for that. First, we have an experienced and ambitious State Attorney who's taken a very active interest in your case. Apparently he has a young daughter at university and isn't keen on the idea of having a rapist wandering the streets of Madison."

Another small white lie, Bobby acknowledged. Rosen had never mentioned anything to her about a teenage daughter, but she thought it might work to good effect.

"We also have a chief of police who, for very good reasons, doesn't like your father. I don't think he'll be easily manipulated or intimidated. Most importantly, the senator will have his own criminal charges to worry about."

"Criminal charges?" Caldwell asked, looking incredulous. "What's he done?"

"I'm guessing you haven't had an up close and personal conversation with your father since the 'incident' last year. He must've been pretty angry when he found out what you'd done. Then, to top things off, you bring more disgrace to the family name by getting yourself drummed out of the army. Imagine his humiliation in having to call in all sorts of favors to make sure you weren't court-marshaled. He probably doesn't want anything to do with you. Am I right?"

Without thinking Caldwell slowly nodded in the affirmative, his face contorted in anger and embarrassment.

"Now, about those criminal charges. With you safely in boot camp, the senator decided to take certain steps to make sure your role in Sumner's death was never discovered. The ironic thing is that in trying to point the finger at Curtis Mansfield, he provided us with all the evidence we need to convict you. I won't bore you with the details, but the clothing you so thoughtfully removed from Sumner's body is now in our possession. On her clothes we've discovered fibers we now know came from your football jacket, as well as the carpeting in the trunk of your father's car. Your father's actions effectively sealed your fate."

Bobby studied Caldwell's face, hoping to read his thoughts. She then took a deep breath and continued.

"By involving himself in the cover-up of the murder, the senator is of course, in a heap of trouble. He'll be charged with obstruction of justice, misuse of a public office, and everything else that the State Attorney's Office can throw at him. He really won't have a lot of time to worry about you, with his own career and freedom at stake. In fact, I anticipate he'll sacrifice you to save his own hide. This probably sounds all too familiar – your father putting his career ahead of you and your needs."

Caldwell's face was now a ghostly white, as the truth of what Bobby was telling him sank in. He licked his lips and his right eyelid fluttered. Finally he said, "Okay, what's in it for me if I cooperate?"

"Ah, now we're getting somewhere. The State Attorney has advised me that in return for your plea of guilty on charges of sexual assault and murder, he's prepared to recommend a reduced prison term in a state institution. With time for good behavior, you'll get out before your old age pension starts. No confession and he'll be seeking the maximum term for felony murder. You'll be put away for a long time in one of those horrible supermax prisons. They really like rich kids in there...."

Bobby paused to let him consider his situation before continuing. "At this point you might be thinking that your lawyer can argue that you were drunk and didn't intend kill Sumner. Unfortunately for you, the very act of raping Sumner followed by her death will, under Wisconsin law, require the court to find you guilty of intentional homicide. You're in a very bad spot, and the State Attorney is offering a sweetheart deal. It won't be repeated once this meeting is concluded."

"What about my father?" Caldwell asked nervously.

She heard Tony's calm voice in her ear bud, "Now, now's the time. Give him the big picture."

Bobby pressed on. "We want him to get what he deserves - hard time in prison. Just think of the satisfaction you'll feel when he has his turn to be disgraced, stripped of power. Never again will he be able to force you to do something you don't want to do, merely to earn his respect or appease his anger."

A flicker of light appeared in Caldwell's eyes. What did it mean? Bobby waited impatiently to find out.

"Okay, let's write up the deal, and I'll tell you what you need to send that asshole to prison."

What Bobby had seen in Caldwell's eyes was the not-so-subtle gleam of revenge.

Chapter 44

Tony was back in the small meeting room, waiting for Bobby to appear and collect him for the next important step in their investigation. In addition to being miserable from his cold, he was feeling increasingly anxious. Things needed to move swiftly to maintain the element of surprise. But this short break in the action did give him a few moments to reflect upon Bobby's interview with Caldwell.

Their psychological profiling of the young man had turned out to be extremely accurate. They knew that Jonathan Caldwell was the only child in a dysfunctional family headed by the overpowering ego of Senator Caldwell. At a young age the boy would have idolized his father, seeking out his love and attention. Like many successful politicians, the senator would've been too busy with his own career to spend time with his son. Tony somehow knew that when they did interact, the son would be under his father's very demanding and critical eye. Experience would teach him that he could never measure up to the expectations of his father. So, after a while, he gave up trying and instead sought out trouble as his way of gaining attention.

It appeared that the senator had reacted to his son's troubles with anger and vindictiveness rather than sympathy and support. Tony knew from Caldwell's actions and behavior that the senator forcing his son to enlist had been the ultimate betrayal in their relationship. He and Bobby had used this knowledge to further drive a wedge between father and son, channeling the younger Caldwell's suppressed feelings of inner turmoil and antagonism into the ultimate betrayal of his father.

Once the plea deal had been completed, Caldwell gave a full statement of what had happened after he'd left the Capital Lounge. As it turned out, Bobby's recounting of events leading up to Sumner's death had been startlingly accurate. While it appeared that her death had been unintended, the rape combined with Caldwell's failure to come forward to the police had effectively sealed his fate.

What was more important was the sequencing of events after the murder. Caldwell indicated he'd driven straight home, all the time worried he might be pulled over by the police. He managed to get there without incident and parked his father's BMW in the garage. He barely remembered to remove Sumner's clothing from the trunk before sneaking back into the house. In the safety of his bedroom he took off his muddy clothes, showered, and drunkenly collapsed into bed.

The next morning he awoke, hung over and somewhat dazed, to find his father standing by his bed. He was holding out a woman's purse and demanded to know who Karen Sumner was and why her purse was in his car.

Caldwell was now sober enough to realize there was little point in lying to his father. Caldwell Sr. had already observed the raw trail of scratches on his neck and face, and once the story of Sumner's disappearance hit the news, he'd know that his son was involved. He slowly told his father what he'd done and pleaded for his help.

His father had at first furiously denounced him, saying he was going to turn him over to the police. But eventually he calmed down and began to carefully interrogate his son about his activities from the night before. He wanted to know how he'd met Sumner, and if anyone else had observed them together. Had he told anyone else about what'd happened? Now believing that his son's role in Sumner's' death might never be discovered, he ordered him to keep quiet and get his ass to boot camp as planned. In Caldwell's words, "my father said he'd take care of everything." The senator had then taken control of Sumner's clothing and her other personal effects.

Tony had pumped his fist in the air upon hearing this, with Denzel giving him an odd look. This was the smoking gun – the direct link they needed to demonstrate that the senator had been involved in the plot to frame Mansfield for murder.

Caldwell had told Bobby that later in the morning he boarded a plane to Fort Bragg in North Carolina, where he reported for duty as his father had instructed. During the first week of training camp, he lived in constant fear, expecting the police to arrive with a warrant for his arrest. He spent his free time searching the Internet, pouring over the headlines relating to the investigation of Sumner's disappearance. He also waited for word from his father on what actions he'd been taking to save him from imprisonment, but there was complete silence. As the week slowly passed without any new developments, he started to calm down.

However, his fears were reignited when Sumner's body was discovered. At this point he seriously considered turning himself in to the police. However, the next day he learned that the police were hot on the trail of the suspected killer, a known sex offender by the name of Curtis Mansfield. He was overwhelmed with relief. As the weeks turned into months, he became more confident that he'd gotten away with murder. This gave him a sense of invincibility - that he was somehow above the law. But he learned this was not the case while on active duty in Iraq. This time his crimes were reported, and he narrowly avoided a court martial before being discharged. Caldwell had told this part of his story in a resigned tone, defeat and humiliation written on his face.

Throughout his entire time in the army, he said, he'd never exchanged a spoken or written word with his father. He was totally in the dark about the senator's efforts to lead the police on a wild goose chase. He'd always assumed Mansfield was the unfortunate victim of shoddy police work. And in many respects, he was probably correct.

Tony then recalled Bobby's final line of questioning. She'd told Caldwell that Sumner's purse and jewelry had never been recovered. She asked if he had any idea where these items might be stored. Caldwell said his father was preoccupied with the threat of a home invasion and had converted a small bedroom into a "panic room" off the master bedroom. A large safe had been installed in this room, which only his father had access to. If any of Sumner's personal effects had been kept by the Senator, that's likely the spot where they'd be found. After Caldwell provided this last piece of information, the interrogation was concluded and he was led away for booking.

Chapter 45
MAY 24 12:30 PM

They'd spent some time debating the best spot to interview Bradley and how Bobby could set up the meeting without raising any suspicions. Bobby had suggested the Coroner's Office, as it was away from police headquarters and outside the earshot of Adelsky. While Tony agreed, he also realized getting Bradley there would present a challenge. It being Saturday, he was likely at the Country Club finishing up his round of golf and getting ready for lunch. Motivating him to come into the city would require some special finesse.

It was Bobby who came up with the idea. After some fine-tuning, she'd called Bradley at the Country Club and tracked him down to the men's lounge. Apologizing for bothering him on the weekend, she explained that a friend on the force had four tickets to the U.S Open next month. Due to financial issues, the officer was now trying to find a buyer to take them off his hands. She didn't have to go any further; Bradley told her not to let "his" tickets fall into anyone else's hands and advised her that he'd be downtown in twenty minutes. She promised to personally escort the officer over to his office to conclude the deal. She and Tony exchanged high fives.

As they walked over to the Public Safety Building, a low-rise concrete edifice that housed the Coroner's Offices, they briefly reviewed tactics for their interrogation of Jim Bradley. Entering the building lobby, Tony felt a shudder of anticipation. He was looking forward to settling some long outstanding scores with Bradley. Despite the heavy cold that was trying to sap all his energy, there was almost a skip in his step as he moved towards the elevator bank.

Bradley's office was located on the second floor. The door to the main reception area was unlocked. Down the hallway, an office door was open and Bobby headed in that direction, motioning Tony to stay back. She walked into the office and cleared her throat to announce her presence. Tony heard Bradley demand, "So where is he? I hope the hell you didn't let him get away!"

"No, he's right here," she replied. This was Bobby's invitation for Tony to join the fray. He sauntered into the office and took a seat. "Hello, Jim. How's the golf game?"

Bradley was behind his desk, an open newspaper and a water bottle in front of him. It was clear that he'd rushed over from the club without changing, as he was still wearing a light yellow golf shirt. His tanned face contrasted with a band of white skin on his forehead left by his sun visor.

The expression on his face instantly changed from anticipation to a grimace of disapproval. "Don't tell me you're the one with the tickets?" he spluttered.

"Nope." Tony flashed Bradley a broad smile.

"Then what are you doing here? I thought I made it clear last time we met that I didn't want you anywhere near me. Please get out of my office." He waved his hand at Tony as if shooing away a fly.

"He's here at my request and will be staying," Bobby said.

Bradley glared at Tony before turning his attention back to Bobby. "Listen, Detective, I'm not sure what's going on here. Is that officer coming with those tickets? If not, I'm out of here."

"Sorry, there are no tickets. But we have another important matter to discuss with you, relating to the Sumner murder investigation."

A look of confusion passed over Bradley's face at the mention of Sumner's name. He quickly recovered and went on the offensive. "What kind of game are you and Deluca pulling here? You lure me downtown with some story about bogus golf tickets, and now you want to discuss a closed murder case? In front of the guy who fucked it all up? Andrade, if you don't explain yourself real quick, I'm going to call your boss and let him kick your ass." Bradley almost spat out the last words.

"You're right, Jim, you've been out of the loop and deserve an explanation," Bobby replied in a soothing voice. "First of all, the Sumner case has been reopened with the approval of Chief Dupree. And Tony has officially returned to the homicide division, at the request of both the chief and the mayor, to assist me in pursuing some new leads in the case. In fact, I'm pleased to announce that Sumner's killer was apprehended this morning and has confessed to the crime. He's now in lock-up, pending the laying of formal charges."

Tony watched Bradley as Bobby delivered these carefully scripted lines. Each statement appeared to deliver a physical as well as psychological blow to the coroner. "You've arrested the killer?" Bradley managed to gasp out.

"Yes... and you know him. Jonathan Caldwell."

Bradley's eyes grew large and he picked up the water bottle, taking a long swig. He was clearly searching for time to collect his thoughts. He finally said, "The senator's son. That's, well, incredible. Are you sure he's the killer?"

"Oh, yes. In addition to the confession, the evidence against him is quite persuasive. Now, there are some other matters relating to this case that we need to review with you. Tony?"

This was Tony's cue and he leaped at the opportunity. "Do you know someone by the name of Matt Riley?" he asked.

He saw this question caught Bradley by surprise, but his innate dislike for Tony seemed to restore his equilibrium. "No, I don't." He smiled tightly.

"He certainly seems to know you. He's provided us with a written statement outlining a series of conversations with you. Here's a copy, I've highlighted the relevant passages. I think you should review it before responding further."

Tony slid the document across the desk. Bradley reluctantly picked it up. He slowly flipped through the several pages, his lips moving as he read the highlighted sections. When he put the document down, there was a flicker of fear and doubt in his eyes.

"Okay, I now recall bumping into this man at a coffee shop. He approached me, said he recognized me from a picture in the newspaper. He indicated he had some information relating to the murder. I didn't like the look of him; he appeared to be more interested in the reward money than anything else. I ended up referring him to the police hotline. The rest of this" – he pointed a long finger at the statement – "is pure fabrication."

"Normally it would be easy to discount the story of a convicted felon. But he's been able to provide us with some additional information that corroborates his story. Now, in Riley's statement he indicates that you provided him with a picture of Curtis Mansfield...."

"I did nothing of the kind." Bradley rose slightly from his chair, placing both hands on the desk in front of him.

"Yes, you did. And fortunately for us, he kept that picture." Tony stood and leaned over the desk, his face barely a foot from Bradley's. He stared into Bradley's eyes and raised his voice. "We've had it analyzed, and guess what? Your fingerprints are all over it. We also know you fixed his drunken driving charge. There's no escaping the truth, Bradley."

Bradley's hands came up from the desk, and for a moment Tony thought he might be throttled by the coroner. Instead, the hands went up to Bradley's face, and he started moaning. Despite the muffled voice, Tony could make out his words. "I knew it. It's finally caught up with me. Why'd I agree to get involved?" Bradley's facade of innocence had totally collapsed. "Shock and awe" went through Tony's mind as he marveled at how quickly Bradley had capitulated.

However, he took pleasure in the situation for only a moment. "Snap out of it, Bradley. Be a big boy," he said without sympathy.

The coroner shuddered and he took a deep breath before lowering his hands. He then collapsed back into his chair, no longer the cocky golf hotshot who'd quickly risen to prominence as Dane County's Coroner.

"You don't know what it's been like, carrying this around for the past nine months," he said, his voice barely above a whisper. "Then we got the new DNA results and Mansfield's body turned up. I could feel the whole thing starting to collapse around me. I haven't been able to get a decent sleep for the past week."

Tony muttered, "Boo hoo," but Bobby placed a warning hand on his arm, signaling that his job was done and to back down. She assumed control of the interview.

"Jim, I'm going to read you your Miranda rights. Then we can talk a bit more, if you want." She extracted a well-worn card from a pocket and read verbatim from it. At the end she said, "Do you understand your rights"?

"Yes," Bradley groaned.

"Good. Now, you've been around long enough to know how this works. Jonathan Caldwell has told us everything we need to know about his involvement in Sumner's death. We've also got a pretty good idea of what went down once he headed off to boot camp. But we need you to fill in the details. Cooperate, and the State Attorney has agreed to give you some latitude in both the charges and sentencing recommendation. If you don't, the charge will be accessory after the fact. That can carry a life-time prison term, as I'm sure you know. We've got Attorney Rosen available to speak with you and provide some assurances. Did you want me to make that call?"

Bradley nodded again, and Bobby punched a number into her cell phone. "Mr. Rosen, this is Detective Andrade. I'm here with Jim Bradley and have explained the situation. He'd like to talk with you."

Bobby paused a moment and then handed the phone to Bradley.

Tony listened intently, trying to decipher the one-sided conversation that was punctuated with a lot of "uh huhs," "that's rights," and lengthy bouts of frowning silence while the State Attorney laid things out. Finally Bradley said, "Yes, I understand. That's acceptable. I appreciate what you've done. Thank you.' He handed the phone back to Bobby.

"Okay, I'm ready. What do you want to know?"

For the next twenty minutes they questioned Bradley on his role in the cover-up of the Sumner murder. They learned he'd been contacted by the senator on a "private matter" the day after Sumner's disappearance was reported to the police. They arranged to meet in a private room at the Country Club where the senator explained that his son had gotten drunk and accidentally killed a girl. He then did something very stupid and tried to hide the body.

The senator indicated he was afraid his son's actions could result in his being found guilty of murder. He asked Bradley for his help in keeping Jonathan out of prison. Bradley knew a bit about Jonathan's troubled background as well as the father's disdain for the son, and figured the senator was taking some liberties with the truth. Still, he'd known the senator most of his life, and his financial and political support had been critical to Bradley getting elected as coroner.

And, Tony thought without saying it aloud, there was also the prospect of future favors from the senator, given the Coroner's own political aspirations.

"So you started to map out a strategy to contain the damage?" Bobby prompted.

"That's right."

"And was Adelsky brought into your plan?" Tony asked.

"No, early on we decided that would be too risky, and probably not necessary. The senator thought there was a good chance the body would never be discovered. However, if it did evolve into a murder investigation, the Caldwell felt the combination of our influence and Adelsky's inexperience would make him relatively easy to control. We were really thrown for a loop when the body was discovered and we learned that you" – he shot a quick look at Tony – "and not Adelsky would be leading the investigation. I told the senator that if you remained in charge there was a good chance you'd ferret out the truth. So we looked for ways to discredit you with the goal of forcing you off the investigation.

"I take it you were the one who removed the security video from my office, and leaked the confidential information on the investigation to that news reporter," Tony said angrily.

"Yes, guilty as charged. The senator also started a whisper campaign against you with his buddies on the Police and Fire Commission. As I said, the plan was to get you fired and replaced by Adelsky."

"You did a masterful job," Tony said between gritted teeth. All those seemingly unrelated events now all fit together into a neat package. "So tell me, how'd you manage to get Adelsky to come along for the ride?"

"I heard through the police grapevine that Rick went ballistic and threatened to quit when he learned you'd be heading up the investigation. We didn't want this to happen, so I paid a visit to his apartment. I commiserated with him and said there were some powerful people in town who thought it was a disgrace that an outsider was in charge of what should have been his investigation. I assured him that the situation would be corrected, but it was going to take some time. I convinced him to go back to work, apologize to the chief, and appear supportive of you. By staying close to the investigation, he'd be in a position to quickly step in when the chief gave him the nod. Adelsky lapped up all my bullshit. "

"That would explain why you both became thick as thieves during the investigation," Tony said.

"Yes, you could say we had a common goal, but with different objectives. It worked very well, as Rick had access to all your investigation reports. He told me you were planning to look into people living in the Madison area who'd been charged or convicted of crimes against women. I suggested he get the jump on you and do his own record search. Mansfield's name was on the list of a select group of sexual offenders Rick dug up. He showed me their police arrest records and mug shots. I liked the sound of Mansfield as a potential suspect and kept his picture. I did a bit more research, found out he lived alone and kept to himself, so I figured it was unlikely he'd have a solid alibi for the night of Sumner's disappearance. That's how he became the mug in this game."

That would also explain how Adelsky's fingerprints ended up on the photo Bradley gave to Riley, Tony thought.

Bradley kept on talking, wanting to unburden himself. "I also suggested to Rick that someone working at the Capital Lounge might somehow be involved in Sumner's death. He did a background check on all the staff who worked the night Sumner was murdered. Once we got Riley's pending drunken driving charge, I was able to use this information as a bargaining chip to get Riley to point the finger at Mansfield."

Bobby and Tony exchanged glances, marking this item off their list. Bobby moved on to the next. "Okay, now we want to know what role you played in Mansfield's disappearance."

"What do you mean?" Bradley asked cautiously.

"I mean someone called Mansfield the night he disappeared, from a pay phone almost across from his apartment, and after that he vamoosed. I'm thinking you're the caller."

Bradley remained silent, his face inscrutable.

"Come on, Jim. I know Rosen warned you the deal was only good if you fully co-operated. You hold back on this, and you're in bigger shit than when we started."

"Okay, okay." Bradley raised both hands in surrender. "Rick phoned me late that day and told me Mansfield had agreed to come in for a medical examination. I wanted to prevent this; I knew the absence of scratch marks on his body could eliminate him as a suspect and perhaps lead the investigation back to Jonathan. I'd also heard about the death threats and that Mansfield was extremely concerned about his safety. I decided to play on his fears and called Mansfield in the middle of the night. I claimed to be a "friend" and told him there were some dangerous people who figured he was responsible for Sumner's death. They planned to snatch him the first chance they got and use whatever force was necessary to get him to confess. I suggested he get out of town until things calmed down. I waited five minutes to let this fester a bit. When I called back, Mansfield was literally out of his mind with fear. I turned up the pressure by telling him that several men were already on the move with a revised plan to force their way into his apartment. Mansfield yelled something unintelligible into the phone and hung up.

"I then waited outside his building and about ten minutes later I saw him pull out of the underground parking. He almost fishtailed in front of me, he was driving so fast. I'd got some of Sumner's clothing from the senator, and took the opportunity to plant them in the apartment trash bin. The rest is pretty much a matter of public record. With both of you removed from the case, it was relatively easy for me to convince Adelsky that Mansfield was the killer and to pay little attention to any evidence that suggested otherwise. The senator played his role by befriending Rick and feeding his ego as needed. That's it."

"Not quite, but we're almost done. We'd like to turn our focus to Jennifer Harding. Did you or the senator have anything to do with her murder?

This question seemed to rouse the old Bradley into action. "What the hell? You can't pin that one on me! I hardly knew her."

Bobby looked over at Tony, and he took control of the questioning. "Listen Bradley, there are an awful lot of coincidences that are hard to explain. For example, you attended a conference earlier this year where she spoke."

"Yeah, that's a real good reason for me to off her," Bradley retorted.

"That's just the start. There's the fact that she was responsible for getting the DNA tests completed. You and the senator may have thought she had another agenda, like trying to find Sumner's real killer. That's why you lured her to Madison and murdered her."

"You're crazy – we did nothing of the sort. We had a report from Adelsky, and everything was under control from his end. No need to panic. Besides, the senator and I were at a charity golf event at the club the night she was murdered, along with about two hundred people. After dinner we drank scotch and played poker until about 3 am. There are a dozen people who can vouch for this. You don't have a chance pinning her death on either of us."

Tony changed course. "Okay, then what about Adelsky? We know they'd been in communication shortly before her death. What can you tell us about the two of them?"

Bradley paused, a contemplative look on his face. "Going back to that conference, I recall Rick saying he thought Harding was pretty hot. He made a joke about wanting to examine her legal briefs. I don't think it went any further than talk. On the other hand, Rick has become quite secretive about his love life since his divorce became front page news in the police department."

He thought a little more. "More recently, I know Rick was pretty upset with her requesting those DNA tests without his permission. He considered it a slap in the face. He said he was going to contact Harding and ask what the hell she was doing. We encouraged him to follow up with her, as we wanted to know her motivation. I understand she sent him back a rather nasty response, which really pissed him off. He told me he had plans for 'that bitch,' but never elaborated. Who knows, maybe he's your killer."

After a moment, Bobby said, "Okay, I think that wraps things up for the time being. We're going to take you back to the Police Department for booking and arraignment. Now, I'm not going to cuff you, but don't try anything funny. And you're not to talk to Rick or anyone else about this conversation."

Chapter 46
MAY 24 2:30 PM

Bobby pushed the doorbell beside the double entry doors to the Caldwell residence. Tony was right behind her, and three uniformed officers and two forensic techs were waiting on the sidewalk leading from the driveway. This was the third phase of today's operation, and a critical one. She should have felt dog tired from her interviews with Caldwell and Bradley, but she was high with adrenaline and caffeine.

Officer Kelly, one of the uniforms, was grinning at her like a little kid. It was Kelly who had secured the murder scene after the discovery of Sumner's body. She'd been impressed then by the young officer and thought it was fitting that he participate in the execution of the search warrant. He was clearly excited at being asked to play a role in the reopened investigation.

The door was opened by a woman Bobby recognized from her photos on the Senator's website. Mrs. Caldwell may have been beautiful at one time, but the aging process, combined with a liberal dose of plastic surgery, gave her thin face the pinched look of an old schoolmarm. She was impeccably dressed in a feminine blouse and linen pants, with Prada shoes that would cost Bobby a week's salary. Mrs. Caldwell peered out at Bobby and then at the entourage behind her, clearly not happy with what she saw.

"What's this about? Has that stupid silent alarm gone off again? I've told Robbie that we should just shut the damn thing off. It's more of a bother than anything."

"Mrs. Caldwell," Bobby broke in, "my name is Detective Andrade. We're not here about any alarm. I have with me a search warrant for your residence and your husband's BMW. These other people are here to assist with the search. Is the senator in?"

Mrs. Caldwell's eyes widened. "A search warrant? This must be a joke, or a mistake. What did you say your name was?"

Bobby repeated her name. She wasn't surprised at Mrs. Caldwell's startled response. This would be the last thing she'd be expecting on a beautiful spring afternoon. "If we could see the senator, I can explain to both of you what's going to happen."

"Robbie? He's on an errand – we're having guests for dinner and he's run off for some Scotch. I'm expecting him at any moment. Why don't you wait until he returns? He'll clear this all up."

Mrs. Caldwell started to close the door, but Tony moved forward and held out an arm to prevent her. "I'm sorry Mrs. Caldwell, but that's not the way it works. We'll need to start without him. Here's a copy of the search warrant. You'll see it allows us full access to your house. I expect we'll take about an hour or perhaps longer. You can remain in the house, but you can't touch anything or get in the way of the officers. The same goes for anyone else currently in the house. Do you understand?"

"No, I don't. I'm planning a party for some very important guests from Washington. We are on a tight schedule that cannot be disturbed. You will not get into my house unless my husband says so!" Her voice was now loud and angry.

This is not going according to plan, Bobby thought, realizing a different tact was required. "May I suggest another option? Now that we're here, with the warrant, signed by a judge, we need to secure your home. If you'll allow us to do that, we can delay the actual search until the senator returns. My partner and I will join you inside, and everyone else can wait outside until the senator arrives. How does that sound?"

Mrs. Caldwell sniffed and her chest heaved up and down. She was still reluctant to allow anyone in the house.

"Maybe we could have some tea until your husband returns. Give everyone a chance to relax," Tony said – a somewhat out of character statement. Mrs. Caldwell gave him the once over, and apparently liked what she saw.

She gave him a brief smile. "Yes, I suppose that's acceptable. My husband shouldn't be more than ten minutes. And a cup of tea would be very good right now. Come this way."

She opened the heavy door just enough to allow Bobby and Tony to squeeze through. The first thing Bobby noticed was the vast expanse of light grey marble flooring with an elaborate inlay. The ceiling looked to be twenty feet high, with cherry moldings, a large bronze chandelier, and an impressive staircase leading to the second floor. She figured most of her own house could fit into this entry area.

They followed Mrs. Caldwell through the foyer and past a long dining room, where a young woman dressed in a housekeeper uniform was setting the table. The plates and cutlery were already in place, and she was now arranging three wine glasses at each spot. She glanced up from her work, clearly wondering who these visitors might be.

Mrs. Caldwell called out, "Ruth, leave that for a moment and make a pot of tea for three. We'll be in the sitting room." Ruth put down the wine glass she'd been polishing and nodded. Bobby lost sight of her as they veered left into a wood-paneled room with floor-to-ceiling bookcases along one wall. Two upholstered reading chairs and a small leather sofa were clustered around a glass-topped coffee table.

"I think we'll be most comfortable here, and we won't disturb the staff as they get set up for the dinner party. Please, take a seat. I have to admit that I'm more than a bit curious by your appearance at our doorstep. What crime has been committed, and why do you think searching our home would be helpful to your investigation? This is really quite extraordinary and comes at a very inopportune time."

Bobby looked over at Tony. The affidavit attached to the warrant contained a number of details of their investigation into Jonathan

Caldwell, enough to convince a judge to authorize the search of his former home. Both documents were now a matter of public record. However, the affidavit contained no mention of the fact that the senator was suspected as being complicit in hiding this crime as well as the frame-up of an innocent person. They didn't want to tip their hand just yet. Bobby also preferred to wait for the senator's return before announcing that their son had just confessed to committing a vicious rape and murder.

"Mrs. Caldwell, I understand your curiosity and concern. However, it's best that we wait until your husband arrives. That way we can answer all of your questions and avoid any misunderstandings."

She raised her eyebrows but didn't press the matter.

"You have a very impressive home," Tony interjected, changing the subject. "When was it built?"

She turned her attention to him. "I'm sorry, I don't think we've been formally introduced."

"My apologies. I'm Tony Deluca, special consultant to the Madison Police Department." Tony suddenly sneezed and quickly apologized, pulling out a Kleenex to blow his nose.

Mrs. Caldwell pulled back into her chair as if to avoid his germs. "Well," she sniffed, "to answer your question, this level was built just after the First World War. When we purchased it, about ten years ago, the real estate agent noted it was in 'original condition,' as if that were a selling point. In reality, the place was literally falling apart. But I saw it had good bones and fell in love with the neighborhood. It took us almost two years to add the second story and restore the rest to its 'original condition,' but it was well worth the effort."

They heard footsteps in the hallway, and Ruth appeared carrying a tray with handsome bone china tea set and cups and saucers for three. The conversation was halted until tea was poured and the housekeeper left again.

"The house is a beauty," Tony continued. "Now you mentioned a silent alarm. Given your husband's political profile, I expect you must worry about attracting unwanted visitors."

Bobby listened with curiosity, wondering where Tony was going with this line of questioning.

"It's my husband who worries, more than me. He became very concerned about break-ins, particularly when we're travelling back and forth to Washington so much. We retained some security consultants who prepared a very extensive report."

"I see. Did they make any other recommendations in addition to the alarm system?"

"Well, you being police officers, I suppose I can tell you. They had us build a special room; I forget what you call it, where we can hide out if necessary."

"A panic room," Bobby interjected, now understanding the purpose of Tony's questions.

"That's right. It has it all, reinforced entry door, special fireproofing and a separate ventilation system. It was frightfully expensive, but my husband insisted it was essential for our safety."

"We hear that more and more wealthy people are doing this." Tony edged the discussion forward. "They store water and food, have an external communication system, and often install a safe to protect valuables. I suppose your consultants recommended this"

"Yes, they did. That safe was a heavy brute, but they still fastened it to the floor and wall to make sure it couldn't be simply carted away. But it is such a pain," she said with a sigh. "Robbie is the only one with the combination. If I want my jewelry I have to ask him to retrieve it. It's gotten to the point where I only keep my heirloom pieces there. Everything else is in an unlocked jewelry box in our bedroom. So much for our grand security measures."

"And no other family members have access to the contents of the safe?" Tony tried to keep a relaxed and friendly tone to his voice.

"Are you kidding? The last thing my husband would do is allow our son anywhere near our valuables and confidential papers. He's probably one of the main reasons we have that safe," she added with a bitter laugh.

Bingo, Bobby thought, looking over at Tony. He didn't meet her eye but took a sip of his hot tea.

Suddenly they were disturbed by a distant shout, followed by the slamming of the front door and the sounds of a struggle, coming from the direction of the front entrance.

Chapter 47
MAY 24 2:50 PM

Tony managed to spill the rest of his tea in his haste to put it down on the coffee table. He followed Bobby out into the hallway on a run, leaving a startled Mrs. Caldwell behind. They headed in the direction of several loud voices, one of them swearing up a storm.

In the entranceway, two officers were wrestling on the marble floor with a heavy-set man. His shirt was pulled out of his pants and halfway over his head, exposing a flabby belly. Officer Kelly stood on the sidelines, glumly watching the action.

Mrs. Caldwell had by now caught up with them. "Stop this hooliganism right now!" she shouted. Her command had the desired effect, as the officers backed away. "Robbie, what in heaven's name is going on?"

The senator slowly got to his feet, looking sheepishly at his wife. "I'm sorry, dear, I didn't know what to think with all these police around. I thought you might have had some trouble while I was gone."

Mrs. Caldwell clucked at him, shaking her head. Then in a softer voice she said, "I'm perfectly fine. Now, straighten yourself out. You look a mess."

He tucked in his shirt and adjusted the collar. One of the buttons had been torn loose in the altercation and dangled by a thread. Then he ran a hand through his hair, taking care to pat it down over his balding spot.

With this lull, Officer Kelly took the opportunity to speak." I'm sorry, Detective," he said to Bobby, "but let me explain. The senator drove up, and when he parked the car I went over to greet him. He became agitated and demanded an explanation for our presence.

I told him the officer in charge was in the house and asked him to wait while I got you. But he bolted past me, heading for the front door. I yelled for him to stop, but he ignored me. You'd told us to secure the premises, and we had no choice but to take him down." Kelly looked miserable, anticipating that the tackling of a senator would signify the end of his brief police career.

"Officer Kelly, you acted quite properly. Senator Caldwell was warned and should have stayed put." Bobby looked directly at Caldwell, no sympathy on her face.

The reactions of the senator and Officer Kelly were diametrically opposed. Kelly breathed a sigh of relief, while Caldwell's lined face turned beet red.

"Now see here," he blustered, "I've already told you I feared for my wife's safety. You had no right to keep me out of my own house. The attack on me was totally irresponsible. You can be assured I will be contacting the appropriate people and lodging a complaint. Your name is Detective Andrade, correct?" He was clearly trying to intimidate Bobby and those supporting her.

"That's right." Bobby looked unfazed. "And I'm sure you recognize my partner, Tony Deluca."

The senator had until now been oblivious to his presence, all attention focused on Bobby. But at the mention of Tony's name, he turned. Tony saw recognition flash in the dark, calculating eyes. The senator's bushy eyebrows rose.

"I wish we could've met under more pleasant circumstances, senator. Actually, I take that back. This is very pleasant for me," Tony said, a tight smile on his face. The senator was silent, sensing danger in responding.

"I'm glad you've finally here, Mr. Caldwell. We're here to execute a search warrant on your car and home. This is a copy for your records. As I have already instructed your wife, you're free to remain in the house and observe. However, please don't try to interfere with our activities."

The senator grabbed the search warrant from Bobby's hand and flipped through to the attached affidavit. He staggered a bit and the color drained from his face until it matched the grey of his hair. "Our son has confessed to murder?"

Mrs. Caldwell let out a small cry and looked like she might collapse. Tony moved to her side and took an arm, leading her to an antique chair in the entryway. He felt a bit of déjà vu, recalling that he'd played a similar role in supporting Mrs. Harding just over a week ago. Mrs. Caldwell sat heavily. "You said murder? Who …?" She couldn't finish her sentence.

"Do you recall the disappearance and death of a university student last fall? Her name was Karen Sumner," Tony said.

"I remember, it was in all the papers." Her voice rose. "I thought they caught her killer. It couldn't have been my Jonathan!"

"Connie, my dear, I'm sure the confession was made under police duress. We'll get him out of this." The senator had recovered from the initial shock and was rallying his legal arguments.

"I think you've helped him too much already," Tony growled through a burning sore throat.

The senator gave him a nervous glance.

Bobby took over. "Mr. Caldwell, we need the keys to your car. I'd then like you to accompany us as we search the house. Mrs. Caldwell, Office Kelly will escort you back to the reading room. I think that's the most comfortable spot for you to wait until we've finished. Is this all understood?"

The group split into three, moving in separate directions. Over the next hour the forensic techs went through the BMW thoroughly, taking various carpet samples, while the rest of the team started in the basement and methodically worked their way up to the second floor.

Despite the overwhelming size of the Caldwell Mansion, their job was made easier by the fastidious and well organized Mrs. Caldwell. Unlike most basements, there was no storage area filled with boxes holding mountains of old photos, discarded clothes and linens, or remembrances of earlier years. All such items were either neatly stacked on tall metal racks, in off-site storage or most likely had been discarded. The main floor was equally well organized, although there were a number of cabinets with drawers and shelves to be carefully sorted through.

The senator observed these activities in silence, while shadowing Tony and keeping a watchful eye on him. At times he appeared ready to say something, but for some reason kept his peace. However, as they moved their search to the top floor of the house, he sidled up beside Tony on the staircase.

In a low whisper, he said, "I've got to give it to you, Deluca. I thought I'd buried you so deep you'd never see the light of day again. I was clearly mistaken. But after this little fiasco turns up nothing, you'll be lucky to even keep that security job of yours." He let out a small chuckle of pleasure.

Tony swung around. "Caldwell, I have to admit I liked you better when you kept your yap shut. But don't worry, I'll still come by and visit you in prison. You'll look good in orange. And who knows – maybe you'll be able to spend more time with your son."

Tony fixed his stare at the man who'd been a proverbial thorn in his side, half expecting a heated retort. However, the senator seemed taken aback by the confident note in Tony's voice and merely pushed past him and up the staircase.

On the second-floor landing, Bobby asked Caldwell to direct them to his son's bedroom. He pointed at a door. "It's a guest bedroom now. Jon moved most things to his condo about a month ago and what he didn't take got thrown out. But go ahead, see for yourself."

Bobby nodded to Johnston and Bryant, who headed towards the guest bedroom. "Okay, now, sir, show us your bedroom."

Caldwell scowled. "Detective Andrade, this is going too far. That's our personal sanctuary and the door is always locked when we aren't in the house. Jon was never allowed in there. What in heaven's name do you think you'll find?" he asked indignantly.

"I remind you that the search warrant is for the entire house." Bobby snapped. "Now, take us to your bedroom, or we'll slow this process right down and still be here to greet your dinner guests."

The senator shook his head in disgust, then grudgingly said, "Follow me." They moved in tandem to the end of the hallway, where Caldwell opened a door that lead to the master bedroom. As was the case with the rest of the house, the room was tastefully decorated and nothing appeared out of place. There was a separate sitting area with a gas fireplace, two comfortable lounge chairs and large bookcase. While the senator watched from the doorway, Bobby, Tony, and Kelly spread throughout the room.

Bobby and Kelly started looking through dresser drawers, while Tony discovered a large walk-in closet with a custom-built wardrobe and shoe organizers. He saw several rows of purses on display and quickly checked for the purse that Karen Sumner's roommate described her carrying the night she died. He wasn't surprised when he didn't find a match. He opened and searched all the drawers, again finding nothing that appeared to belong to the university student. After ten minutes of fruitless searching he moved back to the main bedroom area. Bryant and Johnston had returned and were conferring with Bobby.

"Anything, Tony?" she asked. He shook his head. But if she was disappointed, she didn't show it.

"Okay, senator, we're close to wrapping things up."

Caldwell got up from the bed where he'd been sitting. "It's about time this charade was over. I want you to leave. By this time tomorrow you'll be regretting your decision to come here." He motioned for them to leave and started towards the door.

Bobby stopped him. "Wait a minute, Senator, we're not quite done. We'd like to see the famous panic room before we go."

Chapter 48
MAY 24 4:15 PM

Caldwell slowly turned back to Bobby, his expression showing a mixture of surprise and concern. Tony expected him to deny the existence of this room, or argue that they didn't have the authority to enter and search it. But he seemed to recognize the futility of either approach. "How'd you find out about this?"

"It wasn't that difficult, given our discussions with your son. In fact, we've learned quite a bit from him," Bobby said.

The senator's eyes narrowed. "I think you should be careful with relying on that source. My son is a known liar as well as a confessed killer."

"That's funny – downstairs you accused us of beating that confession out of him," Tony reminded Caldwell. "Now he's a lying murderer. No matter, your wife has already confirmed what he told us. Now stop stalling and show us the room."

Caldwell shrugged and walked to the bookcase in the sitting area. He pushed aside several books and flicked an innocuous-looking light switch. The bookcase swung back to reveal a steel case door with a digital security pad. Without being asked, he punched in a code and turned the lever to open the door, then moved aside to let them enter.

Bobby motioned for only Tony to follow her into the room. "Kelly, you wait with the senator." The lights were on a sensor and illuminated the room as they entered. It was a small room, approximately ten by twelve feet. There was metal shelving against the left wall, stacked full with jugs of water, tins of food and various other survival supplies. On the opposite wall was a bunk bed with folded linens and pillows. In one corner there was a small table

329

covered with a linen cloth, in another Tony recognized a waterless composting toilet – suitable, he guessed, for longer sieges. The room reminded him of a luxurious prison cell.

As they were surveying the room, Mrs. Caldwell's voice drifted in from the master bedroom. She apparently was becoming restless and had come looking for her husband. "Robbie, do you know what time it is? Our guests will be here in less than two hours, and I need to get ready!"

"Now, dear, don't worry. The police are almost done. This is the last room, and as they can see, there is nothing there that points to any crime." While the senator was ostensibly speaking to his wife, Tony knew the comments really were meant for him and Bobby.

"Yes, we're almost done," Bobby called out. "We just need you to open the safe." Bobby was pointing to the linen-covered table. Tony had not recognized its profile in his initial inspection.

The senator suddenly appeared at the door, trying hard to appear casual. "That merely holds my wife's jewelry, our wills and other personal papers. There is really no need…"

"Don't worry, Senator, we already know we're not beneficiaries of your estate," Bobby said dryly. "But to protect your privacy, I'll be the only one looking at its contents, and I don't plan to spend any more time than necessary to confirm what's in there. I understand you're the only one with the combination?"

The senator opened his mouth and quickly shut it. Tony expected Caldwell wanted to deny he had sole access to the safe, but with his wife present, knew she'd likely contradict him. Instead, he strode over to the safe and pulled the tablecloth over his head to prevent them from seeing the combination he was entering. He looked like Casper, the friendly safecracker, Tony thought. The process didn't take long, and when Caldwell re-emerged, the door was open.

Bobby pulled on latex gloves and reached into the safe. She removed a mahogany jewelry box, passports, a stack of folded papers with blue legal covers, insurance policies and an old wallet. No sign of Sumner's purse or silver watch.

Tony felt a keen sense of disappointment, even though he knew this had always been a long shot. They still had plenty on the senator, but physical evidence showing a chain of control from Jonathan to his father would have sealed the deal. Tony put those thoughts aside as Bobby opened the jewelry box. It contained a number of rings and sets of earrings as well as matching gold and diamond Rolex watches for a man and woman. She ruffled through the stack of legal papers and flipped through the insurance policies. When she opened the wallet, Tony could see it was full of Euros and several credit cards.

"Just cash and cards." Bobby looked at Tony and lifted her shoulders in a shrug, returning the items to the safe.

Seeing she was finishing up, the senator walked over. "I told you there was nothing here. Now I want you to get out of our house. I'll be calling your chief to lodge an official complaint. In particular I will note your bullying tactics," he said to Tony.

Bobby ignored the senator's rant and started to push shut the safe door.

Tony felt a buzz of doubt. The senator had been clearly worried about them entering the master bedroom. His stress level rose perceptibly when he learned they knew about the panic room, and one again with the mention of the safe. They must be missing something, an important detail. Whatever it was, it had to do with the safe.

"Bobby, wait a minute," he said with some urgency. She froze and looked at him expectantly. "Let's see that wallet again." She looked puzzled but did as he asked. She held up the brown leather wallet, waiting for further instructions.

"Okay, take a look through the cards."

Bobby flipped through the elite status credit cards, then paused. She extracted a white plastic license that had been buried among them. She examined it and held it out for Tony to see. The license had been issued by the State of Illinois. But it was the picture that sent a shiver of excitement through his body. There was no mistaking the features of Karen Sumner.

Bobby turned to the senator and his wife. "Mrs. Caldwell, it looks like there will be one less guest for dinner tonight. Senator Caldwell, you are under arrest as an accessory to Karen Sumner's murder and obstruction of justice. There may be additional charges laid once the State Attorney has had a chance to review all the evidence against you. You have the right to remain silent…"

Chapter 49
MAY 24 6:15 PM

Bobby's house was in Cherokee Park, above Lake Mendota on the north edge of the city. It was the first time Tony had been in the area, and he had to navigate his way through the maze of roads. His cold had worsened and he now had a heavy cough, his eyes tearing up, and he had difficulty reading the street signs.

Eventually he located Bobby's street and followed it to the very end. Her house was a 1950s colonial on a large lot that backed onto an open green space. The exterior was blue painted clapboard, with a long wooden porch running along the front and connecting to a detached garage. The yard was nicely landscaped and rose bushes bloomed in the front garden. The owner clearly took pride in its appearance.

He parked in the driveway and went to ring the doorbell. Bobby came to the door, somewhat out of breath. "Hi, Tony, I just got here. Senator Caldwell's booking took a bit longer than I expected. What's that in your hand?"

He held up the bottle of champagne. "I thought we could toast bringing the Sumner investigation to an end."

"Good idea. We've got lots to celebrate. Come on in."

The narrow foyer was painted a deep blue that contrasted with the white trim and cream ceramic floor. He followed Bobby into the living room. It faced the back yard, patio doors overlooking a cedar deck and lawn. Beyond that there was a grassy field, with no neighbors in sight.

"Nice place, lots of privacy." Tony reached in his pocket for a tissue and blew his nose.

Bobby gave him a look of sympathy. "Yes, that's what appealed to me when I first saw it. That field has been zoned for parkland, and hopefully I'll always have that open space behind the house. Let me get some glasses and we can sip on some bubbly while I give you the latest."

While he waited, Tony let his gaze wander around the room. A long sofa table displayed a number of framed pictures, and he went over to examine them. Bobby was in many of the pictures, at various stages of her life, the farm where she grew up serving as the backdrop. There were also pictures of an older couple and a number of boys, clearly her parents and brothers.

Bobby returned, glasses clinking in her hand. "Ah, you've discovered the rogues' gallery. My family, as you may have guessed."

"As I recall, you have six brothers?"

"That's right, unless you count me as well. My dad treated me like one of the boys, much to my mother's dismay. He needed all the help he could get. I learned how to fix a harvester and deliver baby calves. However, I won't bore you with my career as a farm hand. Let's open up that champagne."

Tony unraveled the silver foil, eased out the cork and gave a final twist. The cork exploded from the bottle and travelled in an arc, hitting the opposite wall. Champagne started to overflow. "Quick!" He motioned to Bobby to catch it in a glass. "I won't be invited to tend bar in a fine restaurant any time soon."

A moment later both glasses were full. More solemnly, he said, "I would like to propose a toast to the memory of Karen Sumner. May she now rest in peace."

"Amen," Bobby said softly, and they clinked glasses. "Now take a seat and I'll let you know what happened after we left the Caldwell's house."

She went over to an easy chair near the gas fireplace, while Tony took a seat on a leather sofa. He noticed her grimace as she sat down. "Didn't even have time to make my gun off. Damn thing, always poking me." She removed the Smith & Wesson from her holster, putting it on the table beside her chair.

"Okay, what's the latest?" Tony asked with great interest.

"To start off, the other search team got through Jonathan Caldwell's place relatively quickly. He's in a fairly expensive building but he's renting one of the smaller units, about 800 square feet with a bedroom and den. They found the football jacket in his front-entry closet. The officer in charge told me that it had brownish spots on it, which I expect is dried mud from the marsh. It's with forensics now. With Caldwell's confession it's pretty much a foregone conclusion we'll get a match with the fibers on Sumner's clothing."

"But good to have the jacket in case he has a change of heart. What else?"

"I updated the chief about the results of our search. We had an interesting debate over why the senator kept the driver's license. I agree with your theory that he wanted to retain some proof of his son's involvement in Sumner's murder, to maintain his hold over him in the future. Still, it was dangerous for him not to get rid of it. The chief thinks the senator kept it as a memento, or a trophy of sorts. 'Political might overcomes what's right,' or something like that."

"And now evidence in the criminal case against him," Tony said with some satisfaction.

"But the reason I was so late was that someone leaked the fact that we'd arrested the senator and his son. TV vans and plenty of cameras were lined up when I arrived. Rosen was holding an impromptu press conference on the steps of police headquarters. We had to wait and the senator was steaming in the back of the car. He was really pissed off that Rosen was already bragging to the press at his expense."

"Yes, must be quite frustrating for him to see Rosen's political career take a jump forward while his is going up in flames."

"You've got that right. So that's about it, Tony. We scored the Trifecta today – two confessions and enough evidence to build an airtight case against the senator."

Tony nodded in agreement, glowing with satisfaction. "I'd like to propose another toast. To Bobby Andrade, who handled the interrogation of Jonathan Caldwell like a seasoned pro and whose hard work has brought three people to justice. Next step for you is solving the Harding murder."

Bobby flushed a bright pink and her eyes dropped for a moment. She then raised her glass to Tony's.

Chapter 50

Tony glanced at his watch. "I should be heading out. I have a dinner date with Julie and I'm supposed to meet her around seven for pre-dinner cocktails."

He sneezed and reached in his pocket for another tissue, coming up empty; he'd used up the last of his supply. "Do you have any Kleenex around?"

"Sure, there's a box in the bathroom, down the hallway and first door on the right."

He stood up, feeling a bit unsteady. The champagne must be interacting with his cold medicine. He found the bathroom, smallish with light green fixtures and a plain white shower curtain. A sweet scent came from incense sticks floating in a small bowl on the vanity. Beside it was the Kleenex box and he gave his nose a good blow. Looking around, he saw a garbage container in the corner. He balled up the tissue and tried a basketball three-pointer, narrowly missing his mark.

As he bent down to retrieve the wadded Kleenex, his body tensed and a wave of vertigo swept over him. At the same time he was hit by the image of Jennifer Harding's body lying at the bottom of Lake Mendota. A second wave of dizziness overcame him and he dropped to one knee. Images from the past two weeks swirled about in his head.

"Everything okay in there, Tony?" Bobby's concerned voice reached him through the door.

He used the vanity to help pull himself back to his feet. "Sorry, this cold has really knocked me out, I almost fainted." The episode had triggered a severe case of the sweats and he ran cold water on his face. Drying his face and hands with a towel, he left the bathroom, still feeling a bit wobbly.

Bobby was waiting in the hallway, an anxious look on her face. "You really don't look very well, Tony. Maybe you should go to emergency and get checked out."

"No, no, I'll be fine. Let's just go back to the living room for a moment. We can talk a bit more while I have a rest."

Bobby hovered close by as they walked down the hallway and into the living room. She appeared ready to catch him if necessary. "I'll get you some water. Or do you want something hot?"

"Water's fine." Tony heavily dropped back down onto the leather sofa. When Bobby brought him a glass of water, he thanked her and took a long swallow. "Thanks." He made an effort at casualness. "You know, whenever we get together all we seem to do is talk business. I actually know very little about you. Like, Bobby must be short for something else, what's really your first name?"

"Roberta Judith Andrade," she said promptly. "Named after my two grandmothers. I never really liked either name and, with a house full of boys, it seemed natural to go by Bobby. The name has stuck all these years. Now, what else would you like to know?" Her smile was quizzical.

"I'll keep it easy. Are you a sports fan? Football, baseball, the hoops?"

"Not really, this was a real disappointment to my dad. He loves baseball and tried very hard to get me interested."

"Ever been to a game?"

"Oh, yeah. Dad's an avid Minnesota Twins fan. He's taken me to a game or two, but still I find it pretty boring."

Tony felt his heart pounding and the dull pain in the back of his head had escalated to a dazzling headache that brought stars to his eyes. He took another drink of water and started to speak with great deliberation. "You know, typically by the time I'm sitting in front of a killer, I have fit all the pieces together. How it went down and what motivated the deed. I'd have carefully gone over my strategy to lead the suspect to ultimately admit to the crime. However, this time I'm just going to have to wing it."

Bobby's body stiffened. "What are you talking about?"

"Why'd you kill Jennifer Harding?"

"Are you going delirious on me?"

He sadly shook his head. "No, and the question still stands. Why'd you do it?"

Her blue eyes widened and then contracted into slits. She sat perfectly still, carefully considering the situation. Tony felt the room spinning around them.

Finally, she said, "Tony, why would you ever think that? We both know it must've been Adelsky. I really do think we need to get you to emergency. You must be hallucinating."

"I was, until just a minute ago. During my visit to the bathroom I noticed your garbage pail. It has a rather memorable design – pink flower with green fronds. I believe it's part of a matching set with the shower curtain I found wrapped around Harding's body. Of course, it might be a coincidence..."

"Tony, of course it's a coincidence. I got it at Target. There's a million of them out there."

"But then," he went on, "I remembered the St. Christopher's medallion with the engraved initials: "R.A". I'd jumped to the conclusion that the 'R' had to be the first initial of a man's name. In fact, I did think it might stand for 'Rick.' But it's really the first initial for your birth name, Roberta, isn't it? Then there's the baseball cap the killer wore while driving Harding's car back to Chicago. It must've been a present from your dad."

With these words fatigue and anguish washed over Bobby's face. "Ok...right on all counts, almost. But you referred to me as a killer. That part's not true, Tony."

"Okay, so level with me, Bobby. What happened?"

"I need a drink." She reached for the champagne and filled up her glass. "Cheers," she said bitterly.

"Tell me, Bobby."

"You know some of the story," she said hopelessly. "I met Jennifer at that law enforcement conference in Chicago. I was very interested in her presentation, and at the break I approached her with some questions. She had to head back to her office for a meeting, but we arranged to get together later that day, at the hotel bar. We ended up really connecting. We moved from discussing recent court decisions limiting police investigation powers to exchanging personal histories. There was this energy about her that I found really attractive and she felt the same way. We ended up going back to my room. I'd never been with a woman before. It was … quite a revelation."

"So you became lovers."

"Yes, and we remained so until her death. However, we knew we had to keep it very quiet. First of all, we considered ourselves primarily heterosexual. And we were both ambitious and wanted to move up in our careers. Despite all the stories about the acceptance of gays and lesbians in the workplace, there's still a lot of prejudice. We couldn't afford to be branded as lesbians. And my parents are very religious. They simply wouldn't understand. "

"I can understand why you wanted to keep this private. But other than a few phone calls, which you explained, the police weren't able to find any communications between the two of you. How's that possible?" Tony asked, perplexed.

"Cell phones and email. We subscribed to an Internet service that guaranteed all text messages would be deleted from their system within forty-eight hours. Even those phones calls the Chicago police traced were a bit of a mistake. The battery on my cell phone died and Jennifer needed to get hold of me. She had to resort to a regular land line to track me down."

"Your relationship certainly explains why Harding was willing to help with those DNA tests. I always thought the explanation you gave for her doing that was … a bit odd."

"Yes, when I learned those tests hadn't been completed I confided in her. She of course was anxious to provide any support she could, and fortunately her office did have a rape case underway at the time. She was able to use this as an excuse to order the tests."

"How and why did Harding die?" Tony asked gently.

Bobby briefly contemplated her response. "Remember your conversation with Jennifer's ex-boyfriend?"

"Daniel Jayman."

"Uh huh. Jennifer didn't have a totally conventional view of sex. She was very interested in trying out new things. Well, you might say our relationship was part of her ongoing sexual experimentation. Coming from a religious mid-western upbringing, it was a real eye-opener for me. There were a number of different things she wanted to do and she led me along."

Tony suddenly recalled the interview with Jayman. Another part of the puzzle clicked together. "You're the woman in the bar at the Four Seasons Hotel. She sent Jayman over to pick you up."

Bobby nodded, her embarrassment evident. "Jennifer was interested in a threesome, and wanted to test Jayman's sexual appetite at the same time. As you know, he failed miserably on that front. Harding sent him along to her room, and she and I went to another hotel together. That was the end of her relationship with Jayman."

Bobby smiled bleakly at Tony, and then continued. "Shortly after we started seeing each other, Jennifer said she wanted me to try Ecstasy. Her friends told her it heightened their sense of sexual freedom and pleasure. She got her hands on some. I refused to try it – I don't even like taking aspirin. I could get caught in a random drug check and end up fired. Well the stuff just seemed to increase her desire to experiment. She wanted to try erotic asphyxiation. Again, at first I refused…."

Tony felt a sense of revulsion, seeing where Bobby's story was heading.

"...but a couple of weeks ago Jennifer texted me late in the day. She wanted to get together for the night. Normally I'd drive to Chicago to see her or we'd meet somewhere in between. However, I had to work late and Jennifer agreed to drive out here. She'd just won a high profile murder case and she was as high as a kite. She said I had to help her celebrate and finally convinced me to try Ecstasy. You've got to understand, Tony, I'd never even had a toke before. My world went totally out of control. The next thing I remember is waking up in bed with Jennifer's dead body beside me. I can only assume that she got me to try to asphyxiate her and I ended up strangling her." Tears had begun to stream down Bobby's face. "But I can't remember anything. It's all a blank." She choked back sobs. "I would never have intentionally hurt her."

Tony let her cry. He'd returned to the living room without any real plan other than to confront her and find out the truth concerning the circumstances of Harding's death. Even now, with her full confession, he wasn't sure what to do. In truth, Bobby was one of his few friends, and it now appeared that Harding's death had been a tragic accident. Should Bobby suffer the same fate as Jonathan Caldwell? He was filled with doubt and pushed for more information.

"Why didn't you call the police and report what happened?" he asked in a quiet voice.

"Tony, I wish I had. Her death haunts me.... But all I could think about was the humiliation of losing my job, having to face my mom and dad, possibly going to jail. No one knew about our relationship, or that she was even in Madison. So I made a selfish decision to protect myself. I wrapped up her body in my shower curtain and put her in the trunk of the Audi with some bar bells to weigh her down. I changed into dark clothes and the baseball cap. My plan was to drop her body in a deep part of the Yahara River and drive the car back to Chicago."

"Why didn't you just dump the car? Why take the risk of returning it to Chicago?

Bobby gave a rueful smile. They'd discussed the same questions a week ago, but she couldn't answer him then. Now she did. "I didn't want her movements traced to Madison. I thought that if I got the car back into her parents' garage, they'd never know it'd been taken. The police would think she'd disappeared or been killed in the Chicago area. There would be no links back to me. What I didn't count on was the runoff from that big storm being strong enough to pull the weights off her body and wash it into the lake for you to find. Remember I was a total mess when we met at the State Park? By then I knew it could be Jennifer's body, and I was absolutely dreading what was going to happen."

Tony now understood why Bobby had seemed so distant and distracted when they first met, and her emotional reaction when she first saw the body.

"I still couldn't imagine anyone figuring out I was involved with her death. My tracks were so well covered. But the next day when you called to say you'd found some evidence relating to her murder, well that put a chill through me. I was trying to figure out what I'd missed, and then you showed up to our meeting at Starbucks with the medallion. I'd given it to Jennifer about a month before. I left it around her neck so St. Christopher would keep watch over her body. The chain must have broken and was buried in the sand, so all you found was the medallion."

She paused, gathering her thoughts. "When you suggested we work together on the case, I tried to act doubtful. But actually I thought it was the perfect way to manage the situation. I expected the investigation would eventually hit a dead end, but I wanted to keep an eye on you and make sure you didn't stumble onto something that implicated me. When the Sumner investigation got new legs, it was the perfect distraction. I figured I was home free. However, then you mentioned the FBI, and I had to make some contingency plans."

Tony was now deep in his own thoughts. Looking back, it all made perfect sense. Bobby's reaction when she first saw Harding's body, her willingness to allow him to participate in the Sumner investigation, then convincing the chief to retain him as a consultant – it was all meant to keep him occupied, his attention diverted from investigating Harding's murder. He realized how stupid he'd been, going so far as to think Adelsky could be the killer.

"So now you know everything."

Something in the tone of Bobby's voice brought him back to full attention.

"I'm terribly sorry, Tony, but this is the end of the line for our successful partnership." For a moment there was a distracted look on her face, and then she made a decision. She reached for the gun on the table beside her.

Chapter 51
MAY 24 6:40 PM

For a split second Tony considered a frontal assault, charging towards her like a mad bull. But there was little chance of getting to her before she could take deadly aim and fire. Unarmed and in a weakened condition, it appeared he was at her complete mercy.

"So this is the way it ends?" he asked, his body tense and the stress of the situation etched on his face.

"Something like that," she said, the gun trained on him. "Please get up, slowly, and start moving towards the basement door." She motioned with the barrel of the gun.

Tony grudgingly followed her orders, heaving himself from the chair and moving slowly in the direction she'd pointed.

"Keep moving. And please don't do anything foolish."

He nodded and continued towards the basement door. Suddenly his foot caught the edge of the rug and he stumbled. Bobby took a step back, not wanting him to get too close to her. He felt the adrenaline take over as he timed his fall, a shoulder roll, and the kick to her shins.

However, Bobby's quick reaction resulted in him only taking out one of her legs. Rising from a crouch, he desperately launched himself at her. He heard her say, "Tony, no, this isn't – " before he hit her flush in the chest.

She was now on the floor and he was on top of her. But she was big and strong and not about to give in. He used his weight to pin her and maintained his hold on the wrist that controlled the gun. She bucked like a wild horse and he went up in the air and came down hard.

Then there was an explosion of sound, and after that all went quiet.

Chapter 52
MAY 25 11:15 AM

Tony opened his eyes but didn't recognize his surroundings. His brain seemed to be working at half speed. His throat was dry and sore, and there was a dull throbbing pain in his left shoulder. He tried to lift his head, but he didn't seem to have the strength and let it fall back.

Turning his head he saw a plastic tube snaking its way up to a clear bottle of liquid. Behind it was a machine making a steady beeping noise. He was in a hospital.

He felt the presence of someone else in the room. There was a slight scraping of a chair and the shadow of a person blocked the harsh florescent lights.

"Tony, thank God you're awake."

He recognized Julie's voice. At last, something he could relate to. He felt a tremendous relief.

"What happened?" he managed to say. His lips were dry and he sensed rather than heard the raspiness of his own voice.

"You've been shot. It was quite serious. You lost a lot of blood. But you're going to be okay."

Tony felt the room start to whirl and he closed his eyes.

"Get some rest. I'll be here when you wake up." She took his hand and gave it a squeeze.

Tony nodded groggily, and let himself disappear back into the darkness of sleep.

THE NEXT TIME he opened his eyes, a nurse in blue scrubs was fussing about him. Seeing he was awake, she gave him a bright smile. "Welcome back to the world, Mr. Deluca. You gave everyone quite a fright last night. Now, can I get you some water? And how's the shoulder?"

He nodded yes to the water and slowly moved his bandaged shoulder, feeling a sharp stab of pain. The look on his face was all she needed, and she adjusted the morphine drip flowing through the tube into his arm. Then she pulled a roll-out table with a plastic cup with a straw on it within reaching distance.

"That pretty young thing who's been watching over you just stepped out for a washroom break. She'll be back soon. If you need anything else, just give me a buzz." She held up a small cylinder that was plugged into the wall, and placed it on the bed near his uninjured arm.

Then she was gone. A moment later Julie rushed in to the room. "Oh, Tony, I meant to be here when you woke. How're you feeling?"

"Mentally, much brighter than the last time we spoke. But more pain – the nurse has turned up the juice." A memory of the preceding night – Bobby, and the gun – flooded back. But there was a large void; what had happened since? Julie waited patiently, sensing he was trying to bring order to the last twenty-four hours.

"How'd I get here?" he finally asked.

"It's a bit of a long story. Bear with me." She pulled up a chair beside the bed. "When you didn't come to pick me up for dinner, I started to worry. Around 7:30 I called your home, but there was no answer. I then thought you might've been detained at police headquarters and called there. I wasn't sure if the person at the desk would know who you were, so I asked for Bobby. I was put on hold for what felt like half an hour, and then I was put through to Chief Dupree. He started grilling me, wanting to know who I was and why I was trying to get in touch with Detective Andrade. I could tell something was wrong. When he learned you and I had plans for dinner and you were late, he finally told me you were on the way here for emergency surgery. I asked what happened, but he wouldn't tell me anything more. He did say he'd make arrangements for me to be allowed to visit you. I've been here ever since, and still in the dark."

Tony cleared his throat, but she squeezed his hand. "The rest of the story will need to be filled in by the chief, who happens to be pacing outside. There's a big black guy in a suit with him. They're quite anxious to see you. Do you want me to put them off?"

Tony wasn't sure how to respond. He felt like shit and was still trying to make sense of what happened at Bobby's house. On the other hand, there were so many questions he was hoping the chief could answer. Like who found him in time to save his life, and what had happened to Bobby. "No, I need some answers. Let them know I'm ready to see them."

"Okay." Julie brushed the sweaty hair from his forehead and got up.

Chief Dupree came in, followed by an equally tall but younger and slimmer man: Tubman. Tony feebly raised his good arm in a hello.

"Hey, buddy," Tubby grinned. "Good to see you're still kicking. Matching shoulder wounds, eh? You'll be the rage at swim parties. All the girls will want to see the scars."

Tony managed a feeble grin in response.

Dupree moved beside Tony's bed, his face filled with concern. Breaking protocol, the chief addressed him by his first name. "Tony, I'm so glad you pulled through this. Things didn't sound so good when they got you here. How're you feeling?"

"Like a guy who just cheated death, I guess."

Dupree nodded sympathetically. "Well, I hope you don't mind if we talk shop. We're still in the dark about what happened at Detective Andrade's house. She's disappeared, and, well, you've been indisposed."

Tony spoke haltingly, sometimes taking a drink of water to relieve the burning in his throat. He told them about his visit to Bobby's house, the revelations regarding the death of Harding, the struggle and the sound of a discharging gun. Neither the chief nor Tubman interrupted his story, not wanting to tax his energy any more than required.

When he finished, the only noise in the room was the beeping of the heart monitor. The chief's face had a dusky grey pallor.

"Oh my god," said Tubman.

Tony took another painful breath. "Well, you know everything I know. Now tell me, how did I get here? And what's the situation with Bobby?"

Dupree shook off the daze that had taken over him. "Around seven last night we received a 911 call that a man had been shot and was in serious condition. The caller provided directions to a house in Cherokee Park. When the ambulance and police arrived, you were found unconscious on the floor. There was a fair bit of blood, but you were alive, largely due to the tourniquet that had been rather expertly tied around the wound. The police found your wallet and were able to identify you. They'd already determined the house belonged to Detective Andrade. I was contacted and brought up to speed, while you were rushed to the hospital. It was only five minutes later that Ms. Travers called and was put through to me. I thought she might have information on Detective Andrade's whereabouts."

"Who made the 911 call?" Tony asked, already knowing the answer.

"The call itself was placed from a pre-paid cell phone, so I asked to hear the recording. There'd been no attempt to disguise the voice. It was definitely Detective Andrade."

"Have you tracked her down yet?"

"No, but we expect she's out of state by now. Maybe even out of the country. We do know she must have alternative transportation. Her car is still in the garage. The FBI is now involved and so far they haven't turned up anything. There've been no credit charges or calls from her cell phone since yesterday afternoon. We've also completed a thorough search of her house. We found no clues as to where she's going and how she plans to get there. The only thing the investigating officers turned up was this."

Dupree held out an envelope, which he'd apparently been holding since entering the room. "It's a note, addressed to you. Sorry, but given the situation, we took the liberty of reading it." He took out a single sheet of paper, unfolded it and handed it to Tony.

He had difficulty focusing, squinting at the words on the page. It was handwritten in a quick scrawl.

"Did you want me to read it to you?" Dupree asked him.

The chief took the note from his hand. "*Tony – please understand this wasn't the plan. I only meant to tie you up in the basement until I could get far away. I was then going to alert the chief to your location. I'm so sorry. Two horrible accidents involving people I care very much for. I desperately hope you will be okay, and perhaps eventually forgive me for everything. For those reading this letter, please don't come looking for me, I am lost and won't be found.* That's all it says, Tony."

"I have to admit, the 'two horrible accidents' had me stumped, and I had to hope you'd be able to fill me in. In the meantime, this morning I contacted Detective Peters of the Chicago police, to let him know that I was personally assuming control of the Harding investigation. I also thought it was appropriate to give him all the gory details. It was going to come out sooner or later." He emphasized the statement with a resigned shrug.

"Peters got on the phone to me as soon as he heard," Tubman said. "He wasn't aware we'd had any recent contact, but thought I should know what'd happened to my former partner. I would've got here earlier but some nutcase landed an amphibian Cessna on the Interstate just before Janesville. Apparently mistook it for a lake. It tied up traffic for over an hour. Honest," he added, seeing the look on Tony's face.

Something that Tubman said suddenly triggered another memory. "Oh shit," Tony groaned.

"Tony, are you okay?" Julie ducked her head into the room.

"Carla, we made arrangements for brunch this morning. She's probably at the cottage wondering where the hell I am!"

"Oh," Julie responded with relief, "don't worry. You told me she was coming. I managed to get hold of her early this morning before she left. She got here about a half hour ago. She's in the waiting room, with her mother. They would've been here earlier except for some trouble on the interstate."

Tubman shot Tony a *told you so* look but remained silent.

EPILOGUE

Tony drove slowly up the gravel road to the cottage. It was deeply rutted from all the heavy construction equipment that had been moved onto the property. He was late but he couldn't drive any faster for fear of bottoming out the car. Gradually the view opened up until he could see the blue from the lake. When he pulled into the clearing it appeared as if he was in the midst of a battle zone. There were men in hardhats and orange safety vests operating front end loaders, a bulldozer, and several flatbed trucks. The din from the machinery hurt his ears and he rolled up his windows to keep out the smell of diesel fuel.

Part of the cottage roof already lay on the ground. The gaping hole was becoming larger as the men and equipment continued working away. He felt sorry to see what was happening to the place he'd called home for the past year.

A man in his early thirties in the requisite hardhat spotted him and headed over. Tony rolled down his window a few inches.

"Hi, Pete. Sorry, I was delayed by an important phone call that came in just as I was leaving. A new client. I see you've started already."

"Yes, I didn't think we should wait for you, Mr. Deluca. These men and the equipment are too expensive to let sit idle."

"You've got that right. The budget's pretty tight to begin with."

"That's what I thought." Pete's next words were washed out by the sound of falling debris from the roof. He scanned what was happening before turning back to Tony. "I'd better get over there. We're at a critical point and I don't want any of those roof trusses to get loose and damage the lower walls."

"Go ahead. I'll try to stay out of the way. I just wanted to pay my respects to the old girl."

Pete hurried back to manage the ongoing assault on the cottage. Despite the destruction that appeared to be going on around him, Tony was pleased he'd been able to save the cottage from the total teardown that had been proposed by the previous owner. The past year had not been kind to his landlord's business ventures, and he'd become financially over-extended. This had forced him to shelve his plans to build a monstrous house where the cottage now stood. Instead, he'd approached Tony about purchasing the property.

Fortunately, Tony was relatively flush with cash from the settlement of his lawsuit with the city. He'd also received an unexpected gift from Karen Sumner's parents, who'd insisted he take the reward they were offering for information leading to the arrest of their daughter's killer. A long and tortuous year had now passed since Sumner's disappearance and death, but Caldwell was now safely behind bars serving out his sentence. The recent financial windfalls had given Tony the required funds to purchase the cottage.

Tony had originally considered only minor renovations to the cottage, but several events dictated the need to significantly modify his plans. First, there was the press conference where Chief Dupree announced multiple arrests in relation to Karen Sumner's murder and subsequent cover-up. During the press conference Dupree praised Tony for his role in helping the police break open the Sumner case.

With Bobby's disappearance and the demotion of Adelsky to the robberies division, the chief had also hoped to announce that Tony was taking over the homicide division. However, during his time in the hospital, Tony realized he was no longer wanted to resume his police career. Instead, during the barrage of media interviews that resulted from his new-found notoriety, he promoted the formation of his own private detective agency. What he hadn't anticipated was the number of requests he'd receive for his services. He had to quickly find some office space. He was currently operating out of Drake Field's building, but planned to have an office on the ground floor of his enlarged cottage.

The renovation plans had to be further altered when he and Julie decided to move in together and become business partners after she graduated from law school next spring. Following some good-natured negotiations, she convinced him she was destined to become a top criminal lawyer in Madison and deserved top billing on the letterhead. With Julie requiring office and secretarial space, as well as the need for larger living quarters, they'd agreed the ground floor had to be expanded and a second floor added. In less than six months they would be pursuing a new business venture together in their renovated cottage. In the meantime, Julie, Tony, and Sam were living in very close quarters in Julie's apartment, and loving it. It meant that Carla had to stay at a hotel when she came to visit them, but she didn't seem to mind.

As Tony reflected on the past four months, he knew there were still several important loose ends. Senator Caldwell continued the fight for his political life and his freedom. His lawyers were claiming that the senator played no part in covering up the murder of Karen Sumner. They trumpeted to the press that the police case was based solely on the testimony of two confessed criminals, his son and the coroner, and that the lead detective in the case was herself being hunted by the police for her role in another murder and attempted murder. State Attorney Rosen saw a tough fight ahead and had chosen to personally prosecute the case against the senator. As the trial date approached, Tony had spent a fair bit of time with Rosen, going through his testimony. They'd become friends and allies of sorts, and Tony was confident the State Attorney was up to the challenge.

His thoughts often turned to Bobby, who was still at large. He continued to get bits of information from Tubby relating to the FBI search. He learned that she indeed had made contingency arrangements, clearing out her bank account and purchasing a motorcycle several days before Tony confronted her and was shot. There were unsubstantiated rumors that she'd also obtained new ID from one of the gangs she'd become acquainted with during a recent homicide investigation.

There'd been only two breaks in her self-imposed silence. One was a very brief call to her parents to confirm she was fine and missed them badly. The other was a letter, posted from Laredo, Texas, on the Mexican border, to Bill and Mary Harding. It bore a similar message to her note to Tony, apologizing for her role in their daughter's death and asking their forgiveness.

He sometimes pondered what he'd do if Bobby reappeared. There was a time in his life when there would've been no doubts, and she'd quickly have found herself behind bars. But his world was no longer distinguished by the bright contrast between black and white, good and bad. He could clearly see the subtle shadings that filled the world and his own life. And while Bobby's actions couldn't be condoned, her self-imposed exile from family and friends was perhaps a harsher form of justice than any judge or jury could impose.

ABOUT THE AUTHOR

Kevin Wark was born and raised in Toronto, Canada and has been happily married to Sandra for over 30 years. They are the proud owners of JJ, a champion Wheaton Terrier, and Spunky, a rag doll cat with attitude. Kevin is a tax lawyer by training and has previously authored "Everything You Need to Know About Estate Planning" and is a frequent contributor to a variety of publications on subjects relating to tax and estate planning. For the last three years Kevin's been focused on writing his first murder-mystery novel. He was inspired to use Madison Wisconsin as the locale for the book after a motor trip from Toronto to Calgary with Sandy and JJ. He's been back to Madison on several different occasions to gather additional background information for the book and is constantly amazed by the hospitality of Madisonians.

CPSIA information can be obtained at www.ICGtesting.com
Printed in the USA
LVOW04s0849071114

412401LV00006B/16/P